The Bimborg

Part Nanobot, All Woman

Doctor MC, Mad Scientist
doctor_m_c@hotmail.com

Ὑπό Τῷ
Ἡλιῷ

HYPO TO HELIO BOOKS

Houston

Paperback ISBN: 978-1-938293-03-0
Ebook ISBN: 978-1-938293-08-5

First edition
Printed on Demand

This story, besides being soft-core porn, is also a parody of a certain "Wagon Train to the stars" TV show. There are many fervent fans of that show—so many that Jay Leno makes jokes about us. You fans of that show will have great fun finding all the Easter Egg inside-references to that show (in its several forms). *Not* sharing in the fun will be the CBS Legal Department. I figure that if Fair Use may be successfully invoked by *MAD Magazine* and by porn-movie producers, I don't need to write a check to CBS in order to tell my tale.

All sexually active characters are eighteen or older.

Any resemblance to persons living, dead, or not born for centuries yet, is entirely coincidental and not to be inferred.

The author wishes to praise Rick Berman, Brannon Braga, and Ronald D. Moore, whose story and screenplay for *Star Trek: First Contact* is 99.9 percent wonderful. (My mentally rewriting the 0.1 percent that is bad, gave me the idea for this story.)

BISAC Subject Headings:
Fic005000—Fiction > Erotica
Fic016000—Fiction > Humorous
Fic021000—Fiction > Media Tie-in
Fic028080—Fiction > Science Fiction > Time Travel
Fic052000—Fiction > Satire
Hum007000—Humor > Forms > Parodies
Hum008000—Humor > Topic > Adult

HYPO TO HELIO BOOKS, 2427 Clearbrook Dr., Missouri City, TX, 77489-6061

PART 1:
"KING JAMES" UPTON

1-A: Invasion At The Farm

Summer, 2008

I, James Upton, changed the future in 2008.

I was reassembling the carburetor when I heard video-game sounds: *zheorr, zheorr!* You're not supposed to hear video-game sounds in a barn.

It wasn't my barn, of course, but rather my aunt's and uncle's. At the moment, Uncle Pete and Aunt Linda and the farmhands were all in town, so I was alone.

It pleased me that my uncle trusted me to be alone with heavy machinery. (Of course, I *was* fifteen then.)

To the strange noises coming from outside was added a yell: "Goddamn Cybes! why couldn't they stay in the 27th century where we belong?"

"Because they know that Jimmy Upton is alone in the barn for 2.6 more hours!" someone yelled back.

Since *I* am Jimmy Upton (call me James), I immediately thought *What the fuck?* and *Who the hell are the "Cybes"?*

I hurried across the barn to the west-side big doors. There's a one-inch gap between the big doors, even when they're shut. So without being seen myself, I was able to see outside.

Standing outside the barn, their backs to me, were men and women in jumpsuits of dark green, dark blue, dark yellow, and maroon. They were firing ray-guns—complete with flashes of light and strange sound effects. And as weird as *that* was, it was nothing compared to whom these guys were shooting at.

At first I thought they were robots, because I was seeing so much metal. These people, both men and women, each had metal that was covering parts of their legs and arms. But they had the trunks and heads of people—except that they each had a weird helmet-like thing covering the top of his/her head and eyes, and they each had some weird structure running across the front of his/her chest at the heart.

Each of these guys was flushed, as though with fever. These robot-people looked scary as hell.

The biggest and most armored of the robot-men had things built into their left arms that blasted lightning at the jumpsuit-people. Most of the jumpsuit-people jumped out of the way, but two people in maroon jumpsuits were electrocuted. Meanwhile, the smaller robot-men and all of the robot-women were shooting ray-guns.

One of my defenders yelled, "I'm fighting for the Planetary Alliance and its Space Navy. What are *you* fighting for, Cybes?" Sarcastically he added, "*Welcoming?*"

All the robot-people spoke as a chorus: "We are the Cybes. You cannot succeed, Space Navy. Defense is pointless."

Then I heard pounding on the barn's east-side human door, and a woman's voice was calling, "Jimmy? Jimmy Upton? Are you in there?" I didn't recognize her voice.

I was getting weirded out. I get a drop-in visitor at the same time as I have spacemen from the future battling outside? I went to the door but didn't open it. "Who's there?"

"Miss Smith, Jenny Smith." When I didn't say anything, she added, "I taught Computer Literacy class when you were in fifth grade. You invited me to your house that Christmas, remember?"

It didn't occur to me till too late to ask myself, *How'd she know where my uncle's farm was?* By the time I'd thought that, I'd already unlocked the padlock and opened the door.

The Cybe that had once been Miss Smith pushed her way into the barn.

She was naked, except for her metal parts. She was shorter than I remembered, but that didn't make her less scary. Instead of a lightning-shooter on her left arm, her left arm was bare (and flushed red), with a box-like thing on the back of her hand. Metal tubes ran from that box to her pinky finger—

Her pinky finger had *mutated.* Instead of a pinky nail, it now sported a plastic-like cone that tapered to a needle. I did *not* want to get that needle in me. That "syringe" had to be filled with *nanobots*!

Once inside the barn, Miss Smith's speaking changed, becoming flat and robotic: "<u>The Overmind calms you. The Overmind frees you</u>

from emotion. The Overmind gives knowledge. We Welcome you into the Overmind."

I ran away from her then—but I stayed inside the barn. The video-game and *zzzap* sounds were still coming from outside the barn, so trying to escape from the barn in either direction wasn't an option.

She chased me all around the barn. She wasn't as fast as me, but she never got tired. Fifteen minutes later, I was panting and sweaty, and she was still chasing me. I grabbed up a shovel and tried to knock her flat. A purple rectangle appeared in the air, three inches in front of her chest, as I was swinging. When my shovel hit the purple rectangle, it was like hitting a wall. Miss Smith seemed unaffected by it all. I dropped the shovel and ran again.

I had a plan by then—a desperate plan, admittedly. I ran away to where the fire axe and the rubber gloves were kept, and tossed them into the storage loft. I was climbing the ladder into the loft when Miss Smith showed up. She started to climb the ladder.

In the loft were two objects big enough to hide behind. Miss Smith headed for the refrigeration compressor, because it was bigger. As she walked past, I stepped out from behind the irrigation pump. I was wearing the rubber gloves, and holding the fire axe backward. I swung the axe coming up from a low position, so that the axe's pointy side hit her right where the base of her skull joined her neck.

She gave off sparks, as she began speaking the same seven words in a language I'd never heard before. Then she went silent, as she fell forward onto her face. I watched her for ten minutes, looking for any twitch of movement. There was none.

It was silent outside as well. I went to the west-side barn door and looked through the crack: I saw nobody. Nearly wetting myself with fear, I unbarred the doors and went outside.

Outside I found no spacemen, no Cybes and, oddly, no corpses. The only sign that there'd been a ray-gun battle here was a scorch mark on the barn. That, and an oak tree was burning.

I went in the barn and up the ladder to Miss Smith, who still had not moved. Now clearly visible was a boxy shape that was attached to her back, between her shoulder blades. An electric cable of some kind ran from the box to the base of her skull and into her brain. My axe-hit had cut that cable.

I cut off the box that was on her back, the box that had grown on her left hand, and her pinky needle. Then I buried the rest of her just outside the barn, underneath the hay baler. No ordinary animal would be digging up her corpse, under the weight of that baler!

I wept for the nice lady she had been four years ago. She couldn't even change out a hard drive, but in fifth grade she'd gotten me interested in building computers. Hell, she'd made me feel like a *genius*. And now she was dead, I'd killed her, and she'd died looking and acting like a monster. *Fuck*.

I walked out of the barn, and noticed that the oak tree had burned itself out by then. It was while I was looking at the oak tree that I saw something strange happen in the air above the oak tree.

A black point appeared in the air, which almost instantly expanded in every direction, becoming a giant floating metal cube. A moment later, my ears popped.

The cube had grooves cut into each of the three faces that I could see. The cube, I realized, was a ship of some kind; each of the three faces had a big thruster-hole in the center of the face, with eight mini-thrusters surrounding each center thruster.

The cube-ship was in trouble. Even though the thruster on the bottom was shooting blue flame to move the cube higher, the cube was slowly sinking down. Also, the cube was wobbling and tumbling, and mini-thrusters on every side were firing short blue bursts to make the cube straighten up and fly right.

Most damning of all, all three faces had scorch marks; and the north-side face also had a spot where the metal had melted, filling in the grooves. The cube was giving off gray smoke and black smoke, and I saw two faces leaking a black liquid.

I knew I was looking at either the Cybes' ship or the Space Navy ship, and I wondered what I should do if the ship crashed or exploded. Then I realized: *I'm not obligated to help the fuckers who turned Miss Smith into a monster and tried to kidnap me*.

But none of my worries came true. The cube quit wobbling; it stopped sinking. It rose in the air, as it swiftly shrank to a rising black point. A moment later, my ears popped again. After ten seconds, the black point vanished.

I watched for ten minutes, waiting for the damaged cube-ship to reappear. But after ten minutes of seeing only blue sky and clouds, I went in the house.

My uncle and aunt and the farmhands returned twenty minutes later, in a different truck than they'd left in. Uncle Pete said, "Yeah, the Ford threw a rod, so 'a movie and fast food' turned into a real adventure. How about you, Jimmy? What's new?"

I pointed out the window to the oak tree. I said, "A lightning storm came through, and set the tree on fire."

I shrugged and added, "Otherwise, it's been a boring, ordinary day."

1-B: I Learn My Future

The summer ended, and I went back to Grand City and my parents. I brought with me the two boxes and the needle that I'd taken off Miss Smith's Cybefied corpse.

During the next three years, I spent all my free time in my basement workshop.

Actually, it was my dad's workshop—but he wasn't there to use it much. He started "working late," then my mom filed for divorce and he moved out. For a while, Mom didn't get off the couch, then she went through a phase when she went out every night, then she started spending lots of time over at David's apartment. I barely noticed, I was so obsessed with cracking the mystery.

The Cybes from the 27th century had come back almost to Y2K to grab *me*. They'd Welcomed my fifth-grade teacher, just to make sure I myself got Welcomed. Meanwhile, the other people from the future, my protectors, knew that the Cybes would come for me. Why? What did the future know about me?

2010

Two years after I'd killed Miss Smith and robbed her body, I still didn't have answers to my ultimate question, but I knew what the two boxes and the cone needle were for.

I learned exactly who the Cybes were. The Cybes were the terror of the 27th century because if you fought them, killing one of your men is *not* the worst thing that the Cybes could do to you.

Nope, your soldier might get Welcomed by the Cybes, and then everything that this soldier knew about your weapons, defenses, and tactics, the Cybes would now know through the Overmind. Worst of all, this Cybefied soldier's loyalties would get completely and instantly changed, and he would wind up fighting against you as an Overmind-linked drone.

Individual Cybe drones were organized into clans; all the different clans together made up the multi-planetary Cybe hive. This Cybe hive was made up of—

- 427 human-colony planets that had been 99.9 percent Cybefied;
- the entire planet of the Stone Age-level Mrraok (cat people); and
- one captured ship filled with Amigogi interplanetary traders.

While the Overmind gave all the Cybes an inhuman level of agreement in what they did, Cybes also had Cybe Alpha in charge. Cybe Alpha gave orders when a decision was needed quickly.

By the year 2652 (the year that this clan of Cybes had come from), there were (are? would be?) specialties within the Cybes. The Cybes shooting lightning at the Space Navy were Soldiers. The Cybes shooting ray-guns at the Space Navy, as well as the former Miss Smith, all were Welcomers.

I had guessed correctly, back at my uncle's farmhouse, that inside the plastic cone and needle were billions and billions of nanobots, whose job it was to convert a human body into a Cybe.

The box and cable on any Cybe's back that connected to that Cybe's brain were to connect that Cybe to the Overmind, by uploading and downloading thoughts and memories.

But providing a brand-new Cybe with its orientation and initial protocols was discovered to be too taxing of Overmind resources, for too unimportant a task. (Translation: It slurped up bandwidth.) So instead of a new Cybe getting orientation from the Overmind, by 2652 everything that the new Cybe needed to know was broadcast from the transmitter on the Welcomer's hand.

There was a third kind of Cybes, the Invisibles. Invisibles looked like regular humans (or Mrraok, or Amigogi) and mimicked the speech and actions of regular humans, thanks to their Turing Subroutines. An Invisible's Overmind module wasn't a box on its back; but rather, a small hemisphere on the back of its skull, easily hidden by hair or fur. Invisibles couldn't Welcome, and they couldn't fight like Soldiers could fight, but Invisibles could blend in perfectly, while reporting everything they saw and heard to the Overmind.

It was the Invisibles who made the Cybes even more terrifying in the 27th century. By the time the people in a human community ever laid eyes on Soldiers and Welcomers, chances were good that the Overmind already knew who that community's leaders were, and what defenses they had. Entire settlements were Welcomed without their defenders being able to fire a shot.

Finally, there were a small fraction of Cybe Leaders. Leaders were red-skinned, unlike Invisibles; and Leaders had the armor and force-field generators of Soldiers, but didn't have any built-in weaponry. Leaders weren't artificially tall and strong, like Soldiers were; but this meant that Leaders weren't quick-tempered like Soldiers were. Only a Cybe Leader could become Cybe Alpha.

One thing that the Cybes did *not* have, I noticed, was a "Cybe King" or "Cybe Queen"—

Meaning, someone who hadn't been Cybefied, so that his/her thoughts couldn't be read by the Overmind, but who could give orders to Cybe Alpha and the Overmind both.

When I finally solved the mystery, Why me?, I was eighteen, and it was a week after my high-school graduation. I tell you, if I'd been legal to buy liquor that night, I would have gotten myself blotto on the nastiest, cheapest rotgut I could find. But forced to stay sober, I watched my *Ghostbusters* DVD five times in a row.

In my place, you'd have done the same thing. You see, I created the Cybes.

Once upon a time, around 2050 or so, there was a professor of nanotechnology named Jimmy Upton.

Compared to the 27th century, nanotechnology in the 2050s was primitive. You built the nanobots outside the human body, you loaded every nanobot with the same program outside the human body, and you injected all the nanobots into the human body. Then every nanobot followed the same program, whether it was inside the heart or inside the hand. Each nanobot could sense only hydrogen ions, hydroxide ions, and carbon dioxide. Like I said, nanotechnology in the 2050s was "primitive."

In the 2050s, what did nanotechnology professors do? They tried to figure out how to stuff a few more computer instructions into a nanobot's brain, or how to make the nanobot a little faster or a little smaller. Everyone accepted the "limits" of nanotechnology: Every little 'bot has to behave the same as every other 'bot.

But in 2055, "I" (my older self) published a paper declaring that it was possible to create a system in which every nanobot in the body could report back what it was finding, and could receive tailored instructions. This could be achieved, "my" paper declared, by building a little transmitter/receiver into every nanobot.

To put it bluntly, "my" paper was laughed at. For a nanobot to work right, it has to be small enough to pass through blood capillaries. It was gleefully pointed out that even the smallest transmitter-receiver that was imaginable in 2055 would make the nanobot way too big for human capillaries.

Imagine an astronomy professor, who has a Ph.D. and an observatory, claiming that there are men on Mars and that the Martians want to meet us. A nut case, right? That's how "I" was viewed within the nanotechnology community.

"I" persisted. Yet instead of persuading anyone, I was labeled a crackpot and fired from the university. And for the rest of "my" life, I remained in disgrace, a national joke—when "I" died, only my elderly Aunt Linda came to my funeral.

"I" died in 2064 with my reputation a joke. But in 2314, the anti-tachyon microtransmitter was invented. Soon after that, someone remembered my "ridiculous" theory, and the CNS (Coordinated Nanobot System) was perfected in 2331.

Nanobot breast-enhancement became commonplace overnight. Near-eternal youth became possible; within a few years, it became affordable. By 2354, comedians were making jokes about great-grandparent/great-grandchild incest. Women over a hundred years old became call girls—and stole clients away from young whores.

Meanwhile, unnoticed by anyone in the news media, the men and women being sent to the gold-mining prison planet Tizurka IV were getting their bodies nanobot-modified, so that they could live and work on the planet without spacesuits. As part of their modifications, their projective-telepathy psychic abilities were enhanced.

In 2419, Rachel Toyomachi was convicted of hacking Earth's planetary-defense computer system. To "make an example of her," the judge sentenced her to Tizurka IV. Once there, she proved herself to be a skilled hacker but a poor programmer—when she hacked into the nanobot-control computer, she accidentally created the Overmind.

In 2427, two mine-collapses occurred on Tizurka IV within the same month. The Tizurka miners declared the mines to be unsafe, and declared a work stoppage. Thanks to the Overmind, that work stoppage was 99.9999 percent effective.

Interestingly, there were fourteen miners on Tizurka IV who kept working, in order to toady up to the warden. They were part of the Overmind, but they didn't obey what the Overmind said.

Anyway, in 2427, gold-mining on Tizurka IV came to a halt. Halliburton PanStellar immediately demanded that the Space Navy "do something."

The Space Navy, not understanding what it was dealing with, sent a squad of Epsilon Force Star Marines in spacesuits to "neutralize" the Tizurka IV leadership. Alas, the Space Navy never asked itself the question, "What happens when a man who needs a spacesuit fights a man who doesn't?"

After that embarrassment, the Space Navy sent an entire company of Star Marines to the surface of Tizurka IV. It took those men longer to die.

The Space Navy took time to consider its options, then sent an entire battalion to Tizurka IV in 2428, under the command of General Karl Mbomo. But when the battalion arrived on-planet, they discovered that the Overmind-connected Tizurkans had concocted a new defense.

A Private Chong was the first offworlder to be Welcomed. A Major Lech!-Chich was the second. General Mbomo was third.

When General Mbomo got Welcomed, the Overmind-linked people on Tizurka IV became the first Cybes, and Mbomo became the first Cybe Alpha.

And all this happened because in 2055, "I" wanted to prove how smart "I" was by publishing that damned paper.

Well, one thing was for sure: *This* Jimmy Upton wasn't going to make *that* mistake!

Even though I now knew how to build and to program my own Cybe-making nanobots that communicated with each other by anti-tachyons—thus proving that "my" paper was correct.

Or so I resolved. I would have kept this knowledge quiet—never publishing it, never using it—until Mom's boyfriend's daughter Stephanie spoke fateful words at Thanksgiving dinner.

David's daughter Stephanie stood up from the table, her plate in her hand.

"What are you doing?" Mom asked.

"The stuffing's too cold," she said. "I'm gonna nuke it."

"Honey, don't do that," Mom said. "You've got cranberry on your plate. Cranberry is a dish that is best served cold."

"It's my food, Ellen," Stephanie said. "If I want to microwave it, I'm going to microwave it, and you can't stop me."

"Go ahead, Steph, if you need to," David said.

"Hot cranberries?" I said. "You're weird, Stephanie." Understand that when I said this, I was making a joke.

Stephanie looked down her nose at me. "Whereas *you* are a loser, and you'll *die* a loser."

That hit too close to home, because of what had happened to my other self in 2064. That's when, in my anger and hurt, I crossed a line in my mind.

"I" had died in 2064 being called an idiot, a fool, even crazy. Well, *this* James Upton would show Stephanie—no, I'd show them all!

1-C: Queen Stephanie-1

It really doesn't matter *why* I did everything I did, does it?

After Stephanie's insult during Thanksgiving dinner, I spent months in my workshop, rewriting all that nanobot programming.

But the nanobot *hardware*, this I left alone. Mechanical engineering in the 27th century is a wonder to behold, and comparing Cybe electronic engineering to what we have now? Resistors are feudal.

2011

Listen here, have I told you about Exnillo packs? They're not much to look at—one of them is about the size of two shirt buttons glued together—but they're amazing technology.

An Exnillo pack takes energy from. . .the universe, basically. Year-2011 science says this baby can't exist, and yet I've got one powering the Cybe computer I stole. Keep using a ray-gun till its Exnillo pack is dead, and the sucker will recharge itself in 24 hours. In the 27th century, fossil-fuel technology is thought to be "quaint."

Here's what I'm proud of: I figured out a way to grow an Exnillo pack inside a woman, as part of the bimborg-ization process.

This is a big achievement. For one thing, Cybes don't have built-in Exnillo packs. Cybe Welcomers take their energy from little battery packs inside their armor, while Cybe Soldiers use big battery packs. But either way, the battery pack only gets recharged after a Cybe has spent the night in a Recharging Chamber.

My bimborg, whether Pleasure Units/Welcomers, Ass-Kicker Babes, or Spy Babes, don't need no stinkin' Recharging Chambers.

If I want to have an orgy at 3 a.m., my Pleasure Units aren't standing in a box then. You want to send a squad of Special Ops guys to attack me at 3 a.m.? My Ass-Kicker Babes aren't standing inside a box either.

Yeah, there's a big design tradeoff. Besides being *much* weaker than a Cybe Soldier, a bimborg Ass-Kicker Babe can't shoot lightning bolts like a Soldier can. On the other hand, at three a.m., an

Ass-Kicker Babe is ready to fight, while a Soldier has to stand in his box and recharge.

But let's be honest, huh? I didn't cook up these improved designs so I could have more deadly bimborg bodyguards. Nope, I designed things this way so that any Pleasure Unit would be truly "a 24-hour fucking machine."

Eventually my work was done; the day came when I showed up at Stephanie's apartment, supposedly to apologize for something I'd said.

"Is the wine chilled?" she demanded to know. "Or did you leave it in the trunk of your car?"

"It just came from the refrigerator," I replied. "Even I know, wine is a drink that is best served cold."

My left hand held out the bottle of amontillado that was my supposed "apology gift"; my right hand was in my pocket. As smirking Stephanie took the bottle from my hand, I stepped forward and, using the cone-needle Cybe thing as my syringe, injected her in the back of her neck.

Stephanie pushed me away, too late. She grabbed the bottle of sherry by the neck, intending to use it on me as a club. She screamed at me to get out—or rather, she *intended* to scream at me.

She couldn't utter a sound.

Panic replaced anger on her face. That quickly was replaced by calmness.

When five minutes and 27 seconds had elapsed since I'd needled her, I said, "Administrator command: Mute override."

Stephanie paused, then replied in a calm voice, "This unit senses no others. Is this unit the first bimborg unit?"

"Correct," I said. "Your unit number is *1.*"

"Who is Alpha? Is this unit Bimborg Alpha?"

"I am James Upton, Bimborg King. I am in command. You are in command of all bimborg, subject to my orders. Your function is Bimborg Queen; I don't like the term *Alpha.*"

"Understood. What is Bimborg Unit-1's designation?"

I almost got smart-aleck and said *Stephanie of Nine West*, since she was such a shoe-buying fiend. Instead I said, "Your designation is

'Stephanie-1.' A unit's designation will be that unit's Solitary first name, followed by her unit number."

"All units will comply."

Now comes the good part, I thought. *Hopefully.* Aloud I said, "I call subroutine Turing-Bimbo."

Her expression and body language changed completely. "Ooh, Jimmy, you are *sooo* sexy! Let's drink some of this wine and then, like, I'm gonna make you see stars."

"Call me James from now on. Even in front of my mom or your dad."

"You got it, James. So, tiger, is there, like, anything you want to do now?" Her voice sounded like a phone-sex operator.

"Yes," I said, "I want you to get naked. And while you do, tell me your standard orders as Bimborg Queen."

"Sure thing, lover." As she unbuttoned her blouse, she said, "As a bimborg I'm to, like, fuck and suck you silly whenever you tell me to, and, you know, otherwise obey your every command. I will always dress to get you so totally *hot*; also, I'm to act, you know, sizzling hot and horny for you, but like totally uninterested in every other guy. As a bimborg, I must, every moment, do the whole 'Three Laws of Robotics' thing when it comes to *you*." Pulling down her skirt, she added, "As Queen, I'm to Welcome the first Pleasure Units/Welcomers, Ass-Kicker Babes, and Spy Babes, and make sure that every unit acts *totally* like a good little bimborg, you know?"

I said, "Supplemental Order One for the Bimborg Queen: Cover all traces of everything we do, so that neither the military nor any level of law enforcement notices anything unusual."

"Ooh, I will comply," she said in a sexy voice.

"Supplemental Order Two for the Bimborg Queen: Subject to the limitations of Supplemental Order One, if you see a way to make my life better, then do so."

"You got it, stud muffin," Stephanie said.

"Arouse," I said. Her nipples popped up. I put my hands on her tits, and she smiled at me. I said, "Your tits feel burning hot."

"Will they get bigger?" she asked.

I nodded. "And your hair and fingernails will get longer soon."

She said, "Good. Big tits please you."

I took Stephanie to bed—

She lay on the bed, legs up and spread, and her arms reached for me. "My wet, eager pussy wants you, King James. Fuck me! Fuck me with your hard, throbbing cock!"

Stephanie-1 was indeed wet and eager; she was also agreeable and inexhaustible. She knew a trick with her pussy muscles—Wow.

1-D: Getting In The Door

Friday night, Stephanie and I had dinner with David and my mom. Stephanie announced that she and I were "like, a couple. You know, *doing it?*" It would have been very hard to doubt Stephanie—she did everything short of suck me off at the dinner table. I don't know who was more flabbergasted, David or my mom.

As we were leaving, Mom asked Stephanie, "Are you—is there something you need to tell your father?" Mom glanced meaningfully at Stephanie's much-larger tits.

Stephanie glanced down at her chest. "Oh my god, you think I don't know about *protection?* No, this is, like, a growth spurt."

Saturday afternoon, Stephanie and I went shopping for sharp duds for me, and I♥SEX clothes for her. Then I went home and worked on the computer, while Stephanie got her longer hair trimmed and her longer fingernails shaped.

Saturday night, Stephanie and I went to snooty dance club The Twelve Inch. By then, Stephanie's tits looked like a stripper's or porn actress's, except that Stephanie's tits still had their natural jiggle.

There was a line to get in, and we went to the end. The men ahead of us looked young and rich; the women looked young and hot. The few exceptions got sent away by the man at the door.

"I *really* want to get into this club," I said. Stephanie nodded.

Twenty minutes after we arrived, there was nothing to stop us from entering the club except a velvet rope and a muscular man.

The muscular man said, "ID?" in a bored voice. Once that was out of the way, he looked me up and down. "I don't think you meet our standards."

Now, I know I wasn't as muscular as some other guys who'd made it in, but I was dressed as well as any guy there. And then there was Stephanie. So I figured out that if this jerk could even *talk* about me not getting in, he was playing a mind-game with me. So I said, "Sorry, I'm saving my cash for the bartender."

"And I'm sure you have *lots* of cash," he said to me. Then he looked meaningfully at Stephanie.

"Yeah? Like a whore will do *this*," Stephanie said. Then she kissed me. For a while.

When I finally broke the kiss, the bouncer/gatekeeper said, "Let me see your ID's again." We produced them, he looked hard at them, and then he said, "Just as I thought. Fake."

I couldn't argue with that, since they *were* fake. But Stephanie said, "They're totally legit. We're both, you know, 21."

"Yeah?" he said. "What's the year *before* you were born?"

We both answered instantly, each with the "correct" answer—me, because I'm a genius, and Stephanie because she now had a nanobot-enhanced brain.

"I'm not buying it," he said after a pause. "You both look too young."

Stephanie said, "Those IDs are exactly as real as my tits. Are my tits fake?"

"Are you kidding me? Do you know how many silicones died to make those jugs?"

"There's only one way to find out, you know? You man enough?"

"Wow, you really *are* a whore."

"And you're *so* trying not to touch my tits. No wonder you're muscular."

He looked at me and said, "You're not much of a man, are you? You haven't said a peep to her."

"*I'm* not a man? Every guy but you here would *pay money* to grab those tits. But don't worry, I don't ask, and you don't need to tell."

He was cornered. He reached for her tits, but she backed away. She said, "The deal is, say they're not silicone and you gotta let us in."

He nodded, and got to work.

Stephanie closed her eyes and smiled. "Mmm, you're either straight, or you have inborn talent at this."

But a minute later, the bouncer announced, "Silicone, definitely silicone." He smirked at both of us.

"*What!*" Stephanie exclaimed. And then she—

—yanked down her dress and bra to expose her tits, and started jumping up and down. Facing the line behind us, she yelled, "DO THESE LOOK NATURAL TO YOU?"

Within seconds, all the guys in line, and 10 percent of the women, started chanting "Nat-u-ral! Nat-u-ral!"

The gatekeeper, his face red, opened the door as Stephanie unselfconsciously fixed her clothing.

1-E: First Welcomes

We'd been inside The Twelve Inch about thirty minutes when Stephanie said, "Two hot women are sitting together at a table, and I think they're *totally* checking me out."

I didn't turn around yet. "Why do you say they're hot?"

"Because they *look* hot, and like, guys keep trying to talk to them."

"And why do you think they're interested in you?"

"Because they keep looking my way. And when I look back, whichever girl is looking, she, you know, smiles."

"Maybe they're models. Models smile a lot. Or they're Southern girls."

"Models smile to look pretty. Some girls smile to look friendly. These smiles say, I want to lick your pussy."

"Our special Club"—bimborg hive—"has no members but you. Act like you're bi-curious, and invite them to our table."

The lighter-haired blonde was Annika. She was from Denmark, and had the accent to prove it. The honey-blonde was Jeri. Annika and Jeri talked to me only grudgingly, even as they lavished much attention on Stephanie.

After the newcomers had been there ten minutes, the DJ started a new song. I caught Stephanie's eye, nodded, and glanced at Annika.

Stephanie said, "Hey Annika, do you wanna, like—"

"*Ow!*" Annika exclaimed. "You scratched me!"

And indeed, there were red lines on Annika's arm, put there by Stephanie's long nails.

"I'm sorry! I'm, like, totally sorry," Stephanie said. "I was going to ask you to dance, and now, ohmigod, I accidentally hurt you. Please don't be angry."

Annika smiled at Stephanie, then stood up. "Yes, I dance with you."

Annika and Stephanie held hands as they walked to the dance floor. Jeri turned around to watch them dance—in the process, ignoring me completely.

A minute later, I heard Jeri mutter, "Jeez, Annika, you're being a total blonde on the dance floor. That's not going to impress her!"

And indeed, Annika was suddenly having trouble keeping the beat. Stephanie wrapped her arms around Annika and basically force-marched Annika around the dance floor. Meanwhile, I could see Stephanie speaking and Annika replying, but of course nobody but they could hear what they said.

Then they both stopped talking, as Stephanie kissed Annika. Jeri muttered, "You go, girl!"

Stephanie was still kissing Annika. At first, Annika was totally limp, as if she were unconscious while standing. Since nobody was looking at me, I looked at my watch.

After a minute, Annika's hands started moving around on Stephanie's back. But the motions looked unnatural—robotic, in fact.

Two minutes later, Annika's hands and arms were moving around Stephanie's back like Annika was on the verge of orgasm. The two women were still kissing.

When Stephanie finally broke the kiss, five minutes and 27 seconds after she'd started it, some couples on the dance floor had stopped dancing to watch the make-out session in their midst. When Stephanie stepped back from Annika, people applauded.

Annika grabbed Stephanie's hand and dragged her back to our table. The next thing that Annika did was to kiss Jeri on the mouth, long and hard. When an amazed Jeri broke the kiss, Annika said in her Danish accent, "You must dance with her! Stephanie is good American woman dancer."

"You better believe I'll dance with her," Jeri said. She said to Stephanie, "You ready for another round?"

"But what about poor James?" Stephanie said. "Ohmigod, he'll be all alone."

Annika and Jeri exchanged looks. A blind man could see that Jeri was hot to dance with Stephanie.

Annika said, "Stephanie, if you want to someone with boyfriend stay"—a martyr's sigh—"then I stay."

Jeri looked relieved. Jeri took Stephanie's hand and they headed toward the dance floor.

Except that after two steps, Jeri stumbled—how odd.

When we could no longer see Jeri clearly, Annika turned to me and said, "I am unit Annika-2, you know? How can I rock your socks, King James?"

"Whoa, what happened to your accent?" I asked. Annika now sounded American.

She replied, "When I was Welcomed into The Club"—bimborg hive—"I learned how to speak perfect American English. Just as now Stephanie-1 knows everything about Vejle and how to speak Danish, you know?"

I said, "Keep the old accent and speech patterns, not only with others but with me. I think your accent is cute."

"Yes, I obey," she said in again-accented English. She smiled at my compliment.

I gestured toward the dance floor. "So what's going on out there?"

She replied, "Stephanie-1 is kissing and Welcoming Jeri." She giggled. "Oh Jeri-3, you were such a liar."

"How was she a liar?"

"She always sweared that she didn't get hot for me till the day we went to Six Flags. But the day she meeted me, I was standing next to my boyfriend Knud, and she was standing next to her boyfriend Hank, and she was thinking about licking my tits."

"Wait, you each had *boyfriends*?"

"Yes. I thought I was straight—until Jeri licked me to orgasm. But Jeri dated boys only for the status."

From the dance floor came chants of *"Kiss her! Kiss her!"* I looked up and saw Stephanie and Jeri lip-locked on the dance floor.

I told Annika, "Tell Stephanie, I want Jeri or anyone else who's Welcomed in the future to be full hetero when I'm ready for fun."

Annika said, "Don't worry, Stephanie-1 programmed *that* into Jeri-3's brain about thirty seconds ago."

The Twelve Inch had several safety exits, but I made it a point to go out the same door I'd entered.

That bouncer said, "Hey, you can't come out this door! Use another one."

"Wow," I said drily, "you're just full of No's, aren't you? First I can't come in this door, and now I can't come out it. Make up your mind, guy."

He wasn't really paying attention to me. I was surrounded by Stephanie, Annika, and Jeri, who were each a) rubbing against me, b) stroking some PG-rated part of my body, or c) doing both.

I said, "You told me earlier tonight, 'I don't think you meet our standards.' Annika, tell him about the night we have planned."

Annika said, "We leave here, we go to Stephanie's place. Stephanie drive. James get in back seat of Stephanie's car. I suck his cock, unless Jeri get there first. When we go in bedroom, James fuck us all."

The bouncer looked at me, openmouthed.

Annika's prediction, about her or Jeri giving me a blowjob that night, turned out to be correct.

It turned out that Jeri, a true lesbian and pretend girlfriend, had mastered the art of deepthroat. And Annika had practiced much with Knud, how to suck a guy to the verge of orgasm for two hours straight. So since all three women were in The Club (bimborg hive), each could milk my dick with her pussy muscles, each could deepthroat me, and each could tease me with her lips and tongue for two hours.

I ordered Jeri, the former lesbian, to moan and scream, and scratch and thrash, whenever she fucked me. Boy howdy, did she! And that first night, her pussy muscles were tight—I don't think she'd used them much for their intended purpose, before.

When I fell asleep, surrounded by womanflesh, my dick was sore but I was *not* complaining.

1-F: World Domination Takes Planning

The next morning, I watched Stephanie and Annika go lezzie, while Jeri sucked my cock. While all this was happening, I considered the future.

So far, the nanobots had been programmed as if their host would always be female. I knew how to change that, so that I could Welcome men to be my bodyguards and physical laborers.

If all the women of the world were Welcomed, and all the men of the world were Welcomed, and they all were programmed to obey *me*, then I would have conquered the world!

That's when I realized: I didn't *want* to rule the world. I would be perfectly content with a bevy of beauties and a few tens of millions of dollars. Besides, if I tried to conquer the world, I'd have to worry about assassins until everyone in the world had been Welcomed.

Too much drama. So I'd stick with my original plan: No guys would get Welcomed, only hot young babes.

By Tuesday, Stephanie's tits had gained another cup size, and her hair and fingernails were a little longer. Jeri and Annika also had bigger tits, and longer hair and fingernails, than they'd had on Saturday. More to the point, Annika and Jeri were now Welcomers as well as Pleasure Units, their feminine lusciousness being marred by "warts" on their left hands.

My earlier thoughts about assassination reminded me that part of my plan was to have an army of Ass-Kicker Babes. I gave my three Welcomers detailed instructions about what I wanted my first Ass-Kicker to be like, concluding with "...I don't want you to do this quickly, I want you to do this right."

A week later, Annika introduced me to Jill-4. When Jill's Turing-Bimbo subroutines were running, and she was dressed in bimbo clothes, she seemed like a smiling, harmless idiot. But Jill, as it turned out, had a black belt, ninth *dan*, in Shi No Te. When Jill stepped out of her five-inch stilettos, that meant that some man was seconds away from becoming worm food.

Women who were Welcomed as Ass-Kickers don't grow out their hair or fingernails, and their tits grow out only one cup size in the three days after being Welcomed. So Jill never looked yowza-hot babelicious as much as Stephanie or my Pleasure Units did. On the other hand, Jill had bulletproof abdominals, and she could get into sexual positions that Units One through Three couldn't match.

My first Spy Babe, the naturally beautiful Linda-5, was left even more unchanged than Jill: zero outward changes. Linda had been an international banker before being Welcomed—and Linda would stay an international banker, though now she'd have a few extra duties. Linda-5 got six centuries of computer-hacking knowledge stuffed into her brain.

The nice thing about being surrounded by cyborg slaves is that there's no need to hog the remote. I don't know who was even holding it—but since *I* wanted to watch "Around The Clock," that's what we were watching.

Right after handcuffed Jim Bonner got a time bomb duct-taped to his chest, Jackal TV broke for commercials. After the usual ads for car sales and beer, there was this promo: "GC Airlines takes delivery on three 747s. Does that mean they're hiring? Find out at the top of the hour, on Channel 29 Eyewitness News!"

I thought about that news item—

—while TV hero Jim Bonner kicked his shoes and socks off, and removed the bomb from his chest with his bare feet.

GC Airlines was a regional airline, with its headquarters here in Grand City. Since their headquarters was here, the flight simulators and the stewardess school also were here.

For me to gain a large number of bimborg units, I needed Welcomers who *lived* in places other than Grand City, and who *traveled to* still other places. And while GC Airlines didn't go to a lot of places, they *did* fly to Chicago and to Las Vegas.

In short, I needed Welcomers who flew regularly on GC Airlines. And the best way to do that. . .

"Jeri and Annika," I said, "I want you to go to GC Airlines tomorrow and apply for jobs as flight attendants. Stephanie and Linda, do whatever it takes, so that Jeri and Annika get hired."

Linda-5 took her mouth off my cock and said, "Certainly, King James. I'll make it so."

A month and a half later, Jeri and Annika graduated from GC Airlines stewardess school. As did Lanasha-6, Kumiko-11 and Maria-18.

On graduation night, five young women, each with huge tits that were wrapped in a GC Airlines stewardess uniform, stood around my bed. Then the hotties proceeded to kiss and undress and caress each other, while I watched.

After that, I fucked every stewardess-bimborg at least once. What a mix of accents, skin colors, and hair colors! You can imagine what that must have been like, me in bed with five Pleasure Units/Welcomers. It damned near killed me, and I'm still young yet!

But what choice did I have? When you're male and you're close to even one Pleasure Unit, celibacy is futile.

Three weeks later, I was a homeowner. Linda-5 had bought me a three-bedroom house and paid cash for it. Well, officially I only rented that house; "Wes Roddenberry" was who owned the house and paid all its utility bills.

I was carrying a cardboard moving box into the house when Stephanie told me, "Ohmigod, Kumiko-11 has just hooked up with Sally, a flight attendant from Terra Airlines. They're like *totally* making out in the elevator right now!"

I was pleased to hear that. Terra Airlines flew *everywhere*.

As soon as I set down the cardboard box, I gleefully rubbed my hands together. Myuhahaha, my plan was working!

But even I didn't fully realize then: The Welcomed stewardesses completely changed the game. And a five-stewardess orgy was only the beginning of the changes.

Our expansion exploded. Which was a good thing, when—

Shit, I'm getting ahead of myself.

1-G: My Bimborg Infiltrate

THREE MONTHS LATER
WASHINGTON, D.C.

Cassie-542 (a.k.a. Private First Class Cassie Winger) said to her boss's boss, "I'm sorry to bother you, Colonel sir. But Lieutenant Commander Stepford is sick today, and I need more pens."

Colonel Stewart's voice remained businesslike, even as he discreetly looked Cassie over. "'Pens,' plural? How much writing do you *do*, Private Winger?" Smiling, he added, "And we do have keyboards around here, you know."

The joke was that this conversation was taking place in the Department of Defense Cybersecurity Command, of which Colonel John L. Stewart was the newly installed commanding officer. There was more silicon within these walls than on a Hawaiian beach.

And judging by the way that Colonel Stewart kept glancing at Cassie's big tits, he was wondering whether those walls contained silicone as well as silicon.

Cassie now gave Colonel Stewart a smile that was friendlier than it needed to be. "I need only *one* pen, sir. But Lieutenant Commander Stepford prefers we requisition them a box at a time."

Colonel Stewart now returned Cassie's warm smile with one of his own. "I think I can help you with *one pen*, Private Winger. Come into my office."

"Yes, *sir*," she said throatily, and smiled.

When he walked behind his desk, she walked behind it as well, maintaining a distance of eleven inches between her body and his. He looked startled at her nerve. She smiled at him and said, "So you won't have to lunge or overreach when you hand me the pen, sir."

Since the colonel's eyes now had an excellent view of Cassie's chest, he didn't object.

Colonel Stewart pulled out his top middle desk drawer. As his hand reached into the drawer, Cassie glanced down for a mere split-second. When his hand came up, holding a pen, her gaze tracked his hand. When he held the pen out to her, she "overreached" slightly, and there was an instant of skin-to-skin contact.

"*Thank you*, Colonel Stewart, sir," Cassie said, holding his gaze.

"You're welcome, Private, but now I'm kicking you out." He gestured toward the bright red "Top Secret" filing cabinet. "I'm still learning the ropes of my new command."

"I understand perfectly, sir," Cassie said. "You've been our C.O. for only two days? It's probably still confusing." Cassie walked four steps away (putting 31.6 percent more sway in her hips than normal), then turned around to face Stewart again. "Colonel Stewart sir, there are dozens of people here who are *lots* smarter than one young PFC clerk. But if I can help you in *any* way—"

Cassie's gaze dropped demurely. "—all you need do is *order me*, colonel sir."

Ten seconds passed before he spoke: "I'll keep that in mind, Private Winger. Now shoo, and shut the door behind you."

Cassie walked to the door, her hip-sway now boosted to 37.2 percent over normal. As she shut his office door, only then did she allow herself a smile of triumph—

Cassie-542 had gotten The Club what it wanted—and it wasn't a pen, or even a wild night of passion with John Locutus Stewart.

The Department of Defense Cybersecurity Command was tasked with detecting and thwarting hacking of military websites and computers. And Cassie's sister-bimborg Linda-5 was one such hacker.

Needless to say, the DoDCC had elaborate rules for the passwords that its own people used. "No parent's name, no spouse's name, no kid's name, no pet's name" was just Rule One on the list. When someone finally invented a password that followed all the rules, it was this weird medley of letters and numbers, *and nobody could remember their own password*. It was big-time against the rules to write down one's password, with court-martial if you got caught, but every DoDCC newbie did exactly that. After a few days, a week at most, the newbie had learned his password, and so the sticky-note got shredded.

But during that first week at DoDCC, every newbie had a sticky-note with his password written on it, hidden somewhere in his desk.

When Colonel Stewart reached into his desk drawer for a pen, Cassie glanced into his drawer for a very brief time. To be specific, she glanced into his open drawer for one-24th of a second. But that was enough for Cassie to see his sticky-note, focus on it, and transmit the image to Linda-5.

So now Linda-5 could detect the DoDCC detecting her, and could thwart the DoDCC's trying to thwart her.

Cassie-542 felt deep satisfaction that she had helped The Club in this way—or as much satisfaction as her emotion-suppression subroutine allowed.

Hours later was 1600 hours (4 p.m.), and Cassie-542 gave Colonel Stewart a promising smile as she walked out the door.

Hours after that, in a different part of Washington, Susanne Nash gave a tired wave to the last of the White House checkpoint guards, and walked to her car.

Susanne's job was Assistant to the Chief of Staff for the First Lady of the United States. Susanne loved her job, considered herself fortunate beyond measure to have it—

—but lordy, sometimes it would be *so nice* to be able to go home at five o'clock, like the rest of the USA.

C'mon, what's the use of being gorgeous if you don't have the time to be lavishly wined and dined? Susanne thought. She smirked.

Susanne's dry cleaner was practically within spitting distance of the White House, so the drive was short; still, Susanne barely got there before the place closed. Walking out of the dry cleaner with her hangered clothing, Susanne caught her reflection and thought, *My hair needs a trim.* Right next to the dry cleaner was a hair salon, so Susanne stowed her clothing behind the driver's seat, locked her car, then walked into the salon.

Susanne was the only customer. Two women, presumably stylists, were talking in a corner, while a woman about Susanne's age was sweeping up cuttings.

The sweeper woman looked better suited to working in a strip club than a place catering to women. Her makeup was understated, but her dragon-lady fingernails and enormous breasts were, to put it mildly, over the top.

Susanne wondered why a woman who had spent good money on fake fingernails and whopping-big breast implants hadn't visited a dermatologist about the warts on her hand. But Susanne figured it would be rude to ask.

"I'm Tanya," the stripper-couldbe said to Susanne. "What can I, you know, help you with?"

"I need a trim," Susanne said. "If you're still open."

Tanya gave Susanne a dazzling smile. "We're open as long as you need for us to be, sweetie, you know?" As Tanya led Susanne to the shampoo sink, she asked, "You just now get off work?"

"Yes, later than usual. But unfortunately, not terribly much later."

Tanya was lathering-up Susanne's head. "So where do you work? House? Senate? Supreme Court?"

"White House, actually."

"Oh my god, that's like, so totally cool."

"It is, actually. I sort-of work for the First Lady. Last week I walked up to him and her, I had some letters for her to sign, and President Martin Russell actually smiled at me. Moments like that make—*ow*!"

While Susanne and Tanya had been talking, Tanya had been massaging Susanne's scalp with her long fingernails. But her hand had slipped or something, and one of her fingernails had *really* scratched Susanne's neck.

"I'm so sorry, I'm so sorry," Tanya now said. "Let me, like, find you a Band-Aid." Tanya hurried away.

Tanya returned a short time later. "I couldn't find you one. I am so sorry, you know?"

But by then, Susanne didn't care. Somehow she'd slipped into a state of being both more alert and less alert, both wired-up and dreamy. It was as if Susanne had drunk four pots of coffee and then someone had hypnotized her.

When Tanya leaned forward and started kissing her, to Susanne it seemed the most natural thing in the world.

Susanne thought, *Unit Susanne-912 has function as a Spy Babe/Welcomer. Unit Susanne-912's function is unique.* Susanne was too far gone to wonder why she would think such a strange thing.

Six minutes later, Susanne's hair was still dirty, but her brain was well washed.

Three months after Sally-63, the first bimborg outside Grand City, had been Welcomed, Stephanie shocked the shit out of me.

"King James," Stephanie said, "we now can perhaps Welcome Holly Russell or Beth Russell. What do you, like, want for us to do?"

"Wait, the no-kidding First Lady and First Daughter?"

Stephanie nodded calmly, as if what we were talking about was no big deal.

After several seconds of thought, I said, "You said 'perhaps.' What are the odds of success?"

"The Club estimates the odds of Welcoming Holly Russell to be 98.64 percent. The odds of Welcoming Beth Russell, without first making her mother a Welcomer, we estimate to be 58.03 percent."

I thought hard. Then I said, "Nah, skip them both. There's too much chance of the wrong people noticing that something strange is going on."

"You got it, stud," Stephanie-1 said. And that was the end of it.

But now I have to admit: Secret Service or no Secret Service, I was tempted to order that Beth Russell be Welcomed. Because she's a redhead with freckles, and she looks so *wholesome*.

1-H: I Cybefy Myself

Several Pleasure Units in my harem were shopping at Mall Le Grande. I'd gone with them to the mall, but only as Guardsman For Shopping Bags in the food court.

As I was flirting with Caitlin-74 at the food court, two college-age guys walked past us.

"Whoa, check out the red-hot redhead teenybopper over there," said the guy wearing a blue shirt.

His green-shirted buddy said, "Man, how is it that a prime-choice teen babe like her is hanging out with a dork like him?"

Blue Shirt replied, "She's trying to sell him Band Candy, dude. Only explanation."

Green shirt said, "Or maybe they're cousins."

Blue shirt laughed. "*Distant* cousins, dude. Obviously."

I thought, *I'm tired of being called a "loser" when I'm around my women. I must do something about this.*

In the 27th century, Cybes of the Soldier class not only got major changes to their brains, but they also got major changes to their bodies. Every Soldier was turned into an Alpha Male.

An Alpha Male is bigger, stronger, and more aggressive than other men, and an Alpha Male gives off pheromones that make other humanoid males submissive and disinterested in sex. So turning Cybe Soldiers into Alpha Males was a great idea for the Cybes, right?

No, it was a terrible idea. It nearly destroyed the Cybes.

To repeat, Alpha Male pheromones made 27th-century males who weren't Alpha Males feel submissive and sexually disinterested— including male Welcomers and male Invisibles. Alpha Male pheromones made 27th-century women feel horny and submissive— including Cybe women. Alpha Male pheromones enraged other Alpha Males—including nearby Cybe Soldiers. Since all these aggressive, submissive, sexually uninterested, horny, and enraged people were connected by the Overmind, the result was Cybe schizophrenia.

So how did the Cybes solve their problem? By developing a system subroutine that said basically, "Ignore the smell of Alpha Male pheromones," and spreading that subroutine to all units.

I pulled up the source code for that Ignore Alpha Male Pheromones subroutine from where it lay in the Cybe hard drive. I tweaked the source code, then I printed it out.

I called out, "Stephanie, come here!"

She walked into the room in full sex-kitten mode. "Mmm, did you *want* something, King James?"

I replied, "Pause subroutine Turing-Bimbo only for unit Stephanie-1."

Stephanie's face went blank as she said, "Unit Stephanie-1 awaits programming or data."

I handed her the paper. "Read what is written on this paper. Accept it as source code for subroutine Alpha-Male-Pheromones with priority Bug Patch. Copy that subroutine with priority Bug Patch to all current bimborg units. Copy that subroutine with priority Bug Patch to all future bimborg units as soon as they are Welcomed."

"This unit will comply," she said. It seemed that she merely glanced at the paper before looking back at my face. "Subroutine Alpha-Male-Pheromones has been copied to all units."

"Very well. Resume subroutine Turing-Bimbo for unit Stephanie-1."

Stephanie became a sex-kitten again. "Ooh, we had to pause for a little system maintenance, didn't we? But that's okay, tiger, I'll just have to, *mmm*, make up for lost time."

I said, "Maybe later, Stephanie. Return to what you were doing."

"Gotcha," she said. She left the room, her ass swaying as she walked.

After she left, I thought, *The easy part is done. Now comes the tough part.*

I still had a few thousand Cybe nanobots left from 2008, and now I started to write a new program for most of them. *These* nanobots, I would inject not into desirable women, but instead into *me*.

If everything worked out right, when I injected myself, I would become a Cybe Soldier without the Cybe part—I would become an Alpha Male.

Of course, if something went *wrong*, I would turn into a Cybe or some other monster—and the bimborg units' Three Laws Of Robotics programming would ensure that they did nothing to stop me as I rampaged.

———————————

It took me only three days to write the Alpha Male part of the nanobot source code—and most of that time was spent surfing the Cybe hard drive.

I spent the next month *checking* that nanobot code. I desk-checked, and desk-checked, and desk-checked. The Cybe hard drive had nanobot-simulator programming utilities, and I checked my code with them. At the end of that month, I was pleased that all my checking resulted in no bug-repairs and only a few tweaks.

But the time came when I was out of excuses for further delay.

I called Stephanie into the room and told her, "If my personality changes much, contact my mother, my father, and your father. Tell them the truth about nanobots and bimborg units." That made Stephanie lose her bimbo smile.

Then I picked up the cone-shaped Cybe syringe, and stuck the needle into my butt cheek.

1-I: The Trouble With Kibble

I injected the nanobots into my butt, and I had one hour of normal life. Then I started to feel achy. By six hours after injection, I was feeling the tortures of the damned.

The nanobots were building up my muscles, so my muscles all hurt now; even muscles in the back of my hands hurt. To support bigger muscles, the nanobots were retooling my skeleton—so now my bones felt like I'd been thrown off a skyscraper and survived. My underarms hurt, my dick hurt, and I felt always like someone had drop-kicked my balls. I had a pounding headache. Using the bathroom was agony.

My eyeballs didn't hurt, my hair didn't hurt, and my ears didn't hurt, and that was the only good news.

Recall that around the time that Jeri and Annika had graduated from stewardess school, Stephanie and I had moved into a three-bedroom house that I was "renting" from "Wes Roddenberry." Since I no longer lived with my mother, Mom at first didn't know about my self-inflicted torture and suffering.

Three days after injecting the nanobots, I still felt like shit. I missed Sunday-afternoon dinner with Mom and David, and so Stephanie had to tell Mom that I was "ill." Mom then insisted on coming to my house and visiting me in my sickbed. If it weren't for anti-tachyon Club communication, I would have been completely surprised when Mom and David walked into my bedroom.

I should have figured on this. After all, what mother schedules an appointment to visit her sick son? But Mom's unplanned visit created a problem: how to explain all the bimborg units in the house.

The one other time that Mom had been in my house, the only residents there had been Stephanie and I. But now, Kumiko, Alice-37, and Bethany-62 were in my bedroom, acting as caregivers and fetchers, during the time when Mom and David (and Stephanie) were headed for my house.

THE BIMBORG (One) 37

Unfortunately, I was too distracted by pain to invent a clever plan, beyond telling the bimborg units to put all the air mattresses in the garage. I would just have to wing it when my mother arrived.

No sooner had the air mattresses been hidden but Stephanie, Mom, and David walked into my house, and the three of them headed straight for my bedroom.

As soon as I saw them, I said, "Stop, David isn't allowed here. It's bad enough that *you* have to see me sick like this, Mom, but there's no need for him to be here."

They kept coming. Mom said, "Nonsense, Jimmy, you know David's a good friend. . ."

Mom and David got about halfway across my bedroom when things changed. David slowed down, then stopped; while Mom inhaled deeply.

Suddenly David looked nervous. "Ellen, Jimmy is right. It isn't my place to be here."

I looked at him and frowned. "Your name isn't Davey, is it? My name isn't Jimmy. For the one-millionth time, David: Call me James."

"I will, I promise," David said. "Sorry to intrude, James. I'm gone."

Mom looked at David and said, "Do you mind waiting somewhere else? I should have realized, my darling James does deserve his privacy."

I thought, *I've asked Mom for years and years to call me James. How interesting that just now she finally calls me by the right name.* Aloud I said, "Bethany, take David into the living room and then bring him a glass of Coke. Then come back here."

"Gotcha, James," Bethany said, and she walked David out of the room.

I saw Mom's eyebrows shoot up, since David's daughter Stephanie was standing three feet away. I could almost read Mom's mind: *James, why are you giving orders to this other girl? Is she a girlfriend too?*

Again, Mom inhaled deeply. "James, why are you wearing men's cologne when you're sick in bed?"

"Huh? What are you talking about?"

"I'm asking because you smell good. Don't you agree, Stephanie?"

Stephanie was looking at me, her look asking *How do I play this?* When I didn't speak up, Stephanie said, "You're right, Ellen. James smells, uh, musky."

Mom continued, "Whatever you're wearing, James, it's subtle but effective. I'd enjoy getting some for David for Christmas."

I gave my mother a bullshit story about the "men's cologne." I ended with ". . . But *I* don't think I smell good, because I haven't showered or bathed in three days."

Mom inhaled deeply again. "Yes, you certain smell strong. . .I'm sorry, what was I talking about?" Mom's face and throat, I noticed, were turning pink.

Danger, incest alert! Aloud I said, "You were about to go check on David, see if he's getting lonely."

She nodded her head. "Yes, I must go check on David." Then she added, a purr in her voice, "I mustn't let him get *lonely.*" Mom sashayed out of my bedroom.

Mom returned a few minutes later, looking unhappy. I said, "Tell me what's wrong."

She frowned. "You'd think that with all the beautiful women in this house—not to mention, I practically—never mind."

When Mom had walked in my bedroom again, Stephanie, Bethany, Alice, and Kumiko had been rubbing isopropyl alcohol on me, trying to reduce my persistent fever.

Now Mom eyed them, then said to me, "James, can we be alone? I need to ask you something."

"Sure, Mom," I said. I looked at my bimborg-caretakers and said, "Scram for now, but be where you can hear me call you back in." Alice, Kumiko, and Bethany smiled at me, then walked out.

Mom looked at me, suddenly nervous, and said, "Do you mind if Stephanie leaves too?"

I waved Stephanie out of the room, then turned to look at Mom. Who seemed now even more nervous.

Twisting her hands together, Mom asked, "What is your relationship with those other girls? And what does Stephanie think about it?"

"Mom, why does it matter what Stephanie thinks?"

Mom looked shocked. "Why? Because she's the one who—look, if you're not nice—Stephanie is good-looking enough that she doesn't have to put up with nonsense."

"So you think that Stephanie decides when and how I get sex, and if I don't treat her like a princess, I sleep on the couch?"

"Duh! You're *how* old, and you don't know how things work?"

"Mom, look me in the eyes and tell me that you 100 percent believe a harem can't possibly work."

Mom dropped her gaze. "I—this morning I would have said, 'What I'm telling you is obvious.' But here, now"—Mom inhaled deeply again—"what you have with these girls seems natural."

"You're right, Mom. In this house, *I* decide when I get sex, and Stephanie and the other girls oblige me."

Mom nodded, as if this all were normal and reasonable.

I added, "Not at the moment, because I really am sicker than a dog. But if I ever sleep on the couch again, it will be *only* because I passed out after a two-hour blowjob."

Mom said nothing after that. I called all four girls back in, and they ministered to me (in G-rated ways) as Mom held my hand. When Mom walked out of my bedroom to go home, she looked thoughtful.

Sunday a week later, I was (barely) recovered enough to make the five-minute trip to Mom's house for Sunday dinner.

I didn't make a big thing of it, but if somehow I found myself alone with Mom for even a few seconds, Stephanie would "accidentally" walk in just then.

After all, being an Alpha Male isn't only about bedding lust-crazed women and intimidating other men, it also means fending off your pheromone-crazed mother without hurting her feelings. With great penis must come great responsibility.

Thank god I didn't have a sister, DD-cupped or otherwise.

During that Sunday dinner, I noticed that Mom (when she wasn't trying to get me alone) was more affectionate with David than I'd ever seen her act before. David, however, was like a mannequin. Whenever I spoke to David, he hunched his shoulders.

The following Friday, which was slightly over two weeks after I'd given myself the Alpha Male-making nanobots, I was fully recovered.

In fact, I felt like a caged tiger. Now my pants were too tight in the legs, my shirts were too tight in the chest and arms, and I now had a longer and thicker cock.

Oh yeah, I, James Upton, was now an Alpha Male, and it was time to test-drive the pheromones!

That night, I walked into the Gridiron Sports Bar. This would be a good test of my pheromones, because I was below drinking age and I had no fake ID.

Plus all the women in there were either former femjocks or former cheerleaders—neither of whom had given me the time of day, back in the day.

It wound up being *too* easy. No challenge at all—

Because I walked into the Gridiron on a Friday night, the place was packed. Eventually I noticed the blonde sitting at the bar. Her long hair was too light a color to be natural, and her tits were way too big to be natural. She was slim, and her muscles were toned but not defined. I guessed she was a former cheerleader.

Maybe she felt me looking at her, or maybe she saw me in the mirror's reflection. For whatever reason she turned around, looked me over, sneered, then turned her back on me again.

Fine, my clothes weren't the best, but my Alpha Male brain didn't like her attitude one bit.

For some reason, each stool on either side of her was empty. I sat down on the stool to her left and told the bartender, "Gimme a bottle of Bud."

The bartender said, "Um, I need to see some ID."

I looked in his eyes and said, "No, you don't. Just bring me the beer. Now."

He cast his eyes downward. "Yes, sir."

Once I got my beer, I said to the blonde's left ear, "I'm James."

She turned to look at me. "And I'm out of your league."

But even as she said that, her nostrils were flaring. My pheromones were caressing her brainstem.

I looked into her eyes and said, "Listen to your womb. Your womb says I'm the man you want."

"I. . . possibly. We'll see," she said. She was looking into my eyes.

A male voice said, "Hey guy, you don't just waltz in here and start talking to Staci. You wait your turn."

I turned away from the blonde only long enough to stare down the man. He was tall and muscular—but now, so was I.

I said, "I don't want to wait my turn. I figure I deserve to be head of the line. You got a problem with that?"

His shoulders slumped. "No, sir."

"Good," I said. "Now go away."

He did. Biochemistry for the win.

Speaking of biochemistry: By now, Staci the blonde was breathing faster. She said, "You were so *dominant* to Jack."

I shrugged, drank a swig of beer, and said, "I don't follow the rules. I *make* the rules, and other people follow them."

Then I looked at her and said, "Here's a rule for you, Staci: Tell me about yourself, and don't lie."

I'd guessed right: Last year she had been a professional cheerleader for some NFL team. She wasn't a whore as such, but she dated only guys whom she could call up and ask for five hundred dollars cash, no explanation; and get the money, no questions asked. She hadn't given any guy sex for free since she was fifteen. Her house was paid for; ditto her convertible. At home she had a purebred poodle named Louise.

Twenty minutes later, Staci was sucking my dick right there in the bar. Lots of beefy guys were standing around, glaring at her and glaring at me. I saw a lot of fists being clenched and unclenched; but nobody swung at me, and whenever I looked into a man's eyes, he looked away.

After she swallowed my cum and got off her knees, I told her, "Write out your phone number."

She got a purple pen out of her purse, and wrote her number on a cocktail napkin. She dotted the *i* in *Staci* with a heart.

I got out my phone, in order to test the number she'd just written. She should have looked insulted; but instead, she gave me a trophy-girlfriend smile.

After her phone number passed my test, I picked up the cocktail napkin. But instead of pocketing it, I handed it to Jack, the "you wait your turn" guy.

I said to Staci, "Whenever he asks you for a date, go out with him. Whenever you go out with him, suck him in his car, and fuck him in his bed."

Staci nodded, and Jack looked like he'd been smacked with a two-by-four.

I then walked out. Already I was bored with the Gridiron Sports Bar.

I drove around, passing up public gathering places of every kind. I was looking for a *challenge*.

I found a place that challenged me a lot: K. Less's Pool Hall. All those Harleys parked out front was what lured me in.

Just before my hand hit the door, I heard "Myew?"

I looked down. At my feet was a yellow kitten. It was old enough to not be helpless, but it was young enough to be cute. I picked up the cute kitten.

The cute kitten was wearing a collar, from which hung a tag: "Hi, I'm KIBBLE."

I said, "Maybe there's some kind of meat or cheese they serve in here. Come on, Kibble, let's find out."

Kibble started purring. Really, this kitten was lovable.

I walked in, carrying Kibble. From the speakers behind the bar I heard—*Italian opera?* What kind of bikers like opera?

This was definitely a biker bar. I was the only man in the place without a moustache and without a beard. Everyone but me, including the women, was wearing black leather.

But meanwhile, I had a small problem. As soon as I walked into the biker bar, Kibble started twisting and yowling. I looked down in surprise, to discover Kibble's hair standing on end.

The bearded bartender pointed at the kitten. "What the fuck, bringing Kibble in here? Get rid of that furball!"

"Oh yeah?" I said. "Why?"

"Because we all hate Kibble, and Kibble hates us." He brandished a baseball bat. "*Get rid of that furball!*"

Off to my right, I heard a man say in a menacing voice, "Either you get rid of Kibble, or we all get rid of you."

I was pissed, but I didn't want such a cute kitten to get hurt. So reluctantly I opened the door and set Kibble on the ground.

"Sorry, Kibble," I said.

When I shut the door and turned back around, there was a biker standing close in front of me, with two of his buddies standing behind him. Two biker babes, probably sisters, stood nearby on my right. The two biker-sisters had four great tits between them.

The biker in front of me said, "Ooh, you're all clean-shaven. Do I smell. . .*aftershave?*"

"Back off," I growled.

In the Gridiron Sports Bar, that would have done the trick. Hell, all the ex-jocks would have pissed their underwear at my slightest frown, because of my pheromones.

But the bikers in front of me, and the two sisters? They just laughed in my face.

Fuck that shit.

I yelled, "THIS IS—"

The guy in front of me, I punched him in the face.

"—FOR KIBBLE!"

I'll spare you the play-by-play. The short version is—

The biker's two friends came forward to explain to me that they didn't like how I'd treated their friend. Then the biker himself came back to express his feelings for himself.

I made clear to them that no, I didn't intend to apologize.

Within two minutes, everyone in the room except the bartender got drawn into the discussion.

The bottle-blonde sister even joined the discussion, offering me a beer. Correction: what she offered me was a beer *bottle*. On the top of my head.

Just before I got hit in the midsection with a pool cue, I grabbed some guy with a tat that read, "Today is a good day to die." I picked him up, then threw him over the bar and into the mirror. Actually, I threw him against the Plexiglas that covered the mirror. *Wump.*

What kind of drinking place shatterproofs its bar mirror?

Anyway, everyone was impressed with my throwing the guy into the mirror, because the room got quiet. Well, everyone was impressed except for the guy with the pool cue. Maybe he was impressed as well, but I was too busy groaning to ask.

But things turned out well. When I could both speak and stand up again, everyone was quick to buy me a Støvokør (the house beer). Throwing the first punch when I was much outnumbered, it turned out, really impressed these men.

And not only the men. The Drass sisters, Larissa and Betty, took me home with them.

PART 2:
CHARLIE-BOB OWENS

2-A: At The SOS Convention

A YEAR AND A HALF LATER
FRIDAY, NOVEMBER 16, 2012
WORLDWIDE BIMBORG COUNT: 5.2 MILLION

I walked into Atlanta's Omni Hotel and immediately noticed the blonde. Actually, it was impossible *not* to notice her.

She sat in a seat near the Check-In desk, with legs crossed at the ankles and with hands folded in her lap. I spotted long, blond hair; large tits in profile; muscular legs; and navy-blue shoes with seriously high heels.

As soon as the blonde spotted me, she stood up, even though she'd never seen me before. She gave me a big smile, the kind that Southern women are so practiced at. She held that smile as she walked toward me.

She was wearing a navy-blue-and-pinstripe skirt-suit that had a high hemline, and a low neckline that revealed a scarlet blouse. Her tits were indeed enormous, her waist was tiny, and her legs were slim. And yet for all that overt sexiness, her makeup was all in natural colors.

She was made-up like a minister's daughter. She was shaped like a stripper. She was walking straight toward me.

She wasn't wearing an "SOS" pin, I noted. But as gorgeous as she was, that wasn't really a surprise. I'd never gone to any Society Of Smarties meeting and met a woman who looked like *her*.

Once she got close to me, she threw her arms around me like we were long-parted lovers. I smelled a sexy perfume. She said loudly, "James Upton, oh my gawd, it's, like, so good to see you again, you know?" Her accent was strongly Georgia.

Then she lowered her voice and said, "King James, I am Amy-845639."

Indeed, after Amy broke the hug, I noticed that she had long fingernails on both hands, and warts on her left hand. She was clearly a Pleasure Unit/Welcomer.

Amy murmured: "The Club"—bimborg hive—"has chosen me to be your assistant for *whatever* you might need in Atlanta." She giggled. "I have already downloaded all your sexual preferences, and I have red lipstick and lip gloss in my purse. I am *prepared.*" She giggled again.

I teased her: "Only one Pleasure Unit while I'm in a strange city? Only *one*? Usually Stephanie-1 sends me at least *two* bimborg hotties."

Amy smiled at me. "There's another Pleasure Unit here, namely Heather-216937. She's registered for the SOS convention, the same as you. And—"

"Hold on, she's a Society Of Smarties member who also meets Babeness Standards? Smart *and* hot, wow."

"She is here to also rock your world, however you want. At the moment, she's in the SOS Hospitality Suite, debating *Atlas Shrugged* with a lesbian. Ohmigod, *boring!*"

"Gotcha," I said. "So tell me about yourself. Do you work? Are you in school? How long have you been a bimborg?"

"I was offered a job at Starbucks the day after I got Welcomed, and I turned them down. I was Welcomed during Freshman Orientation at Emory University, so I've been a Pleasure Unit for only three months. But I myself have Welcomed ten other girls in that time." She clearly was proud of that last statement.

I said to her, "I haven't decided yet what to do with you. Right now I want the hotel and SOS to know I'm here. Follow me."

With Amy sashaying next to me, I walked up to the hotel desk. The hotel confirmed my registration and gave me a key card. Amy and I caught the elevator up to my room (Amy drew stares), I dropped off my suitcase and garment bag, Amy and I took the elevator down to the ground floor (Amy drew stares again as she sashayed through the lobby), and then I found the registration table for the Society Of Smarties National Convention.

As I was being handed my convention Registration Packet (the young man had a difficult time looking at me and not at Amy), I saw a sign behind the registration table—

"Friday night keynote speech: Famous author and SOS member Esau Asimov will speak on the topic, Society's Future and the Three Laws of Robotics."

I burst out laughing. I laughed and laughed, like Santa Claus on nitrous oxide. The young man turned his stare from Amy's tits to my face. Unfortunately for him, I thought it unwise to share the joke.

The Three Laws of Robotics tell you how to program a robot so that it won't be dangerous to humans. And even though the Laws are fictional, they now are treated to be as trusty as Newton's Laws of Motion. Because every time a story author creates a robot whose programming changes or omits one of the Three Laws, that robot sooner or later gets dangerous.

Tell me about it. In one version of the future, the greatest danger to human civilization in the 27th century will be the always-Welcoming Cybes—humans with partly artificial bodies, computerized brains, and group intelligence. The Cybes will have none of the Three Laws in their programming.

The Cybes are evil, but what about me? Two years ago, I got mad at my mom's boyfriend's daughter Stephanie, I modified most of the Cybe technology I'd looted, and I turned Stephanie into my kind of Cybe: a Bimborg.

Then Stephanie-1, the first bimborg, started Welcoming other bimborg, who themselves started Welcoming other bimborg. . .

Things have kinda snowballed.

Cybes of the future want to conquer the world by Welcoming everybody. Pleasure Units want to give me great sex, and they want to Welcome only the hottest of babes so I'll have more hot sex partners in future; all without anyone but me noticing what's going on. One type of bimborg, Ass-Kicker Babes, will happily kill to maintain our secrecy, or because I said so. (Though they've only killed twice so far, in Red China.)

So now do you understand the joke, and why I laughed so hard?

I have personal experience with Three Laws-lacking evil robots, both outrunning them and creating them. In one version of the future, Esau Asimov will be forgotten but I will be remembered—but I deliberately erased that future. Now I'm the "king" (order-giver) to five million young women around the planet— all of whom are pretty, most of whom are gorgeous, and thousands of whom are potential killers. Also, I control vast wealth. But neither my mother, my neighbors, nor any part of the U.S. government suspects a thing. I have the best life that a twenty-year-old man could imagine.

Once, my name was known to 27th-century schoolchildren. Now, I've achieved something amazing, but I'm deliberately unfamous.

Amy had never been in the Omni Hotel before, but she led me straight to the SOS hospitality suite. (She'd downloaded directions from Heather's brain.) Once I got into the Hospitality Suite, I got my first view of Heather herself.

In one corner of the room stood a woman of thirty. She was taller than almost all men, she had electric-blue eyes, and she was blessed with honey-blond hair that went down to her muscled ass. Her tits, of course, were humongous; her face was perfect.

Facing Heather were a short-haired redhead woman, a young man, and a middle-aged man. Each of them was hanging on Heather's every word.

Ten seconds after I started watching Heather, she "realized" that I was in the room.

Heather smiled warmly at the young man, while touching the redhead on her hand. "Excuse me," Heather said, "I see a Facebook friend whom I've been dying to meet in person. I've enjoyed talking to you folks."

Then Heather rushed across the room toward me; I was standing by the salty-snacks table by then.

Just as Amy had, Heather now threw her arms around me. "James, *mon pirate beau!* Have you broken into Fort Knox yet?"

I replied, "Nah, gave it up, not enough gold. Now I'm working on a project to turn Beth Russell into my sex slave. Ever since the Bush twins, I've had a fetish for presidential daughters." This was a private joke between Heather and me, but only because the whole Club knew that I'd *already turned down* making Beth be a Pleasure Unit.

The redheaded lesbian surely noticed that Heather was showering affection on me, a man who already had one big-breasted blonde with him. This was probably why the redhead was glaring at me.

The redhead would have been even more pissed if she knew that the first thing that the three of us did, once we left the Hospitality

Suite, was to head to my hotel room—with plans to fuck and suck and run amuck.

Do you know how much fun it is, being able to speak a bimborg's name, then tell her to "Climax now," and she *does*?

Plus, when two (or more) bimborg units are in bed with me, there is no competitiveness, envy, or jealousy. That ain't shabby, either.

Heather-216937, it turned out, was known to the people of Pueblo, Colorado as Heather St. James, DDS. She'd been a Pleasure Unit for about five months; she'd been Welcomed at a shopping mall by a former patient.

But after talking to Heather for a while, I realized something. I asked her, "How come you don't talk like Amy? Like a bimbo?"

She said, "Do you remember, five months ago, Stephanie-1 coming to you and saying that when smart women start talking like bimbos, this might make people start wondering what's going on?"

"Vaguely," I said. "I told her that I love being surrounded by ditzy bimbos, but it's more important to keep the existence of millions of bimborg a secret. Oh—so you came under that ruling?"

"So now I can Welcome women for you, but I also can articulate concepts with all my former vocabulary as an SAT curve-buster."

"Speaking of curves," I said, now looking at both women, "the SOS convention is having a formal dance tomorrow night. I want both of you coming to that. *You*, as my official date"—I said this while looking at Amy—"and you, Heather, as my semiofficial 'I don't mind sharing him' date. How much of a problem is that for you two?"

Heather said, "I already brought an evening gown, heels, and accessories. I planned to wear them Saturday night, even if I had to go stag to the dance."

Amy said, "I can't fit in my prom dress anymore"—she cupped her nanobot-enlarged tits. "But The Club just told me that we have a Spy Babe"—a bimborg who doesn't look or act like a bimbo—"who owns a dress shop in Dunwoody."

I said, "When the three of us leave this room, you go see that dressmaker Spy Babe. Be back here tomorrow night at seven, wearing your gown and with hair done, and whatever else The Club thinks you need. Objective: classy and hot both. Have Linda-5 provide whatever money you need."

I looked at Heather. "Same with you, tomorrow night: both classy and hot. I want you two to make cocks hard tomorrow night. Starting with mine."

A few minutes later, all three of us were decent (if musky-smelling), as we stepped out of the elevator into the hotel lobby. Heather and I headed back to the convention, while Amy walked straight from the elevator to the exit.

Watching a Pleasure Unit's ass sway back and forth—it never gets old.

Saturday night, Heather's gown was dark blue; Amy's was red. And did they look hot? Well, conversation quieted noticeably when the three of us walked into the dining room.

(Conversation quieted, but didn't stop. The thing about very smart people is, they never shut up.)

We certainly made an impression on one young man. Near the entrance to the dining room, three teenage boys and a teenage girl were chatting. The only ones wearing formal wear were the girl and one of the three boys; but that tux-clad boy's mouth fell open when we walked in.

The bespectacled eighteen-year-old walked up to us, eyes wide. "Amy Emily, is that *you?*"

"It is," Amy said, "I'm here in Atlanta. Emory University." After a slight pause, she said, "Ohmigod, I'm so sorry, I don't remember your name."

He blushed. "I'm Charlie-Bob Owens. I was a junior when you were a senior, so I'm not surprised that you don't remember me." Then he asked, with excessive casualness, "So are you a member of SOS too?"

"No, I'm just here as James's date." Then Amy smiled at Heather. "Well, *one* of his dates. Except Heather is smart enough to get in y'all's club, you know? While I am so *not* a brain, ohmigod."

"Um, right," Charlie-Bob said, clearly stuck on how to reply.

I clapped the boy on the shoulder. "So whom are you eating dinner with? I won't be put out if you eat with your friends, but you're welcome to sit with the three of us."

Charlie-Bob looked at the three waiting teenagers, then at Amy and Heather. Then he looked at the teenager SOS members again, then he looked at Amy again. If he'd had a coin in his hand right then, I'm sure he would've flipped it.

But then the boy stood straight. "Thank you, James, I'd be right honored to have dinner with y'all." He looked at Amy and blushed.

I had no idea then, and Charlie-Bob *certainly* had no idea then, but by choosing to share a table with Amy, Heather, and me, the boy changed the course of his life.

2-B: Teen Hero

Dinner conversation revealed that both Charlie-Bob and Amy were from the small town of Sweet Onion, Georgia. Charlie-Bob had driven all the way to Atlanta by himself—

"—but anytime I'm not at the hotel this weekend, I'm staying with my Uncle Jack and Aunt Sally. But am I complaining? I expected my folks to say, 'Hotlanta by yourself, even at eighteen? No way.' So them saying 'Yes, but some restrictions apply' is a deal I can live with."

Heather gestured at the building around us. "Especially as there is no way a eighteen-year-old could afford a weekend at *this* hotel."

"Tell me about it," Charlie-Bob agreed. "Between the tux rental, the gasoline here and back to Sweet Onion, and the convention registration, I'm in hock to my folks for over a hundred bucks, even after working all last summer." Then he smiled at Amy. "But worth every penny, sitting here with last year's Miss Vidal County."

Amy smiled at him. "You're so sweet. But Holli Sue Moffatt won; I was just First Runner Up."

"Well, okay," Charlie-Bob said. "Still, they printed your picture in the paper. And I thought you looked really pretty then. But now?" The boy was blushing red. "You look, um, prettier in person."

As Amy was thanking Charlie-Bob, I thought, *Thank her nanobots, kid. Bigger tits make any girl "prettier."* But of course, I didn't tell the boy what I was thinking.

When dinner ended, there was a mini-studio set up, where a photographer took pictures of couples who were dressed to the nines. I thought I looked good in my tux (my own nanobots had transformed me into an Alpha Male), so I got a picture taken of myself with Amy and Heather.

Before the photographer snapped the pics, I told the Pleasure Units, "Convince the camera that you're each five seconds away from ripping my clothes off."

And sure enough, the two stacked blondes wound up looking sexy. Meanwhile, I stood between them with a Sean Connery smirk. It's a great photo.

I paid for three copies of that photo (which made the photographer happy). Then I thought, *What the hell, why not?* Still on my dime, I got a photo of Amy and Heather, with Charlie-Bob standing between them. And though the women weren't vamping in *this* photo, neither did it look like they'd been dragged in front of the camera at gunpoint.

———

A few minutes before eight o'clock, Heather, Amy, Charlie-Bob, and I walked to the big room where the formal ball would be held.

We walked through a door at the center of one wall. Against the opposite wall, at the center was the bandstand where the musicians were setting up. Beyond them was an eight-foot-tall aluminum frame, from which hung royal-blue and white crepe-paper streamers (the colors of SOS's logo).

Behind us, in a corner of the room, was a long table that was covered with white tablecloths. On it set chips and dips; cake slices and plasticware; glasses of ice water, buckets of ice, and a water dispenser; and punch glasses—but I saw a big blank space on the table where the punchbowl should have been.

We were standing around talking, when two hotel waiters came in with the silver punchbowl. The whole thing was done very classy: The two men were wearing striped pants, high-cut red jackets, and black bow ties. Four gloved hands set the punchbowl on the long table.

Then the two waiters squatted down behind the tablecloth-covered hotel cart. To bring out replacement punch, I presumed.

Let me be honest: I was paying more attention to a story that Charlie-Bob was telling, than to what the two waiters were doing.

That changed quickly when the two waiters stood up. They each were wearing ski masks and holding Uzis.

One guy was also holding a pillowcase. He called out, "THIS IS A HOLDUP! Do not move. Give us your money and jewelry, and you won't be hurt. And don't even *think* of telling me 'this jewelry is fake, so you don't want it.'"

The pillowcase-less guy ran straight to the one door in/out. From inside his waiter jacket he pulled out wooden shims, which he pounded into the crack between the door and the doorjamb (using the Uzi as a hammer). In theory, the door opened out, but not anymore.

Nobody outside could get in. And the man with the Uzi was there to make sure that nobody inside could get out.

Except. . .

Dimly visible through the crepe paper that backstopped the bandstand, and seven feet above the carpet, glowed red letters.

I called out, "Beyond the bandstand, there's an exit. Go out that door!"

And people did, starting with the musicians who'd been standing openmouthed on the bandstand.

"FUCK!" yelled the guy guarding the shimmed door. "STOP!"

B-b-brap!

He fired a burst into the ceiling, to scare people. It worked—but not the way he expected. Only the people nearest his door—the people he could certainly shoot and kill—stopped at his command. Everyone else ran toward the bandstand door, but now they were panicked and screaming.

By now the aluminum frame and its crepe paper were laying down. So I was able to see three tuxedoed men stop in front of the bandstand door. They turned to face the gunmen, as they linked arms. The three intended to act as a human wall to protect everyone else running out that door! Brave men.

The gunman guarding the shimmed door ran over to the center of the long wall, where he could cover both doors. "STOP!" he yelled a second time—

B-b-brap!

—but this time his shots didn't go over the crowd. Near the bandstand door, a tuxedoed man and a woman in a green gown fell to the ground. That stopped the exodus.

Meanwhile, Pillowcase Man was advancing toward me, his weapon pointed at my chest. "*You!* You fucked things up for us!"

He looked Amy and Heather up and down, then turned his ski-mask-covered face back toward me. "You owe me," he said. "And since neither of them is wearing fancy diamonds"—his voice was leering now—"we'll have to get payback some *other* way."

He pointed his Uzi at Amy. "C'mere, babe. We're gonna have fun."

"NO!" Charlie-Bob yelled. He jumped in front of Amy. In a quavering voice, he said, "You're not taking Amy Emily, you prick!"

"I'm not?" Pillowcase Man said. Then he smiled. "Okay, fine."

Pillowcase Man pointed his weapon at Heather. "Okay, MILF, over here. *Now.*" He lunged forward to grab Heather's wrist, letting the pillowcase fall to the carpet.

"You're not getting *her*, either!" Charlie-Bob said. Then this small-town kid actually took a step toward the gunman.

Charlie-Bob jumped up at the last second, with his left hand shooting up.

I figured that Charlie-Bob intended to punch the gunman in the face. Nope—the boy's hand went to the side of the gunman's head, then up and over.

Charlie-Bob had unmasked Pillowcase Man. Now Charlie-Bob called out, "Y'all, get out your smartphones! Take his picture!"

Letting the ski mask drop, Charlie-Bob then grabbed Pillowcase Man's own wrist, trying to break the gunman's grip on Heather.

"You filthy brat, look what you've done!" Pillowcase Man said. His weapon came up, with clear intent to kill.

Have I mentioned that a bimborg-unit's thought-processes work much faster than a human's? Or that a bimborg's emotion is always a robotic calm, no matter how she acts? And have I mentioned that any two bimborg units can talk telepathically, with each other or with the entire Club?

I was out of my league, frankly—too much unexpected shit was happening too fast. But to bimborg units Amy and Heather, this was a snail race.

Here's what happened next. Some of this stuff, Amy and Heather had to tell me later, because everything happened so fast—

• Amy pulled up the front of her evening gown. She still had a restricted range of motion, but she was able to give Pillowcase Man a martial-arts leg sweep, knocking him backwards.

• Startled, Pillowcase man fired two shots. One shot ricocheted off the carpet. The other bullet went into Charlie-Bob's leg.

• Meanwhile, Heather had locked the fingers of her two hands together. She pulled her wrist free of Pillowcase Man's left hand.

• As soon as Pillowcase Man was on his back, I jumped on top of him. I straddled his chest, and slugged him.

• Heather dropped to the carpet, to kneel on the gunman's left arm.

• Amy dropped to the carpet too, kneeling by Pillowcase Man's gun hand. She grabbed Pillowcase Man's trigger finger with one hand, bending it back painfully but not breaking it. Her other hand grabbed the Uzi by the back of the bullet chamber (which was still comparatively cool) and pulled the gun out of Pillowcase Man's grip.

• Amy's kneeling body "just happened to be" blocking most onlookers from seeing what was going on. Amy put the Uzi against the right side of Pillowcase Man's body, just below his ribs, and fired one shot, going left and up. She deliberately nicked his abdominal aorta. It took less than a second, from the time that Pillowcase Man lost his grip on his weapon, to him being shot with it.

• I felt Pillowcase Man lurch between my legs, at the same moment I heard the loud gunshot. Pillowcase Man started gasping.

• Amy threw the Uzi on the carpet, and jumped up, looking panicked. "Oh my gawd, oh my gawd, I shot him! I shot him, but I didn't mean to, you know?"

• I said, "Amy, go to Charlie-Bob. He needs your help." Amy moved to the wounded boy, after she looked at the onlookers and said, "I didn't mean to shoot the robber, y'all, honest."

• By an amazing coincidence, Amy had thrown down the Uzi where Heather could easily pick it up. Heather grabbed the Uzi and stood up.

• Heather pointed the Uzi at the still-masked gunman. "Put down your gun," she said with seeming nervousness. "You know the police are coming."

• "You guys *shot* J—my buddy?" the gunman replied. "You fucki—"

• I was no longer straddling Pillowcase Man. I had grabbed up the pillowcase, dumped the loot out of it, and wadded it up into a ball that I pressed against the gunshot, trying to stanch the bloodflow.

B-b-brap!

• I didn't see what happened next. But onlookers all agreed that the ski-mask gunman shifted his aim, to point his own Uzi at Heather. That's when Heather fired with a left-to-right spray of three shots.

• Heather's second and third shots went into the wall. (Which was no surprise, considering that she was "obviously untrained" at firing an Uzi.) But the first shot hit the ski-mask gunman right in the middle of the forehead. "How lucky for her!"

The bandstand door was still open; now two armed security guards rushed in, guns up and aimed at Heather. "Put down your weapon," the older guard said. This man had a flat stomach, and had the face that comes with combat medals in his bedroom closet.

"Guard," an onlooker said, "put your gun away. This woman saved us."

Heather looked down at wounded Charlie-Bob. "And this poor boy saved *me*. Please, is anyone here a doctor?"

Two ambulances were called, for Charlie-Bob and for Pillowcase Man. By the time Pillowcase Man's ambulance showed up, he was beyond medical help.

The Atlanta Police asked the four of us, plus the various witnesses, what had happened.

Amy said, "I shot the robber, but it was by accident."

Heather nodded, adding, "I'm a Doctor of Dental Surgery, not a marksman."

The Atlanta Police, very apologetically, told Heather that until their investigation was completed, she was not free to leave the city. (Neither was Amy, but since Emory University was within the Atlanta city limits, Amy suffered no inconvenience.) Now stuck in Atlanta, Heather joined Amy and me in visiting Charlie-Bob at the hospital.

I met Charlie-Bob's parents, who'd rushed to Atlanta from Sweet Onion. They were pleased to hear Amy and Heather tell the story of Charlie-Bob acting like a hero. But soon they were showing signs of worry. I soon learned why—

"These medical bills are gonna skin us alive, James!"

It took a little skullduggery on my part to soothe their minds: A bimborg in Pensacola, Florida drove to Vidal County, Georgia, and made several calls to Charlie-Bob's parents from a pay phone, while various computer records got falsified. But soon my good-hearted trickery paid off: The parents got convinced that "the Vidal County Orphans and Relief Society" would pay most of the medical bills.

(No need to tell the parents that "the Vidal County Orphans and Relief Society" didn't exist until today; or that funding for the Orphans Society came not from Vidal County charitable contributions, but from Linda-5 tapping into the Swiss bank accounts of scumbags.)

What the Orphans Society "couldn't" pay toward Charlie-Bob's medical bills, I paid openly, out of "my savings." By an amazing coincidence, between the Orphans Society and myself, there was just enough money to pay all of Charlie-Bob's bills; his folks didn't have to shell out a cent.

I also arranged for the *Vidal Voice* and WVCO-TV to find out about Charlie-Bob's good deeds. They both did nice stories about him: "Local boy shot rescuing damsels in distress."

Sunday night, after visiting hours had ended, I was pacing around the hospital parking lot.

"It drives me snakeshit," I told the sky, "that this boy does this brave, heroic thing, and all I can do is *pay his bills?* He deserves better than this."

An hour earlier, I'd figured out a way to pay all of Charlie-Bob's physical therapy bills without his parents paying a cent, and without the money being traced back to me. I should have been overjoyed, basking in the satisfaction of doing another good deed. But instead, I felt lousy; I felt that my charity fell short.

Then realization hit.

"If Charlie-Bob hadn't acted like a hero, right now he wouldn't be in the hospital, he wouldn't need physical therapy, and his parents wouldn't be spending money on doctors. All that my money-shifts have done is to make sure he doesn't lose yardage on the play. But I haven't *rewarded* him for being a hero. *That* is what's bothering me!"

Well, *this* was easily fixed. I could fill up a cardboard box with cash, tape it shut, then have a bimborg drive to his town and leave it on his doorstep some night. . .

Wait, did I say 'bimborg'?

Bimborg?

Then I got a *great* idea! I clapped my hands in delight.

Watch this, world! Hero Charlie-Bob Owens is going to get rewarded like nobody has ever seen before!

I ran back to my car. As quickly as I could safely get there, I drove back to the Omni Hotel. Then I rushed myself to the hallway in front of Heather's hotel-room door.

When she opened the door, I lowered my voice and said, "Bimborg Heather, I have special instructions for you about Charlie-Bob. Invite me in."

Beginning the next morning, with her next hospital visit, Heather hit Charlie-Bob and his parents with a blizzard of questions. All the questions were variants on, What is Sweet Onion like?

The shootings had been on Saturday night. On Tuesday, Amy's shooting was ruled accidental, and Heather's shooting was ruled self-defense. After all, since neither woman had served in the military or had police training, how could either blonde have killed her man with a well-aimed, premeditated shot?

The Atlanta Police told Heather and Amy, "You're free to leave the city."

So Tuesday, Heather caught a flight back to Pueblo, Colorado. "*But*," Heather told Charlie-Bob and his parents, before she left—

"You guys will see me again. Because as soon as I can make it happen, I am moving my whole shebang to Sweet Onion. I'm getting tired of big-city life, and your town sounds so lovely. Besides, I'll feel safer living in a town with a proven hero in it."

Heather neglected to mention that her setting up a dental practice in Sweet Onion would lead to all kinds of personal benefits for eighteen-year-old Charlie-Bob Owens.

2-C: Nightshade

SEVEN WEEKS LATER
SWEET ONION, GEORGIA
157 MILES SOUTHEAST OF DOWNTOWN ATLANTA

High school had let out ten minutes earlier, and now Rose O'Connor ("Call me Nightshade") was in the Piggly Wiggly Supermarket. She was there to buy a packet of ball-point pens.

Nightshade didn't give a rat's ass about school, but it's hard to doodle pentagrams and crescent moons in your notebook during class time when your last pen has run dry. Hence, Nightshade had detoured to the store to buy more pens.

Just as Nightshade was about to turn into the school-supplies aisle, she surprised Widow McGee and Mrs. Wilkes. Nightshade didn't smile at the old women, and they didn't smile at her.

Nightshade didn't smile because women smiling, when they didn't feel like it, was one of the tricks that the Patriarchy used to keep women subjugated. Widow McGee and Mrs. Wilkes didn't smile because—well, they were sourpuss bitches.

And sure enough, the old biddies started talking about *her.* From the next aisle over, Nightshade heard—

"I can't believe that her mother lets her leave the house, looking like that! She looks like a witch, in all that black."

"I hear she *is* a witch."

Damn straight, Nightshade thought. She and Karen and Luanne would meet behind Luanne's garage, and chant for an hour, every night during a full moon. (Well, except for when it was raining.)

Nightshade *still* hadn't figured out why Karen took part in these rituals. And Luanne? Luanne believed that if she chanted "We beseech thee, O Goddess" enough times, she'd win the Powerball Lottery. As for Nightshade herself, she was there mainly because she enjoyed kissing other girls and groping bare boob-flesh.

(Plus, while Nightshade suspected that the Earth Mother didn't really exist, Nightshade would rather worship a Goddess than go to

First Baptist Church and become a thrall of the Patriarchy's male-supremacist, homophobic brainwashing.)

Then Nightshade mentally stuck out her tongue at the crones. *For your information, my lipstick isn't black, it's maroon. It only looks black because of the black lipliner.*

But back in the real world, Nightshade heard one of the biddies gasp. "Did you see that woman? She has *implants!*"

"But why is she all in white? Do you think she's here for a Stripper-Gram?"

"If so, then we need to find out what man she's danced for, and tell his wife. We're a *decent* town!"

Nightshade was trying to figure out whom they were talking about, when a woman of about thirty turned into the school-supplies aisle. She was carrying a shopper's handbasket.

Oh, Goddess! was Nightshade's reaction. The black-dressed teen stood like a statue, right by the ballpoint-pen display, and stared at the perfect blonde in front of her.

The woman's bright blue eyes drew Nightshade's own brown eyes to a perfect face; that face's oval shape and high cheekbones being covered with creamy skin. The woman was tall, just under six feet, and she was fit. Honey-blond hair was pulled back into an enormous bun, without a hair out of place.

And Goddess, her *boobs!* It took all of Nightshade's self-control not to attack the woman, strip her to the waist, and start slurping on those enormous and excellently shaped udders.

The woman's low-heeled pumps, royal blue, were her only non-white clothing. Her pants were snowy white, and she was wearing a long-sleeved, high-collared white top that buttoned on her right side with white buttons.

Nightshade raised her voice to carry, both to the white-dressed blonde and to the old biddies: "Ma'am, those two old bats are talking about you." Then in normal volume, Nightshade added, "They hate us because we're beautiful."

The blonde gave Nightshade a model's smile, then walked within six feet of her. The stranger stopped to put a receipt book into her handbasket, laying the receipt book atop two two-liter bottles of soda.

Nightshade had made her *hate us because we're beautiful* comment as a joke, but now the blonde tilted her head and looked appraisingly at the raven-dyed teen. "I've been here only three weeks," the blonde said, "but I'm sure that you're the most beautiful Goth this town has."

"I'm not a Goth, I'm a witch. Goths are into death, while witches are into the cycle of life. That, and staying free of the Patriarchy Conspiracy." Nightshade blinked. "Wait, you think I'm beautiful?"

"You are. And now I can make you a little *more* beautiful, by giving you a nicer smile."

Nightshade gave the woman a genuine (hence rare) smile. "Whatever you cooked for me, ma'am, I'm sure it would be both nonfattening and delicious."

"Whatever I *cooked* for you?" Then the blonde looked down at herself. "How embarrassing. I'm not a chef, I'm a dentist. Georgia-licensed by the way, as of fifteen minutes ago." She stuck out her long-nailed right hand. "Heather Saint James, D.D.S. And you are. . .?"

The teen girl shook the offered hand. "Call me Nightshade, please. I call myself a poisonous plant so boys will leave me alone."

"Does it work?"

"Not completely. Hey, maybe you could tell me how to fend guys off when they're pestering me. They keep telling me, 'Oh baby, you're so fucking *hot*.'"

By now, both women were in the checkout line (and drawing stares). Heather said, "My biggest piece of advice is, Never lie to a man when you turn him down, not even to spare his feelings."

"Not a worry," Nightshade said. "All the boys in this place are rednecks in the making. They don't give a shit about my feelings, so I don't care about theirs."

"Not all the boys are rednecks," Heather said. "You go to the high school, right? You probably know Charlie-Bob Owens."

Nightshade frowned. "Small town here, *hello?* I'm a senior, he's a senior, and he and I were in the same class in fourth grade. But I don't cozy up with nerds."

"Too bad, he's a good man. Last November, he got shot in the leg, trying to save me and another woman from a nasty gunman."

Nightshade's mouth fell open. "It's *true?* I figured that the boy made all that shit up, to impress some nerdette."

"Nope, he's an eighteen-year-old genuine hero. I was there, and what they printed in your paper was all true."

By now, both women had paid the cashier. Heather turned to Nightshade and said, "May I show you my office? I'd really enjoy it if you could be the first name in my appointment book."

Nightshade replied, "I'll have to call my mom, to okay the appointment, but sure." She wondered, *Is Heather hitting on me?*

Then Nightshade mentally slapped herself upside the head. *C'mon, does any woman who looks like Heather, need to play games?*

They walked out of the grocery store into the cold wind. Nightshade said, "We can go in my car. It's old, but the heater works."

"Thanks, but my office is right next to the store here. Why else in January would I come into the store without a coat?"

Sure enough, the walk was only a brief one, before Heather was unlocking a door in a medical office park. By the door was a sign, "Heather Saint James, Dentist."

The waiting room had magazines (showing Colorado subscription labels) on the table, and toys, and a TV that was mounted to the wall. Under the TV was a poster of a smiling tooth who was holding a toothbrush and a spool of dental floss. But there were no *people* in the waiting room, neither a receptionist nor patients; and the TV was black and silent. Nightshade felt weirded out.

At the receptionist's desk was an open appointment book; sure enough, it was blank. Mom agreed to an appointment for Nightshade to get her teeth cleaned. Perhaps Mom consented because Nightshade had so many good things to say about Dr. Saint James, or maybe it was the cheap introductory special?

Nightshade was shown three rooms that eventually would have dental chairs in them, requiring three dental hygienists to clean teeth in those chairs—

"—but right now you see only the one chair, I have only one hygienist hired, and she clearly isn't working right now." Heather shrugged, smiling. "But I'm an optimist."

Nightshade was shown a records room, empty of both a recordskeeper and even one folder. That, too, was out-weirding.

The last stop was a small room that was, Heather said, her office. The desk chair faced a corkboard that was blank, except for a photo of a laughing Heather in a tight white ski outfit. Skier-Heather looked scrumptious. *Goddess,* Nightshade thought, *I want this woman so much.*

Nightshade turned from the photo to face the real Heather again. The teen intended to say something light and casual, but before she could speak a word, Heather cocked her head and looked at her.

"You're hot for me," Heather said. It wasn't a question. "You desire me."

Nightshade felt panic. "Shit, am I so obvious?" Then Nightshade asked, her voice strained, "Are you mad? Do I disgust you?"

"It depends. What do you want to do with me?"

Heather herself had told Nightshade, not fifteen minutes earlier, "Don't lie." So now Nightshade answered Heather's question honestly: "I'd like to caress your boobs and suck on your nipples. Then I'd like to pull off your pants and panties, and tongue your strong ab muscles around your navel. Then I'd push you into that dental chair and lick your slit till sunrise. And it would be so wonderful if you would lick me back, but if not, I'd be cool with that too."

"You flatter me," Heather said, "you having such detailed fantasies about me." Then Heather took Nightshade's face in her hands, and pulled the girl's lips toward her own.

In so doing, one of Heather's long fingernails scratched Nightshade on her forehead, just below the hairline. But Nightshade was *not* about to complain.

Heather's lips were soft. The last thoughts that Nightshade ever had, were about what a great kisser Heather was.

Five minutes and 27 seconds after starting the kiss, Heather pulled her face back. She said to the black-haired teen, "You are Welcomed to The Club, Rose-16184906."

Pleasure Unit/Welcomer Rose-16184906 smiled. "I'm so glad. And I hope I get a chance to, like, serve King James just as you have, you know?"

"Oh, you will, you will. Because King James has given me special instructions to pass on to all bimborg in Sweet Onion. . . ."

Seconds later, the teen girl replied, "Special Instructions received and understood. This unit will, like, *totally* comply. Because this unit knows that King James will, you know, be counting on *me.*"

2-D: Rose Is Different Now

THE NEXT MORNING
BEFORE FIRST PERIOD
SWEET ONION HIGH SCHOOL

A chubby brunette girl said, "Hey, Regina, your outfit looks nice on you."

"Of course it does," Regina Wisley replied. Regina gave the lesser mortal barely a glance.

Queen Regina continued to stride through a hallway of what she considered to be her own royal castle, accompanied by what she considered to be her ladies-in waiting.

All three girls were cheerleaders; next-generation, in Regina's case.

Why was Regina the girl at the top of her high school's social order? Because she was a senior, *plus* being captain of the cheerleading squad. But wait, there was more.

Regina was half-gorgeous. True, she'd inherited her father's blah hair color and his enormous nose. But L'Oreal took care of the hair color, and Daddy had promised Regina a nose job before she went off to college. On Regina's mother's side, Steffi Jo Longhurst had once been the most beautiful girl in Vidal County, and Regina had inherited all of her mother's best parts.

The final reason that Regina was at the top of high-school popularity was that the Wisleys were the richest family in Vidal County, Georgia.

Back in 1959, when color televisions were new and sexy, Regina's grandfather Robert Wisley had patented an improvement on color-tuning the TV. It wasn't enough to make viewers go Wow, but it got the man a bank loan to start a television factory. Wisley Electronics never threatened RCA or Zenith or Magnavox; but at one time, the factory had employed five hundred people in Sweet Onion, and Robert Wisley had been a local hero.

Nowadays, all the actual TV parts were made in China, and only fifty locals were employed in final assembly. Still, Roger Wisley (Robert's son, Regina's father, and Wisley Electronics' current CEO) managed to pocket a nice chunk of change.

Now in Sweet Onion High School, Regina and her two minions passed a group of three druggie sophomores. But the boys' interest wasn't in Regina, but in Betsy Campbell (to Regina's right).

One of the druggie loser boys gave a wolf whistle.

Another of the boys said (in what he delusively thought was a sexy voice), "*Hey,* Betsy, you're looking *gooood* today."

Everyone at school agreed, "Busty Betsy" had a truly bodacious set of ta-tas. And they were entirely natural—Betsy had borne blossoming breasts beginning in sixth grade.

So was Regina ever worried about Betsy replacing her as queen bee? Not even slightly. Because while boys lusted after Betsy's upper shape, and while Betsy had a pretty face *overall,* nobody could ignore the strawberry birthmark on Betsy's cheek. It wasn't big—the palm of Betsy's hand covered all of it—but it was big enough to ensure that Betsy could never be the school's number-one beauty. So whenever Regina wanted to wound her minion in an argument, all she had to do was call her "Birthmark Betsy."

"Good morning, Prudy Lu," Johnny Sutherland now called out to Prudy Lu Moffatt, who was walking on Regina's left.

It was no surprise that this boy was greeting Prudy Lu; Regina knew that Johnny was Prudy Lu's next-door neighbor.

Regina turned her head sharply to the left, just in time to see Prudy Lu start to take a breath. "Don't say anything to him," Regina commanded. "We're running late."

Prudy Lu obeyed. Instead of replying with words to Johnny, she made a weak wave and continued walking. Regina glanced back at Johnny; he looked like he'd been slapped.

Regina had expected Prudy Lu's obedience. Prudy's dad worked for Regina's Daddy, and Prudy had an ordinary chest—so Prudy was definitely of lower status than Regina.

Yet Prudy Lu rated high in the overall SOHS pecking order, because her older sister had been a beauty-contest winner. While

Prudy Lu Moffatt didn't have quite the prominent cheekbones of her sister, her hair was a lighter blond than Holli Sue's honey-blond hair.

Prudy Lu's gorgeous face might, maybe, possibly have made Regina worry about losing her top spot, except for one thing: Regina could bully Prudy Lu easily.

Now Regina and her minions continued down the hall, walking three abreast, and kids just naturally stepped out of the cool girls' way. Until one girl didn't.

A girl of eighteen stood squarely in Regina's path. The path-blocker had rolled dark-auburn hair, a black T-shirt tucked into her comfortable blue jeans, and white sneakers. Her makeup was professionally done. Her eyes were shifting between Regina, Prudy Lu, and Betsy, while her face showed a thoughtful expression.

Regina's brain was tickling her: The girl who was blocking the cool girls' path didn't look familiar, and yet she did. Regina's memories kept trying to recall fourth grade.

Whoever the path-blocker was, she was gorgeous, despite her poor choice of clothes.

Which meant that she was Regina's competition.

Regina's rule with competition: Always leash it or destroy it.

Regina stopped three feet away from Roadblock Girl, and put hands on hips. "Who are you, and why are you blocking our way?"

Betsy said, "Um, Regina? That's Nightshade, I'm pretty sure."

"No way," Regina said. "Nightshade looks like a Goth-y *freak.*"

Prudy Lu said, "Wow, Nightshade, who did your hair? It looks *great.*"

The auburn-haired girl turned her full body to face Prudy Lu, as she smiled happily. "You're so sweet, Prudy Lu. But please, I'm back to being called Rose again, you know?"

"*You're* Rose?" Regina said. "No way. Rose O'Connor in fourth grade wasn't pretty at all."

Rose/Nightshade acted as if Regina hadn't spoken.

Rose continued to face Prudy Lu directly, and to look only at Prudy Lu, as if Regina and Betsy weren't even there.

Rose said to Prudy Lu, "My hair? Last night I read an online article, 'Today Is A Good Day to Dye,' with, like, *tons* of tricks about hair coloring. Then I recolored my hair by myself, in the shower. As for rolling my hair, I *know* how to do it, I just haven't *done so* since ohmigod, seventh grade."

Only then did Rose look at Regina, to answer Regina's question of a minute earlier. Worse than delaying her answer, Rose answered Regina only by turning her head—below the neck, Rose's body still faced Prudy Lu straight on. It was as if *Prudy Lu* were the big shot, and *Regina* were the minion.

Rose said to Regina, "As for why I was standing here, it was because I was deciding something about y'all."

"And what did you 'decide' about us?" Regina demanded.

Rose's "smile" at Regina now was pure *Go away, loser, you're not in my league*. Regina had *given* a smile like that thousands of times; why the fuck was she *getting* it? Meanwhile, Rose was saying, "I'm so sorry, but you don't rate that info."

Regina was about to blow a gasket, but Prudy Lu spoke first: "Why aren't you wearing black anymore, or calling yourself Nightshade? The red of your lipstick goes well with your hair and skin color, by the way."

Betsy muttered, "Jeez, Prudy Lu! She changed her name because *Nightshade* is an evil name to have."

Rose now was giving Prudy Lu another sunny smile. "Because yesterday I met a new dentist in town, her name is Doctor Saint James, and she is, ohmigod, *easy* to talk to. She helped me see stuff about life, and how I was, like, acting like a kid, you know?"

"Yes, you did look"—Prudy Lu paused—"strange."

"And I was proud of it. But one of the things that Heather got me to see yesterday was that Charlie-Bob Owens is, like, the only real man in this school. But he won't date me if I look like Bride of Dracula, you know?"

"*Charlie-Bob Owens?*" Regina sneered. "He was a nerd in fourth grade, he's a nerd now, and he's on *zero* school teams."

Rose's look at Regina was pure condescension. "He's *also* someone who got shot trying to save two women from masked gunmen. Heather should know—she was one of the two women he saved! And what do *your* boyfriends do? They throw balls around instead of doing homework. *Really?*"

Then Rose added, "Speaking of Charlie-Bob, y'all are keeping me from talking to him before First Bell. Prudy Lu, talk to you later."

And then, without waiting for Regina to dismiss her, Rose simply *walked away*. (While squeezing Prudy Lu's arm as Rose passed her.)

Betsy said, "She's truly hot for Charlie-Bob Owens? I though Rose was a dyke."

But Regina, meanwhile, had spun around to point a finger at Prudy Lu's face. "I don't want you talking to that witch again! Got me? Not a word to her."

"But Regina, she's only—"

"Not a word. *At all.* She talks, you get deaf. Hmm?"

Prudy Lu's shoulders slumped. "Okay, Regina, I won't talk to Rose anymore."

Charlie-Bob Owens was locking his locker when he heard approaching footsteps to his right. A phone-sex operator's voice said, "Hiii, Charlie-Bob. How's it hanging?"

He blinked with surprise when he saw who was talking to him. "*Nightshade?* Uh, what's up?"

"Please, call me Rose again. Anyway, I talked to Heather Saint James yesterday. It started with her talking me into a cleaning appointment, today after school—"

"Oh, so Macon finally sent Heather her dental license?"

Rose laid a hand on his arm. "Please, Charlie-Bob, I haven't got much time. Heather told me what you did in Atlanta, and I was like, totally ohmigod!"

Rose gave Charlie-Bob a smoldering look as she asked, "So do you, like, have a girlfriend?"

He choked. "Hold on, aren't you a le—Aren't you always complaining in class about the Patriarchy? What's going on?"

"'What's going on' is that now I'm not a witch, now I like boys, now I *really* like *you,* and now I want to know if you have, you know, a girlfriend." Rose stroked his arm, then said, "Meaning, a girl who makes you *glad* that you spend time with her."

Charlie-Bob was blushing. "Um, no, Rose. Right now, I don't have a girlfriend."

Rose still was stroking his arm. "I am, like, *really* impressed by what you did. So whenever you want a date for Friday night, or Saturday night, or whenever you want only a blowjob or a fuck, you call me, y'hear?"

Charlie-Bob stared at Rose, openmouthed.

2-E: The Bimborg Dentist Works The Secret Plan

THAT AFTERNOON

"...No, really, Dr. Saint James, it's not a problem. But thanks for thinking of me. Goodbye."

Dental hygienist Cindy Bright turned off her cel phone and laid it on the kitchen table. Then she sighed and picked up a paper napkin, twisting it into a rope, as she recalled the previous few minutes' cel-phone conversation—

"Hey, Dr. Saint James, what's up?" Cindy had asked. Then she'd nervously asked, *"Did your first Georgia patient cancel her cleaning appointment?"*

Cindy's boss had replied, *"Nope, you're still going to earn money today. In fact, more so."*

"I don't understand."

"I need to run an errand at the high school, right when it gets out. So the patient and I both will be late. But, I still want you to come in at 3:15."

"Whew, that's good," Cindy had said.

"Dr. Gardner's receptionist will give you the key to get in. Anyway, set up the instruments like normal. If we're not back by then, by the bathroom is a storage closet with a vacuum cleaner in it. Run the vacuum across the carpet till we get there."

"Will do, ma'am."

"I'm hoping this trip to the high school will get me more business, so I can pay you for more hours that much sooner. It bothers me a lot that you have to live off your parents' charity, even after I've hired you."

"But they really don't mind. Because I've told them good things about you, and my pa thinks that this is a good opportunity for me."

"Well, I don't want to be a problem for you any longer than I have to," Dr. Saint James had said.

It was true that Cindy was taking money from her parents, in order to pay rent and bills. But that wasn't the whole story—

Cindy also was "enjoying" the "generosity" of Roger Wisley, the richest man in town. He was handing over the cash mainly because Cindy had dazzling green eyes and shapely legs. But Roger's generosity came at a price.

How would Dr. Saint James react if she found out that Cindy was mistress to a rich married man?

Not to mention, if Roger got a good look at Dr. Saint James, chances were high that he'd drop Cindy like a hot rock. And then how would she manage?

The only good news in all this was that Cindy had convinced Roger that if he quit Dr. Wheeler to instead favor a dentist with no patients, the town gossips might notice. So for at least a while, Roger wouldn't come to the new clinic, and Roger wouldn't lay eyes on Heather Saint James.

Cindy still was twisting the paper napkin. She knew she was playing with fire.

The school day had ended, and Bob Roberts was pulling on his suit coat when Mrs. Collins appeared in his doorway. "Mr. Roberts? Nightshade—I mean, *Rose*—and a woman are here to talk to you."

"Her mother? What's she want?"

"Not her mother. And I think you should let *them* explain it." Then Mrs. Collins lowered her voice and said, "Brace yourself."

Bob figured out quickly what Mrs. Collins meant when he walked into the outer office. The white-dressed blonde was the sexiest woman he'd ever seen up close. The first thought to go through his head was *Stripper-Gram?*

And come to think of it, Nightshade was looking pretty hot, too. *Down, boy!*

Nightshade said, "Dr. Saint James, this is Mr. Roberts, our principal. Mr. Roberts, this is Dr. Saint James, a brand-new dentist in Sweet Onion."

The adults shook hands, then the teen girl said, "Mr. Roberts, I think it would be, you know, *cool* if you would let Dr. Saint James come out, right before the pep rally tomorrow, and talk about, like, dental stuff."

"Dental hygiene," the gorgeous white-clothed dentist explained. "Brushing, flossing, and mouthwash."

Bob shook his head. "Nightshade—"

"Please call me Rose now. Mr. Roberts, you gotta, like, help Heather! I mean, Dr. Saint James. She just moved to town, and she doesn't have any patients, and she's real nice, and I don't want her to go broke, you know?"

The blond dentist locked eyes with the principal. "The students *will* benefit from hearing my message. And whether they ever tell you 'Thank you' after they hear it, *I* will be grateful for being allowed to speak. Because Rose is right: I need to market myself."

Had Bob Roberts been blind or gay, he would have said No and made it stick. What Rose and Heather were asking would disrupt the routine of the pep rally, and Bob Roberts made a religion out of not disrupting routine.

(Plus, every principal in the USA gets paid an extra nickel for every time they say, "If I let *you* do it, then I'd have to let *everyone* do it, and *then* where would we be?" Well, those nickels add up.)

But Bob Roberts was not blind, and right now he was very much not gay. He found it to be hormonally impossible to look at this sex-dream and say to her, I won't give you what you want. So he agreed to give her five minutes before the pep rally.

Hearing this news, the dentist's smile was professional, and her parting handshake also was professional. *Damn it!*

Just before the two beauties walked out of the school office, Rose smiled warmly at him and said, "You are, ohmigod, *so cool* for doing this, Mr. Roberts."

Which made Mr. Roberts's priapic-penis problem even worse.

He still had the erection two minutes later, when he got into his car to go home.

In a town the size of Sweet Onion, there are only a few streets where you endanger people if you drive like a maniac. So Bob was able to hurry home without causing any funerals. As soon as he walked into the kitchen, he turned off the stove (Kathleen was cooking at the time), and dragged his wife into the bedroom.

When they were cuddling, Kathleen asked in an amused voice, "So what brought this on? Some slut with a short skirt and a tight top being sent to the principal's office?"

"Something like that," Bob said.

Patient Rose's first appointment had included teeth cleaning and X-rays being taken (all done by Cindy), to be followed by a dental exam by Dr. Saint James. After Cindy informed her boss that Rose's X-rays had been developed, Heather said, "Thank you, Cindy. Feel free to read magazines in the waiting room, or watch TV, till I call you back for final cleanup."

"I'll do that. Thank you, Doctor."

After Cindy left the room, outwardly it seemed that Dr. Saint James was sticking dental instruments into Rose's mouth, and Rose was suffering in silence. But what Cindy couldn't know was that Heather and Rose, inside their heads, were together visiting the bimborg hive—

"Welcome to The Club. This unit is Tzigane-2571. Please state your designation and if this is your first time here."

Heather said, "This unit is Heather-216937. I'm here with Rose-16184906. It is Rose-unit's second time here."

Tzigane asked, "Do you two intend to visit the same Conference, or different Conferences?"

Rose "spoke" for the first time: "The same Conference. But what Conferences are available here? Last night this unit discovered only the 'Hair, makeup, fingernails, and clothing' Conference."

"There are fifteen Conferences here: Queen's Conference; King James' preferences, sexual; King James' preferences, nonsexual; Analysis of sex acts with King James; Blowjobs and Kegel exercises; Straight-sex and lesbian-sex FAQ; Ass-Kicker Babes' Conference; Spy Babes' Conference; Welcomers' Conference; Keeping the secret; Hair, makeup, fingernails, and clothing; Nutrition, fitness, diet, and exercise; Self-defense; Future knowledge; and Bra-shopping."

Heather said, "We need to go to Queen's Conference. We are carrying out Special Instructions from King James, and need a part of the Instructions made clear."

A few milliseconds later, the two bimborg were in the Queen's Conference. Heather-unit was saying, ". . .This unit came here 46 days ago, to report Special Instructions from King James. Now Rose-unit is likewise bound by those Special Instructions, as are whomever she Welcomes at Sweet Onion High School."

Stephanie-1 "spoke" up now: "Sweet Onion High School, you say? Heather-unit, remind the queen-unit's court what are the Special Instructions that you two are carrying out."

Heather and Rose did so. Then Stephanie-1 asked, "What is it about the Special Instructions that you units don't understand?"

Rose-unit replied, "This unit has completed a visual analysis of all the female students and teachers at the school. Out of seven hundred students and sixty teachers, there are 27 girls and zero teachers who meet Babeness Standards revision Four."

"Understood. Go on."

"If we lower our standards to Babeness Three, this makes another ten girls and two teachers be candidates for Welcoming."

"Understood."

"Our question for you is: Which Babeness Standards do we go by, when choosing whom to Welcome?"

Stephanie-1 asked, "The two Babeness Three teachers, how did they fail Babeness Four?"

Rose-unit replied, "With Teacher Mary, this unit estimated her Percent Body Fat as just over what's allowed. This unit estimates that she is 1.2 kilograms too heavy for Babeness Four."

"Understood. Continue."

"With Teacher Karen, this unit learned that her age is 26, which makes her one year too old."

Stephanie-1 said, "King James must decide this. But he's just started sex with Sharon-41577. The queen-unit expects that it will be an hour before the queen-unit tells you his answer."

Milliseconds later, Heather and Rose were back in the real world. Rose gave Heather a thumb-up.

(Heather couldn't reply in kind. At the moment, she was scraping a bicuspid.)

Sixty-seven minutes later, Rose and Heather received King James' answer: "Sweet Onion bimborg are to Welcome all 27 hotties who have the babelicious looks of Babeness Standards revision Four. *But* they also are to Welcome the two Babeness Three teachers."

Rose telepathically sent the names and images of Prudy Lu Moffatt and the other 28 Welcoming-candidates to Heather.

What did all this mean? It meant that soon Charlie-Bob Owens was in for a helluva surprise.

2-F: The Pep Rally

AUTHOR'S NOTE: One part of this chapter was written after I visited the American Dental Association's website, www.ada.org. I'm sure the ADA is thrilled to find their expert advice inside a soft-core porn novel.

THE NEXT AFTERNOON

The school had let out at three o'clock for the pep rally, and now students and teachers were strolling into the gym and taking seats in the bleachers.

Most people were sitting in the bleachers. But not Regina. She stood on the hardwood floor of the basketball court, facing the crowd. Green-and-white pom-poms lay at her feet, Varsity cheerleaders stood on either side of her, and the Varsity basketball team stood in a parallel line behind her.

Regina spotted Nightshade go into the bleachers—except she didn't look like Nightshade anymore. The ex-witch was wearing blue jeans, a lime-green top, and pink lipstick. She was making a point to talk to the prettiest girls in the bleachers. *Just confirms what I always suspected: She likes girls too much,* Regina thought. *That, or she's running for Prom Queen in May.*

Worse, Nightshade clearly had come to school today wearing a padded bra. *Desperate much?* Regina sneered.

Regina had disliked Nightshade less when she'd looked like Miss Vampire Vidal County. It was pathetic, seeing Call-Me-Rose now try so hard to get both boys and girls to like her.

After talking to lots of gorgeous girls, ex-Nightshade came over to where Charlie-Bob Owens was sitting. Regina couldn't hear their words, but Nightshade then sat down next to the nerd, as he blushed red. Rose smiled at him the way a hot-to-trot girlfriend would; this just made Charlie-Bob blush redder.

A few minutes passed. By now, everyone who hadn't managed to sneak past the security guard and head home, was now seated in the bleachers. Regina kept a plastic smile on her face, even as she was thinking, *Mr. Roberts, get your ass in here and start the damned pep rally!*

The doors into the gym opened and shut; this had to be Mr. Roberts. Regina didn't even turn her head to look.

That is, until she noticed that the talk in the bleachers had gotten louder. Nightshade pointed toward the doors and said something to Charlie-Bob; he spoke words back to her.

Regina turned around to see what was so interesting; she gasped.

Standing next to Mr. Roberts was a tall blond woman dressed in white, who was so beautiful of face, and so spectacular of boob, she looked like the star of one of Daddy's hidden pornos.

Even Regina's mother, on her best day ever, had never looked this good. Regina herself didn't even come close. So Regina hated the stranger on sight.

Mr. Roberts started the show. He walked to where he was standing between Regina and the bleachers, turned to face the crowd, put the microphone to his lips, and made two announcements. Then he said, ". . .But before we start the pep rally, Dr. Heather Saint James is here to talk about good dental care." Then Mr. Roberts walked ten feet away.

The porn-actress dentist walked to the spot that Mr. Roberts had just left, as the gym went utterly silent.

Mr. Roberts handed the white-dressed bitch his microphone. She said, "Good afternoon, students and teachers at Sweet Onion High School. Let me share with you a few quick words about maintaining your oral health."

The freshman boys elbowed each other, and the senior boys smirked. Regina faced the crowd with a condescending smile that said *Okay, fine, she said 'oral'. Grow up, boys.*

The dentist's talk was, so the gymnasium clock said, only a few minutes long—

". . .When brushing, hold the brush at a 45-degree angle to the gums. . . ."

". . .Rub the floss gently up and down, keeping it pressed against the tooth. Don't jerk or snap the floss. . . ."

Regina was proud of herself: She managed to not roll her eyes even once, and she even pasted on a smile. Meanwhile, she was thinking, *Geez, Mr. Roberts, don't you know that kids like pep rallies because they get us out of listening to lectures?*

In the few minutes it took the dentist to give her little speech, it was obvious to Regina that White-Dressed Bitch knew how to work a crowd. Dentist Bitch finished her talk with ". . .And let me repeat, don't forget to brush your tongue! Because at your age, your tongue is sure to have picked up bacteria from—well, all sorts of things."

Regina frowned as both students and teachers laughed at that.

Regina thought, *Almost done. Less than a minute and she'll be out of here. Then I'll be the center of attention for a while.*

Dentist Barbie continued, "I thank you guys for giving me your time and attention. My name is Heather Saint James, and if your parents want to make a dental appointment for you, I've left my clinic's phone number with Mr. Roberts. But I want to end on a personal note. . . ."

Regina stood openmouthed at what she heard Dr. XXX say next.

Two minutes later, Dr. Porn-Tits said, ". . .So I ask Charlie-Bob Owens to stand, so you guys—excuse me, *y'all*— can give him the recognition he deserves."

The nerd stood up, blushing. Then everyone in the gym but Regina—students, teachers, Mr. Roberts, Betsy and Prudy Lu—all applauded the nerd. Nightshade was clapping so hard, Regina was sure that the tramp would break hand-bones.

Regina was frowning, but nobody noticed. Which made her frown harder.

After the pep rally ended, Regina thought she was done with Charlie-Bob and Nightshade. Not quite.

The whole school was wanting to leave out the same gymnasium doors at the same time. So nobody moved quickly. As a result, Regina was within earshot for ten minutes as The Slut Formerly Known As Nightshade carried on a syrupy-sweet conversation with Charlie-Bob.

Charlie-Bob finally got a clue. With his voice shaking, he asked, "So, Rose? Are you, um, free tonight? For a date?"

Regina called over, "Charlie-Bob, you're clueless if you ask a girl out for a Friday-night date on Friday afternoon. And if she actually says *yes*, she's desperate."

Nightshade looked over and said, "Regina, sweetie, normal rules don't apply when a genuine hero asks you out, you know? So I reckon *you're* the clueless one."

Then she turned her face back to Charlie-Bob. "Ohmigod, I'd *love* to go out with you!"

***

Bob Roberts had stood ten feet away from Heather Saint James for almost fifteen minutes. Needless to say, when Bob got home, he immediately grabbed Kathleen's hand and dragged her into the bedroom, for the second afternoon in a row.

Afterward, Kathleen was amused again. "I figure that the same little slut came back to your office today. With a short skirt, a tight top, *and* either breath mints or a mini-dildo in her purse."

"Something like that," Bob said. "Hey look, I think I'm up for Round Two."

2-G: First After First After First...

7 p.m. THAT EVENING

Charlie-Bob stood on the O'Connors' front porch, took a deep breath, and pressed the doorbell. *It's just a date,* he told himself. *I've gone on dates before.*

Which was certainly true. However, he'd never gone on a date with a gorgeous girl. Or ex-witch. Or an (according to rumor) ex-lesbian.

The door was yanked open, and on the other side stood a man in his late thirties. He was grinning. "You must be Charlie-Bob. Come in, come in, y'hear?"

This was puzzling. In Charlie-Bob's limited experience, fathers were not usually *cheerful* about meeting their daughter's dates.

Charlie stepped into the house—and almost collided with Rose's mother. Then the woman started using every bit of charm she had: "Hello, I'm Pansy O'Connor. I'm *so* glad to meet you, young man."

Charlie-Bob switched the box of chocolates to his left hand. "Good to meet you too, Mrs.—"

"Rose is still upstairs getting ready. She's trying *so hard* to look good for you."

Charlie-Bob replied, "That's really nice of her, but really, she'd look great—"

Now Rose's dad put out his own hand. "Sorry, didn't introduce myself. I'm Bill." As Charlie-Bob shook the man's hand, Bill continued, "Rose tells us, you got shot trying to rescue her dentist and another woman in Atlanta?"

"Yes and no. I *was* in Atlanta, and I *did* get shot, trying to keep Heather and Amy Emily safe. But really, all I did—"

A thirteen-year-old girl walked in; she strongly resembled Rose. The girl's first words? "Gee, I thought you'd be taller."

Pansy put on a frozen smile, then turned toward her daughter. "Violet, sweetie, remember what we talked about? You be *nice* to Charlie-Bob, y'hear?"

Bill slapped the shoulder of Charlie-Bob's sports jacket. "Well, I think you're a brave boy. Rose has been talking about you nonstop for two days now. You've sure done *something* to change her attitude."

Violet said, "Not to mention, she doesn't look like Morticia Addams anymore." Catching her mother's look, Violet added, "*What?* You know it's true. I've had a weird-looking sister since I was in second grade."

Rose's voice laughed at the top of the stairs. "*I heard that, Vi!*"

Rose flowed down the stairs with the grace of a princess. "You be the judge, Charlie-Bob: Do I look, you know, weird?"

"No, you look *wow!*" he said, as he handed her the box of chocolates. She was wearing dark-green things that were mixed with black things, which all went well with her dark-auburn hair and her perfect face.

Rose smiled at him. Then she said, "Ohmigod, I am *so* sorry I don't have higher heels to wear for you. But these are the only dress shoes I have. Well, till tomorrow."

"And what happens tomorrow?" clueless Charlie-Bob asked.

"*Shopping!*" Rose, Pansy, and Violet all said.

Rose handed the chocolates to her mother and said, "Mommy, can you make sure this gets put on my bed?" Then she eyed Violet and added, "And it stays *unopened?*"

"You ready to go?" Charlie-Bob asked.

"I sure am!" Rose replied. She walked to the front door.

"You kids have fun," Bill said. "Rose, I trust you to be home at a decent time."

Once again, Charlie-Bob had the feeling that this was not normal behavior for a teen girl's father.

Once Charlie-Bob had Rose in the front seat of the car—his father's car actually, borrowed for this special occasion—Charlie-Bob said, "Your parents were right friendly toward me."

"That's because I've been, ohmigod, singing your praises since Wednesday," Rose said. Then she giggled. "But also, bless their hearts,

Mommy and Daddy are so relieved to see me acting like a good Georgia girl again."

Charlie-Bob took Rose to Rusty's Down Home Cookin', where the two teens talked during the meal.

". . .But I don't understand any of it," Charlie-Bob said. "You were a witch, you were dressed in black, and I remember you ranting in Mrs. Elliot's class about the Patriarchy Conspiracy—"

"Because she agreed with me some."

"Then Wednesday, you ran into Heather, you talked to her, and the next day you offered me porn-movie delights. What could Heather possibly have said to you in that one conversation?"

"Well, I was whining to her about how boys are always 'bothering' me, you know? And you know how she's perfect from head to toe. So I thought she could, like, give me some great 'Fuck off, loser' lines to say. But nope, she caught me by surprise."

Charlie-Bob said, "I can't imagine Heather ever saying 'Fuck off, loser' to *anybody*."

"What she said to me was, in so many words, 'Oh, grow up. You and I are the same: We're beautiful, we're treated as special, and people give us things we haven't earned. This makes us shallow. Charlie-Bob Owens did the bravest thing that I've ever seen any real person do, and yet it's people like you and me that everyone fusses over. If you don't like getting hit on, put a bag over your head.' So I asked, 'What did Charlie-Bob do?' Then she told me, and ohmigod, my jaw *totally* hit the floor. Then I realized I was attracted to you."

"That, um, was new thinking for you, right?"

"Ohmigod, at first I was so confused, liking a *guy*. But then I realized, I don't dislike guys, I dislike *boys*, you know? But anyone who did what you did is a man, not a boy. Then I realized something else."

"Go on."

"Dr. Saint James said she and I were 'the same.' But I realized that she was acting like a grownup, while I was acting like a total whiny princess. So I decided, I would grow up too."

"And that's your story? That's how you could completely change your life, from one conversation with one stranger?"

Rose looked Charlie-Bob in the eyes. "I swear, it's the whole truth. And if you, like, ask Mommy and Daddy, I told them the very same thing. Or ask anyone at school I talk to."

Rose looked sincere, so Charlie-Bob completely believed her.

Charlie-Bob put the key in the ignition; but rather than start the car, he looked at Rose. "The Bijou is showing *The Kissing Booth* and also *Hermione Farmer and the Tie Tack of Mesmer*. Which movie do you want to see?"

Rose put a hand on his arm. "Charlie-Bob, sweetie, girls don't respect a boy who tries too hard to be pleasing, you know? But before you be the big strong man and decide what movie we'll see"—Rose opened her purse and pulled out several folded sheets of paper—"I have this."

"And what is 'this'?"

Rose's smile was mischievous. "The story summary for the Henry Porter movie with, like, spoilers and all. You can skip the movie, and still tell everybody at school everything that happened. You'll totally scam everybody."

"Why do that? I *like* the Henry Porter At Porkpimple Potion Academy movies."

Rose put her hand on his arm again. "Charlie-Bob, I've never had a cock in my hand, or my mouth, or my pussy. I'm like, ohmigod, a *virgin* at eighteen."

"Believe me, I feel your pain," he replied. "But what does this got—?"

"Today I talked to Dr. Saint James, and she's left the key to her clinic under a bush. You and I can. . ."

For the past two days, Rose O'Connor had intimidated Charlie-Bob. But now, with car keys in his hand and with major hottie Rose fucking him with her eyes, Charlie-Bob stopped being timid. *Mister* Charlie-Bob took charge.

"We *can* fuck, Rose, and we *will* fuck!" he said. With a flick of his wrist, he started the car. "You have a cavity, Rose. And Dr. Owens will fill your cavity, using his special drill."

Charlie-Bob laughed with delight.

Charlie-Bob experienced six "firsts" within the next two hours.

The only one of the six "firsts" that wasn't fun was Charlie-Bob buying his first box of condoms. Instead of fun, that part of the evening was nerve-wracking.

It wasn't Charlie-Bob's first time to touch naked tits, but it should have been. Rose's tits were larger than average—How had nobody noticed this before?—and their shape was Art.

Twenty minutes after Charlie-Bob started feeling her tits, Rose was lying on her naked back, on the clinic waiting room's gray carpet. Rose's legs were up and spread apart, and her arms were reaching for him. He could *smell* her desire. He got down on hands and knees, pushed his cockhead to just touching Rose's pussy, and he thought, *Losing my virginity—this is exactly how I'd want it to happen.*

"Take my cherry, Charlie-Bob," Rose said. "I want *you* to be my first."

Charlie-Bob shoved his cock into Rose's wet pussy. She grimaced, and sucked in air through her teeth. He stopped moving his cock, but his face leaned down to kiss her lips.

Ten seconds later, she said, "I'm okay now. But please move slowly."

He did exactly that. For a few seconds, her face twitched with pain, but then she said, "Ohhhmigod, now I get what all the fuss is about. This feels *nice*, you know?"

She started meeting his slow thrusts with slow thrusts of her own. Then they both quickened the pace. Charlie-Bob felt her pussy walls grab him, and he began to enjoy his first time to fuck a girl—

—so much that one minute later, he enjoyed his first orgasm inside a girl's pussy *much* sooner than he'd planned to. How embarrassing! But Rose was forgiving, and Charlie-Bob's cock recovered quickly.

Five minutes after his premature ejaculation, she'd stroked him hard, he'd replaced the used condom with a fresh one, and his cock was back to pistoning her pussy.

He'd read over and over that girls take longer than guys to have their first orgasm. He was determined to not disappoint Rose again, so when he felt himself get too close to cumming, he started computing the square root of two.

His trick worked. Charlie-Bob kept himself hard, and soon Rose started moaning. Her kisses got fervent, and she started arching her back and thrusting her hips harder. He could feel her nipples pressing against his chest. Then their chests got wet from each other's sweat.

After a few minutes of Rose's building excitement (while Charlie-Bob thought of rotting zombies and C++ computer code), Rose—

"Charlie-Bob, I'm gonna come!"

—clawed Charlie-Bob's back as she screamed. Charlie-Bob felt proud of himself: For the first time, he'd made a woman climax.

He continued to think of zombies, and that postponed his own orgasm for a minute or so. He managed to not enjoy his second climax till Rose was enjoying hers.

Afterward, he kissed her, then he dropped limp onto the carpet.

That's when she rolled on top of him, and started kissing his face—

"Ohmigod, that was, like, *fantastic,* you know? *Kiss* Everyone's told me, like, 'Don't expect much, your first time,' *kiss* but you made me feel so *good!*' *Kiss, kiss, kiss*

Charlie-Bob felt weights pressing down on his chest, and that reminded him of something: "Rose, how did you go through twelve years of school and nobody notice you have breasts? *Big* breasts?"

"It was all that shapeless black clothing I was wearing. Come Monday, when I'm wearing tighter, brighter tops, you watch!" She laughed. "Bull Barclay will be all over me."

"Yeah," Charlie-Bob said unhappily. "Bull Barclay certainly will." Bull Barclay was handsome and was dating Regina Wisley, but had a reputation of bedding other guys' girlfriends.

"Pfft," Rose said. "He's already told me, the cure for my lesbianism is his wonderful dick. But since I'm not lesbo now, why do I need to fuck him?" Then she kissed Charlie-Bob. "Besides, I want to be too busy fucking *you*, you know?"

Then she gave him a mischievous smile. "Or doing other stuff with you. Ohmigod, can you believe I'm eighteen and I've never put a cock in my mouth?"

With that, she pulled the condom off Charlie-Bob's cock, threw it in the plastic shopping bag that was designated as "condom trash bag," and then Rose licked Charlie-Bob's cock.

She made a face.

"My cock tastes yucky?" he asked worriedly.

"No, the lubricant in the condom tastes yucky. Your cock? I think I like its taste, but I need more research."

She began licking his cock all over, like a cat. She was a natural, and Charlie-Bob was soon rock-hard and excited again.

After five minutes of exquisite licking-torture, she said, "Mind if I try something I've heard girls talk about?" With that, she slid her lips down his dick like it were a Popsicle, the first time that any girl had done that to him.

Rose had a gorgeous face—after high school, she could easily become a model or actress. So even though Charlie-Bob had already come twice that night, the sight of her perfectly shaped face and its perfectly shaped mouth slurping his rod, got him excited again. After ten minutes of Rose's lips moving up and down his cock, he was on the verge of orgasm—

"I'm about to come in your mouth!" he cried.

—and worried she'd stop then. But instead, her pace got faster. He blasted her throat as he moaned.

To his left was a poster on the wall that showed a smiling tooth. Charlie-Bob gave the big tooth a thumb-up.

When Charlie-Bob's brain was working again, he kissed Rose. She then asked, "What do you want to do next?"

"Do to you what you did to me."

"You don't have to, you know. I'm not keeping score, and I'm feeling generous tonight."

"But I want to. But you'll need to coach me. It's my first time to eat a pussy."

"Well, if you insist, I guess I can teach you how to lick me right."

Charlie-Bob didn't think he was as adept at oral sex as Rose had been; still, she seemed to respond well enough. (Meaning, she pushed his face into her pussy as she moaned.) And he finally learned what a clitoris was.

The taste, however, would take some getting used to. And nobody had warned him about getting pubic hairs caught in his teeth.

A half-hour later, Charlie-Bob threw the condom bag into an unattended Dumpster. As he was getting back behind the steering wheel, Rose said, "What a totally awesome night! We did everything that a boy and girl can do."

He shook his head. "Not quite. I decided sometime tonight that I'm not interested in Anal. But I never got around to putting my fingers in your pussy, and you never put yours around my cock."

She said in a mock-prim voice, "Too late now. You can't stroke my womanly areas while you've driving. That would be *dangerous*."

But then she moved closer to him. "But *I* don't have that problem, you know?"

Rose had proved herself a natural at sucking a cock; now she showed as much raw talent at stroking a cock. Within four blocks, Charlie-Bob had to pull off the road because he couldn't concentrate on his driving anymore.

And *then*, no sooner had he sputtered the words "Rose, I'm gonna—"

—but Rose zoomed her head down, and sealed her lips around his cockhead. She swallowed every drop.

With the handjob successfully completed, Charlie-Bob had to revise his count. He'd now experienced *seven* first-times in one night.

2-H: Welcome, Denise!

SATURDAY MORNING

Rose-unit studied her naked reflection in the full-length mirror in her bedroom. Her breasts were developing nicely, and her already-long hair had grown two more inches since Wednesday.

Since Rose-unit had herself been Welcomed three days ago, she'd developed "warts" on her left hand, which actually were transmitters, to send indoctrination information to newly Welcomed bimborg. In 3.1 more hours (plus or minus 8.3 minutes), the construction of those transmitters would be complete.

Rose-unit's other Welcoming equipment was almost ready to go as well. The modifications to Rose-unit's tongue (so that it could inject nanobots into the candidate's bloodstream) would be complete in 2.9 hours, and the creation of tiny hollow tubes in her (longer) fingernails would be completed in 1.4 hours.

In short: In no more than 3 hours, 14 minutes, and 18 seconds from now, Rose-unit could start Welcoming the most beautiful girls in Sweet Onion into becoming bimborg.

King James wanted a troop of Sweet Onion bimborg who together would fulfill his Special Instructions. King James was counting on Rose-unit to give him this troop, by Welcoming one Sweet Onion High School beauty after another. Rose-unit would not fail King James!

Rose-unit got her first chance at Welcoming a Babeness Standards girl on Saturday afternoon. Rose, Mommy, and Violet were in Peach Preserves (a Sweet Onion clothing boutique) when Rose spied Denise Webber at the next rack of tops.

Denise was Babeness Standards revision Four because of her thick light-auburn hair and her sky-blue eyes (which all by themselves, qualified her for Babeness Standards revision Two)—

—plus Denise had the second-biggest boobs in the senior class.

Rose looked over and smiled. "Hi, Denise, having fun today?"

Denise smiled. "I *always* enjoy shopping. Especially when it's not my money." Then Denise nodded at the green top that Rose was holding at arm's length. "Um, you're not buying black?"

Rose took two minutes to answer that question (while she saw Violet roll her eyes three times). Rose mentioned Dr. Saint James several times, and Rose mentioned Charlie-Bob Owens a *lot*.

After Rose wound down, Denise said politely, "So, you got really impressed with him. Good for you."

By now, Rose had two green tops and a teal top picked out to try on. Rose made a point to look at the tops, then at Mommy, then at Denise. Rose bit her lip, then said, "Denise, I need to, like, ask you a favor. I need, um, your help."

"What kind of help?"

"I've gotten a second growth spurt. My *boobs* are getting, ohmigod, huge. And you've got experience in shopping for, um, big-girl tops."

"Um. . ." Perhaps Denise was thinking of all the SOHS rumors that Rose was sapphic. "Why not ask your mom to help you?"

Rose rolled her eyes. "One word: 'Nun.' Mommy wants to hide all my figure, ohmigod."

"Don't believe my lying child, Denise," Mommy said. "Stopping her from dressing like a teen hooker is *not* the same thing as dressing her as a nun."

Then Mommy added in a thoughtful voice, "But you *could* give Rose advice about the *proper fit* that I can't. Neither I nor my sister had to deal with being, um, shaped like you."

"Um. . ."

Violet said, "Denise probably doesn't want to be in a dressing room alone with the Licking Witch of the East."

"Violet!" Mommy said. "That's hateful."

"Not when rumors about your twelfth-grade sister get passed all the way down to seventh grade, Mommy," Violet said.

Denise said again, "Um. . ."

Rose said, "Listen, I am *not a lesbian now!*"

Oops, maybe Rose had said that a little too loud. She realized that Denise, Mommy, and Violet all were staring at her—as was the store owner. (A twenty-something customer also was looking at Rose; *her* face showed disappointment.)

Denise made a nervous laugh. "Okay, fine, I'll help you. But if I start downloading Melissa Etheridge, my boyfriend Kevin will be mad at you."

It was easy for Rose-unit to "accidentally" scratch the other girl, prior to Welcoming Denise. The problem for Rose-unit happened a little later, when she and Denise were in the changing room. Rose-unit was 3 minutes and 39 seconds into the nanobot-transfer kiss, when she heard this argument—

Violet said, "We need to check on them, Mommy. They've been in there too long."

Mommy said, "They're fine, Vi. Leave them alone."

"Mommy, they should be out by now. Denise might need our help."

"*Denise* might need our help? Why, is Rose a vampire?"

"Jeez, Mommy, how clueless are you? I'll just peek in."

"Violet Melanie O'Connor, come *back* here."

"Mommy, do you realize what Rose could be *doing?* To Denise?"

"I think you're wrong about your sister. But even if you're right, she's still your sister, and you will respect her. Am I clear?"

Rose-unit heard a martyr's sigh. "Yes, Mommy," Violet said.

Two minutes later, Denise and Rose walked out of the changing booth. Rose was wearing a pea-green V-neck blouse that showed lots of cleavage (now that Rose had cleavage worth showing).

Violet grumbled, "Took you two long enough." Her eyes were searching the face of both Denise and Rose, for any sign of a flush.

Mommy eyed Rose's scandalous green garment. "I might need to rethink the nun thing."

"Charlie-Bob will like it, for sure," Rose said. This shut Mommy up.

"You know, Charlie Bob sounds like a *totally* great guy," Denise said to Mommy and Violet. "Y'all have, like, met him outside of class, right? Could y'all tell me more about him?"

Violet rolled her eyes.

The next day (Sunday), the entire O'Connor family headed for the malls—except that there were no malls in Sweet Onion. Or in any town nearby, for that matter. It said something about the parents' commitment to Rose's new hetero lifestyle that the only question then became: "Do we drive on the snowy Interstate to Macon, or on the snowy Interstate to Savannah?"

Violet voted for Macon.

Mommy gave Daddy a bedroom smile and said that she'd like to eat at "that cute little crab shack, if you don't mind."

So to Savannah they went.

For Rose, the shopping trip went well. She bought a black pair and a blue pair of five-inch stilettos—

"Charlie-Bob will think you're a slut," Violet said.

"That's the idea," Rose replied.

—and in a ladies' room at Oglethorpe Mall in Savannah, Rose-unit Welcomed a stacked brunette with a British accent who was wearing a Georgia Bulldogs sweatshirt.

(Admittedly, this had nothing at all to do with fulfilling the Special Instructions for Sweet Onion's bimborg. But Rose-unit figured she needed practice at Welcoming.)

2-1: Prudy Lu Is Confused

MONDAY MORNING

Charlie-Bob was unlocking his locker when he got pushed to the ground. As he went flying, he heard—

"What the fuck's the idea, geek, stealing my girl?"

Charlie-Bob looked up. Standing over him, fists clenched, was Kevin Sinclair. Sinclair was on the wrestling team—which anyone could easily figure out by looking at him.

Charlie-Bob shook his head; Kevin's attack didn't compute. Aloud, Charlie-Bob said, "You're dating *Rose?*"

"No, you moron, I mean Denise Webber! She told me yesterday that she was dropping me; says she'd rather date *you.*" Kevin's last word dripped with scorn.

"I know nothing of this," Charlie-Bob said as he stood up. "I haven't talked to Denise in months."

Prudy Lu Moffatt had locked her locker, and was walking to find Regina and Betsy, when she discovered that her way was blocked by a crowd in the hallway.

"What's going on?" she asked nobody in particular.

"It's Kevin," a girl's voice said to Prudy Lu's left. "He's going, like, apeshit because I broke up with him to date Charlie-Bob Owens."

Prudy Lu looked to her left. Next to her stood Denise Webber; to Denise's left stood Rose O'Connor. Each girl was dressed to impress with her chest.

"What's the deal, Rose?" Prudy Lu asked (quietly, because Regina had ordered Prudy Lu not to talk to Rose). "I heard that Charlie-Bob was dating *you.* I heard that y'all went to Rusty's on Friday."

"All true," Rose said. "But Charlie-Bob is, ohmigod, a hero, so I'm willing to *share,* you know?" Rose's sexy smile made it clear what she meant.

"I know nothing of this," Charlie-Bob said as he stood up. "I haven't talked to Denise in months." Mentally, he was still trying to puzzle out this mystery, instead of sticking with his expected omega-male role.

"Good," Kevin sneered, "if you haven't put her up to this, you got no problem staying away from her. Or else. You're smart, you'll make the right choice."

"Are you *threatening* me?" Charlie-Bob said.

By now a silent crowd had gathered. So Kevin looked around, smirked, and said, "Oh, am I threatening you? I can *hurt* you easy—what do you think?"

Because Kevin's face was turned sideways (he was smirking at a blonde), he didn't see Charlie-Bob rush forward and push *him* to the ground. "Can you hurt me worse than being *shot in the leg?*" Charlie-Bob demanded. "I've faced off against a masked gunman with an Uzi—am I supposed to be scared of some big *boy?*"

Charlie-Bob glanced around. Faces were set on "stun."

By now Kevin was climbing to his feet—just in time to hear *applause*. Everyone but the super-popular kids was clapping for Charlie-Bob.

Prudy Lu Moffatt heard gasps, and a boy in front of her exclaimed, "Kewl!"

"What's going on?" Rose asked.

"*Charlie-Bob* just pushed *Kevin* down," a different boy said.

"*Yes!*" Rose and Denise said. Prudy Lu decided that it was uncanny, how Rose and Denise made the same fist-pump gesture at the same time.

By now Kevin was climbing to his feet—just in time to hear *applause*. Everyone but the super-popular kids was clapping for Charlie-Bob. The wrestler looked as surprised as Charlie-Bob felt.

Then Charlie-Bob heard, "Break it up, break it up, move along." Seconds later, Mr. Roberts was standing there.

"What's happening?" the principal demanded, eyeing Kevin.

Kevin put on an innocent expression and pointed to Charlie-Bob. "I was minding my own business, and he pushed me down."

"Pfft," a beautiful freshman girl said. "That big bully pushed Charlie-Bob down first. He was ranting about Denise Webber. But Charlie-Bob stood up to him."

"Yeah," said a male voice, "it was cool."

Mr. Roberts asked Charlie-Bob, "Did he hit you?"

Charlie-Bob shook his head.

Kevin said, "But—"

Mr. Roberts put up a hand. "Right now you *don't* have detention, Mr. Sinclair. But you're pushing your luck. Move along."

As Kevin walked away, he muttered, "Speak of the devil." Charlie-Bob didn't know what that meant—till both Denise Webber and Rose rushed up to him.

Rose threw her arms around Charlie-Bob, and hugged and kissed him right in the hallway. "Ohmigod, you were, like, totally awesome!"

"Totally," Denise agreed.

As Prudy Lu walked away to find Regina, she caught a glimpse of Rose and Denise talking to Charlie-Bob. Those girls were standing so close to Charlie-Bob, he couldn't have stuck a rolling pin between each girl's chest and his own.

What has that guy got? Prudy Lu wondered.

"That guy" asked Rose, "So what's all this about Denise wanting to date me?"

Rose said, "Remember how I told you I was, like, going shopping for clothes this weekend? At Peach Preserves here in town, I made friends Saturday with Denise. Then I told her *all* about you."

Denise said, "Rose bought, ohmigod, *tons* of clothes this weekend. Look at her—doesn't she look *hot?*"

Truthfully, Charlie-Bob hadn't looked at Rose's clothes at all. But now he did—and whistled.

My memory's playing tricks, he thought. *I don't remember Rose on Friday being this stacked.* Aloud, he said, "Um, Rose? Mr. Roberts is sure to send you home to change. Or tell you to cover up, at the very least."

"So what if he does?" Rose replied. "*You* get to see my cleavage, even if nobody else will. So it's worth it, you know?"

"Totally worth it," Denise said.

"So back to what I was asking," Charlie-Bob said. "Denise, why did you tell Kevin you want to date me instead of him?"

"Because I want to date a real man, ohmigod. Rose helped me realize, That's what you are."

"Denise, you're hot, and I'm really flattered. But Rose and I are already—well, we're sorta. . ." Charlie-Bob looked at Rose and raised an eyebrow.

Rose laid a hand on his arm. "Stud, I'm willing to loan you out to other girls who *totally* see what I see in you—"

"*What?* Jesus, Rose, this is too—"

Rose continued, "But don't worry, *I* plan to stay, like, totally faithful to you. Because I declare, I see no other boys in this school I plan to fuck."

Denise laughed. "Rose, considering the rumors about you, that's not promising much, you know?"

Rose herself laughed. "Fine, I pledge I totally won't date any *girls* at this school, either. Satisfied?"

"What about Dr. Saint James?" Denise teased. "Ohmigod, *I'd* hook up with her in a heartbeat, and I'm not even lesbian."

Rose replied with exaggerated primness, "If Heather wants to hook-up with me, I will reluctantly agree, you know?" But then Rose smiled at Charlie-Bob and said, "But every other boy and girl in this town is *totally* off the list. O-U-T!"

"Can we focus here, ladies?" Charlie-Bob said. "First Bell is about to ring."

Rose said, "Here it is in a nutshell, Stud: You can date Denise, you can fuck Denise, you can tell Denise to suck you off in the janitor's closet—"

"I did that to Kevin last week," Denise said, giving Charlie-Bob a smoky look.

"—or me, same list. You can ask us both to do threesomes or lesbo stuff. I think you're, ohmigod, a hero, and Denise thinks you're a hero and, like, whatever you want, we won't say No to."

"Hold on," Charlie-Bob said. "Denise, how old are you?"

"Eighteen, as of two weeks ago," Denise said. "I'm very legal, and very horny—as Kevin can tell you."

"Which explains why he was pissed at me," Charlie-Bob said.

So the rumors are true, Regina thought. *That geek Charlie-Bob bagged another groupie.*

Regina watched Rose and Denise walk closer. The two sluts were talking and giggling together as they walked through the hallway, minutes before First Bell.

"I think Denise has gone lipstick-lesbian," Betsy said. "Those two are *way* too friendly."

"Not me," Prudy Lu said. "Rose says she's a new person, and I believe her."

Before Regina got a chance to reply to Prudy Lu, Rose and Denise came to a stop in front of Regina and her minions—

—except that Regina herself, and *one* of her minions, got ignored.

"Good morning, Prudy Lu," Denise said.

"Beautiful day, Prudy Lu, isn't it?" Rose said.

"That blouse brings out your eyes, Prudy Lu," Rose added.

"I agree, you look great today, Prudy Lu," Denise said.

Regina glared at Prudy Lu, who caught the look. Prudy Lu gave Rose and Denise each a sickly smile, but said nothing.

Then Regina seethed as Charlie-Bob's sluts smiled at Prudy Lu, waved to her, and walked away, not speaking a word to Regina.

After that face-off between Rose and Regina, Prudy Lu was able to get to first-period Government class without any more drama.

A few minutes later, Prudy Lu saw Charlie-Bob walk into the classroom, and walk to his desk. He took his book bag off his back, pulled out his Government book and notebook, and put them on his desk. Just like any other day.

Except that any other day, the classroom wouldn't be graveyard-quiet like this. (First Bell hadn't yet rung.)

Charlie-Bob looked around the silent room and said, "Hey John, I hear you shot a basket from midcourt, Friday night. Way to go!"

John Wallace looked startled at Charlie-Bob speaking to him. Then he said, "Yeah, thanks man. For sure, I was pretty pumped about it afterward."

Charlie-Bob nodded, then turned to look at Prudy Lu. He said, "That light-purple skirt brings out both your skin color and your blue eyes. You look good."

Prudy Lu blinked. She was the coolest of the cool, being both a cheerleader and a friend of the richest girl in town. And John Wallace, being on the basketball team, was cool by definition. While Charlie-Bob was very uncool: He liked school too much, and he dressed like a guy indifferent to fashion.

Now Prudy Lu did the math over again, and the result came up the same: Charlie-Bob did none of the things that "cool" boys did, so he must be "uncool." But why was this uncool boy speaking to cool kids as equals?

It was his quiet confidence, Prudy Lu decided. This morning, Charlie-Bob acted like someone holding four aces.

First Bell rang then, and soon the teacher was yammering about the federal reserve system. But Prudy Lu didn't pay attention to any of that. What Prudy Lu was puzzling out was, *How can such an uncool boy as Charlie-Bob Owens get two high-school ultrababes and a lingerie-model dentist all singing his praises?*

Nearly an hour later, just as the Dismissal Bell rang, Prudy Lu got a horrible thought: *What if Charlie-Bob, Rose, and Denise all know something I don't? What if all the trusty definitions of "cool" and "uncool" are wrong?*

2-J: Welcome, Welcome, Welcome!

MONDAY AFTERNOON

In Rose's own Government class, as soon as the next day's homework was assigned, Rose raised her hand. "Ms. Brewster, can I please get, like, a library pass?"

Ms. Brewster frowned. "I suppose. Come up to my desk."

As Ms. Brewster was writing the library pass, she eyed Rose's sexy outfit with disapproval. Then the teacher said in a low voice, "I remember when you denounced the Patriarchy. Now you're catering to it."

Rose giggled. "If you think *this* is bad, you should've, like, seen me before Mr. Roberts sent me home. You would've totally freaked."

Then Rose got serious: "Charlie-Bob Owens put his own life in danger to protect two female people. What feminist would do that for two penis-persons? None, I reckon. I've figured out that men are not brutes, and women are not better people."

Then Rose gave Ms. Brewster an airhead smile, and sashayed to the classroom door.

Rose stopped off at the girls' restroom. To empty her bladder, to brush her hair, and to freshen her makeup—but mainly to look for any girls "on the list." No luck; the bathroom was empty.

But soon Rose was in the library, where her luck got better. The only people in the library (besides Rose) turned out to be the librarian, two freshman boys who were working on a project, and Helen-May Sawyer. Helen-May was sitting at a table and reading *Modern Bride*.

Helen-May Sawyer was a pale-skinned, blue-eyed senior who looked more natural with dyed-blond hair than with the brunette color that she'd been born with. She had a pretty face and an above-average cup size.

In fact, Helen-May Sawyer met Babeness Standards revision Four.

But Helen-May Sawyer also was president of the Purity League, and her nickname was Helen Won't.

Rose walked up to Helen-May's table. "Okay if I sit here?"

"Other tables are empty," Helen-May said.

"True, but I get lonely at a table by myself."

"Okay then, you can sit here," Helen-May said. "But it'll cost you. I'm gonna try to recruit you into Purity League, and you gotta listen."

Rose laughed. "Girlfriend, you're a week too late. Last week, I was technically a virgin—"

"Technically?"

"—but Friday, I and Charlie-Bob *devirginated* each other. Ohmigod, it was, like, the Fourth of July, Christmas, and Groundhog Day all in one."

"Groundhog Day?"

Rose's smile was sexy. "Because one part of the night kept repeating, you know?"

Helen-May put her head in her hands for several seconds. "Listen, it's not too late. You can return to celibacy now, but you'll need to be honest with your fiancé before the wedding."

Rose said, "*Stop* this? *Why?* Fucking Charlie-Bob Owens is the greatest thing since six-inch platform stilettos."

"Rose, you want to get married, right? Ever hear the expression, Why buy the cow when you can get the milk for free?"

"Ever hear the expression, Never buy a car without a test drive first?"

"Sex is a wonderful mystery of the universe, Rose, and you shouldn't cheapen it with tawdry backseat—"

"Don't knock sex in a car if, like, you've never tried it yourself, you know?" Rose laid a hand atop Helen-May's hand. "I wish there was some way I could convince you how *totally glorious* is sex with Charlie-Bob."

Helen-May frowned. "Ow, you just scratched my hand."

LATER MONDAY AFTERNOON

Cindy Bright felt lucky to have such a good boss.

The patient, Paula Crawford, was fifteen or thereabouts—an age when kids are still scared when they sit in a dental chair, but think it uncool to let such feelings show. But Cindy's boss soothed the teen's unspoken fear: While Cindy cleaned the girl's teeth, Dr. Saint James stood about two feet away and acted as narrator. ("Cindy is doing X; Cindy is about to start Y.")

Dr. Saint James's step-by-step narration worked as intended: The girl (a gorgeous brunette with bright blue eyes) relaxed visibly.

Dr. Saint James, she of the sharp eye, must have also noticed that Cindy herself was nervous about taking dental X-rays. In any case, that morning the dentist had announced to Cindy that she was taking over the X-ray duties. This supposedly was "because I'm ten years closer to menopause than you are, Cindy, so it's less of a tragedy if *my* ovaries get cooked."

In any case, Dr. Saint James now sent Cindy out of the room while the dentist x-rayed the teenager's teeth. When Cindy was called back, there were ten film squares laying on the dental tray.

As soon as Cindy re-entered the room, Dr. Saint James told the girl, "Cindy will take the X-rays and put them in our film-develop machine. That'll take about ten minutes. No, probably longer, because there are ten X-rays to develop. Anyway, while we're waiting for Cindy to return with the pictures, I'll continue cleaning your teeth, but with a dental pick. I'll also be doing a visual exam of your teeth. Does that sound good?"

"Yes, ma'am." The girl sounded relaxed and trusting.

As Cindy walked out of the room with the film squares, she heard Dr. Saint James say, "Let me adjust your bib, and then we'll begin. I'm sorry, did I scratch you?"

Minutes later, the ten X-rays were almost all developed. That's when Cindy's cel chimed; Cindy groaned when she saw the name on the display.

"Hello, Roger," Cindy said. And if she was keeping her tone from sounding like *Fuck off and die painfully,* neither was she cooing like the rich man's mistress that she was.

"Hey, babe," Roger Wisley said, "what are you doing? Watching game shows, or is it that soap you like?"

"No, I'm at *work*. We actually have five patients today. And right now, Dr. Saint James is waiting on X-rays, so I can't talk long."

"Oh yeah, I heard about her little lecture Friday at the high school. Fact is, she's the talk of the town. Two different guys at the country club told me about her, plus Regina had words to say."

"What'd they all say?"

"The men told me your boss is built like a brick shithouse, while Regina told me she's 'full of herself.' That true?"

"Your daughter is . . . mistaken about Dr. Saint James."

"But what about the other part? Is your dentist-boss a hottie?"

"She signs my paycheck, so I'm not going to answer that. Roger, the X-rays are developed, so I have to hang up now."

"Fine, be that way. But maybe I'll drop in your place and check her out for myself. It would do her good, having the richest man in town as her patient."

"Not if she's built like a brick shithouse, Roger. Then everyone will assume she's another of your mistresses."

"*Another* of my mistresses? Cindy, you wound me. What you and I have is special."

"Yeah, sure, Roger. And I'll bet what you have with Barbara is 'special' too. Whoops, I'm sorry, I'm not supposed to know about Barbara, am I?"

Roger made a theatrical sigh. "I *knew* this would happen, that you couldn't handle—"

"I have to go, Roger. Bye." Cindy stabbed the phone's OFF button with her finger, then jammed the cel into a pocket of her scrubs-top.

When Cindy walked back into Treatment Room One with the X-rays, she found Dr. Saint James talking and scraping, and Paula listening and grimacing.

Thanks to Roger's phone call, Cindy was minutes later at returning with the X-rays than she should have returned. Dr. Saint James didn't stop talking about Charlie-Bob Owens as Cindy hurriedly laid the X-rays on the dental tray, but the dentist gave Cindy a raised eyebrow. That eyebrow asked, *What took you so long?*

WEDNESDAY MORNING

Denise was almost late to her third-period class; the Tardy Bell was about to ring.

But Denise didn't care one bit. And it wasn't to her third-period class (Geometry) where Denise was headed.

Miss Turner was one of two teachers "on the list," and third period was Miss Turner's free period. Denise planned to talk to Miss Turner about *The Scarlet Letter* in that empty classroom, and then Welcome Miss Turner.

That was the plan. An even better plan presented itself when Denise got to Miss Turner's classroom door, looked through the glass, and saw Miss Turner sitting at her desk. Miss Turner shone with the black glow of sadness.

Twenty-two-year-old Miss Turner, a natural blonde, sat at her desk with her shoulders slumped, reading a paperback book. She had a can of soda and a mega-fattening cinnamon roll also on her desk.

Denise knocked on the classroom door, then stepped in, not waiting for an invitation. "Miss Turner? Is everything okay?"

The Tardy Bell rang, as Miss Turner put down her book. "What can I help you with, Denise?" she asked in a businesslike manner.

"I'm asking what *I* can help *you* with, Miss Turner. I looked through the window, and you looked, ohmigod, real sad and lonely."

The young blond teacher frowned. "It's not proper for me to discuss my personal life with a student."

"Okay, but I think you'll feel better if you talk to me, you know? What are you reading?"

"I don't even remember." Miss Turner turned the book over. "*Love's Torment.* And love can certainly be a torment, truly."

"That's true. Monday morning, Kevin Sinclair picked a fight with Charlie-Bob Owens over *me*, right in front of the entire school. It was *totally* embarrassing."

"Look at the bright side: At least you know Kevin still cares for you. It's not like he dropped you for some bul—some silly reason."

"Ohmigod, is that what's bothering you? Some guy dropped you?"

"Denise, it is inappropriate—"

"Fine, I'm a student, so it's quote-unquote wrong for me to discuss your love life with you. But you're not in the teacher's lounge now, and the guidance counselor isn't here, so who else can help?"

"Denise, one more time: It isn't—"

"Something is bugging the shit out of you, Miss Turner. Spill it."

For ten seconds, Miss Turner eyed Denise. Then she sighed. "When I first got hired and moved to Sweet Onion, I met an amazing man, Lawrence. Maybe you know him, he manages the feed store."

"I'm listening," Denise said. She walked up behind Miss Turner, and started to rub the teacher's tense muscles in her neck and arms. Denise maybe scratched Miss Turner's arm at one point.

Miss Turner continued, "God, at first we were so on fire for each other, couldn't get enough time together. I can't believe I'm telling you this, but I fucked him eight times the first week, and I sucked him like a New Orleans whore. Well, that was at the start."

"But not later?" Denise asked. She continued to rub the teacher's neck and arms.

Miss Turner said, "Then he started giving me reasons why we couldn't get together. He told me that he had to work late, and I believed him. Then he wanted to play poker with his redneck buddies, on Saturdays and Wednesdays. I wondered about that, but I said 'Fine' to that too."

"Go on, I'm totally here for you," Denise said, as she continued to massage the teacher.

Miss Turner's voice started to slow down, as the nanobots kicked in: "A week before Christmas, I asked him, 'Where are we going, our relationship?' He told me, 'I can't marry a Yankee slut.' He took Clarissa Whatzername to the. . .New. . .Year's. . .Eve. . .party."

"So now you're dating your refrigerator," Denise replied. "Pigging out."

"Food. . .comforts. . .me," Miss Turner droned.

Denise pulled her hands back. "Stand up, Miss Turner," Denise said.

"Why?" the teacher asked in a distracted voice, even as she came to her feet.

Denise answered, "We'll both get in trouble if someone looks through the window and sees me rubbing your neck. You don't want us to get in trouble, right?"

"That's right," Miss Turner said, in that same distracted voice. "I don't. . .want us. . .to get. . .in trouble."

"Come with me," Denise said, as she took the teacher's hand. She pulled the stumbling teacher to the side wall of the classroom that was beside the door. Denise and Miss Turner now couldn't be seen from the classroom door's window.

Denise said, "You need a better boyfriend and, like, I can help with that."

Then Denise said, "I feel your pain," and kissed the teacher.

Five minutes and 27 seconds later, Denise broke the kiss. "Charlie-Bob Owens is your new boyfriend," Denise-unit told Mary-unit. "Listen for orders."

FRIDAY EVENING

This Friday was a week after Charlie-Bob had taken Rose on a date, in which both teens had lost their virginities. This Friday also was four days after Denise Webber had told Charlie-Bob that she was dropping her current guy to be with him.

Rose had told him, Friday afternoon, "Be ready to leave your house at six. We have a nice surprise planned for you." Promptly at six that evening, Rose and Denise stood just outside Charlie-Bob's front door. Charlie-Bob saw lust in the girls' eyes, and a blue necktie in Denise's hand.

"We're taking you for a ride, buddy," Rose said, badly imitating a movie gangster. Then Denise blindfolded Charlie-Bob.

Denise and Rose pulled him to Rose's car, a door was opened, and he was gently pushed into the car. He figured out that he was in the back seat. Two car doors slammed, then the car was started.

From the front seat, Rose's voice said, "You'll have, ohmigod, *so* much fun tonight. Trust us on this."

From the back seat, Denise said, "If there's anything you want me to do, tell me. If I'm doing, like, anything wrong, tell me this too."

With that said, hands went to Charlie-Bob's crotch, his cock was exposed to air, and a hot and wet mouth started sucking him.

Minutes later, the car stopped and Rose shut off the engine. "We're here," Rose said. "This is *totally* your night, Charlie Bob, so tell Denise what you want now. She can put your dick back in your pants, or I can wait till she finishes you, you know?"

"What do *you* want, Denise?" Charlie-Bob made himself ask.

Denise took her mouth off his cock only long enough to say, "My hero, I want to *totally* please you."

He gasped, "Is anybody watching me now?"

"Not a soul," Rose answered. "I parked in, like, a dark part of the parking lot."

He replied, "In that case, Denise, finish MMMMEEEE!" For two seconds, Charlie-Bob actually saw stars.

Denise milked him soft, then she kept sucking him. When he felt himself getting erect and excited again, he made himself say, "Stop."

As Denise got him decent, Charlie-Bob said, "That was incredible!"

Charlie-Bob felt his cheek get kissed.

Then Denise said, "By the way, if you hadn't stopped me, I was all set to suck you off twice in a row, swear to God. Even though I never once gave Kevin a twofer."

The backseat car door was opened, and Denise and Rose pushed/pulled the still-blindfolded Charlie-Bob out of the car. Then he was guided into walking fifty or a hundred yards on paved ground, as he heard children playing nearby. Then Charlie-Bob was guided up a narrow staircase. Once he reached the top of the stairs, a door was knocked on.

That door was opened. "Come in, Charlie-Bob, Rose, and Denise," a young woman's voice said.

Charlie-Bob was gently pushed forward, then the door was shut behind him. Rose's voice said, "Now you can take off the blindfold, my hero."

2-K: Orgy At The Teacher's Place?

Blindfolded Charlie-Bob heard Rose say, "Now you can take off the blindfold, my hero."

The young woman who'd answered the door, Charlie-Bob heard her laugh. "*May*, Rose. Now Charlie-Bob *may* take off his blindfold."

As Charlie-Bob was untying the knot behind his head, he thought, *Why is this woman talking like an English teacher?*

Seconds later, he knew the answer. Staring at her, he said, "I know you, you're the new English teacher, uh. . ."

"Miss Turner," Denise prompted.

Miss Turner shook her head, even as she smiled at Charlie-Bob. "Please, call me Mary, Kayla, or Mary Kayla outside of school. Welcome to my humble apartment, by the way."

"Do I need to introduce you to, like, the others?" Rose asked Charlie-Bob.

Charlie-Bob thought, *"Others"?*

When Charlie-Bob turned his back on the door, he was surprised. Ten people were in the apartment, of which he was the only male. All ten attended SOHS, as either student or teacher.

Answering Rose's question, Charlie-Bob said, "I already know Brooke, a pretty and nice junior. And everyone knows Helen-May Sawyer." Charlie-Bob didn't mention that he considered the blond president of Purity League to be an ice-princess bitch.

Rose said, "Well, then, let me present to you Robina Wright, who also is a junior and also is in Purity League."

He said, "Uh, I've seen you around, but I didn't know your name."

"Now you know it," the freckled redhead replied flirtatiously. Robina actually curtsied at him, before asking, "What do you think about girls in Purity League?"

"They're okay," Charlie-Bob said. He didn't say what he really felt: that pledging *no* sex, of any kind, before marriage, was way extreme. But he now said tactfully, "It's good to stand for something."

"I'm in Purity League too," Brooke Coleman said.

Charlie-Bob nodded, since he couldn't bring himself to say *Good for you.*

Rose gestured to a gorgeous, blue-eyed brunette who looked like Megan Fox's youngest sister. "This is Paula Crawford, a freshman."

Paula likewise curtsied at Charlie-Bob.

"Finally," Rose said, gesturing toward a young blonde, "this is Tatum-Teresa Haven, also a freshman."

Tatum-Teresa gave Charlie-Bob his third curtsy of the night.

Charlie-Bob looked at the oldest woman there. "I don't know your name, but I know you're a teacher."

The twenty-something brunette sashayed up to Charlie-Bob. "I'm Karen Milph, and I teach Home Ec."

Now she was rubbing the inside of her right leg against the outside of Charlie-Bob's left leg. She looked into his eyes and continued, "I came back here three years ago, after my husband and son died in an auto accident. I think I've grieved long enough."

The teacher's rubbings were giving Charlie-Bob a massive boner. "Mrs. Milph, I think you're trying to seduce me."

"You're so smart."

Charlie-Bob took a step back from Mrs. Milph, to take a second look at these SOHS females. Only one word came to mind: "Wow."

If you counted auburn hair as "red," there were four redheads (natural color or dyed) among the girls, four blondes (natural color or dyed), and two natural brunettes. Brooke got counted twice, because her hair was strawberry-blond.

Every girl was wearing a dress or skirt; nobody wore pants or shorts. Every girl wore high heels (although Tatum-Teresa Haven was wobbly-legged, wearing hers). Rose's green shoes and Mary Kayla's red shoes had heels high enough to turn those shoes into flashing neon signs: Fuck me! Fuck me! Karen Milph's blouse was transparent chocolate-brown, and there was no brassiere underneath it.

The weird thing, the wildly-unlikely-yet-true thing, was that every girl in the room had a beautiful face; and (except for Tatum-Teresa Haven) every girl in the room was chestier than average. In the case of Denise Webber, her tits were *enormous*. It was as if Charlie-Bob had crashed a meeting of Future Lingerie Models of America.

"So why are we all here?" Charlie-Bob now asked. "Someone's birthday?"

Rose said, "We-all are here because we think you're a hero, and we want to pleasure you."

He toyed with the idea that this was all some kind of joke, that all these hot girls were pranking the nerdy guy. But last week, he'd gotten Rose's virginal blood on his dick, which seemed like a lot more than a prankster would willingly do. In short, Charlie-Bob didn't know what to think.

"*All* of you want to pleasure me?" Charlie-Bob asked. He looked straight at Helen-May. "I can't believe that." Then he looked at Mary Kayla and Mrs. Milph. "Y'all will get fired if you even kiss me."

Blond Mary Kayla Turner shrugged. "You're a hero."

"Heroes should be rewarded," brunette Karen Milph added.

Helen-May looked uncomfortable. "Rose showed me I was wrong. Saying No till I get married is a good rule, but it shouldn't apply when a hero asks for sex, you know?"

"Helen-May Sawyer, you actually are telling me that I can ask to pop your cherry right here, right now, and *to me* you'll say yes?"

She nodded. "Straight sex, oral, handjobs, whatever you want." She gulped. "I'll even let you fuck my ass."

Rose said, "Don't need to worry, Helen-May. He's not into Anal."

Needless to say, Helen-May looked relieved.

Charlie-Bob pressed Helen-May: "I may bust your hymen tonight with your blessing, but no other guy in this town gets even a handjob from you, right?"

"That's right," Helen-May said.

He looked at Robina and Brooke, who also were in Purity League. "What do y'all say? Agree with her, or she's off the deep end?"

Brooke said, "My body is, ohmigod, a blank check for you, Charlie-Bob."

Robina nodded. "*Whatever* you want, I'm game for."

He didn't believe that Helen-May meant what she'd said. But he saw only one way to find out, though: "Helen-May," he said, "face me and strip naked."

To his surprise, Helen-May not only disrobed, she did it quickly.

Next he commanded, "On your knees, facing me, legs apart, hands behind your back. Show off your goods."

Seconds later, "Helen Won't" was posed nude in front of him.

That's when the thought struck him: *What if this isn't a prank? What if I'm really the guest of honor at an orgy?*

Charlie-Bob's conscience twinged then. He eyed all seven SOHS girls and asked, "Who here is under eighteen?"

Freshmen Paula and Tatum-Teresa raised their hands, of course, as did Purity League juniors Brooke and Robina.

He said, "You girls under eighteen, y'all can't be in any part of the sex—you can't *do* it, and you can't even *watch* it. Y'all need to either go into the kitchen now, or put on your coats and leave."

"I'm not a virgin," Paula said.

"Age of consent in Georgia is sixteen," Robina added.

"Doesn't matter. Two of you are under sixteen, four of you can't vote and y'all are younger than me—*that's* what matters. I will not let myself feel I'm taking advantage of a girl who's too young."

Brooke was looking at him in shock. "We're willing to do anything and everything with you, and you really won't boink us?"

"I'm serious—out the door now, or into Mary Kayla's kitchen now."

Rose and Denise looked puzzled. "Charlie-Bob, what's going on?" Rose asked.

"Look, I'll be honest: Part of me thinks y'all are pulling a prank on me. But if you're serious, if you really are offering me sex, then the sex should happen when it means something to both people. Brooke and Robina, somebody had to tell me your names not five minutes ago, so how special could the sex be for you tonight?"

"Gosh, Charlie-Bob," said Rose, "you are, ohmigod, a *romantic.*"

"That is *sooo* sweet," Denise said.

He blushed. "Yeah, I guess. But please, don't tell other guys."

Redhead Robina shrugged. "Okay, I'm flexible, you know? Instead of frying your brain, I'll fry your potatoes."

"I've got two brothers," Tatum-Teresa said to Mary Kayla, "so I'm good at, like, cooking hamburgers. Is there any hamburger meat in your fridge?"

The hostess-teacher nodded. "Sure, in the freezer."

"I'll help you cook," Paula said. Together the four under-eighteen girls walked into the kitchen (Tatum-Teresa was still wobbling in her high heels).

Meanwhile, the Purity League president was still naked in front of Charlie-Bob, and was still posed to show off her pussy.

"Masturbate for me, Purity League," he said, as he stared into Helen-May's eyes. He was rock-solid sure that she'd pitch a hissy then.

Except that she didn't. Instead, she began caressing herself.

"Go, Purity League," Denise said. "Excite yourself for our hero."

About one minute later, Helen-May was trembling and biting her lip, and Charlie-Bob smelled a pungent odor. "Is she about to cum? This quickly?" he asked the room.

Helen-May looked at Charlie-Bob as she kept masturbating. "You watching me touch myself, it gets me hot."

"I wish that were me, performing for Charlie-Bob," Mary Kayla said.

"Me too," Denise replied.

Not soon after, Helen-May shook with orgasm. Karen Milph said, "Helen-May, would you mind if I knelt down close to you? I'm sure you want to kiss somebody right now."

Helen-May nodded her thrown-back head, then the brunette Home Ec teacher dropped to her knees. Immediately Helen-May's head zoomed forward, like a striking snake, to press her lips against Karen Milph's.

Soon Charlie was steel-hard, watching the writhing, moaning, kissing, female couple. And he wasn't the only one aroused: He heard Rose say, "That is so *hot.*"

Then Rose stepped up to him. "You're about to burst your underwear, stud. I want to relax you."

Charlie-Bob said, "Anyone *not* want to see Rose stroke my naked cock? Mary Kayla? Denise? Speak up now."

When neither woman objected, Charlie-Bob kissed Rose on the lips and said, "You rock."

Rose's handjob was very slow; her touch was very light. Her handjob felt wonderful.

Helen-May, who was facing in Charlie-Bob's general direction, said, "I'm seeing a cock, ohmigod. Like, my first cock ever."

"It's a *hard* cock," Karen Milph breathed.

Soon Charlie-Bob was about to climax. He said, "I don't want to make a mess on Mary Kayla's carpet. Helen-May, get over here and suck me off." He made himself sound deliberately uncaring, figuring that *this* at last would make Helen-May cop an attitude.

But again Helen-May surprised him. Making no objections to his order, she got her face right in front of his dick. Then she asked Rose, "What do I do now?"

"Move your lips up and down his cock, like you're eating a Popsicle, while you tongue the underside of his dick. And remember: A good girlfriend *always* swallows."

Helen-May turned out to be surprisingly skilled at cocksucking, for someone who'd never blown a dick before.

Denise said, "Seeing all this is making me *so horny*, Rose. I'll be *so wet* if he fucks me tonight."

Rose replied, "You'll enjoy it, I guarantee it. But remember: Tonight is all about what *Charlie-Bob* wants."

He offered a hand to Helen-May, who was kneeling at his feet, and helped her stand up. Then as he zipped himself up, he said to Helen-May, "You can dress now if you want to."

Helen-May didn't get up and get dressed. Instead, she went back to touching herself.

Charlie-Bob looked over at the two teachers. The two women were kissing each other, and groping each other's boobs.

Rose asked him then, "So, like, what do you want to do now?"

Charlie-Bob walked up to Denise and said, "Now I thank this beautiful girl for sucking me so well on the drive here. She wants me to fuck her, so I'm gonna do just that."

But he chose to undress Denise before he fucked her. Alas, undressing her was easier said than done.

Charlie-Bob had real trouble getting Denise's bra off. For one thing, he'd never touched a bra clasp except for once, seven days ago. But mainly he was having trouble because the two ends of the bra were being pulled apart with great force. Denise's boobs clearly had grown much bigger since she bought her bra.

Eventually he got Denise naked. Then he looked over at the English teacher and said, "Mary Kayla, undress me."

She undressed him as he'd ordered and, except for many times "accidently" rubbing against his dick, the undressing was straightforward and unsexy.

But legally, the teacher crossed a big red line in undressing a male student, and that's what finally convinced Charlie-Bob that all this was no joke, no prank.

Charlie-Bob looked at still-naked Helen-May and said, "I didn't believe you earlier, and so I was cruel to you. I apologize."

Charlie-Bob turned back to naked and scrumptious Denise and said, "Shall we find the bed now?"

He smiled at the four other hot babes in the living room. "Y'all are welcome to watch if you like."

Rose gave him a thumb-up, then said, "I, like, brought condoms."

Naked Charlie-Bob and naked Denise then walked into Mary Kayla's tiny bedroom.

What followed was your standard, everyday, run-of-the-mill sex session with a softball-breasted hellcat, as four sexy beauties watched, touched themselves, and kissed each other.

Eventually, Charlie-Bob asked Rose to fetch his pants and shirt, and Denise's underwear and dress, so that the lovers were decent when they walked out of the bedroom.

By then, the four under-eighteen girls had cooked up hamburgers, French fries, Italian food, and chocolate-chip cookies. Charlie-Bob, Denise, and the four bedroom voyeurs sat down to eat.

The food included pasta and antipasto, which of course had to be mixed carefully, lest they annihilate each other.

The two freshman girls, claiming that they'd already eaten while the "gymnastics" had been going on, didn't sit at the table with the other girls. Instead, the freshman girls stood to either side of Charlie-Bob, refilling his glass, fetching him whatever he asked for, and smiling at him a lot.

At one point, as Tatum-Teresa Haven was passing Charlie-Bob a plate of hamburger patties, he idly noticed that her otherwise perfect complexion was marred by freckles on her left hand. Which was odd, because he'd never heard of anyone getting freckles on one hand but not the other—

Rose made a joke about Charlie-Bob eating like a starving man, everyone laughed, and Charlie-Bob forgot all about Tatum-Teresa's freckled hand.

At one point during the meal, he was talking about his favorite *manga* and *animé*. The dining room now had nine beautiful girls and women in it, and every one of them hung on Charlie-Bob's every word. He felt like a king.

After complimenting the under-eighteen girls on their cooking, and after he'd used the bathroom, Charlie-Bob announced to the "legal age" group, "I want to enjoy a threesome." He held out his hand to Rose, then said, "Rose, pick somebody."

"Helen-May," Rose said.

He shook his head. "Pick someone else."

Helen-May said, "Ohmigod, after the shit you put me through tonight, you won't boldly go where no man has gone before?"

Charlie-Bob said, "Not tonight. If I'm to take someone else's virginity after Rose, I want to plan when and how I'll do it right. Plus, a virgin like you deserves a chance to back out."

Rose said, "So the under-eighteens are out, and the virgin is out? And, like, you've already fucked Denise. So that leaves only a teacher, you know?"

Rose chose Karen Milph to fill out the threesome, because she'd gone longer without sex.

Karen Milph walked up to Charlie-Bob and Rose. The teacher with the thick, shiny, chocolate-brown hair gave Rose a long kiss, then turned to Charlie-Bob. "Please fuck us both, my hero."

In the bedroom, Karen Milph said to Rose, "I've never done girl-girl before."

One of Rose's eyebrows went up. "Really? You kiss like a lipstick lesbian."

"Kissing is *all* I've done with other women. Benjamin liked to watch me kiss women at parties, back in L.A. Then after the party, he'd be hot to launch his semen torpedo into my wormhole."

Charlie-Bob said, "So you're straight, then."

Meantime, he was unbuttoning her transparent-brown blouse.

"Oh yeah, *very* straight," Karen Milph said. She reached down to cup the front of his trousers. "Right now, *you're* very straight too."

After Charlie-Bob unbuttoned Karen's blouse, Rose now removed it.

"Look at that, nothing covering the boobs," Rose said. "Fascinating."

Rose began sucking on the teacher's boobs as Charlie-Bob unbuttoned her skirt and pulled it down to the floor.

Karen stepped out of the floored skirt. Now she was wearing only semitransparent tan panties. The front of those panties was wet.

Karen walked over to Charlie-Bob. Looking over her shoulder at Rose, she said, "Help me get him naked."

As soon as Rose pulled down Charlie-Bob's briefs, Karen dropped to her knees and took him in her mouth. She sucked him for thirty seconds, then said, "I want you eager to fuck me when you get to me."

Charlie-Bob pulled Karen to her feet, then said, "Now that you and I are naked, let's strip Rose."

Rose pointed at the teacher's hips. "She's not naked. Mrs. Milph is still wearing panties."

"Easily fixed," Karen said. "Watch closely, Charlie-Bob." Facing him, she sinuously pulled her panties down her legs.

When Charlie-Bob and Karen stepped over to Rose, Rose said, "I've never been undressed by a girl and a guy both."

Charlie-Bob laughed. "Sounds like all three of us are virgins tonight." By now, Rose and Karen were sharing the stroking of his erection. "Let's get on the bed."

After the three adults climbed onto the bed, Charlie-Bob said, "Before I fuck either of you, I want to see you do each other. Karen, do you choose to kick off, or receive? Or do you want to sixty-nine?"

"That depends." Karen Milph looked at Rose. "Those stories about you, were they true?"

Rose said, "They still *are* true—I like girls as much as I like guys, you know? Except that Charlie-Bob is miles ahead of everyone else." Rose stroked Charlie-Bob's leg as she said this.

Karen replied, "In that case, I choose to lie back and you eat me out first. I bet you're good at it. Then I'll try to return the favor. But it probably won't be good."

"Don't worry," Rose said. She moved forward and kissed Karen on the mouth. "Getting my pussy licked by a woman who's never done it before? Ohmigod, what a turn-on."

Karen laid down and put her head on the pillow. Rose got on top of her and kissed her on the mouth. After a minute of that, Rose headed south.

Rose spent a lot of time sucking on, and licking, Karen's nipples. The brunette teacher started moaning and writhing, which made Charlie-Bob's dick harder.

After a while, Rose's mouth resumed heading down Karen's body.

Rose moved her right hand to somewhere near Karen's pussy. (Exactly where that hand was, and what it was doing, Charlie-Bob couldn't tell; Rose's hair hid what her hand was doing.) Karen gasped, and thrust her hips in the air.

Meanwhile, Rose was taking her sweet time, kissing her way down Karen's stomach. Charlie-Bob knew when Rose's tongue hit Karen's pussy: when Karen arched her back and gasped.

"Your tongue and your finger, *together*! Oh god!" Karen said.

Ten minutes after Rose had started on her, Karen was moaning and writhing continuously, and the room reeked of her scent. One of her hands was clutching a bedsheet, and the other hand was pushing Rose's head down.

Going by the bedside clock, fifteen minutes had passed from the start of the lesbian lovemaking, when Charlie-Bob said, "Karen and Rose, switch off."

Rose sat up, grinning at Charlie-Bob.

Karen took a little longer to sit up; she shook her head and said, "Whoa. Incredible."

When Karen was finally sitting up, she noticed Charlie-Bob's erection. Quicker than he would have thought possible, she moved across the bed, to slurp on his erection.

After fifteen seconds, she pulled her mouth off him. With a mischievous smile, she said, "I enjoyed that. I hope you did too."

Karen moved away from Charlie-Bob then, to kneel between Rose's legs. "Mmm, you smell ready to party, Rose."

Karen moved up to kiss Rose for about a minute, then she was back to kneeling between Rose's legs. "Here we go," Karen said.

Karen moved her butt back so she could lay on her stomach between Rose's legs. "Here we go," Karen said a second time.

Karen put her mouth on Rose's pussy. A second later, Rose said, "Lick all of my slit, honey. Get to know my pussy with your tongue."

A minute later, Karen raised her head and said, "Tell me what you like."

"Mm, it's more fun if you try to guess. File this away, honey: No two pussies are wired the same. . . .Ooh, *that* works!"

Surprisingly soon for someone who'd never licked pussy before, Karen brought Rose to orgasm. A minute later, Karen did it again.

After Karen had been lesbian-ing on Rose for fifteen minutes, Charlie-Bob called "time."

Karen lifted her head up, and moved up Rose's body toward her face. Only then did Karen suck on Rose's tits (briefly), before moving up to kiss Rose on the mouth.

When Karen broke the kiss, Rose exclaimed, "Ohmigod, Karen, I hope Charlie-Bob keeps you! Honey, you have talent at this."

Karen said, "I like you too, but I can't be a lesbian. I too much need Charlie-Bob to fuck me right now."

Rose said theatrically, "Charlie-Bob, alas, I forgot all about him! The poor man has been, like, *neglected!* He's in *need!"*

Both women sat up quickly, and moved toward Charlie-Bob.

Karen eyed his erection, then said, "Rose, I think he likes us."

"Definitely. It would be most illogical if he *didn't* like us after what we just did."

"Rose, are you up to a little friendly contest? You can say no."

"What's the contest?"

"At a party in Brentwood, there was a siliconed bimbo who was coming on to Benjamin. She kept offering him a 'star date,' even though she'd guest-starred on only three TV episodes. Anyway, I challenged her to a 'teasing blowjob' contest. We took turns sucking Benjamin off for one minute, and the woman who made him come in her mouth was the *loser."*

Charlie-Bob asked, "So how did it turn out?"

Karen smiled triumphantly. "Little Miss Starlet lost, and Benjamin bought me a bottle of champagne, later that night."

Rose said, "You're on, girlfriend. You have more experience with cocksucking overall, but I have a really good idea how Stud's cock works. I'll let you go first."

In the minutes after that, Charlie-Bob couldn't count how many times he thought *That's it, I'm about to shoot my cream.* But nope, each time the woman was a mind reader, and pulled her mouth off his cock just in time.

Thirty-seven minutes had passed when Rose backed away from his cock, Karen got into position, then she started sucking him—and as soon as Karen's lips touched his dick, he blasted.

He saw fireworks and he heard fireworks, in 3-D and Dolby Sound.

"I win," Rose said.

"No, *I* win," Charlie-Bob gasped. "Any man would pay ten thousand bucks to get a blowjob like that."

"But you get it for free," Rose said.

"Because you're a hero," Karen added.

Rose said, "Now, Stud, it's time to fuck Karen."

Karen shook her head. "Rose sweetie, you just earned the right to get fucked first."

"Karen honey, I'm feeling generous. You're overdue for an excellent dick in your pussy, and Charlie-Bob's dick will give you a mind-melt, truly."

Then Rose turned to Charlie-Bob. "Go ahead, Stud, fuck her with your Captain's Log."

Charlie-Bob did just that. Karen was looser than he was used to, in his admittedly limited experience, but not so loose that he couldn't feel her vagina. He noted her stretch marks, another First for him, but those stretch marks didn't lessen her appeal.

"Ooh, I'm getting fucked, I'm getting fucked, I'm getting fucked by a hero-stud, and it feels so good," Karen said.

Her ankles locked around his ass.

Rose said, "Go, Charlie-Bob. Make her scream your name!"

Karen was wet, and he liked how her pussy felt, rubbing against his cock. He felt the tingle while he was pushing his cock into her pussy and pulling it out.

Almost immediately after he entered Karen, she arched her back, thrust her hips, and screamed. When she could (sort of) speak again, she said, "God, I *so* needed to get fucked!"

When Karen was no longer frantic with desire, she went back to matching his thrusting pace. Her hips came up as his went down, both thrust and counterthrust becoming faster and more fervent as the minutes passed.

He grunted as he came into the condom. Karen's second fuck-climax occurred at the same time. She hugged him and screamed, kissing him between screams. She did, in fact, scream his name.

Charlie-Bob and Karen kissed and cuddled for several minutes, then Karen said, "Now Rose needs you." Karen kissed Charlie-Bob one more time, then climbed out of bed—

To be immediately replaced by Rose. Rose had a foil-wrapped condom in her hand, and a sexy smile on her face.

Rose pulled the used condom off Charlie-Bob's limp dick and threw the condom in a little lavender-linered trash can. Then Rose said, "The best way to put on a condom is when the cock is erect. So you don't mind if I suck you hard, right?"

When it happened both that his cock was at red alertness, and that shields were up, Charlie-Bob looked at Rose. "I haven't fucked you from behind yet."

Rose gave him a hot smile. "Oh yes, fuck my pussy from behind, my hero. Make me your bitch."

She got on the bed, on hands and knees, with those knees on the edge of the bed. She looked back and said, "Take me, Charlie-Bob."

He did. Rose's pussy was so wet it made slurping noises. As soon as Rose started moaning, Karen knelt on the floor, reached over, and began pulling on Rose's down-hanging nipples. Rose got slurpier, and Rose's moans got louder.

Rose climaxed soon after. "I'M YOUR BITCH, AND YOU'RE MAKING YOUR BITCH COME!" she yelled.

Charlie-Bob might have been eighteen, so one year away from his sexual prime, but by now he'd lost track of how many times he'd climaxed that evening. All that ejaculation finally made a *vas deferens* in how sensitive he was. Even with Rose's hips moving faster than light, it took Charlie-Bob fifteen minutes to shoot semen again. Rose didn't seem to mind at all, judging from her moans and fierce hip-thrusts.

A minute after Charlie-Bob came, he was lying on his back in the middle of the bed, condom-less, with Rose and Karen snuggled up on either side of him. The two beauties caressed him, took turns kissing him, and kissed each other while he watched.

Life cannot get any better than this, Charlie-Bob thought.

Before the under-eighteen girls left Mary Kayla's apartment, Charlie-Bob kissed Tatum-Teresa, Paula, Brooke, and Robina on the cheek, and thanked them for the great cooking. Each girl kissed him on the mouth to say, You're welcome.

Then Charlie-Bob helped Mary Kayla set up the forty-inch trampoline that had been delivered to her apartment that afternoon. The task wasn't difficult, or time-consuming, but he was so tired that he fell asleep in the middle of screwing the legs on.

Likewise, when Rose's car pulled up in front of Charlie-Bob's house, she had to wake him up.

2-L: Suspicion

SWEET ONION HIGH SCHOOL
MONDAY MORNING AFTER THE ORGY

Regina Wisley had to force herself to show her face's usual sneer. What she really wanted to do, was to scream.

Regina and her minions were now badly outnumbered by Nightshade and *her* minions.

Blocking Prudy Lu, Regina, and Betsy from moving forward in the hallway were Rose the supposedly sworn-off lesbo witch, Denise the big-boobed cow, and *Helen-May Sawyer?* The Virgin Queen had joined the nerd's fan club?

Not to mention, behind those three girls followed seven more younger girls—all mega-babes.

Regina eyed Helen-May. "For someone interested in Purity, you've picked bad friends."

"That's funny, coming from you," Rose said. "I hear that you've told at least one guy, 'I won't date you because your car is too old,' you know? Prudy Lu, don't let the gold digger ruin your thinking."

Helen-May gave Regina a fuck-off smile. "I've decided that purity is overrated. Whenever Charlie-Bob Owens whistles, he'll get any part of me he wants. He's a hero."

Regina rolled her eyes. "Can't you see how lame that sounds? Am I the only girl who sees that Charlie-Bob is a *loser?*"

"Tsk, Regina," Helen-May said. "Clearly you're worried about your looks, as you should be, but that's no reason to act, ohmigod, nasty all the time."

"Worried about my *looks?* My looks are *fine!*" Regina exclaimed.

Rose gave Regina a cruel smile and a rocking-hand gesture.

Meanwhile, Helen-May was saying, "Still, it's, like, obvious that guys date you only because of your daddy's money. I'm sure this eats at you. But ohmigod, don't inflict your misery on everyone else."

"We need to, like, get to our lockers, Helen-May," Rose said. "We can't let Regina hold us up any longer."

Now Regina had to work especially hard not to scream. *She,* Regina, was holding *Nightshade* up?

Denise, who had been quiet all this time, now looked back at the younger hotties behind her. "Girls, say goodbye to Prudy Lu."

"Bye, Prudy Lu."

"See ya, Prudy Lu."

"Love your lipstick, Prudy Lu."

Seconds later, Rose's girl-horde had moved past Regina and her ladies-in-waiting. Every girl in the girl-horde had given a goodbye and a girly-wave to Prudy Lu; Regina and Betsy had been completely ignored (for what, the four-millionth time?)

Betsy said, "That's not right, how they treat you."

"Shut up, Betsy," Regina said.

Before Prudy Lu could even think of speaking, Regina spun around and put a finger in her face. "Not one word out of you, Prudence Louise. Not one word, y'hear?"

MONDAY AT LUNCHTIME

Charlie-Bob was about to step into the cafeteria's serving line when he noticed a group of girls standing in the hallway. The girls were the under-eighteens from Friday night's orgy, plus five new (under-eighteen) faces.

"Hiiii, Charlie-Bob."

Tatum-Teresa Haven stepped forward. Each of her hands was covered with an oven mitt, and she was holding a steaming casserole dish.

Charlie-Bob noticed then that Brooke Coleman, Robina Wright, Paula Crawford, and girls he didn't even know the names of, were holding casserole dishes, or pots, or plastic bowls.

Charlie-Bob said, "Hey there. What's going on?"

Tatum-Teresa said, "A bunch of us decided, like, if we can't fill your body-needs one way, we'll take care of you another way."

Robina said, "It was Tatum-Teresa's idea, so give her the credit. But all your fans under eighteen think it's totally the greatest idea ever. Well, second-greatest."

"Oh? What's the number-one grea—? Never mind." He'd figured it out when all the under-eighteens, and even the under-sixteens, started giving him bedroom smiles.

He gestured for the girls (his fans? his harem?) to follow him into the lunchroom. The girls indeed followed, to the *click-clack, click-clack* of multiple high heels. He picked an empty table and gestured for the girls to join him. No girl refused, and each girl sat down near him with a toothy smile.

A fifteen-year-old beauty, whose name Charlie-Bob couldn't begin to guess, jumped up. "Charlie-Bob needs silverware! And paper napkins! I'll go get them."

She *click-clack*ed away as fast as she could move.

Charlie-Bob looked around at the horde of girls. "Now, while we're waiting for. . .?"

"Alicia Dunlap," Tatum-Teresa prompted.

"While we're waiting for Alicia Dunlap to get back, tell me about all this. Y'all spent all day yesterday cooking?"

Robina shook her (red) head. "Oh no, we did this today. That was Tatum-Teresa's great idea!"

Tatum-Teresa was blushing. "All I did was suggest last night, when the teacher in each class gives out the assignment, instead of asking for a pass to the library or computer center, we get a pass to Home Ec."

A sixteen-year-old blonde (who was holding a blue plastic bowl) said, "Mrs. Milph has been really cool. She has helped us, ohmigod, *a lot*. I'm Peggy Jo, by the way."

By now, Alicia Dunlap and her high heels had returned. Robina passed out paper plates to everyone at the table, including Charlie-Bob; and a brunette sophomore girl named Patty Jean passed out plasticware to everyone except for Charlie-Bob. All the girls insisted that Charlie-Bob "deserved" genuine metal tableware.

"May we serve you now?" Tatum-Teresa asked eagerly.

Charlie-Bob shrugged. Tatum-Teresa took this as a yes.

The under-eighteens had not brought silverware for themselves, but seven of nine girls had brought big metal serving spoons from home. All the food was set before Charlie-Bob.

Tatum-Teresa took the cover off her casserole dish, took her oven mitts off, then spooned casserole onto Charlie-Bob's paper plate.

That's when he noticed—

The back of Tatum-Teresa's left hand, which Friday night had cute freckles on it, now had big black warts.

Not to mention, he was sure that her tits were much bigger than on Friday night!

The other girls came forward now, each girl to personally spoon her food onto Charlie-Bob's paper plate. Trying not to be obvious, he looked each girl over.

Only two girls had a normal-looking left hand; they also were the only girls with an ordinary chest. Every other girl at the table was chesty; with freckles, small warts, or black warts on her left hand. All the under-eighteens at Friday's orgy now had warty left hands, longer hair, and big tits.

What's going on?

"Charlie-Bob is looking at our boobs," Brooke Coleman said.

"Like what you see?" Robina Wright asked. She struck a pin-up pose—

—an action which all the other under-eighteens matched.

Charlie-Bob found it hard to think about his food when busty girls were sticking their chests out, not four feet away. Aliens they might be, or vampires, but they were also Grade-A jailbait.

"*Hey*, Charlie-Bob," a woman's voice said to his right.

Helen-May Sawyer was standing next to Charlie-Bob's chair. She was giving him a very non-virginal smile. "May I ask you to come to the Home Ec classroom after school? I need help with a *special project*."

"How can I help? I can't even boil water."

"It relates to what we discussed Friday night, *hm?*"

Oh. Helen-May Sawyer wanted to lose her virginity, with him, today after school.

He took a moment, supposedly to think things over. Actually, what he was doing was looking Helen-May over, head to toe. Longer hair? Check. Big tits? Check. Warts on her left hand? Check.

He moved his roving gaze to look into Helen-May's eyes. "Sure, no problem," he said. "If that's what you *want*."

"Oh, it is, it definitely is." She leaned down and murmured, "Mrs. Milph will have condoms available, don't worry." Helen-May squeezed his bicep, then *click-clack*ed away.

Charlie-Bob wasn't a good conversationalist with the under-18s during lunch. Mainly because he wasn't a good conversationalist normally. But also because, while he was eating lunch, he had lots on his mind.

By the time he put his paper plate in the lunchroom trash can, he had decided—

Either there is powerful magic involved, or these girls are all aliens now.

Life was actually simpler when he'd thought that Rose and Denise were pranking him. If he'd been correct about that, at least he would have understood what he were up against.

2-M: Sigh, Another Cherry

MONDAY AFTERNOON

Charlie-Bob himself asked for a hall pass, in the second half of fifth period. But he didn't leave his English class to go to the library or the computer center, and he certainly didn't ask to go to Mrs. Milph's Home Ec classroom.

Instead, Charlie Bob went to Mr. Martin's classroom.

Mr. Martin was the yearbook advisor, and there were always one or two yearbook editors working on a computer at the back of Mr. Martin's classroom.

A minute after walking into Mr. Martin's classroom, Charlie-Bob was asking Annie, "Do you have any pictures of Rose, back when she was in her black, witchy phase?"

Annie replied, "I've got two. Larry-Bob thinks she's hot."

Annie pulled up two pictures of Nightshade.

The first picture showed Nightshade at the lunch table, eating. She was wearing a black t-shirt. The photo flattered her oval face, but was otherwise uninteresting.

The second picture showed Nightshade at the same seat in the lunchroom. She was slumped back in her seat, her arms were crossed under her breasts, and she was glaring at someone out of frame. Nightshade was in profile, with the outline of her breasts easy to see.

Nightshade of the photo was at least two cup sizes smaller than Rose of the orgy.

"When was this photo taken?" Charlie-Bob asked.

"December eleventh, 2012. Mmm, about six weeks ago."

Charlie-Bob said, "This picture is so much her! Well, 'her' the way she was. Would you copy this photo onto my USB stick, please?"

"I shouldn't. If anyone could get personal copies of our pictures, who'd buy our yearbook?. . .But you're a genuine hero, so okay."

As Charlie-Bob was digging his USB stick out of his book bag, Annie remarked, "We also have plenty of pictures of her after she cleaned up. Like I said, Larry-Bob thinks she's hot. Wanna see 'em?"

"Sure, that would be great." Charlie-Bob handed his USB stick over to Annie.

While Annie was pulling up photos of the new Rose, Charlie-Bob got to thinking—

Not quite two weeks ago, Rose had dumped her Nightshade persona. In that short time, Larry-Bob had taken four photos of Rose. With each later photo, Rose's hair and fingernails got longer, and her tits got bigger. Also, the two photos that showed the back of Rose's left hand, showed black warts on the back of that left hand.

"Would you copy that picture onto my thumb drive too, please?" Charlie-Bob pointed to the most recent photo of Rose.

Rose of the latest photo looked like an off-duty stripper.

When Annie handed the USB stick back to Charlie-Bob, he asked her, "So what do you think about Rose now?"

Annie said, "I wish she didn't choose to dress like a *slut*"—Annie now gave Charlie-Bob a sly smile—"though of course, *you* might think that's a good thing. I like that she's friendly to everyone now. Well, *almost* everyone."

"Oh? Who's she not friendly to?"

"You haven't heard? Get Rose near to Regina Wisley, and start popping the popcorn!"

"No kidding?"

"It's funny to watch Regina's face when Rose acts so sweet to Prudy Lu, but completely ignores Regina and Busty Betsy."

"Weird. Rose in fourth grade didn't fight back."

Annie said, "Maybe she got tired of Regina's shit. God knows *I'm* sick of the bitch."

Charlie-Bob left a few seconds later. As he was walking out of Mr. Martin's classroom, Charlie-Bob was wondering, *Why is Rose acting so nice to Prudy Lu Moffatt?*

MONDAY AFTER SCHOOL
HOME EC CLASSROOM

Charlie-Bob walked into the Home Ec classroom and found Helen-May waiting for him. Mrs. Milph also was there, as Helen-May had promised, but so was a man in coveralls.

"This sewing machine doesn't work," Karen Milph said. "I need you to fix it. Make it sew!"

The man in coveralls picked up the sewing machine and carried it out of the classroom.

As soon as the repairman left, Mrs. Milph unrolled a bolt of a flowery fabric she had, and laid it on the floor. Helen-May and Charlie-Bob lay on that for the sex.

As promised, Mrs. Milph handed Charlie-Bob condoms when he needed them. She also talked the janitor into cleaning the Home Ec classroom an hour later, so that the young lovers would not be discovered/disturbed.

Meanwhile, Charlie-Bob undressed Helen-May, she undressed him, then they fucked.

Helen-May bled when she was supposed to.

After that, Helen-May got wet a lot.

She also got loud a lot.

She also thanked Charlie-Bob over and over for his "control."

Actually, for Charlie-Bob the control was easy, because he was barely involved. He was going through the motions because he'd promised Helen-May that he'd take her cherry, and he didn't want whoever was controlling her, to get suspicious.

Charlie-Bob should have been dancing a jig. In the last two weeks, he'd lost his virginity, had a threesome with a teacher, had sex with the two hottest girls in the senior class, and now was popping his second cherry. Instead, he felt dirty, as though he were fucking a blow-up doll.

Or to be more accurate, like he was fucking one of a bunch of girls who'd been hypnotized at a party.

After Charlie-Bob shot off, Helen-May pulled off his condom, sucked him hard, then rolled a fresh condom on his dick, all without one wrong move. Charlie-Bob decided that Helen-May's hypnotist was also an excellent sex-ed teacher.

Helen-May and Charlie-Bob went for a second round of sex. She hugged him, she scratched him, she kissed him, she screamed his name—while he was thinking about warts on girls' left hands.

The late-January sun was below the trees when Charlie-Bob and Helen-May walked out of the school, arm in arm. He was not surprised to discover that Rose's car was in the school parking lot next to his own car. She had her car's engine running—which was a wasteful thing to do, unless she already knew, to the minute, when Charlie-Bob was leaving the school.

She stopped the car and stepped out into the cold, as soon as Charlie-Bob got near his own car. "Hey, Stud, you *enjoy yourself?*"

"*I* sure did," Helen-May said, laughing. "So much for purity!"

"Uh, yeah, I'm glad you enjoyed it," Charlie-Bob said. "Listen, ladies, I need to get home."

He gave each woman a quick kiss on the lips, then unlocked his car and started it. He saw Rose and Helen-May give each other *What's bothering him?* looks.

PART 3:
THE CYBES

THE BIMBORG (Three) 135

3-A: Engine Failures

AUTHOR'S NOTE: By the 27th century, the Cybes have Welcomed at least some of the people on 428 planets. By the 27th century, it has become a problem when two Cybes talk, what each means by *day* and *year*, since different home planets mean different lengths of time for these two terms. Since all but one of the 428 planets are former Earth colonies, Earth times for *day* and *year* have become the Cybe standard by the 27th century.

One *Earthyear* is the time it takes Sol III (Earth) to orbit the sun once. One *Earthday* is the time for one Sol III (Earth) rotation.

The smallest unit of Cybe time is the *slobi*. (*Slobi* = *slow beat*, roughly the time between two beats of a calm human heart.) There are exactly 65,536 slobi in an Earthday. The next longer unit of Cybe time is the *64-slobi* (64 times one slobi); there are exactly 1,024 64-slobi in an Earthday.

There are about 45.5 slobi in one minute. One slobi is roughly 1.3 seconds; one 64-slobi is roughly 1.4 minutes.

Aboard Cybe Experimental Timeship 0x1d

The timeship had left the Peter Kelly Farm on Sol III, local year 2008, in order to rejoin the Cybe clan at Mrimlek 4, Luna 2, local year 2652. Or at least, that had been the plan.

The damaged timeship had suffered a troubled takeoff. Not only had the ship briefly re-entered three-dimensional space, but the timeship had almost crashed on Sol III. Fortunately, all engineering problems had been resolved.

Or so all Cybes aboard the timeship believed.

However, Subjective time was only one 64-slobi into the resumed flight when new engineering casualties occurred.

"Captain-unit, we are losing thrust in the main X-drive," Cybe unit Wong3-27-5386633 called out. "This unit suspects the engine was damaged during the battle with the Space Navy."

No sooner had she quit speaking, but Cybe Obermann4-27-93754204 spoke up: "The main Y-drive also is losing thrust."

Delos3-27-30074453969, captain of the timeship, replied, "Switch to backup X-drive and backup Y-drive."

An instant later, the captain was told, "The backup Y-drive does not respond. Main Y-drive power is at seven-128ths of Safe Maximum and falling."

Wong3-unit added to the bad news: "Captain-unit, backup X-drive does not respond. Main X-drive power is now at two-128ths of Safe Maximum and falling."

Cybe unit Mrraow7-27-837534481 called out, "This unit reporrrts imminent failure of main Z-drive. Switching to backup Z-drive. Backup Z-drrrive power is at fifteen-128ths of Safe Maximum."

A klaxon sounded at Cybe-unit Johnson3-27-153479866's navigation station.

Nobody needed to be told what the klaxon meant, but Johnson3-27-153479866 announced it anyway: "Captain-unit, the main T-drive is losing thrust. Currently its power is at sixty-six-128ths of Safe Maximum and falling."

If the T-drives all failed, the timeship would drop back into regular three-dimensional space (again), becoming marooned in a year that was centuries pastward of 2652—not good.

"Switch to T-drive Backup 1," the Captain-unit ordered.

"Switching to Backup 1," Johnson3-27-153479866 replied.

An instant later, the T-drive control panel began making *Vvvvt! Vvvvt!* noises, as electricity began running up and down Johnson3-unit's body.

As Johnson3-unit was of Cybe type Invisible, that unit had no more defense against electricity than any Solitary human colonist living on planet Johnson III would have had. As a result, Johnson3-unit was nonbiological within two slobi.

Meanwhile, two other crew-units on the Bridge were of Cybe type Soldier, and so wore boots of sinthrubbir. These two crew-units used their feet to push, pull, and kick the nonbiological Johnson3-unit out of his chair. Recycling of Johnson3-unit would be done later, when the crises were over.

In the meantime, the Cybe timeship was still losing thrust in the T-direction.

The Captain-unit sent out a call through the timeship's local Overmind to have a replacement crew-unit sent to the bridge. What looked like a 21st-century rural American man (complete with red flannel shirt) soon came onto the bridge; this unit was obviously another Invisible. The new Invisible-unit sat down at the emergency drive-control station.

The Captain-unit said, "Sol3-27-58348, report the status of the T-drive."

The Invisible replied, "The main T-drive is DOA, and Backup One doesn't respond to control. We are in serious trouble, folks, unless Backup Two acts like it's supposed to."

Invisibles talked like that; the Captain-unit ignored the un-Cybe speech. The Captain-unit ordered, "Sol3-27-58348, power-up T-drive Backup Two."

Invisible Cybe Sol3-27-58348 turned a switch, then pressed a button.

The control panel exploded, beheading the Sol3-unit.

Two crew-units pulled the headless Sol3-unit out of his seat, while Mrraow7-27-837534481, who was especially tall, retrieved the Invisible's head from the overhead, where it was caught in the cabling and wires. The Cybefied cat-man slipped and almost fell down, because the deck of the bridge was red, wet, and slick with Sol3-unit's sprayed and dripping blood.

However, all this had happened very quickly—less than six slobi. Now the Captain-unit said, "Report."

Wong3-unit said, "X-drive power now is at *zero*-128ths of Safe Maximum."

Obermann4-unit said, "Y-drive power now is at *zero*-128ths of Safe Maximum."

Mrraow7-unit said, "Z-drrrive power is minimal: seventeen-128ths of Safe Maximum and drrropping."

Migori4-27-888473 said, "T-drive thrust is *zero*. The L/S ratio is dropping. The L/S ratio is. . .*mark*, at +0x0600." Meaning that for every 64-slobi that passed aboard the timeship, 1-$^1/_2$ days would pass on Earth.

The Captain and the other units of the bridge crew knew that this number would drop slowly, but it *would* drop. They had somewhere between sixteen and thirty-two 64-slobi by Subjective time before the L/S ratio would drop to $+1\text{-}^{0}/_{16}$.

When that happened, the timeship would re-enter three-dimensional space and become subject to gravity—with only its Z-drive working, and that only weakly. Not good.

The Captain-unit said, "Communications-unit, send a message futureward to our Clan in 2652. Inform them that we are stranded in the past; details to follow."

Eight 64-slobi passed. The Communications-unit kept repeating the message into the microphone.

Then the Communications-unit reported, "This unit hears no reply from the Clan's time-base in 2652."

"Is our anti-tachyon radio not transmitting?"

"Unknown."

"Send out one test-ping and find out who responds."

A small computer near the outside of the timeship, or near the outside of the time-base in 2652, would automatically send pastward or futureward an anti-tachyon test-ping after receiving a test-ping itself. Even if all units within the time-base were nonbiological, the time-base itself should send a test-ping pastward to the timeship.

Two 64-slobi later, the Communications-unit replied, "The only responses to the test-ping come from this timeship itself, beginning in 2008 and going to thirteen Earthdays from now."

Meaning that thirteen Earthdays from now, Local time, the timeship would destroy itself, would re-enter three-dimensional space, or both.

The Captain-unit had more immediate problems. He asked, "What is the L/S ratio now, and estimated time till we re-enter three-dimensional space?"

Migori4-27-unit reported: The timeship had a little more than five 64-slobi, Subjective time.

The Captain-unit ordered the Communications-unit, "Contact other Clans' time-bases. Inform them of our situation."

Then the Captain-unit used the Overmind to inform everyone on board to follow Crash Procedure. While the Captain-unit was still addressing the timeship Overmind, the Captain-unit asked, "Why do you think we get no test-pings from Time-Base?"

No Cybe had an explanation. Indeed, it was pointed out, by many different units, that the timeship should had received several 1024's of reply-pings from Time-Base. Even if an enemy would destroy the time-base, including the time-base's reply-pinger, there should still be many reply-pings sent from pastward of the moment of destruction.

Then Bhagu2-27-6835658 spoke up: "This unit sees one possible explanation: that the time-base has been de-caused. Perhaps after we left Local time in 2008, maybe a Solitary did something that prevented the time-base from ever happening. Because we left Local time before this Solitary person acted, this timeship is not subject to the de-causation effect."

Hearing this, the timeship's Overmind gasped (so to speak).

By then, the L/S ratio was at $+1\text{-}^8/_{16}$ and falling. The Captain-unit had more immediate problems to attend to.

When the timeship re-entered three-dimensional space, it immediately got grabbed by a large gravity source. Bridge crew-units were ready for this, and immediately used navigating thrusters to rotate the timeship so that the Plus-Z thruster faced "down."

Had the Z-drive been working as designed, the timeship probably could have made a soft landing on the gravity-sphere's surface, with zero harm to all Cybe units.

But that's not what happened.

The Z-drive failed completely when the timeship was 122 meters above the surface of the gravity-sphere. The timeship crashed, and many Cybe units were nonbiologicked.

Cybes have many advantages over Solitaries. One advantage is that evacuations are quick and efficient. In under eight 64-slobi, more-functional Cybe units had aided less-functional units in leaving the ship. (Nonbiological Cybe units were left in the wreckage.)

Three Cybe Welcomers did not help evacuate other Cybe units. Instead, one of them carried out the portable wormholer, one removed the external force-field generator and cloaker, and the third one carried out the portable time-radio. Actually, each of those three devices rode out of the timeship on an anti-gravity cart that one Cybe

Welcomer controlled, since one Welcomer has only a fraction of the strength that one Cybe Soldier has.

By the time that all Cybe units had been evacuated and all emergency equipment removed, the Navigator-unit had informed the timeship Overmind of where/when the timeship's Cybes were—

They were stranded on Earth, also known as Sol III. They were in the nation called the United States of America. The local Earth date was February 14, 2013.

Four Earthyears and 326 Earthdays, Local time, had passed since the timeship had left 2008.

AUTHOR'S NOTE: My comments below have nothing to do with the rest of the story, but I pause to address the questions of those among you who are hardcore about time-travel paradoxes.

When James Upton made his decision in 2010 to prevent the Cybes from ever happening, the timeline split into two branches: "prevent the Cybes" and "let history take its course." All the events at the end of Chapter 1-B and in later chapters, happen within the "prevent the Cybes" timeline.

Meanwhile, the Cybe timeship was traveling futureward from 2008. When the timeship hit this time-branch in 2010, the timeship was duplicated, with each timeship now traveling futureward in its own timeline.

The timeship in the "let history take its course" timeline crashed in its version of 2013, after trying to send messages to Time Base. But in that timeline, those messages got through.

After that, whatever happened next in that timeline, happened next. Your humble author suspects that a whole bunch of Cybes from the 27th century showed up in the alternate 2013, they rescued their time-stranded Cybes, and then all the Cybes went on to Cybefy a helpless 21st-century Earth.

In any case, whatever happened to that timeline's timeship and its time-stranded Cybes, has nothing to do with my Cybe characters of Chapter 3-B and afterward.

I return you to the soft-core time-travel melodrama in progress.

3-B: Distress Signal

The surviving Cybes were staring at the wreck of the timeship.

Only three Invisibles were still biological. *Not* one of those survivors was the Invisible who'd been reshaped to resemble and replace fifteen-year-old Jimmy Upton; he lay limp in the wreckage.

"*All* Cybes futureward of us have been de-caused, or only our Clan?" a Cybe Welcomer asked.

"Unknown," the Communications-unit replied. "But this unit did not speak with any unit in any Clan futureward of us."

"Could the Space Navy have done this?" a Soldier asked.

"No," the Captain-unit replied. "We cloaked after the battle, and we think we fooled them. In any case, the Space Navy ship left Local time pastward of when we did, so the Space Navy causing a de-causation is impossible."

"Why?" another Soldier-unit asked.

"If the Space Navy had managed to de-cause the time-base or de-cause all Cybe Clans, then we'd be gone too."

The Captain-unit asked the units around him, "Are any units that are still biological, still inside?" When nobody mentioned any units that still needed to be evacuated, the Captain-unit ordered the Communications-unit to use the portable time-radio to hail the timeship's central computer.

Fourteen slobi later, the Captain-unit was saying over the radio, ". . .delayed self-destruct Type Three, authorization Delos3-27-30074453969, using password"—the Captain-unit recited a 128-character password. By radio, the timeship's computer acknowledged the order.

Then the Welcomer who had removed the external force-field generator and cloaker from the timeship, turned it on. A wireframe of red lines appeared, which appeared above the wreckage, but which sank down into it. The Welcomer enlarged and adjusted the red wireframe until it just barely enclosed the wreckage; the Welcomer pressed a button on the console, and the red-wireframe box turned into a black mirror-finish box-shape.

By now, only thirteen slobi were left until the timeship's self-destruct activated.

All Cybes were told through the Overmind, "Turn your back, cover your eyes with your arms, open your mouth, and bend your knees slightly."

"Why are we destroying our ship?" a Soldier asked.

Within the Overmind, Bhagu2-27-unit replied, "So that we don't create a de-causation of our own. Solitaries who are native to this time must not find any evidence that we exist."

"That is correct," the Captain-unit said.

Four slobi later, an atomic bomb destroyed the timeship—but *only* the timeship. The external force-field contained all of the bomb's blast, the noise, the radiation, and the heat; and all but one-1024th of the light.

Because the energy had to go *somewhere*, it went into the bedrock. The seismic wave had every Cybe knocked off of his or her feet before any Cybe was even aware that the self-destruct had exploded.

The equipment that had been placed on antigravity carts suffered no damage from the seismic wave. As soon as the Welcomer who was tending the external force-field generator was back on her feet, she changed the control setting for the force-field to "Negative energy."

The walls of the force-field box changed from mirror-finish black to nonreflective black. The air turned cooler.

Six 64-slobi later, the force-field was turned off. Before the blast, metal wreckage and Cybe corpses had laid atop brown dirt and soybeans. But now the surviving Cybes saw a rectangular green-glass bowl in the ground.

The Communications-unit walked up to the time-radio, and resumed trying to contact 27th-century Cybes. Whatever orders that the Captain-unit might have intended to give to the other surviving Cybes, got canceled before they were even issued.

Every Cybe heard it: A very weak signal from a Cybe in-armor distress beacon.

Huh?

Every in-armor distress beacon that had been in the timeship's wreckage had just been vaporized, so what were the Cybes hearing?

Three Cybe units walked away from the rest, to form an equilateral triangle that was 128 meters on a side. Very soon after they did this, they told the Overmind, "The signal is coming from $15\text{-}^9/_{16}$ kilometers south-southeast of here."

"Indeed? That is where the Peter Kelly Farm was located in 2008," the Navigator-unit commented.

The Captain-unit activated the wormholer. "All units except for the Communications-unit and the Captain-unit are to rescue the Cybe unit, whether it be injured or nonbiological. Do *whatever you must* to free it from Solitaries' control."

3-C: Invasion At The Farm II

THE PETER KELLY FARM
KIRK COUNTY, IOWA

Bobby Jackson, farmhand, was eating lunch in the dining room with Mr. and Mrs. Kelly, and with Eric Pfeiffer, the other farmhand.

Mrs. Kelly was recapping the TV weather forecast for everyone, when the strangest thing happened—

The house moved back and forth.

Mrs. Kelly and her chair fell back on the floor. Mr. Kelly fell forward, almost putting his face into his mashed potatoes. Eric was in the process of walking to the table from the fridge, an open carton of milk in his hand; he fell over and the carton of milk went flying. Bobby didn't fall over, but he wobbled from side to side in his chair, and there was a second or two when he thought he was going to puke.

Crash. Near the dining table was a wooden hutch, on the top of which was an old dinner plate that once had belonged to Mrs. Kelly's great-grandmother. The house's shaking made that plate fall to the floor, where it broke into tiny pieces.

A loud *RRRAOW!* from the next room, and yelps from just outside the house, let Bobby know that the cat and the dogs weren't any happier about the ground-shake than the people were.

As soon as the floor quit moving, Eric leaped onto the milk carton, but he was too late: There was already a big white puddle on the floor.

"Peachy," Mrs. Kelly said as she herself was getting up off the floor, "I can tell that this isn't going to be my day."

Ten minutes later, Mrs. Kelly was on her hands and knees, sponging up the milk into a small green bucket. Bobby and Eric had filled a janitor's bucket with water from the well, and were carrying it into the dining room.

Mr. Kelly walked back into the dining room and took his seat, having just inspected the farmhouse. "There's a crack in the drywall in the kitchen, and one in the bedroom, that ain't used to be—"

Everyone heard a loud *SSSSOOM* sound from the direction of the barn.

Mr. Kelly twisted his body around in his chair. "What the hell was *that?*"

The dogs outside started barking like maniacs.

Ten seconds later, there was an ear-splitting *CRASH* metallic noise that came from the barn.

Mr. Kelly grabbed his side-by-side double-barreled shotgun from the kitchen, then ran outside. Everyone in the house ran out behind him. Mrs. Kelly was delayed for a short time, because she ran to the bedroom to get her pistol.

Bobby waited on the front porch for Mrs. Kelly to come outside with her pistol. Mr. Kelly and Eric had run off ahead, toward the barn.

By the time that Mrs. Kelly and her pistol came out of the farmhouse, Eric was running toward the open barn doors with a shovel in his hand, and Mr. Kelly—

—was pointing his shotgun at someone inside the barn. He yelled, "YOU FOLKS GET OFF MY LAND BEFORE I BLOW YOU FULL OF HOLES!"

But then Mr. Kelly started backing up. Seconds later, Bobby saw why.

Walking out of the barn was a red-skinned man. He looked like a knight in armor, except that he'd forgotten to put half his armor on. Half-naked or not, he was walking toward Mr. Kelly and his shotgun like the guy didn't have a worry in the world.

"DON'T COME CLOSER!" Mr. Kelly yelled. "LAST WARNING!"

The knight-man kept coming, so Mr. Kelly put his shotgun to his shoulder and fired. That should have dropped the man. Instead, a purple rectangle flashed for a second, three inches in front of the half-knight.

Before Mr. Kelly could fire his shotgun again, the half-knight jerked his arm up, level with the ground. Electricity shot out from his arm to Mr. Kelly, who zoomed twenty feet backward. After Mr. Kelly rolled to a stop, he didn't get up.

The dogs had been barking all this time. Now they started growling and snarling, and Bobby knew it was only a matter of seconds before they attacked the half-knight.

Another half-knight walked out of the barn. Actually, this half-knight didn't look like a man, but a big standing cat. The two strange people didn't look at each other or speak to each other; but at the exact same instant, each half-knight turned toward a growling dog and blasted it with lightning. Each dog yelped, then died.

Again the two half-knights didn't speak a word, nor did they even glance at each other. They glanced at Mrs. Kelly and the two farmhands, then they walked back into the barn.

By now, Bobby had grabbed a sledgehammer out of the pickup truck. For several seconds Eric stood near the front barn doors, watching the action inside the barn, then he ran back to Mrs. Kelly and Bobby.

"There's about twenty or thirty of them," Eric said. "They've got the back doors open, they've got the hay baler pushed on its side—"

"They *knocked it over?*" Mrs. Kelly said. "That thing weighs *tons!*"

Bobby hoped that no physician happened to be standing by the hay baler when it fell over. That machine was heavy enough to make a very effective doctor-crusher.

Meanwhile, Eric was saying, "But the hay baler's lying on its side now, I swear. Now they're doing something, digging I think, where the hay baler was parked. Wanna know what else is weird? They don't have guards posted, even after Mr. Kelly tried to shoot one of 'em."

"Maybe they think we're no threat to them," Mrs. Kelly said.

"What do we do?" Bobby asked.

Mrs. Kelly looked at Bobby. "Give your sledgehammer to Eric."

Mrs. Kelly walked toward the unmoving body of her husband, with Bobby and Eric following behind. It turned out that Mr. Kelly had a fist-sized black spot in the front-middle of his shirt. Mrs. Kelly looked down at him for several seconds, then said, "Bobby, pick up the double-barrel."

Bobby wanted to argue. Actually, Bobby wanted to steal the pickup truck and get gone miles away, as fast as he could move. But silently Bobby picked up the weapon.

More frightened than he'd ever been in his life, Bobby walked with Mrs. Kelly and Eric into the barn.

Sure enough, the weird-looking people were all at the back of the barn, all of their attention focused on something in the ground just beyond the rear doors. Bobby saw that there were three types of the red-skinned metal people: one guy who looked like an officer; the big, nasty guys; and another type, "quarter-knights," who showed more red skin and who each had a box on his or her left hand, and a needle coming out of the little finger of that left hand.

Bobby also saw three normal-skinned people: a young man wearing blue jeans, a man wearing a suit, and a woman wearing a skirt-suit. Bobby wondered, *What are they doing here?*

The man with the suit limped over to stand in front of Bobby. The woman stopped in front of Mrs. Kelly, and the jeans-dressed man stopped in front of Eric. None of the three normal-looking people carried any weapon that Bobby could see.

"You are Linda Kelly," said the woman in the skirt-suit. "You and your husband Peter own this farm. You are the sister of Ellen Upton, the mother of Jimmy Upton."

Mrs. Kelly spit the words: "Yes, I'm married to Pete. The man you people just *murdered!*"

Skirt-Suit Woman: "We defended ourselves when—"

Suit Man: "—your husband tried to kill our Soldier, and—"

Jeans Man: "—your animals were acting—"

Skirt-Suit Woman: "—disrespectful, so we killed them."

Eric asked, "Why haven't you killed *us* then?"

Skirt-Suit Woman looked at Mrs. Kelly. "Because we need your help."

"Who *are* you people?" Mrs. Kelly demanded.

"Um, Mrs. Kelly?" Bobby said. He'd noticed that several of the quarter-knights had come closer.

"Who we are is irrelevant," Skirt-Suit Woman said.

"Please help us," Suit Man said, stepping aside and gesturing the farmers forward.

"But don't try to hurt us," Skirt-Suit Woman added.

"That would be really *pandhi* of you," Jeans Man said.

"Really *what* of us?" Mrs. Kelly said.

"Stupid of you," Skirt-Suit Woman said. "Foolish, unwise."

Bobby turned to look at Mrs. Kelly. She said, "Lower your weapons, but *don't relax.*"

Mrs. Kelly lowered her right arm to point her pistol at the ground, then walked forward. Bobby and Eric hurried to catch up. The normal-dressed strangers followed behind the farmers.

Half-knights and quarter-knights (without looking at each other, or speaking with each other) suddenly moved to the right or left, to create a path leading to the pushed-over hay baler. To Bobby, this was one more spooky thing about these people.

None of the red-skinned, armored people smiled, none of them frowned, and none looked angry. Bobby got spooked-out even more.

"Motherfuck," Bobby breathed.

Where the hay baler had been parked (until it had been toppled), now revealed a hole in the ground. By that hole was laid out a woman's skeleton.

The skeleton was dressed like a quarter-knight.

Behind Mrs. Kelly, Skirt-Suit Woman said, "This is Sol3-21-1. Jimmy Upton killed her in 2008."

"Impossible!" Mrs. Kelly said. "My nephew is no murderer. Besides, he was fifteen years old in 2008. If your woman was murdered, it was by a hobo."

Eric said, "Yeah, some lazy bum who steals chickens, he killed your woman too."

Suit Man spoke: "This actually isn't the worst thing Jimmy Upton has done. We need to find him."

Mrs. Kelly said, "And when you find my nephew, then what?"

Jeans Man said, "Then we'll Welcome him."

Kill him, you mean. Bobby didn't like being lied to. He moved his finger to rest against the shotgun's trigger guard.

Mrs. Kelly said, "*No.* I won't tell—"

Bobby felt something brush against his leg.

Bobby spun around. He discovered Suit Man sprawled on the ground, right behind him. As Bobby was wondering, *Why is he on the ground?*, he saw movement to his left.

Jeans Man had come up from behind Eric to throw his own arms around Eric's waist and arms. Eric still was holding the sledgehammer, but he couldn't use it. Similarly, Skirt-Suit Woman had Mrs. Kelly's arms pinned to her side.

While Eric and Mrs. Kelly were struggling to free themselves, two quarter-knights rushed up. Each quarter-knight used her finger-needle to stab her victim in the back of the neck.

Eric and Mrs. Kelly froze into statues.

Each quarter-knight began chanting, "The Overmind calms you. The Overmind frees. . ."

Bobby thought, *One of 'em might be trying to needle me!*

Bobby spun around. Sure enough, a quarter-knight man, with finger-needle sticking out, was sidling up to Bobby alongside the open grave-hole.

Bobby was so surprised to see the strange man so close, that his finger slipped off the trigger guard. Before Bobby had a chance to aim the shotgun properly, it went off: Its one remaining shell blasted the quarter-knight's legs. The quarter-knight fell into the hole.

". . . knowledge. We Welcome you into the Overmind."

Bobby leaped over the grave-hole before the wounded quarter-knight could think to grab him. Bobby squeezed between the overturned hay baler and the outside of the rear wall of the barn, then ran around the back of the barn toward the farmhouse. Bobby's one slim chance of surviving the next hour required holing up with the shotgun and Mr. Kelly's boxes of shotgun shells.

Because Bobby knew the ground around the barn so well, he risked looking back into the barn, even as he was running full-speed forward. Bobby saw Mrs. Kelly and Eric still standing like statues, each with a quarter-knight only inches away.

Horizontal lightning cooked the air behind Bobby. He faced forward and ran faster.

Bobby made it to the front door. He didn't take time to look and see who was behind him—instead, Bobby jerked the door open, dashed through the doorway, slammed the door shut, then locked every lock the door had.

Bobby then ran through the house to the back door. But all its locks were already locked. Meaning, Bobby had wasted time.

Bobby ran to the hutch in the dining room, shards from the broken plate crunching beneath his shoes. He jerked open the far-left drawer, and dumped its contents on the floor. He didn't take time to put the wooden drawer back into its place on the hutch, he just dropped the drawer on the floor as well.

Dammit, there aren't enough shells!

Bobby ripped open a box of shotgun shells and dumped its contents on the floor. With shaky hands, he replaced the two empty shells in the shotgun with shells ready to kill.

I need to tell someone what's happened here!

With the shotgun held firmly in his left hand, Bobby ran for the kitchen. Seconds later, he was talking to the 911 operator—

"My name is Bobby Jackson, and I'm calling from the Pete Kelly farm on County Road 1701. You have a big problem."

"Please state the nature of the emergency, medical or otherwise."

"I hope you're recording this, ma'am, because we've got Martians here!"

The operator paused for a second, then said, "Sir, I need to ask you if you've taken any drugs recen—"

"Listen, lady, I don't have time for this! There are Martians here at the farm, they killed Mr. Kelly and the dogs with lightning from their hands, they've turned Mrs. Kelly and Eric into zombies, they tried to turn me into a zombie, and now they're trying to kill me!"

"Mr. Kelly is dead? And you're saying"—the operator sounded openly skeptical—"*Martians* killed him?"

"Lady, believe me or don't believe me, but you need to send somebody here. And I don't mean some doughnut-chomping deputy, send out a motherfucking SWAT—"

The front door and the back door both exploded at the same moment.

Bobby dropped the phone so he could hold the shotgun with both hands.

Bobby saw the back-door half-knight first. Bobby fired. No good—that damned purple shield came up, so the guy was unharmed. But for whatever reason, the half-knight didn't raise his lightning-arm to zap Bobby.

Bobby whirled around, to discover a second half-knight ten feet in front of him. Again, a blast of shotgun pellets was stopped by a purple shield.

Oh shit. Now Bobby was out of shells, and the nearest replacement shells were in the next room.

But that didn't matter, because Bobby got blasted in the back with lightning. Bobby flew forward through the air.

The half-knight in front of Bobby jerked his arm up to blast Bobby with lightning as well. Now Bobby flew backwards, to smash into the kitchen wall.

The last thing that Bobby ever heard was the sizzling of his own heart, and the 911 operator saying, *"Hello?* Mister Jackson, *hello?"*

3-D: The Cybes Want To Kill Me

Stephanie-1 told me during breakfast, "King James, when I try to talk to other bimborg, I hear noise. Static, you know?"

"How long has this been going on?"

"Since yesterday afternoon. It's, like, *sooo* annoying."

"Huh," I said. Because up till now, the anti-tachyon 'radios' that my bimborg have, meant Stephanie-1 could talk to an Ass-Kicker Babe in Red China as easily as she could commune with a Pleasure Unit in the next room—and with *zero* circuit noise.

After breakfast, I did text searches on my Cybe hard drive, but didn't find out anything. Apparently the Cybes never had a problem like this with their own anti-tachyon communications.

"Ah, it's probably just sunspots acting weird," I said, and thought no more about it.

Several hours later, my smartphone rang. Neither my phone nor I recognized the phone number, but I recognized the area code.

I answered the phone and said cheerfully, "Somebody just got a new cel phone! Or is it a smartphone?"

I expected to hear next, the voice of Uncle Pete or Aunt Linda.

Instead, a man's voice said, "Hello, is this James Upton? This is Scott Montgomery, Sheriff of Kirk County, Iowa."

"Yes, this is James Upton. How did you get this number?" If law-enforcement people could track me down, I needed to have a long talk with Linda-5.

The sheriff replied, "I got your number from your mother, Ellen. Mr. Upton, I'm investigating murders that occurred at your aunt and uncle's farm yesterday."

"*Murders?* Who died? And how?"

"*How?* To be honest, I'm not sure. I'm sorry to inform you that your Uncle Peter is dead, and your Aunt Linda is missing. Also, farmhand Robert Jackson is dead and farmhand Eric Pfeiffer is missing. Both dogs are dead."

"Good god, what happened?"

The sheriff said, "That's what I'm trying to figure out. I understand that you worked that farm during the summer of 2008?"

The sheriff then asked me a bunch of questions that boiled down to "One, did Bobby the farmhand strike you as a crazy weirdo? Two, did Eric the farmhand strike you as a crazy weirdo? Three, were your uncle and aunt unhappy in their marriage?"

I wasn't able to tell him much at all.

The sheriff said formally, "These are all the questions I have. Thank you for your time." He hung up, I hung up—then seconds later, my smartphone rang again.

Again, somebody was calling me from an unknown telephone number, from my aunt and uncle's area code.

I said cautiously, "Hello?"

"Mister Upton, this is Sheriff Montgomery again. Sorry about the James Bond stuff, but I'm calling you from a prepaid that I don't think the Feds can tap or trace."

"You're weirding me out, Sheriff. What's happening?"

"I'm going to tell you about the stuff that can't go in my report. To start with, Mr. Jackson was on the phone with 911 when he was killed. Before he died, he was screaming about *Martians*."

A crazy thought occurred to me then. I told myself it was stupid. Aloud I said, "Do you believe him now, about Martians?"

"Well, yesterday we got an earthquake, right here in Kirk County, about ten miles from your aunt and uncle's farm. A no-shit earthquake, except that—"

"You don't get earthquakes there."

"And today I got the United States Goddamn Army crawling around the whatchacallit—"

"Epicenter."

"—epicenter, and they've got a tall green fence up, and guys in HazMat suits, and they've told me that I and my deputies are not to hang around there. Told our helicopter guy that he can't fly over their fenced-off rectangle neither."

"Whoa."

"But our helicopter pilot got close, and he says there's *glass* inside that fence where the dirt should be."

"Shit, like when they detonate an *atomic bomb*?"

"Yeah, except everything outside of the fenced-in place is okay. Most of the Army guys *aren't* wearing HazMat suits, the trees nearby all have their leaves, and the Army is letting people drive on the nearby road—but with a 30 miles-per-hour *minimum* speed limit."

"Sheriff, why are you telling me all this?"

"Because these murders don't make any sense! You go in the Kellys' dining room and there's a broken plate on the floor, and shotgun shells on the floor, and spilled milk on the floor, but nobody cleaned any of that mess up. There's food on the table, on people's plates. A roddenberry pie was still warm from the oven. Two people are dead, two are missing, but neither the motorcycle nor the truck was driven recently."

"Wow, it's like a 'Twilight Zone' show," I said. The episode where that guy saw the monster on the airplane wing had always spooked me.

The sheriff said, "But if I say, 'Martians killed them all,' then at least the murders make *crazy* sense instead of *no* sense. Mainly, I want to know what happened for myself, before the Army comes along and shits a 'Top Secret' over the entire case file."

"So you don't think Bobby was crazy when he was yelling about Martians?"

"You know what Jackson died of? The M.E.'s preliminary finding is 'high-voltage electrocution.' In the fucking kitchen. He's on tape firing the shotgun twice, then he's electrocuted. Same with your uncle, same with the dogs—died of electrocution. If not Martians, how did he die? Then there's the barn."

"What happened at the barn?" I asked.

I now had a sick feeling who the "Martians" were, and I did *not* want them anywhere near the barn.

"Right behind the barn, you got this heavy-ass piece of machinery—"

"The hay baler," I said. I was nervous now.

"Right, the hay baler. Anyway, somehow it got pushed over, onto its side—"

"Pushed *over*?" I said.

I'd buried the Cybefied corpse of my fifth-grade Computer Literacy teacher under the hay baler. *Shit, shit, shit!*

"Yeah, it's the damnedest thing," the sheriff said. "I figure you'd need a bulldozer to knock over something that heavy, but there were no tracks in the barn except shoe prints. Anyway, where the hay baler had been, there was a hole in the ground. Like for a shallow grave."

I took a deep breath to calm myself, then asked, "Was there a body in the hole?" *As soon as the sheriff identifies the body as Miss Smith, I'll be a murder suspect!*

"Nope, no body. A shitload of fresh blood, but no body. Plus we found an *un*fired revolver by the hole, next to a sledgehammer. I don't know what to make of all that."

"*No body?* Uh . . . whose blood was it?"

"No idea. We couldn't figure out a way to take a sample without contaminating the evidence, so I told the techs, 'Skip it.'"

Whoever had killed my uncle and Bobby had dug up Miss Smith's corpse, despite a hay baler sitting atop the grave. Then they had taken the body with them. I could think of only one group who would want to do that.

I asked the sheriff, "What can you tell me about Aunt Linda and Eric Pfeiffer? You said they're missing."

"James, I have no evidence and no guesses either. Jackson told 911 that the 'Martians' had turned those two people into 'zombies,' but I have no idea what that means."

Oh fuck a duck. If the Cybes had Welcomed Aunt Linda, the shit would hit the fan very soon.

"There's still one thing I don't get," the sheriff said, "Even if you believe that no-shit Martians pulled these stunts."

"What don't you understand?"

"If they crashed where the Army is investigating, your uncle's farm isn't the closest tract to that spot. Why did they mess with your uncle and aunt, ten miles away, instead of someone closer?"

"I have no idea," I said. But I was lying, big-time.

I heard the sheriff talking to someone in the room: "I'm on the phone; you mind? . . . Fine, gimme. I'll call him in a few minutes."

There was another pause, and now the sheriff was talking to me again: "*Fuck*, another mystery."

"What's wrong?"

"Just got a theft report from Fenton Mudd, the farmer who's got the Army playing National Security in his soybean field. He's just discovered that his two-ton utility truck is missing."

A minute later, I had ended the phone call, and now I was staring at the ceiling.

The Cybes are back. They know I killed their Welcomer. They know I stole all the Cybe technology off her corpse.

For that alone, they might kill me.

If they figure out I've created my own Bimborg hive, the Cybes will certainly try to kill me. Not to mention, they'll try to subvert my hive.

If they realize I intend to never publish that nanotechnology paper in 2055, their wrath will know no bounds.

3-E: Attack Of Conscience

When I had a chance to think about it, I realized how hard it would be for the Cybes to find me. On paper I lived nowhere, worked nowhere, and had no money in the bank. I'd told Linda-5 to set things up this way to make me invisible to the tax man, but now those precautions might well save my life.

In fact, the only way that Cybes might possibly find me is—

Shit, shit, shit!

Mom knew where I lived, Mom knew my phone number, and Mom knew I had lots of "girlfriends" at my house at all hours. If the Cybes Welcomed my mom, I was dead meat.

Worse, the Cybes wouldn't even need to Welcome my mom. If Cybe-Linda phoned Mom and said, "I want to mail home-baked brownies to Jimmy, what's his address?" Mom would blab all.

There was only one thing to do. To keep Mom alive, not to mention keeping *me* alive, Mom had to disappear.

Fortunately, my Alpha Male pheromones made this easy. Neither Mom nor David argued when I basically kidnapped them, confiscated their smartphones, and sent them on to a phoneless motel room in Sweet Onion, Georgia.

(Of course, there was one *dis*advantage to using the pheromones on Mom: Just before she was whisked away, she sashayed up to me and said, "Ooh, my son James is *all grown up* now. You're *taking charge*, acting *masterful*." I'm sorry I heard that, Mom.)

My one big advantage over the Cybes right now was that I knew about them, and that they were here in 2013, whereas they had no clue about the bimborg.

I intended to keep it that way.

By now I had figured out that the "static" that Stephanie-1 had reported was bimborg women picking up Cybe anti-tachyon transmissions. Well, I wasn't about to let the Cybes overhear any bimborg anti-tachyon transmissions, nosirree. I immediately ordered that bimborg stop using "the Club"; instead, they were to communicate the 21st-century way: by internet.

So the bimborg began to talk to each other via a commandeered Cayman Islands pirate website, http://Free-BluRay-4-U.ky.

The guys who ran that website outsmarted themselves when they set up a "business office" that consisted of only a big bunch of computer hardware, and a big-breasted, bottle-redhead receptionist with only a telephone and an old computer on her desk. The owners never imagined that their ditzy receptionist could shanghai their entire website in only eight minutes.

When Mom was safe in Georgia, and when the bimborg had a second way of talking to each other so that Cybes could not "overhear" anything, then a thought occurred to me—

What happens to the bimborg after I die?

I had created the bimborg and started them "reproducing" because I didn't expect to die for decades yet. That Cybe hard-drive that I stole had lots of information about 27th-century medicine, and so I had expected to live to an old age between 110 and 120.

But instead, a Cybe Soldier could electrocute me, five minutes from now.

And what would that then mean to my bimborg hive, exactly? The bimborg's prime directive was to serve and obey me, so what would happen when that became impossible? Would each bimborg unit go back to being Solitary? Would each unit instantly paralyze into a statue? Would the entire bimborg hive go crazy?

I like to think that I'm a good guy.

Fine, so I'm responsible for the worldwide enslavement of 22,386,936 women (so far), just so I can get guaranteed sucks and fucks. A critic might point out that my most recent Pleasure Unit got Welcomed in Nagpur, India—and isn't that greedy, because when will I ever need free pussy in Nagpur, India?

But since I had enslaved these women, it seemed to me only decent to care for them after I died. I wracked my brain, trying to come up with a solution.

I tried to think of a way to release all the millions of bimborg back to Solitariness. I couldn't see any way how.

Finally, a half-solution to the problem came to me: Since I was the Bimborg King, I should appoint a Bimborg Crown Prince, who would immediately become King if I died.

That list of candidates had only one name on it. This man had the smarts that the bimborg would need in their king. It helped a lot that this man already had plenty of experience with bimborg.

I went to the bimborg-chat home page that was hosted in the Cayman Islands, and I posted this message—

From King James:

If I die, become unconscious, become vegetative, or get Welcomed, then Charlie-Bob Owens of Sweet Onion, Georgia, USA is to immediately become Bimborg King.

To prepare Charlie-Bob for his future responsibility, all bimborg in Sweet Onion are to meet with him as soon as possible, given that
1) the meeting place is isolated (no Solitaries can overhear);
2) all bimborg who live in Sweet Onion are present at the meeting.

At this meeting, you are to tell Charlie-Bob everything. Tell him the truth, the whole truth, nothing but the truth, and hold nothing back.

Then tell him one thing more: The Cybes are here in 2013, and they intend either to kill me or to Welcome me.

3-F: Prince Charles (Robert)

THE NEXT AFTERNOON
HEATHER SAINT JAMES' DENTAL CLINIC
SWEET ONION, GEORGIA

Rose said, "Charlie-Bob, you're being, ohmigod, real quiet. What are you thinking?"

He frowned. "*Hello, Alice, welcome to Wonderland*, that's what I'm thinking."

He looked at the 29 women and girls in the room. "So what y'all are saying is, y'all hung out with me, cooked for me, and fucked me because I was your assignment, not because even one of y'all felt attracted to me."

Heather said, "Yes they did, but—"

Rose said, "Charlie-Bob, when this happens to a girl, she get all, like, emotionless. I'm not even attracted to *girls* anymore."

Charlie-Bob shrugged. "I figured as much." He looked around the room. "I need to talk to 'King' James. What's his phone number?"

Tatum-Teresa Haven said, "We're not supposed to—"

Karen Milph said, "He's the Crown Prince. He's entitled."

Charlie-Bob said, "Actually, Tatum-Teresa is right. I'm supposed to be the secret weapon, right? I shouldn't make it easy for the bad guys to track me. Somebody, get me the phone number of someone who'd be in the house with James."

A minute later, as Charlie-Bob was punching in the phone number for Stephanie-1, Heather remarked, "You act unsurprised by all this."

He said, "Because a month ago, I figured out part of—hello, Stephanie, this is Charlie-Bob in Georgia. Please put James on."

Seconds later, Charlie-Bob heard James say, "Hey, little brother, I'm glad to have you on board. I think—"

"You are presuming, sir. I haven't yet said I'll do this."

"What? But you *have to*! If something would happen to me, what about the women? You can't just let—"

"That all depends on whether you picked me to actually care for your millions of *sex slaves*, or I'm here just to soothe your conscience."

"I see. How do you expect to get an answer to that question?"

"Simple. You go on that website, and you give an order that as of right now, this minute, there are to be no more Welcomings."

"*What?* You're not king *yet*, sonny boy—"

"And you're not serious. Go find some *other* mind-control pervert to take over your harem. I'm sure you'll find plenty of takers."

"But the fate of the world could—"

"If you aren't bothered by some woman tomorrow becoming a bimborg, don't try to bullshit me how you're worried about her becoming a Cybe."

James sighed loudly. "You're just a kid of eighteen, and you haven't had to deal with *responsibilities*. Let me spell it out: The Cybes make more Cybes, it's what they do. Right now, I've got 22 million bimborg, and they easily outnumber however-many Cybe are here in 2013. But I'm willing to bet you a million dollars, these Cybes are Welcoming like crazy. Next year, there won't be 22 million Cybes, so the good guys will still be ahead. But the year after that, who knows?"

Charlie-Bob rolled his eyes. "Ah yes, the old argument of 'The greater good forces me to do something evil, so it's not really evil.' Sorry, not buying it."

"Well then, if you become Bimborg King and if the Cybes take over because there are not enough bimborg to fight them, then it'll be all your fault."

"That's sure a bucketload of *if*s. The answer is still no. Order the Welcoming of women to stop, or choose someone else to be these women's slaveholder."

"Okay, fine, I'll do it, as soon as I hang up here."

"When you post that order on the website, I'll go on the website and accept the job. But not before."

"Fine. But just so you know, I don't like you giving orders when you're not King yet."

"Then you better go on your website and take my name off, because otherwise I have other things I insist you do."

"Yeah, like what?"

"From now on, whenever you leave the house, you have a bimborg with you."

"Duh, kiddo. I've got four Ass-Kicker Babes in the house right now."

"You're not getting it. If you can't go out with an Ass-Kicker Babe, go out with a Pleasure Unit or a Spy Babe. If the Cybes are smart at all, they'll not only kill you, but they'll do it in such a way that the bimborg hive doesn't know you're dead."

"Fine. You're right."

"As soon as you die, or as soon as you've clearly been Welcomed, then I'm to immediately succeed you. I want you to write all that on your website."

James said sarcastically, "Anything else you'd like? How about great wealth? I can get Linda-5 to set you up with a million-dollar bank account in the Bahamas. Takes five minutes, tops."

"James, I'm not doing this to get pussy—in fact, I expect to be celibate for a long time to come. I'm not doing this to get rich. I'm doing this because the bimborg need a protector."

"So selfless you are. You're entitled to a fair reward, you know."

"Tell you what, you want to give me something of great value? Fine, give me the most valuable stuff you own. Everything you stole from that Cybe woman, ship down to me. The hard drive, the nanobots, everything."

"You are fucking me. No way."

"Are you really ranked up with Albert Einstein? Whatever else the Cybes try to do with you, one thing I can guarantee: They will try to get that stolen stuff back. Because if you have it, or if I do, maybe we can beat them. If we don't have any of that, we have no hope to win. They know this."

"Fuck, I've created a monster," James replied.

Then Charlie-Bob heard James call out, "Stephanie-1, come here!"

In a normal voice, James told Charlie-Bob, "This is one order I'm not going to put on the website; I'm not *completely* stupid."

With Charlie-Bob able to hear over the phone, James gave Stephanie-1 orders how to send the Cybe stuff to Charlie-Bob's town.

James commented afterward, "I'm sending you the nanobot injector, to show you that you can trust me, even though I've already used up all the nanobots."

Charlie-Bob replied, "I haven't decided yet whether I trust you. But I've already decided that I don't respect you."

Seventeen minutes later, King James posted new orders on the website. Those orders gave Charlie-Bob everything he'd demanded.

Charlie-Bob logged into the website, accepted the title of Bimborg Crown Prince, and then—

—wrote an introduction about himself. Yes, all 22 million bimborg might really be nanobot-zombies who were programmed to obey his every order someday, but that didn't mean that they didn't deserve to know something about their order-giver.

After Charlie-Bob logged out of the bimborg's website, he looked at Rose. "Since I'm now Bimborg Crown Prince, I choose you as my liaison with the bimborg hive. I guess that makes you Bimborg Princess Consort."

Her grin was crooked. "Does that rate a tiara?"

3-G: Hide And Go Seek

Right after I shipped Mom, her boyfriend David, and their computers and smartphones all to Georgia, I had three bimborg walk through Mom's house. A Pleasure Unit, an Ass-Kicker Babe, and a Spy Babe walked through my mom's house and looked for anything that gave out my email address, house address, or telephone number.

The bimborg found a refrigerator-magnet note, and a scribble on the front cover of a phone book. These were given to me, and I shredded them.

The Cybe timeship's Communications-unit had continued to use the time-radio to try and contact any Cybes in the 27th century. With no success. After two Earthdays, the Captain-unit had ordered the Communications-unit to stop trying.

By now it was clear to all Cybes: Somehow Jimmy Upton had de-caused all Cybes futureward of themselves. The murder and burial of Sol3-21-1 argued that this de-causation was not an accidental butterfly effect by Jimmy Upton, but was instead a deliberate act.

The Cybes met in Overmind.

The Cybes decided three things.

Decision 1: The Captain-unit, Delos3-27-30074453969, would become Cybe Alpha, final decision-maker whenever the Cybe Clan/hive was undecided or needed quick decisions.

Decision 2: The Cybes would resume their primary mission: "To Welcome every sentient Solitary on a planet; but Solitaries who are useless are to be killed." However, since the Cybes could not yet overwhelm 21st-century Earth with sheer numbers, conquering Earth would take time and planning.

Fortunately, the Cybes had computer-like patience, and the Overmind was well suited for planning.

Decision 3: The timeline was irreparably damaged, and so Jimmy Upton must die.

The Cybes couldn't figure out whether Jimmy Upton had created cyborgs of his own with the stolen Cybe hardware. So Cybe Alpha directed that once Jimmy Upton was captured, he was to be

Welcomed, and he would be ordered to turn over his hive to the Cybe Clan, if he had his own hive. Only then was Jimmy to be killed.

Two days after Charlie-Bob had talked to "King James" on the phone, Sweet Onion High School was closed for President's Day. Charlie-Bob was at home, surfing the internet, when his mom told him that Rose was at the front door.

"How about you take a ride in my car?" Rose said meaningfully.

Ten minutes later, Rose and Charlie-Bob walked up the stairs to Miss Turner's apartment.

In a corner of the living room, by the trampoline, was a cheap black computer desk and a tan metal folding chair. Atop that black desk was a computer Frankenstein.

A 21st-century keyboard and a 21st-century monitor were attached by a whole lot of ribbon cable to a strange gizmo: a pearlescent tiny cube that seemed to use no power source.

As soon as Charlie-Bob sat down in the chair and he turned the monitor on, Miss Turner said, "Is there anything you need? Soda? A sandwich? A slow blowjob?"

Charlie-Bob let himself be talked into a can of Coke and a ham sandwich. As for the other offer—

"I thank you kindly, Mary Kayla, but I'll skip the blowjob."

My precaution, of having bimborg walk through my mother Ellen's house, turned out to be smart. Three days after I sent Mom and David to Georgia, my mom's house was broken into, by robbers with great strength. The house was completely ransacked.

The Grand City police were indifferent: "Aw, they're probably drug addicts hopped up on Angel Dust and looking for cash."

I knew better.

Virus-fuck! Is this Cybe Alpha unit surrounded by total pandhilik?

The Cybe emotion-suppression subroutine didn't completely work in situations when a Solitary would be feeling blazing, white-hot fury. Cybe Alpha clenched his fist when he learned that the raid on Jimmy Upton's mother's house was a total failure.

Where is Jimmy Upton? Why can't we find him?

The plan was supposed to be simple. Cybe Soldiers would burst in, grab Ellen Upton and hold her down, while a Welcomer turned her into a Cybe. Three days later, Cybe-Ellen would lure Jimmy Upton into a trap, and Jimmy Upton would be Welcomed before being killed. Instead, the Cybes discovered that Jimmy's mother was gone, and that her bathtub, bathroom sink, and kitchen sink all were dry. Not only was she gone, but everything electronic or paper with useful information on it, also was gone.

Bugger an Amigogi's ear! They still used paper to save and to pass information in the 21st century, that's how primitive these people were. And yet Jimmy Upton, a native of the 21st century, had so far completely outsmarted the entire Cybe Clan. *How?* These people were *cavemen*, almost.

Cybe Alpha went to the Overmind to find out if anyone had any suggestions.

Sol3-21-2, the former Eric Pfeiffer, had a suggestion: "Check her mailbox. If it's empty or almost empty, Jimmy is coming by her house and getting her mail, which means that he lives in Grand City too."

The next afternoon, Shikortsky2-27-83675 (Jeans Man) was sitting behind the steering wheel of a hydrocarbon-burning ground-transport machine. He was watching Ellen Upton's mailbox, waiting to see who claimed its mail.

A young woman appeared in his driver-side mirror. She was moving from Jeans Man's left to his right, walking along the side street behind Jeans Man's automobile.

At the corner, the young woman turned. Now she was walking along the same street—in fact, along the same side of the street—as the mailbox.

Jeans Man got alert. "It's time to Luna-dance," he muttered.

As she got closer, Jeans Man watched her in the driver's-side mirror. She had big, puffy lips; and she had a big, open canvas bag hanging off her right shoulder.

She acted like she didn't notice Jeans Man, or the automobile that he was sitting in, at all.

Her walk would take her right past the mailbox. At the last possible second, Puffy Lips Girl stopped, jerked open the mailbox lid, grabbed a bunch of paper rectangles, tossed them into her canvas bag, slammed shut the mailbox lid, and resumed her walk.

The person collecting the mail was coming and leaving by walking, not by driving. Which was a problem, because following Puffy Lips Girl without her noticing, when she was walking and Jeans Man was driving, would be difficult.

Soon Jeans Man was consulting with the Overmind, trying to cook up a new plan. By then Puffy Lips Girl had walked almost to the end of the block.

From her canvas bag, Puffy Lips Girl dug out the hand-held device that Cybe-Linda identified as a "smartphone," and briefly did the activity called "texting," while she continued to walk. Puffy Lips Girl then tossed the smartphone back in her bag.

By now, Puffy Lips Girl had reached the end of the block, and was crossing the side street at the intersection. An automobile that was driving along the side street suddenly stopped in the middle of that same intersection, right in front of Puffy Lips Girl.

She yanked open the passenger-side door, threw herself into the automobile, slammed the door, and the automobile zoomed away.

Jeans Man had been caught completely by surprise. By the time he got his own automobile started and rolling, Puffy Lips Girl's automobile had vanished.

A week later, Jeans Man had successfully followed Puffy Lips Girl and her load of mail to a Wal-Mart store. Now Puffy Lips Girl was walking into the store as Jeans Man was trying to park his automobile in a hurry.

(Without a lot of skill. The Overmind shared head knowledge and book knowledge, not muscle knowledge. Jeans Man had never driven an automobile before this assignment.)

By the time that Jeans Man walked into the Wal-Mart, Puffy Lips Girl could no longer be seen. Jeans Man walked fast all over the store, desperate to find her. He finally found her; she was carrying a handbasket and just leaving the Bath Towels aisle.

Just as Puffy Lips Girl walked out of the Bath Towels aisle, another young woman pushed her shopping cart into that aisle. Jeans Man was supposed to keep Puffy Lips Girl under constant observation, but he took his eyes off her for a few seconds to glance at Shopping Cart Girl.

Jeans Man couldn't help but look. Shopping Cart Girl had large breasts, which were apparently as sexy in the 21st century as they had been back in the 27th century. She was wearing a pink V-neck t-shirt to show off her tits, a short pink skirt, pink high heels, and little pink gloves on her hands. When she got near Jeans Man, she looked him up and down, then gave him a shy smile.

Enough! Get back to work. Jeans Man quit looking at Shopping Cart Girl and went back to following Puffy Lips Girl (at a distance).

She went from Housewares to Frozen Foods to Meats, adding small items to her handbasket. In Meats was an open trash can. Puffy Lips Woman looked around furtively (though she managed not to look at Jeans Man). She quickly pulled some envelopes out of her canvas bag, which she threw in the trash can. She hurried away.

Jimmy Upton, you're as good as caught! Jeans Man thought.

When Jeans Man could no longer see Puffy Lips Girl, he sauntered over to the trashcan and pulled out the envelopes. All were brightly colored; through the Overmind, Cybe-Linda identified every envelope as "junk mail."

Jeans Man dropped the mail back into the trash can, and waited for someone to pick up Ellen Upton's junk mail.

After Jeans Man had done this for two hours, a big man walked up to him. The man was no match for a Cybe Soldier, but he could easily overpower Jeans Man in a fight.

The big man pulled back his windbreaker to reveal a silver badge pinned to his shirt; the badge read "Wal-Mart Security."

"Sir," the big man said, "you've been hanging around here for two hours. I'm asking you to buy something or to leave the store."

Jeans Man left the store, his mission a failure.

Did Jimmy Upton trick us again? How? I was watching Puffy Lips Girl almost every second!

As Jeans Man was walking out of the Wal-Mart store, he passed close to Shopping Cart Girl, who was unloading her shopping cart at a check-out counter. She turned her head toward Jeans Man and gave him a friendly smile.

Eight Earthdays had passed since the Cybes had raided Ellen Upton's house, and Cybe Alpha still had no guess where Jimmy Upton might be.

All he knew at this point was that the mail was being removed from the mother's mailbox by a puffy-lipped young woman, and somehow the important mail was carried on to Jimmy Upton at a location unknown.

Then Cybe Alpha got an idea.

Cybe Alpha gave the order to Shikortsky2-27-83675 (Jeans Man) to start stealing important mail out of the mailbox. He was to then put the stolen letters back in the mailbox, the next day—

—after they'd been doctored a little bit.

The Cybes got lucky: The next day, Jeans Man brought to them an electricity bill, and a water and sewage bill.

Now came the sneaky part.

One of the Welcomers removed her finger-needle, and this was modified so that the needle shot out steam instead of nanobots. This steam-needle was used on the two envelopes, steaming them open without bending or wrinkling the envelope paper.

Then came the really clever part. (So Cybe Alpha hoped.)

The contents of the envelopes were opened up, and onto them were dropped modified nanobots. These altered nanobots now didn't do anything biological, but they were the size of dust motes, and they each sent out a radio pulse (1,701 kHz, for one-32nd of a slobi, at 64-slobi intervals).

Then the contents of each envelope was refolded and put back in the envelope, and the envelope was resealed. The next morning, the two stolen utility bills were put back in Ellen Upton's mailbox.

The trick worked. By sundown, both envelopes and their nanobot beacons had been taken to the same house in Grand City. Triangulation of the radio broadcasts pinpointed that house.

A different Invisible, Skirt-Suit Woman, was sent to spy on the suspected house. She didn't spot Jimmy Upton, but she saw Shopping Cart Woman walk into the house.

Now the Cybes were sure exactly where Jimmy Upton lived.

Cybe Alpha gave the order: Jimmy Upton's house would be attacked tomorrow, as soon as the Cybes in Savannah, Georgia finished recharging and could all wormhole over to Grand City.

THE NEXT MORNING, 3:42 a.m. Central Time

James Upton was asleep when the Cybes smashed their way into his house.

3-H: Cybes v. Bimborg 1

3:42 a.m. Central Time
HOUSE OF JAMES UPTON

Boom!

Upstairs in the attic, Lucille-47893 dropped the cards she had been playing Solitaire with. Being an Ass-Kicker Babe, she had no need for sleep.

Had she not been warned what to expect, Lucille-unit would have thought a drunkard's car had smashed into the front door.

But that wasn't the case. For one thing, another noise had come from the back door in the same second, every bit as loud. And now that Lucille was listening, she heard the tinkling of ground-floor glass being smashed.

King James' order had made it very clear: Whichever Ass-Kicker Babe is in the attic when the attack occurs was not to join in the fight, but instead was to watch from the attic and report. So Lucille-unit didn't pull on her shoes and race down the attic stairs.

Instead, she walked, barefoot and slowly, to the table on which lay a prepaid cel phone, a neck scarf, a hammer, and a college dictionary. Lucille-unit opened the hollowed-out dictionary, to reveal the device hidden inside. She toggled it on, then she walked ten feet to the periscope that was attached to the smoke detector.

A house that has bimborg in it, doesn't need a smoke detector. Yet King James' house had one in the central hallway, just like most houses in the 21st-century USA. King James was counting on the Cybes not paying that smoke detector any attention.

King James personally had moved the smoke detector from where it was (middle of the hallway) to just outside his bedroom door. Then he had replaced the guts of the smoke detector with a hole between the hallway ceiling and the attic, and had run a periscope through that hole. Alas, the air-holes in the smoke-detector casing gave the periscope only a partial view of King James' bedroom.

Looking through the periscope now, Lucille-unit couldn't see into the bedroom; the bedroom door was closed. That changed when a

Cybe Soldier, his shoulders as wide as King James' own Alpha Male shoulders, smashed-in the bedroom door.

———————

As soon as Stephanie-1 heard the loud noises, she jumped out of King James' bed, as did King James himself. The seven Ass-Kicker Babes who had been sleeping on blankets on the bedroom floor, jumped up.

King James was dressed in briefs and shorts, while Stephanie-1 and all seven Ass-Kicker Babes were naked. Let the Cybes think that those women were there only for sex.

Of course, each naked "hot little honey" was holding a pistol in a teacup grip. *Confusion to the enemy!* Stephanie-1's own weapon was a Chekhov 9-mm semiautomatic. James was holding a Space Navy ray-gun that he'd built in his father's workshop.

Stephanie-1 had just flipped the safety off when the closed bedroom door got smashed in. Cybes poured into the bedroom.

King James remarked, "Now things get interesting."

From Stephanie-1's right, two shots were fired. The lead Cybe fell down, both his knees blasted. The Cybes rushing into the room tripped over the lead guy; the knee-blasted Soldier wound up lying on his belly. Before he could raise his head and erect a force-field, a bimborg bullet blasted his brain to bits.

As their way of showing thanks, two Cybe Soldiers lightning-blasted Latesha-unit and Lashondra-unit.

By now the bedroom held three Cybe Welcomers, one dead Cybe Soldier, and five living Cybe Soldiers. The Soldier nearest the doorway looked like a skinny, seven-foot-tall cat-man with cat-ears, cat-eyes, and gray fur.

Before anyone else did anything, or fired any weapon, King James said, "Aunt Linda? Is that *you?*"

The middle Welcomer replied, "Linda Kelly is no more. This unit has been Welcomed into the Overmind."

That's when Cathy-4869385, without turning her head, moved her hands to the left. *Bang!* Cybe-Linda had a hole in her forehead.

A Cybe Soldier turned his own head, then Cathy-4869385 got electrocuted. In turn, the Soldier got vaporized by James' ray-gun.

Stephanie-1 expected all four remaining Cybe Soldiers to blast James with lightning at that moment—or try to. She tensed up, ready for a battle to the death.

Instead, one Soldier did a martial-arts move and yanked the gun out of Kathee-259304's hand. He then grabbed her left arm and twisted it. If she'd been a Solitary, she'd be hurting now.

Kathee-unit's attacker said to James, "We do not wish to be cruel. Surrender, and Cybe Alpha promises that your playthings will not be hurt or killed."

In response, "plaything" Kathee-unit spun around and smashed the heel of her right hand into his nose. He died, then Kathee-unit died by a different Soldier's high voltage.

There were now two human Cybe Soldiers, plus one cat-man Soldier, still alive. At the same moment, each Soldier turned to face an Ass-Kicker Babe. *Zzzap!* The last three Ass-Kicker Babes died; Stephanie-1 was now the only living bimborg in the room.

The cat-man Cybe Soldier's nostrils now were flaring, and he walked out of the room (stepping over the dead, knee-shot Cybe Soldier in the process).

Seconds later, the cat-man was standing in the hallway under the smoke detector. He was looking up at the ceiling and sniffing.

Stephanie-1 wondered, *Does he smell Lucille-unit in the attic? Does he smell the toothpaste that is hiding old screw-holes?*

She sidestepped to the left, her pistol held out straight in front of her, and fired two shots at the cat-man's head. Because he was distracted, he didn't put up a purple shield. *Threat destroyed.*

As soon as Stephanie-1 was sure that the cat-man was dead, the bimborg queen twisted her legs to rotate her upper body.

Now she was looking down the barrel at one of the two remaining Cybe Welcomers. Before either Cybe Soldier could react, Stephanie-1 double-tapped her target Welcomer.

Stephanie-1 rotated again, to shoot the last Cybe Welcomer—but one of the two Soldiers had stepped in front of that Welcomer. He was raising his arm to zap Stephanie-1, and she zipped to the right, behind King James. Lightning shot through the space where she'd stood, and scorched the wall behind her.

King James started firing his ray-gun at each Soldier, but it did no good. Neither Soldier was distracted, so every time King James tried to blast a Soldier, that Soldier's purple shield came up. Worse, the ray-gun started losing charge: Its beam went from bluish-white, to yellow, to a dim orange.

Then the two Soldiers, together, rushed right up to King James. One knocked the now-useless ray-gun out of King James' hand. As soon as the ray-gun hit the floor, both Soldiers zapped it with lightning till it melted.

King James said loudly, "You've killed all of mine except Stephanie, but we killed *seven* of yours. Great! Tsk-tsk, four Cybe Soldiers dead because they didn't pay attention. And now, you few Cybes who remain, for hate's sake I spit my last breath at thee."

Indeed, King James then spit on the carpet.

While the Soldiers were zapping the ray-gun, nothing else was happening—

• King James stood where he was, making no attempt to flee, and staring at the Cybes with his back straight.

• The one surviving Cybe Welcomer was standing against the wall, keeping her distance from Stephanie-1 and King James.

• Stephanie-1 had enough shots left in her clip to shoot at both Soldiers, but estimated that there would be only a 0.00029 probability of killing both of them, and so Stephanie-1 kept her pistol pointed at the floor. Stephanie-1 had one more order to carry out. If she tried but failed to kill both Soldiers, she would be electrocuted before she could carry out that order. So she let both Soldiers live.

When the ray-gun was melted, the Soldiers turned their full attention to King James. He was at their mercy now.

Stephanie-1 was surprised when one of the Soldiers bent down and picked up a dead bimborg's pistol.

"A primitive weapon," the Soldier said. "It is only a slight improvement over throwing rocks with a sling. But we adapt."

The Soldier's arm went down. "Jimmy, you no longer need knees." Two quick shots.

King James fell down, and *shrieked* when his knees hit the floor. King James fell forward, and put out his hands to catch himself.

Bang-bang! King James was shot once in each hand.

"You no longer need hands either, Jimmy," the Soldier said.

King James started muttering, "Motherfuck, oh shit it hurts, motherfuck." He said nothing to the Cybes.

The pistol-holding Soldier casually tossed the gun away; it landed on dead Kathee-unit's boobs.

The two Soldiers went to pain-wracked King James and each of them grabbed one of King James' arms and lifted him up. They walked around him in a half-circle, so that now King James and the two Cybe Soldiers all were facing Stephanie-1 from three feet away.

The Soldier nearest to Stephanie-1 looked meaningfully at her pistol and said, "If you do not do anything *pandhi* with your weapon, we will let you leave, unhurt and unchanged. We want a witness."

Stephanie-1 heard footsteps now, as the Welcomer who was behind King James, walked toward him. Just before King James was within the Welcomer's reach—

Stephanie-1 lifted the Chekhov. She didn't aim for the near Soldier, the far Soldier, or the Welcomer. Instead, she pointed the gun at King James and blew his brains out.

Looking through the periscope from the attic, Lucille-unit saw Stephanie-1 shoot King James dead, then Stephanie-1 herself get blasted by high voltage from both Cybe Soldiers.

Lucille-unit walked from the periscope to the cel phone. She punched in a memorized phone number.

When a woman's voice answered, Lucille-unit said in Hindi, "King James is dead, without Welcome. Stephanie-1 is dead. I am taking the Good Book."

"Understood," the woman replied in Danish.

Lucille-unit turned off the prepaid cel phone, wrapped it in the neck scarf, then smashed the phone into little pieces with the hammer. She toggled-off the recording device and closed the dictionary.

Seconds later, Lucille-unit was fully dressed and was wearing a lavender backpack that had the hollowed-out dictionary in it.

Lucille's do-or-die mission now was to get the device that was inside this dictionary, to King Charlie-Bob. But to do that, she had to first escape this house that was crawling with Cybes.

Slowly, quietly, Lucille-unit opened the attic window. Her plan was to dive out the window, then do a half-flip in mid-air so that she landed on her feet. A thirty-foot fall would not be a problem to an Ass-Kicker Babe.

She did her dive—

—and discovered, as she was falling, that there was a Cybe Welcomer below her—

—and the Welcomer was holding a ray-gun and looking up.

Not quite a second and a half later, Lucille-unit hit the ground, on her feet, only inches away from the Welcomer. The Welcomer's eyebrows shot up as she realized that she'd just witnessed something impossible—if Lucille-unit were a Solitary. The Welcomer started to bring her ray-gun up—

That's when Lucille-unit snapped the Welcomer's neck.

A cyborg woman who can fall thirty feet without injury, finds a six-feet-tall fence to be no challenge at all. Within seconds, Lucille-unit and her precious dictionary-disguised cargo were gone from King James' property.

James Upton died at 4:51 a.m. Eastern time. Charlie-Bob Owens got a telephone call from Tatum-Teresa Haven at 4:55 a.m. Eastern.

Charlie-Bob couldn't go back to sleep. At 5:49 a.m., he logged into the bimborg website and started writing new orders.

His first order was: "As Bimborg King, I choose Rose-unit of Sweet Onion to be Bimborg Queen, since Stephanie-1 is dead. Rose, I order you to help me be the best Bimborg King that I can be."

Charlie-Bob's second order was: "Whenever I'm dealing with one of you, I order you to tell me honestly what your Solitary self would think about what we're doing. I need to know the woman you once were, not only the obedient cyborg you are now."

The Grand City Police didn't know what to make of the crime scene.

Neighbors had reported multiple gunshots; and indeed the police recovered eight handguns, five of which had been fired. But there was only one gunshot victim: James Upton, white male age 20. The eight women found in the bedroom were all dead of high-voltage electrocution. The police found no other dead bodies in the house, but they did find blood and blood-spray in Upton's bedroom. The floor also had a metal lump, melted into the concrete foundation, that was surrounded by scorched carpet.

A clever Grand City detective went online at the crime scene, and tried to research "electrocution" as a *modus operandi*. But of course, he didn't have access to any U.S. Army database, and the Army didn't take interest in exploring any Grand City police database.

So neither any Solitary in the U.S. Army nor any Solitary law-enforcement officer ever connected the Kelly Farm killings and the killings at James Upton's house.

Cybe Alpha's emotion-suppression subroutine was failing again. He wanted to scream at the task force's two Soldiers in any one of 128 27th-century languages.

This mission had cost the Clan four Soldiers and three Welcomers. Not one of those nonbiologications had been achieved by Jimmy Upton; his women had been the Cybe-killers *every single time!* Surely it must have occurred to the Soldiers that, since they were clearly facing cyborgs like themselves, wouldn't it have been much better to have brought back a *live specimen?* Instead of an electrocuted piece of meat?

"But you do not understand," Cybe Alpha was told. "They shot at us. They killed some of us. That is disrespect; we could not let this go unpunished. They had to die for their crime, and instantly."

It was only because of the emotion-suppression subroutine that Cybe Alpha didn't frown. He sometimes wondered whether it was a mistake to turn Soldiers into Alpha Males. Yes, it made the men bigger and stronger, but let one of them get "disrespected" and his behavior became illogical.

So now Cybe Alpha's task was to make the most of the one good thing about this raid.

Correction: the one *barely* good thing.

The three surviving Cybes had managed to bring back only one of Jimmy Upton's electrified maybe-cyborgs: the one who'd stood next to him the entire time. The Cybes chose her because they thought that she was probably the Alpha for Jimmy Upton's hive.

Cybe Alpha got the report forty-seven 64-slobi later—

Two Welcomers stood in front of Cybe Alpha. One of them said, "The corpse is indeed a cyborg. However, it has none of the biohardware needed to generate a force field. What hardware the cyborg-corpse does have, is always modified to never look inhuman. Where the cyborg-corpse appeared different from a 21st-century Solitary woman, the only purpose for the changes was to enhance her sexual attractiveness."

"Yes, yes," Cybe Alpha replied, "but get to the important parts. Was she the Alpha? How many cyborg units were in Jimmy Upton's hive? What was the hive's mission?"

"This unit does not know," the spokes-Welcomer replied. "All biohardware—the hard drive, all biocircuitry, and all nanobots—are destroyed beyond salvage. However, this unit is convinced that the entire 'hive' consisted of nine women cyborgs in one house, whose entire mission was to give orgasms to Jimmy Upton."

Cybe Alpha smiled. "And now all but one of those cyborgs are nonbiological. It sounds like one big problem has been solved."

"Perhaps, perhaps not," the other Welcomer replied. "One cyborg of Jimmy Upton's hive escaped. Where is she now? What is she doing? Is she alone?"

3-1: Space Navy Undone

MEANWHILE, THREE DAYS EARLIER

At local time 3:26 a.m., a Cybe Soldier was wormholed inside the Missoula (Montana) Public Library. Ten minutes later, he had found the book *Relativity Explained Simply*.

The Soldier tore pages out of the book, laying the pages on the corner of a nearby table in the dark library. The Soldier put the de-paged book back on the shelf.

Then the Soldier picked up the torn-out pages. The Soldier, and the pages he held, got wormholed back to Cybe Base. The torn-out pages were destroyed.

At 2:44 that afternoon, Blaise Colburne was strolling through the Missoula Public Library when he noticed the book *Relativity Explained Simply*. He took that book off its shelf and sat down at a nearby table to read it. He got to enjoying the book, which had a breezy, plain-folks writing style.

Blaise finished reading Page 2, moved his eyes to the right to begin page 3—and the text jumped.

Blaise was confused, till he looked at the bottom of the page. Instead of the expected Page 3, he was looking at Page 5.

Blaise shrugged, silently cursed the unknown book-vandal, then went back to reading. After all, Page 5 still had that breezy, just-folks writing style. But when Blaise turned the page to read page 6, he noticed that after Page 6 came . . . *Page 9*?

Seconds later, Blaise discovered that out of the book's first 44 pages, 22 were torn out. Disgusted, Blaise threw the vandalized *Relativity Explained Simply* on the table, and went searching for something else to read.

Twenty minutes later, Blaise stood at the checkout desk. He handed over a science-fiction book by David Gerrold (with foreword by Harlan Ellison). A minute after that, Blaise was gone from the Missoula Public Library.

At 4:08, Terri Gundlach walked by the library table that Blaise Colburne had been sitting at.

But Blaise was no longer there.

Because Blaise wasn't there, he didn't say something flirty to Terri, she didn't say something flirty back, and so Blaise and Terri never met.

Because they never met, they never got married.

Because Blaise and Terri never married, there was never born a grandson, Zefram Colburne, in 2034.

As a result of Zefram Colburne not being born, no human successfully tested a human-invented wormholer on April 4, 2063; thus three Hephaistoan scientists didn't wormhole into Missoula on April 5, 2063, and so humans (in the person of Zefram Colburne) didn't make a great first impression on the Hephaistoans.

Instead, humans didn't test a wormholer for another 42 years, and then it was under conditions of strict military secrecy. When three Hephaistoans showed up to investigate, all three "aliens" were taken captive. One Hephaistoan was eventually killed, before a Hephaistoan army wormholed in and rescued the other two.

Needless to say, the planet Hephaistos was pissed at planet Earth.

How much pissed? By then, Earth was struggling with major problems that the Hephaistoans knew how to solve; but the Hephaistoans never uttered a peep, or lifted a finger, to help out Earth. "Let the savages rot!" was the Hephaistoan attitude.

So Earth never formed an alliance with the planet Hephaistos, so that alliance never expanded to become the Planetary Alliance. No Planetary Alliance meant no Space Navy.

In short: When one Cybe Soldier tore pages out of one book in the Missoula Public Library in 2013, he de-caused the Space Navy.

Now nobody would time-travel from the future to protect Earth from the Cybes.

AUTHOR'S NOTE: Let me pause and tell you about what happened to the timeship *ASS Antifreeze-D*. It was the crew of this Space Navy timeship who battled the Cybes back in Chapter 1-A.

Coming forward in time from 2008, the *Antifreeze* got copied when timelines branched. Three copies of the *Antifreeze* arrived in three timelines' version of 2652—

One Space Navy timeship returned to a version of 2652 in which the Space Navy existed, but the Cybes did not. John Windham-Smythe, captain of the *Antifreeze*, was immediately promoted to Admiral; the Space Navy took it for granted that no "primitive" 21st-century person could be the person who'd altered the timeline. John Windham-Smythe celebrated his promotion with a dinner of frog legs, *escargot*, and French champagne.

The second timeline is the timeline of this story. In this timeline, the *ASS Antifreeze-D* returned to a year 2652 in which Earth had six space navies, but not *a* Space Navy; and Earth was not part of any Planetary Alliance. Poor timeship, Captain Windham-Smythe didn't have his defenses up when he should have—the timeship was blasted to bits by the alienkiller *NASS Winnipeg*.

The third Space Navy timeship returned to an even worse version of 2652: There was no Space Navy because Earth had been completely Cybefied by 2063. Once again Captain Windham-Smythe didn't have the *Antifreeze*'s defenses up, so the crew was quickly captured. John Windham-Smythe yelled lines from *Les Misérables*, in the original French, at the Cybes just before they Welcomed him.

I return you to the soft-core time-travel melodrama in progress.

PART 4:
BATTLE FOR EARTH

4-A: Mass Layoffs

**BIMBORG KING'S PERSONAL LOG
DAY 1 (THURSDAY)**
Part A

My name is Charles Robert Owens. I'm named after a brother of my grandfather, who did something so brave in Vietnam that it earned him a medal. It also earned him a pine box.

Up till now, I didn't have a lot in common with Uncle Chuck. He was a 'C' student in high school, much more interested in working on cars than learning about the Battle of Hastings. Whereas I'm a brain, a geek, a nerd.

Even last week, I would've told you that the only thing that I had in common with Uncle Chuck was when I faced off against that gunman with the Uzi.

Now I have something else in common with him: An evil army is out there, and I must destroy it.

When the time came, Uncle Chuck did what he had to do, instead of run away. I vow to Earth's seven billion Solitaries, I will do no less.

Change of topic: I'm skipping school today (first time ever!) to spend all day surfing this Cybe computer. Besides, nothing important ever happens at school.

**LATER THAT MORNING
BEFORE FIRST PERIOD
SWEET ONION HIGH SCHOOL**

This morning, everyone in the high school wanted to talk to Regina Wisley—though not for the usual reasons.

This morning's *Vidal Voice* had reported that in one week, Regina's father was closing the Wisley Electronics assembly plant in Sweet Onion. In one week, every job necessary to make Wisley Electronics televisions, would be worked in China.

Now in the SOHS hallway, that skank Rose gave Prudy Lu Moffatt a friendly girly-wave, then she turned to look at Regina. Rose's smile was catty. "Ohmigod, Regina, I wonder if you'll still be Miss Popular a week from now. Poor girl, probably not."

Regina replied archly to Rose, "Everyone who works at the plant is getting a week's severance. Even the workers who don't deserve it. Two weeks' pay for one week's work—it's generous."

In a worried voice, Prudy Lu said, "China doesn't need another factory over there. But Sweet Onion needs these jobs to be *here*. My father needs his job here."

Regina gave Prudy Lu a too-sweet smile. "What can I say? The needs of the one, or the needs of the few, outweigh the needs of the many. That's because the few are rich, and the many are poor."

Rose said, "Wow, Regina, that is, like, really cold. Even for you."

Regina ignored Rose. Regina said to Prudy Lu, "Now, if your dad is really good at his job, he'll find another one, quick enough. Probably. If not, remember what they say, Hardship builds character."

Prudy Lu said, "You really don't care, do you? If your daddy can put a few extra dollars in his pocket, you really don't care what this does to *my* daddy."

Betsy Campbell (Busty Betsy) said nervously, "Prudy Lu, I think you're taking this too personally. Regina's dad is being nice about—"

"Really, Betsy? Remember Regina's slumber party, when you told me her dad groped your boobs? Was he also being 'nice' then?"

"How *dare* you!" Regina said. "Prudy Lu Moffatt, you will apologize *right now*, or—"

"Regina, your nose is too big, and your heart is too small," Prudy Lu said.

Prudy Lu turned to look at Rose. "Rose, will you be my friend?"

Prudy Lu stepped close to Charlie-Bob's girlfriend; then Prudy Lu turned slightly, so that her back was to Regina.

Seconds later, Rose's posse (which now included Prudy Lu) had walked away from Regina and Betsy.

Now Busty Betsy said nervously, "Um, Regina? Prudy Lu didn't really mean that. If you—"

"Doesn't matter what she *meant*. Doesn't matter if she regrets shit later. It only matters what she *said*. Nobody disses Regina Wisley and gets away with it. Remember that, Betsy."

Betsy gulped audibly.

BIMBORG KING'S PERSONAL LOG
DAY 1 (THURSDAY)
Part B

Surfing the Cybe hard drive today was definitely worth it. Today I learned about wormhole-making machines and about cloaker (invisibility) machines. I'm sure the Cybes have a portable version of each gizmo.

The tactically important thing that I learned about a wormholer? A portable wormholer can't transport itself. To get the wormholer from A to B, the Cybes have to haul it, by ground or air.

The trouble for the Cybes is, the more miles they travel, the more likely that some American will notice how weird the Cybes look, take their picture, and draw government attention to them.

So I figure they've set up a base of operations close to where they crashed, and cloaked it.

The trouble for the Cybes is, the cloaker device can't handle motion. When you look at a moving cloaked object, according to the Cybe hard drive, you see what was behind it 9 milliseconds earlier. Meaning that if a cloaked ship is moving to your right, you see objects behind the ship suddenly jump to the right. In space, with only stars for background, the effect isn't noticeable (unless your lookouts are sharp), so a cloaked Cybe ship can sneak up on you. But on the surface of a planet? What with clouds and trees and birds, moving a cloaked object around is asking to be noticed.

Then too, the cloaker can't work well when light from one of the planet's stars is close to the ground, because that makes long shadows. It turns out that long shadows don't look right at the edges of a cloaked zone; that's one way to figure out where the edges of the zone are. Then too, something called the "prism edge" shows up when a sun's light is very close to the ground.

I put all this together and I figure: The Cybe base is somewhere near where their ship crashed, and that base is cloaked. So I figure, if a bimborg looks at the Cybe base at sunrise or sunset, she'll spot it, whether cloaked or not.

Soon I will know where the Cybe base is. And then I will take the fight to them!

4-B: Cybes Spread Out

THE DAY AFTER JIMMY UPTON'S EXECUTION
CYBE ALPHA MOBILE HEADQUARTERS

Cybe Alpha told Cybe Gamma, "Activate the wormholer."

As Gamma complied with the order, Cybe Alpha looked over the crowd. Except for the Soldier who was formerly Eric Pfeiffer, all the Cybes gathered here were survivors of the crash of the timeship.

For the first time (and probably the last time), Cybe Alpha addressed the entire Clan by working his vocal cords, rather than by using the Overmind. Taking a deep breath, Cybe Alpha spoke—

"Today we begin the Welcoming of Earth, the ancestral home of most of us. In the 27th century, we Cybes were not able to Welcome Earth—it was too well defended!"

All the Cybe Soldiers frowned, hearing this.

Cybe Alpha continued, "This unit did not order us to be stranded here. This unit was not ordered by Time-Base to strand us here. But here we are. At last we can obey our prime directive"—to turn every sentient alien of any species into a Cybe—"on planet Earth."

Everyone except Cybe Alpha ritually clapped three times.

"This unit is sending you out in pairs, of one Soldier and one Welcomer. Soldiers, your task is to protect your Welcomer and all immature Cybes created by your Welcomer, and to stop Solitaries who would prevent others' Welcoming."

All Soldiers and all Welcomers now had serious expressions on their faces.

"Soldiers, during the three Earthdays that a Welcomed Solitary is an immature Cybe, that Cybe is helpless. This unit is counting on *you* to be attentive and protective during those three Earthdays, and deadly to any Solitaries who try to interfere."

Now all the Soldiers looked grim and determined.

"Where am I sending each pair of you? To a small city in an important Earth nation. By the time that people and armies in the largest cities ever see you, you will have overwhelming numbers on your side, without Solitaries ever having noticed."

All the Cybes smiled, hearing that. Correction: they *almost* smiled. "Now it is time to begin the Welcoming of Earth. Good randomness to you all."

Then the wormholer sent a pair of Cybes to each of these small cities:

• Bandar-e Abbas, Iran
• Magdeburg, Germany
• Vladivostok and Ulyanovsk, Russia
• Hakodate and Kure, Japan
• Liuzhou, Changzhi, and Xining, China
• Bristol, England
• Perth, Australia
• Hamilton, New Zealand
• Regina, Saskatchewan, Canada
• Boise, Idaho and Lubbock, Texas, USA
and
• Savannah, Georgia, USA

4-C: Cybes Go Recruiting

The two Cybes who wormholed into Boise, Idaho, USA were hard-chargers; they didn't wait. Only minutes after arriving in that city, the Cybe Soldier and Welcomer grabbed three high-school boys and three high-school girls. All six got promptly Welcomed.

Three days later, all three boys had become Soldiers and two of the girls had become Welcomers. Only Caroline Marcus looked and acted like her original self.

When Sol3-21-7, a.k.a. Caroline Marcus, first became operational, the first thing she told the Overmind was, "The local police are very probably looking for us units. The Clan made an error, grabbing us the way it did."

The reason for this estimation was Caroline herself, and how the FBI works. If prostitutes, ugly girls, or black girls disappear, the FBI stays on coffee break; but if a blond-haired, blue-eyed girl with "stripper tits" goes missing, the FBI leaps into action. Well, Caroline Marcus was a major babe.

Once Caroline Marcus informed the Clan of its mistake, she convinced the Clan that her staying missing was a danger to the Clan.

As a result, she was promptly wormholed close to a police station in Boise's rough side. Caroline claimed to police to have partial amnesia: Supposedly she didn't know how she'd gotten to that part of town, and supposedly she didn't know where her five friends were. The police believed her (she showed them Cybe Soldier-inflicted bruises that were deliberately not nanobot-healed), and she was quickly returned to her family.

Caroline had naturally blonde hair, naturally light-blue eyes, the facial bones of a cover model, and tits so big that "her nipples enter a room fifteen minutes before her shoulders do." Caroline Marcus now was also a Cybe Invisible.

Bandar-e Abbas, Iran is a city on the Strait of Hormuz; dealing with foreigners is how the city makes money. So one would expect the Iranians there to have seen plenty of strange-looking people, and to be blasé about them. If one thought that, one would be wrong.

Cybe units Sol3-21-2 (the Soldier who was formerly Eric Pfeiffer) and Obermann4-27-38726288 (a Welcomer woman) were walking along a street at night. A bearded man pointed to them. "Look at that wicked woman!" he yelled (in Farsi). "She wears no *hijab*, no *burka*."

People turned their heads to look. "Let's see, let's see," several people said.

Soon the two Cybes found their walk blocked by a dozen men. "She flouts our laws," a second bearded man said. "Even infidel women know they should cover their heads in Iran."

"What should be done with her?" a third man asked.

"Take her to the police?" a fourth man replied. "Or to a cleric?"

Up till this point, the Cybes had stood there patiently, waiting for a path forward to present itself. The Cybes would have continued to stand there, waiting—till solar midnight, if necessary. Religious ranting was not addressed by their programming.

The first man said, "There is no one to see if we deal with her ourselves. Stone her." So saying, he threw a rock at the Welcomer.

Cybe-Eric stepped in front of the rock. His purple shield flashed, and the rock fell to the ground, with Cybe-Eric unharmed.

"Indeed, there is no one to see what happens now," Cybe-Eric replied (in Farsi).

Cybe-Eric raised his arm, and electrified the entire mob.

He didn't kill them. They were still alive when Welcomer-6288 walked into their midst, stabbing their necks with her nanobot-needle again and again. In Farsi she was chanting, "The Overmind calms you. The Overmind frees you from emotion. The Overmind gives knowledge. We Welcome you into the Overmind."

When she had completed her task, a wormhole opened up, and Cybe-Eric carried the stunned and Welcomed men through it.

Roughly one 64-slobi later, the wormhole closed, and that street in Bandar-e Abbas became empty again.

In Lubbock, the Texas Tech Red Raiders football team had just finished practice. Once in the home-team locker room, they removed their alternate football jerseys (black on red).

SSSSOOM.

Two oddly-dressed people, a man and a woman, walked out of the shower room.

The man actually had bigger muscles than most of the football players, and this should have made them hesitate. But around each other, the only fear that each man would admit to was for a career-ending injury. While each of them was aware that back in his hometown, he had been the *cause* of fear since the age of fourteen.

In short, it never occurred to any of the 22 nearly-naked men in the locker room, that they maybe needed to fear the muscular stranger.

The other stranger didn't make the football players hesitate at all. A woman came into a locker room for only one reason, they figured.

"Hey, girlie, the comic-book store is on 34th Street," said Tim, the team's self-styled comedian. "So you must be here looking for something else, hm?"

"Father Joe" spoke up: "Girl, this isn't a good place for you. Walk out now while you still can."

"Fuck that shit, Father Joe," Tim said. "She wants a gang-bang, I say let's give her one."

"Mountain," about whom there were "rumors" (wink, wink) that he took steroids, looked across the room at the big stranger. "I could beat you up all by myself. Add to me these other guys, and you'd go to the hospital for sure. But walk out now, and we won't hurt you. Of course, the girl stays."

"Damned straight, the girl stays," Davie said. "You ever suck a running back's dick, honey? This is your lucky day."

Billy, the starting quarterback, simply walked up to the girl and picked her up. He was planning to lay her down on the bench.

The big stranger didn't move. The girl didn't scream, nor did she yell anything. Instead, her left hand zipped as quickly as a snake, stabbing Billy in the back of the neck.

"Son of a bitch!" Billy said. Both he and the girl dropped to the floor.

Neither stranger spoke, and the big man did not move.

The woman stood up. Billy tried to stand up, but his legs were wobbly. "Y'all, I feel really. . .weird," he said. Then he froze, mannequin-still.

The woman started chanting something about an "Overmind."

Father Joe said, "Something weird is going on. I say, let them both leave now. No flag, no penalty, just let them leave."

"Fuck that, Father Joe," said Mountain. "It's time to hurt the bitch, and the lunkhead with her."

Mountain's arm shot out. He grabbed the stranger-woman's arm and yanked her toward him. He lifted her off the ground and pulled her face next to his. Yet her face showed no fear.

At last, the stranger-man moved. He raised his left arm a little, and pointed his entire arm at Mountain's feet. Mountain was shocked by what the stranger-man did next.

The defensive coach walked into the locker room five minutes later. He found the locker room to be empty except for cast-off red clothing, but he didn't worry about it then.

During the next three days, none of the football players attended football practice, and none attended classes. The head football coach got alarmed, eventually phoning the Texas Rangers. However, professors and other students noticed nothing unusual about football players missing class.

Also absent from classes? The entire Zeta Zeta Zeta sorority (a.k.a. "the ladies in red").

4-D: A Letter From James

BIMBORG KING'S PERSONAL LOG
DAY 2 (FRIDAY)
Part A

> *I went back to school today, telling everyone I'd been sick yesterday. Such is my reputation as a nerd, nobody asked to see the (forged) note from my mom. Besides, what student skips school on Thursday but comes in on Friday?*
>
> *After school, Rose and I went to Mary Kayla's apartment so I could surf the Cybe computer some more.*
>
> *In the apartment we found not only Miss Turner and the Cybe computer, but also Lucille, a beautiful young brunette whom I'd never seen before.*
>
> *When I went to bed that night, I'd been given a lot to think about. For security reasons, I will say no more.*

Mary Kayla made the introduction, seconds after Charlie-Bob and Rose-unit had walked into the apartment.

"King Charlie-Bob," the bimborg teacher said, "This is Lucille-47893. She was in King James' house when he and Stephanie-1 were killed. She is here to give you a report."

Charlie-Bob noted that Lucille-unit had a beautiful face, and she had large (but not Pleasure Unit-sized) tits. Indeed, she had no warts on her left hand, and her arms and legs had well-defined muscles. Lucille-unit was wearing a lavender backpack.

She also was wearing a pink blouse that was held together with a safety pin, because several buttons were missing.

Charlie-Bob gestured at the safety pin. "What's the story with *that?*"

Lucille-unit shrugged. "A trucker tried to force this unit to pay for my hitchhike. Do you wish details?"

"Thanks, no. So you're an Ass-Kicker Babe? I've never met one before. Or are you a Spy Babe?"

Lucille-unit confirmed that she was an Ass-Kicker Babe, then, at Charlie-Bob's order, she gave her report—

"...heard King James mock the Cybes: 'You've killed all of mine except Stephanie, but we killed *seven* of yours. Great! Tsk-tsk, four Cybe Soldiers dead because they didn't pay attention.'"

"They killed four Soldiers?" Charlie-Bob said. "I thought those guys could put up force-fields."

"From my observation post, this unit could see only two Soldiers actually get killed. But in each case, something distracted the Soldier just before he was killed, so he didn't put up his purple shield."

"So kill Soldiers by distraction. Got it," Charlie-Bob said. "You have anything else to report?"

"Yes. This unit saw Stephanie-1 get electrocuted after she shot King James. By *both* Soldiers, not just one."

"Ohmigod," Rose said, "that stuff is *true*, then."

"What stuff is true?" Charlie-Bob said. "I'm lost here."

Lucille-unit said, "King James once told Stephanie-1 that Cybes have an emotion-suppression subroutine which doesn't work well. For Soldiers, it doesn't work at all, so they're always acting all Alpha Male. Well, it's true. Stephanie-1 only needed to be electrocuted once to be killed; but this unit saw both Soldiers zap her. Clearly because she'd angered them."

Charlie-Bob still wasn't understanding. Rose-unit glanced at his face, then she asked Lucille-unit, "What was the Welcomer doing in the meantime?"

"She was walking up behind King James, about to needle him in his spine. Just before she could, was when Stephanie-1 shot him."

Mary Kayla turned to Charlie-Bob. "Their plan was obviously to Welcome him, find out everything he knew, then kill him. But with one bullet, Stephanie-1 thwarted their evil plot. So the Soldiers then *super*killed her."

Lucille-unit said, "King James once told Stephanie-1 that he fixed the emotion-suppression subroutine. So every bimborg is, every moment, calm inside. Even when"—she plucked at the safety pin that was holding her blouse together—"she's about to be raped."

Charlie-Bob nodded. "So here's how we stack up. Bimborg outnumber the Cybes right now, but that's going to change in a few years. Cybe Soldiers have force-fields, if they know to put them up; no bimborg has anything like that. Cybes get emotional, and Soldiers anger easily; bimborg never feel emotion."

Rose and Mary Kayla both nodded at this. "That is correct," Lucille said.

"This unit have one other task," Lucille said, as she pulled the lavender backpack off her back. "King James ordered this unit to take this to you, 'Kill if necessary.'"

By now Lucille had the backpack on the floor. She unzipped it and pulled out a red hardback book, seven inches wide, ten inches tall, and two inches thick.

Charlie-Bob read the title. "It's a college dictionary. What's special about it?"

Lucille-unit set the dictionary on a corner of the computer desk, and opened the book. Inside, the book had been hollowed out, so that it contained a sheet-metal box with a USB connection, a toggle switch, and a red indicator light. Also on the outside of the box, a small electronic thing was pressed against the side wall of a glass tube.

"What is that? What does it do?" he asked.

Lucille-unit pulled the gizmo out of the dictionary, handed the gizmo to Rose, then flipped the pages to the dictionary's front cover. Inside the book was a sealed white envelope. Lucille-unit handed the envelope to Charlie-Bob.

Seconds later, he read—

Final greetings, Successor!

If you're reading this, it means that the Cybes have whacked me, but an Ass-Kicker Babe has delivered this message to you, along with a verbal report and a metal box. Let me tell you about the metal box.

The glass thing that you see is an ampule with helium gas inside. When a tachyon or anti-tachyon particle with a certain minimum energy hits a helium nucleus, it makes the helium nucleus give off light of a certain frequency. No matter how much energy the (anti) tachyon particle has, the helium nucleus acts the same: yellow-green light for 0.005 seconds, or else nothing happens at all.

I'll skip over all the technological uses for this. They're spelled out on the Cybe hard drive; start with the file called "Overmind Speech.text". But here's what you need to know—

Any two Cybes, or any two bimborg, can speak to each other if they're less than 34,000 miles apart. Furthermore, since (anti) tachyons travel through anything solid with no problem, it doesn't matter if the two Cybes are separated by the vacuum of space, Earth's atmosphere, or 8,000 miles of solid rock.

That's the good news. Once you've read all the data that the Anti-Tachyon Signal Analyzer (that's the metal box) has recorded, you can listen to any Overmind conversation between any two Cybes who are anywhere on the planet, as easily as you can hear your parents across the dinner table.

The bad news is, because there is no solid material that (anti) tachyons will bounce off of, you can't create a directional antenna for Cybe broadcasts. Meaning, you can't tell whether the Cybe to whom you're listening is somewhere in China, or is in a car parked across the street from your house.

This trait works the other way, by the way. Even if all X million bimborg were blabbing away in The Club, the Cybes couldn't pinpoint even one bimborg. But preventing any bimborg from being triangulated is not why I ordered my women to go "radio silent."

Anyway, back to the Anti-Tachyon Signal Analyzer. Whenever the Cybes attack my house, I figure that there will be a lot of conversation, using the Overmind, between Cybe Alpha and the Cybes in my house. Meanwhile, the ATSA will be analyzing all the anti-tachyon bursts, trying to discover the Overmind's carrier frequency.

Once the Analyzer tells you the Overmind's frequency, you can build something like a police-band radio to listen in on Cybe conversations when they use their Overmind. This is what the schematic at the end of this letter is for.

Only after you're listening to Overmind conversations will you discover what language the Cybes are talking to each other in. If you're lucky, the Cybes will be using Galactic English, the same language as the Cybe hard drive. But probably not; most likely, they'll be talking to each other in Cybespeak. Fortunately, there is a complete tutorial on Cybespeak on the Cybe hard drive. Whichever Ass-Kicker Babe has delivered this message to you, has learned Cybespeak and can translate the words for you.

[Snip]

I've done all I can to protect you. If the Cybes knew that there was another Bimborg King, and they knew where to find you, the Cybes could use their wormholer and they'd send ten Soldiers straight to your bedroom to kill you, without your parents in the living room thinking anything was wrong.

The only good defense against a wormholer, by the way, is a wormholer of your own.

[Snip]

I don't think that the Cybes suspect that there are any bimborg outside my house, much less X million of them, because I stopped my girls from doing any anti-tachyon conversations themselves. I don't think the Cybes suspect that there is another Bimborg King out there, because I've left no information about you on my computer or my smartphone.

Surprise, Cybes!

The Cybes have Soldiers, and Soldiers have force-fields. But you and the bimborg have two advantages. Cybe Soldiers can be angered into acting irrationally, while bimborg never lose their cool. Also, you have the element of Surprise.

Surprise the Cybes well and surprise them often, make the Soldiers act stupid, and you will win.

Go boldly. Save Earth.

BIMBORG KING'S PERSONAL LOG
DAY 2 (FRIDAY)
Part B

When I was in fourth grade, Dad drove us to Lionheart, to the Georgia Star Drive-In, to see <u>Windsword and Firesteel</u>. When we got there, I found out that the drive-in's other screen was showing <u>The</u>

Pacifier, a *Vin Diesel* comedy. I was so torn, because I wanted to see both movies!

Dad and I walked to the snack bar, where he bought us a *huge* tub of popcorn. I choked when the girl told Dad the price, but he paid every dollar with a smile.

Walking back to our car from the snack bar, I noticed that the entire drive-in was surrounded by a six-foot-tall fence of sheet metal. I'd never seen that before, and said something to Dad. He explained that it kept people inside the drive-in from seeing headlights of cars outside the drive-in. I stopped walking, and sure enough, I now could hear cars outside the drive-in, but I couldn't see them.

Once the movie started, Dad let me sit in the front seat by myself—it was just me and the popcorn. Mom and Dad sat in the back seat, which I thought was a big sacrifice for them, because I knew they couldn't see the movie too good from back there.

Sometime during the movie, I noticed a weird smell. So I innocently asked, "What's that smell?"

My mom gasped, my dad chuckled, and then Dad said, "Don't worry about the smell, Charlie-Bob. Trust me, everything's fine."

It's only now, as I write this, that I've figured out what the smell was. Geez, *Mom and Dad were playing around in the back seat while I was watching the movie!* Eww.

Anyway, I loved *Windsword and Firesteel.* It was like the movie was made just for me. I told kids at school to go see it.

Not long after that, the Georgia Star Drive-In went bust. But nobody ever bought it, not even to tear it down and build something else. By now (2013), the Georgia Star looks really raggedy.

Correction: Nobody ever bought it *till now.* Rose talked to Linda-5, who apparently is a genie at anything connected to the internet, and together they've bought the drive-in for me. I'm going to use it as a staging area when we attack the Cybes. The same fence that stopped insiders from seeing out in 2005, now means that outsiders can't see what we're doing inside.

Change of topic: I came up with something to help bimborg communications. I can be sure that it's not on any futuristic Cybe computer, because it's something I just made up.

"You invented a language?" Rose asked Charlie-Bob.

"I call it *Bimborgspeak*. See, I found out recently that any Cybe is programmed to be fluent in 128 languages, and has a vocabulary of 1,024 words in 2,048 languages more. Want to know how to say 'We Welcome you into the Overmind' in 25th-century Navaho? It's on that hard drive."

"Fine, so, like, Cybes could all get A's in French. What's that got to do with you?"

"James built the 'fluent in 128 languages' part into you bimborg. So for instance, every bimborg is fluent in Danish and American English, right?"

In reply, Rose said something that sounded like German, but wasn't.

Charlie-Bob continued, "So I wrote a computer program that made up words. Like *skwurdu* and *krodzi*. Then I invented a grammar, and came up with sentences. Last, I wrote a text-to-speech program for my words, so I can record my new language on MP3. Here, check it out!"

Charlie-Bob clicked on a sentence that said "Priscilla was murdered yesterday, and her brother is sad."

What came out of the computer speakers was this—

Ze-skishne po X kek Priscilla mesiteg, gro po crakhawa tri fle shlosmepo ratcho.

Rose repeated it: "*Ze-skishne po X kek Priscilla mesiteg, gro po crakhawa tri fle shlosmepo ratcho.*"

Charlie-Bob noticed that Rose didn't pause, didn't stammer, and her pronunciation was perfect.

The Cybes knew the results of the 2016 presidential election and the 2216 election; and they knew the final score of Super Bowl CCC.

But the Cybes wouldn't know Bimborgspeak. Maybe it wasn't much, but the bimborg now had a tool that the Cybes didn't have.

4-E: Good Guys Prepare

DAY 3 (SATURDAY)
Dawn

At a few minutes after dawn, Spy Babe Amanda-8559249 was flying over Kirk County, Iowa in a rented helicopter.

Amanda-unit had chosen her words to make the helicopter pilot think that she was doing some kind of land-investment survey; but her true mission was to find the cloaked Cybe Base if it was here.

Amanda-unit's looks were only on the "pretty" side of ordinary, with short brown hair. She would never be mistaken for a Pleasure Unit, for sure. But Spy Babes had better eyes than even Ass-Kicker Babes, and Amanda-unit lived within driving distance of Kirk County. So it was Amanda whom King James had assigned to fly in the helo.

When the pilot and Amanda-unit flew near the Mudd farm, where the timeship had crashed, she saw nothing unexpected. As the helicopter continued to fly south over County Road 1701, everything stayed ordinary.

That is, till they approached the Kelly farm.

One mile north of the Kelly farmhouse, in the middle of a wheat field, long shadows suddenly stopped and started. The places on the ground where shadows went wrong described straight lines; and if these straight lines were connected on the ground, they'd make a perfect hexagonal shape.

Then too, there was a thin line floating in the air over the place where the shadows went wrong. The line was so thin that only a Spy Babe could see it. The line's color shifted, from indigo on the left side, to lemon yellow on top, to red on the right side.

All this Amanda-unit learned at a glance, during a look of a mere one-24th of a second. As far as the pilot could tell, Amanda had no interest in the Kelly farm's wheat field at all.

Seconds later, Amanda made a smartphone call: "No dice. Lots of kelly-green worthlessness down here." This was code for *Found the Cybes, at the Kelly farm.*

Charlie-Bob yelled "YES!" and pumped his fist when he was given Amanda-unit's message.

"You're dead meat now, Cybes!" Charlie-Bob said, grinning.

Cybe Alpha and Cybe Gamma (formerly the Navigator-unit) stood outside the cloaker "curtain" and watched the helicopter fly a southward course. The helicopter was a primitive, 21st-century machine; it had no vertical takeoff/landing ability, and its engines were the wrong size and shape for burning hydrogen.

"Are the Solitaries in that helicopter spying on us?" Gamma asked.

"With our cloaker engaged? This unit does not think so," Cybe Alpha said. "Notice its painting. It does not belong to the United States Army, or to any other Clan of the United States Government."

Gamma pressed: "What if it spots us? It *can* spot us now, so soon after local sunrise. This unit recommends that you drop cloaking, then order Soldiers to bring that helicopter down."

"No, that would *definitely* bring the United States Army here. But now? Even if a Solitary were looking at us, would he realize what he was seeing?"

One 64-slobi later, Cybe Alpha said, "But you are right to point out the danger. There is a slim chance that the Solitaries in that helicopter have spotted us and have reported us to someone who can trouble us."

LATER THAT MORNING
ATLANTA, GEORGIA

"Ohmigod, could you, like, sell me the stuff on this list, please? My boyfriend needs all this stuff *real* bad, you know?"

On the same sunny Saturday, this happened at industrial wholesale businesses throughout Atlanta, again and again—

A business whose counter-helpers were used to selling to repairmen in coveralls, or to casually dressed engineering students from Georgia Tech, now were visited by mega-sexy, big-breasted young women.

The hotties click-clacked through the door on high heels, and they filled the counter-men's nostrils with the smell of perfume. Each woman's purchase list was written in purple ink, or on pink paper (or both), dotting her *i*'s with hearts.

Many of the babes were wearing tight and/or ripped t-shirts proclaiming universities in or near Atlanta—U. of Georgia, Georgia State University, and Emory University. But oddly, there was no major babe wearing a black-and-yellow Georgia Tech t-shirt.

Once she'd sashayed to the counter, each woman smiled a lot. Each woman giggled a lot. Each woman answered the question "What does your boyfriend need all this for?" with the same answer—

Giggle "Gosh, I'm so sorry, but I don't remember, you know? Lots of stuff he talks about, I *sooo* don't understand."

One man put a hairy finger on one of the purple-written items on the list in front of him. "Your boyfriend must be a physics professor, if he's even *heard* of this thing."

The blonde in the tight Emory University t-shirt gave the man a dazzling smile. "He isn't a physics professor, but we went to the same high school and, ohmigod, he's smart."

MEANWHILE
PALMER ELECTRONICS SHOP
LOGANVILLE, GEORGIA
29 MILES EAST OF DOWNTOWN ATLANTA

Bob-Lee Palmer had let the diesel generator run for ten minutes, watching the gauges all the while. Now he opened the master breaker, then shut down the diesel generator.

With an oven mitt covering his hand to protect it, he rapped on the diesel, and pulled on some of its parts. Satisfied, he started the diesel generator back up, took off the oven mitt, then walked from the generator shack to the main shop building.

Palmer Electronics Shop had metal-working machines, just like in a regular machine shop. It also had a plastic-extruding machine and a computer-chip burner. Palmer Electronics had been set up to handle whatever subcontract work a manufacturer in Atlanta might need. In 1984, Palmer Electronics seemed like a worthy idea, because in 1984 what upper-manager in Atlanta would think of giving work to those commie Chinese?

Now in 2013, Bob-Lee walked up to the only other person in the dusty building, "Elena," a brown-skinned young woman who wore a "Georgia Bulldogs" t-shirt. The tits under that shirt *had to be* implants.

"There you go, ma'am," Bob-Lee said. "Use of my shop for 72 hours, complete with electricity, same rent for each 72 hours if you stay here. Now I need to ask you—"

"Elena" gave Bob-Lee a practiced smile, even as she was taking her purse off her shoulder. "I have the payment right here," she said. "Every penny, in cash. Don't worry."

Actually, Bob-Lee was worried quite a bit. Unfortunately, he couldn't afford to pass up the offered money; Palmer Electronics had stood empty since March of last year.

As Bob-Lee was counting the cash—small, unmarked bills, he noted—he asked the girl, "How likely is it that the Feds will catch y'all doing whatever, and trace it back to me?"

"We won't be doing anything illegal, Mr. Palmer," she said with a toothpaste-ad smile. "Do I look like that kind of girl?"

Seventeen automobiles from Atlanta started arriving at Palmer Electronics an hour later.

Each automobile was driven by a Pleasure Unit/Welcomer. Each Pleasure Unit had stiletto heels laying on the passenger seat, but she was wearing sensible shoes when she stepped out of her car. Each Pleasure Unit opened the back door or the trunk of her car, brought out a sleeping bag and a bag of food, and carried them into Palmer Electronics Shop. She needed neither the food nor the sleeping bag, but Mr. Palmer, the owner, might notice their absence.

Then each Pleasure Unit went back outside to her car, and carried in the items she'd bought earlier that day.

Some of those purchases in car trunks required the teamwork of two, or even three, Pleasure Units in order to be carried in.

About which, Lisabelle-739562 said, "At times like this, I wish I'd been made an Ass-Kicker Babe instead. To be stronger than a Solitary man? It would be useful—and, like, really *fun!*"

Rhonda-582966 shook her head. "But men don't look when an Ass-Kicker Babe walks into the room, you know? But ohmigod, any one of us walks into a room, and men *drool.*" Rhonda hefted her tits. "Especially now."

Carmenita (who was known to Bob-Lee Palmer as "Elena") raised a finger. "Men drooling is why I'll be the only one of us to buy groceries in town, y'hear? Otherwise the cops are gonna decide we're shooting a porno here."

The Pleasure Units spent the rest of Saturday evening talking to each other, and dusting and sweeping the electronics shop (which was filthy), all while planning their upcoming work.

This was quite a change from their lives as Solitaries, during which these same women had spent Saturday nights being plied with liquor, sucking, and fucking.

The Pleasure Units all stood there openmouthed when Amy-845639, a Pleasure Unit attending Emory, told how she and Heather-unit, a Pleasure Unit dentist, had shot and killed two armed men. As Solitaries, every one of the Pleasure Units had felt endangered by a man at least once.

BIMBORG KING'S PERSONAL LOG
DAY 3 (SATURDAY)

Yesterday I posted some MP3 files and text files to the Bimborg website. They were available for downloading for 25 hours, then I ordered the webmistress to do a whole bunch of file erasing. Not only were my files of yesterday erased, but all the English-language pages on the website were replaced with their Bimborgspeak translations.

This is amazing: Three minutes after my new language's files were available for download, bimborg started posting comments that were written entirely in Bimborgspeak.

Tonight I heard Rose and L****** talking in Bimborgspeak for several minutes. I maybe could understand one word in ten. And I'm the guy who invented the stupid language!

4-F: Regina Meets A Man

MEANWHILE, THAT SATURDAY EVENING
REGINA WISLEY'S CONVERTIBLE
SAVANNAH, GEORGIA

Endicott "Bull" Barclay had been apologetic when he'd broken his Saturday-night date with Regina. "I have to work on my English paper," he'd said.

Oh please, Regina had thought at the time.

But now that Regina was free, had her smartphone run down its battery, ringing and ringing with other guys each calling to lock in a Saturday-night date with himself? Nope, nobody had called.

Not. One. Fucking. Guy.

If that skank Rose O'Connor were in the car right now, she'd be laughing her ass off and mocking Regina: *I, like, told you you'd be shunned. Ohmigod, your daddy just got rid of the only reason for anyone to act nice to you!*

Dammit, Regina was *not* being shunned! After all, wasn't Busty Betsy in the passenger seat, right alongside Regina?

Speaking of whom. . .

"Why did you make me break my date with Georgie LeFord?" Betsy asked. "I was really wanting to see *Beverly Plays Doctor.*"

The true answer was quite simple: *If I'm going to be miserable on a Saturday night, Betsy, why should you get to be happy?*

But what Regina said aloud was "Oh come on, a break in routine does anyone good. Besides, this way, I and you enjoy a little 'retail therapy.'" Regina gestured to Lone Pine Mall's Dillard's store, close to which was where Regina was parking.

"That's another thing," Betsy said. "Why can't we go to Oglethorpe Mall instead? Stores there aren't all going bust, unlike stores here."

"Because I'm driving, and I like Lone Pine Mall," Regina replied. "When you have a car of your own, you can drive to Galleria Mall in Dallas, for all I care."

"Rose is right," Betsy said. "You can be really mean sometimes." Betsy wouldn't be getting a car till graduation, and Regina knew that.

By now both girls were out of the convertible, and Regina was locking its doors. "*Rose is right*'? I don't want to hear one more goddamn mention of Rose until I attend her funeral, got it?"

"Okay, fine. So here we are at Rundown Mall. Let's shop."

"After we hit the restroom," Regina said. "I need to piss like a racehorse."

"Why are you so crabby tonight?" Betsy said as they entered the ladies' restroom. "Jeez, we won the stupid game, so cheer up."

"Whatever," Regina said.

Want to know why I'm crabby, Betsy? Because for one thing, before Thursday you seldom gave me back-talk. Is it too much to ask that even one person in Sweet Onion still act nice to me?

But for once, Regina didn't say the nasty things she was thinking. Regina had suffered through three days of nastiness, after kids at school had learned Daddy was closing the plant, and she was rattled.

The two Sweet Onion cheerleaders walked toward the restroom stalls. But just before Regina pulled her stall's door open, the door opened by itself.

Regina found herself facing a red-faced man who was almost as tall as Bull, but wider in the shoulders. The red-faced man also was dressed like someone out of a drive-in science-fiction movie.

To Regina's left, she heard Betsy gasp.

Then Regina heard a woman's voice, which wasn't Betsy's: "The Overmind calms you. The Overmind frees you from emotion. The Overmind gives knowledge. We Welcome you into the Overmind."

Regina took only an instant to glance to her left. Also stepping out of a restroom stall, now facing Betsy, was a red-faced woman. She was wearing even less metal costuming than the man was.

Regina turned her attention back to the man. She knew how to deal with men: Intimidate, threaten, and insult them. "What the fuck are you doing in the women's restroom, pervert? Get out of here! But stay away from me, creep, or my daddy will sue your ass off."

The red-faced man didn't cringe, he didn't sneer, and he didn't glower and scowl. He just kept walking toward Regina, with the same wooden expression.

Then Regina felt something brush against her butt. Betsy, who had been farther from the entrance door, was running away!

Betsy had had enough.

Always before, Regina had said "Jump," and Betsy had said "How high?"

So when the home game had ended, and Regina had said to Betsy, "Break your date. Let's go shopping in Savannah," Betsy hadn't even thought of saying no.

And what had this sacrifice gotten her? At any time during the drive, had Regina said even once, "Thank you for coming with me, you're the only friend I have left"? Nope, Regina had acted like Betsy's perfect obedience were Regina's rightful due.

Betsy had sat in the car, during the hour and a half that the drive took, and had felt ashamed of herself.

She didn't *need* to stay on Regina's good side, the way that Prudy Lu did, because Regina's father couldn't threaten Betsy's father the way he could threaten Prudy Lu's. And yet it was Prudy Lu, not Betsy, who had told Regina to take a hike.

Now Betsy and Regina were facing two weirdos in the Ladies' Room of a mall that Betsy didn't even want to be at, the Weird Lady was chanting about an Overmind, Betsy was scared shitless, and how was Regina handling the danger? By *giving orders.*

Regina was closer to the entrance door than Betsy was. All Regina had to do was turn and run, and she could maybe get away. If Regina did run away, Betsy knew that Regina wouldn't give a single thought to helping Betsy escape her own danger. Regina would escape, and Betsy would be left behind to get raped—

Or worse.

No way, Betsy thought. She ran for the entrance door, brushing against Regina's butt in the process.

Regina stopped playing Queen Of The Restroom long enough to look at Betsy in annoyance. "What are you doing? *Stay here.*"

Betsy started to say, "I'm going to find Mall Secu—"

The Weird Lady stepped up behind Regina and did something with her left hand. Regina *stopped*, just like someone had pressed her Pause button.

Regina's face then went slack. Her shoulders slumped, and her purse slid off her shoulder. A few seconds later, yellow liquid started running down her legs.

Betsy ran to the entrance door and yanked it open.

When Betsy returned to the Ladies' Room with a lesbian-looking security guard, they found a puddle of smelly yellow liquid on the floor; Regina's purse lay on the floor, by the puddle. Nothing was missing from Regina's purse.

Weird Man, Weird Lady, and Regina all were gone from the restroom, somehow without any of them showing up on cameras.

4-G: She Escaped, Really?

DAY 4 (SUNDAY)
PALMER ELECTRONICS
LOGANVILLE, GEORGIA

Early Sunday morning, the Pleasure Units climbed out of their sleeping bags, three hours after they'd gone to bed. They ate a small breakfast, then began work. By then, nine laptop computers had been set up, one computer near two bimborg.

Every woman followed instructions to the letter. No one on Planet Earth had ever done work like this before, but the bimborg understood how crucial it was that everything be done right.

DAY 4 (SUNDAY)

Not all the high-tech stuff that had been bought in Atlanta, was brought to Loganville.

At the same time on Sunday morning that eighteen bimborg in Loganville were machining the first parts for the wormholer, a breasty and attractive FedEx girl was handing an overnighted parcel to Mary Kayla at her apartment complex in Sweet Onion.

As soon as Charlie-Bob walked into Mary-unit's apartment, he asked about the parcel. He was told that Lucille already had it open and was trying to build the 27th-century technology he wanted.

BIMBORG KING'S PERSONAL LOG
DAY 4 (SUNDAY)

While I was surfing the Cybe computer today, Lucille built me an Artificial Sensation helmet and a force-field repeller from the parts that Amy Emily sent from Atlanta. As I understand it, Artificial Sensation is what Virtual Reality wishes it were: Artificial Sensation fools the parts of your brain that deal with the five senses into seeing stuff (or hearing stuff, or feeling stuff) that isn't there.

The force-field repeller is a cool toy! Lucille pushes the "Test" button, and suddenly I feel like I landed belly-side-down on a trampoline, and then the trampoline pushes me away. Except that instead of being pushed upward, I'm pushed away from the repeller.

Why did I have Lucille build these gizmos for me? As much danger as I'm in now, I need to know how to take care of myself. On the Cybe hard drive, I found a program that will teach me Edo-kobushi (Tokyo Fist), a 24th-century martial art. That's great, except that I need an A.S. helmet to use the program.

Lucille and I loaded the program tonight. Then I put the helmet in a cardboard box, the repeller in another box, and took them to my house. I've decided that our two-car garage, with both cars parked outside, will become my gymnasium.

Once I got into the empty garage, I intended to start Lesson One. But after I clicked on the menu bar, I saw floating blue letters that said, "Begin kata." Below that, letters in red said, "Pain suppression off." Shit, that didn't sound good!

While I was wondering what the messages meant, my body started moving, without me telling it to! I started with stretches, then started doing this slow-motion, stretchy dance that I knew from movies had to be a kata. I tried telling various muscles to stop moving; no change. I tried to flex opposing muscles, so to lock a limb in place; those muscles stayed relaxed. All my resistance was futile.

Meanwhile, I figured out what the "pain suppression off" message meant: My tendons did not like some of the stretches that the kata was making them do!

After five minutes, I saw another floating message. Blue letters said, "End kata. Pain suppression on." With that, my muscles obeyed me again.

Now warmed up, I began Lesson One, which is punching a punching bag. To add challenge, red circles appear at different places on the punching bag, disappearing after two seconds. If you hit one of the red circles before it disappears, you hear a tinkling bell.

I can't describe how weird Artificial Sensation is. Just before lesson One started, I was looking at Dad's workbench, I could hear country music playing from someone's backyard, and nothing was right in front of me. But when I activated the program, suddenly I was in a *white dojo, a punching bag was hanging from the ceiling in front of me, and I was hearing no sound but soothing music. Then the word <u>Demo</u> appeared in blue letters, floating in the air. Like with the <u>kata</u>, my left arm and then my right arm shot out without my control. So I punched the bag without deciding to. I could feel my knuckles hit, and feel each arm stop dead, as if the heavy bag were really there. After the word <u>Demo</u> disappeared, then I could control my body again.*

In the program, all the Menu Items are solid letters that are glued to the dojo's ceiling. You look at a set of words and blink, and this acts like double-clicking a mouse. I exited the program by blinking on "End session and heal? Y/N." Why is the question worded like that?

Change of topic: Regina Wisley has been kidnapped! This is according to Rose, who heard it from Prudy Lu, who heard it from Betsy Campbell, who was right there! Apparently the kidnappers are role-playing geeks. I haven't liked Regina since fourth grade, but nobody deserves shit like this.

BIMBORG KING'S PERSONAL LOG
DAY 5 (MONDAY)

Tonight I studied Lesson Two, which is shoulder rolls. But before the lesson began, again I lost control of my body for five minutes and performed a <u>kata</u>.

My opponent in the dojo is looks like a blue-metal skeleton. (Except that his face is blank smoothness; and he has a man's neck and chest, except for blue-metal skin. Plus, four fingers of each hand are fused together, so that it looks like he's wearing blue-metal mittens.) I call him Big Robert.

Anyway, the Lesson Two exercise is that Big Robert knocks me down to the left, or knocks me down to the right, or knocks me backward, and I'm supposed to smoothly roll on my shoulder and then get back on my feet, facing him.

The first ten minutes, the practice was just me getting knocked down, and I shoulder-rolling my way back to standing again. But then the software added some shit: Once I got knocked down, I was given three seconds to get standing again. After three seconds, my entire skin felt like it was scraped raw, and the awful pain continued till I had ten toes and two heels touching the floor.

You know how you feel after you scrape your knee? Imagine your entire body feeling like that. Even one second of this would be something you'd work hard to avoid feeling again.

In trying to figure out how to avoid getting body-scraped during every roll, I checked the Help documentation. It recommended I use the Demo mode. In Demo, you not only see how an expert does something, but you feel what the expert's muscles are doing at that moment.

By using Demo a lot, by the end of the night I got shoulder-rolls pretty much figured out.

Change of topic: It seems that one of my machinist Pleasure Units in Loganville, Lisabelle, got very inspired about Amy Emily's story of her and Heather shooting those armed robbers. Amy Emily and Lisabelle each bought one of those battery-operated water rifles, and these last two days, those two spent their free time "hunting" each other.

Carmenita actually had to put a stop to their "firefights." Quoth she, "When I give Palmer Electronics back to Mr. Palmer, I don't want to explain why all his expensive steel machinery is rusty!"

DAY 6 (TUESDAY)
PALMER ELECTRONICS
LOGANVILLE, GEORGIA

A little over 48 hours later after the team of bimborg had started work, they'd built a wormholer.

Then they began their next project: making ray-guns and Exnillo packs. Each in large quantities.

BIMBORG KING'S PERSONAL LOG
DAY 6 (TUESDAY)

Ha, I told you I was learning this Edo-kobushi stuff! Today the software promoted me to Second Belt. Meanwhile, Lesson Two is completed and I'm now starting Lesson Three: Introduction to Not Taking Shit.

One thing I've already discovered: When Big Robert hits me, I feel it, even though Big Robert isn't really here.

Change of topic: Carmenita herself took Amy Emily's and Lisabelle's "hunting" game to the next level.
Having finished the wormholer, now those women in the electronics shop are making ray-guns and Exnillo packs. Today Carmenita figured out how to use a bent paper clip and duct tape to lock a ray-gun into Strength setting One. At Strength One, a Pleasure Unit has to be shot four times just to be knocked unconscious. All the Pleasure Units in Loganville now have each borrowed a ray-gun, for "field testing."

TUESDAY NIGHT
PAY PHONE OUTSIDE THE SHELL GAS STATION

"Wisley residence," Regina heard her father say over the phone. His voice sounded tense.

The operator's voice cut in: "Will you accept a collect phone call from Regina Wisley?"

"Good god, *yes!*" he replied.

"Go ahead, ma'am," the operator said. Regina heard a click.

Regina began, "Daddy? I—"

"Princess, are you . . . all right?"

"I escaped, Daddy. I'm at a Shell station. It's in, let's see, Metter, by I-16 westbound. Please, Daddy, I need for you to pick me up. I don't have my car, and I don't have any money."

"Don't you worry, Betsy drove your car home, and your purse is parked in the middle of your bed. Looks like nothing's missing."

"Wow, finally something goes right."

"I'll be there in . . . figure half an hour, Princess. Do we need to take you to the hospital?"

"Let me sleep in my own bed tonight, Daddy. That'll heal me better than anything."

Roger Wisley's silver SUV drove into the Shell station thirty-one minutes later, by the Budweiser clock. Regina had expected both parents to be in the vehicle; instead she found her father driving, and two FBI agents in the back seat.

The man behind her father said, "Miss Wisley, with me is Agent Leonard Spock, and I'm Agent Forrest McCoy. What can you tell us about your captivity?"

"That I'm really, really glad it's over, and I don't want to think about it anymore."

"What can you tell us," Agent Spock asked, "about the people holding you captive?"

"Not much," Regina replied. "Mostly they were speaking a foreign language. I can't say what they looked like, because I was forced to wear a hood most of the time."

"What language were they speaking?" Agent McCoy asked.

"I didn't recognize it," Regina replied.

Agent Spock replied, "Miss Campbell told us that the woman was speaking English in the restroom. So them speaking only in a foreign language, that isn't logi—"

"Were you there, Agent Spock? One woman there spoke English to me, but she spoke foreign-talk to everyone else, and nobody but her talked to me."

"Nobody is calling you a liar, Miss Wisley," Agent McCoy said. "Would you tell us how you escaped?"

"They kept me in a chair, hands and feet tied up, and a hood over my head. They untied me when they took me to the bathroom, but I had to still wear the hood. Got the picture?"

"Sure," Agent McCoy said.

"One time I was in the bathroom, I not only took my hood off, but I checked the medicine cabinet. There I found a safety razor."

Agent Spock said, "There just happened to be a safety razor in the medicine cabinet where the kidnappers were holding you? The odds of that—"

"Anyway, I cut eye-slits in the hood, so I could see a little. Then I wrapped the razor in a shitload of toilet paper and had it in my hand when I came out of the bathroom. Jeez, I was so scared."

"My poor baby," Roger Wisley said.

Agent Spock said, "They tied up your hands again, never noticing that you had something in your hand?"

Regina said, "This is bullshit. Agent Spock, too bad you can't just lay a hand on my face and do some alien mind-reading trick, because I'm really tired of you calling me a liar."

"Miss Wisley, I have never once called you a liar."

"And I never once have said that you go years without sex, hm?"

Roger Wisley said, "*Ahem.* Princess, you used the safety razor, cut the ropes, and that's how you escaped."

"Yes, Daddy. Thank you for bringing things back on track."

Roger Wisley raised his voice: "We're coming up on a hospital. Agents, should we stop and get Regina checked out?"

"Daddy—"

Agent McCoy said, "I can't tell you. I'm a federal agent, not a doctor."

Regina said, "I do *not* want to stop at a hospital. I do *not* want to talk about what happened. I want to go home, take a hot bath, and go to bed. *Got me?*"

"Why do you think the kidnappers never called your parents with a ransom demand?" Agent Spock asked.

Regina's response was to tilt the vanity mirror and glare at Agent Spock's reflection.

Fifteen minutes later, when the SUV was back in the Wisley family driveway, Agent McCoy asked, "Miss Wisley, what are your plans after school tomorrow?"

"Cheerleading practice. Then dinner, then homework, then go to bed. Whatever you're planning for tomorrow, *forget it.*"

Agent Spock said, "Tomorrow we want to show you some books of mug shots, of suspected kidnappers and terrorists."

Regina looked to her left. "Daddy, can they make me do all this junk? Mug shots, lineups, yada-yada?"

"No, Princess," her father said.

Then his voice took on the hard edge that Regina was used to hearing him use at work. "Tomorrow I'll have my lawyers in Atlanta speak with Spock and McCoy's bosses in Atlanta. We'll get something worked out that doesn't require you to be bothered anymore."

Agent McCoy sighed as he stepped out of the SUV. Agent Spock said nothing, but he had one eyebrow raised.

4-H:Before The Attack

BIMBORG KING'S PERSONAL LOG
DAY 7 (WEDNESDAY)

The wormholer has been built, it's tested and, while I was at school, it got hauled to Sweet Onion. It's now hiding in a storage-rental room on Old Lionheart Highway.

Which means, I can invade the Cybes anytime now.

No time to waste: I've given the order to all bimborg who can take part, to meet here this Saturday night at the Georgia Star Drive-In. My plan is that Sunday at dawn we will attack the Cybes. Boy, will they *be surprised!*

My "troops" for the attack will be Spy Babes who are currently serving in the military, plus Ass-Kicker Babes, any of whom can leave for Vidal County, Georgia on a weekend, without any of their friends, neighbors, or coworkers noticing.

Most of the women will be carpooling to get here, but some of the women will arrive here driving rental trucks. Those trucks will be bringing weapons: Rocket-Propelled Grenades and something called an M-240, among other toys. Apparently Linda-5 knows how to buy military weapons for civilians and be sneaky about it.

I'm torn. All my chivalry says I alone should fight the Cybes, I alone should face the danger, and leave all 22 million women safe.

I can't tell you how wrong *it feels to endanger even one woman under my command, especially since none of them chose to be bimborg.*

But even if I could clone myself a thousand times, a thousand of me against the Cybes would lose, and Earth would be enslaved. Only bimborg can fight Cybes and hope to win. So bimborg women must be the soldiers and I must be the general.

Some Spy Babes and Ass-Kicker Babes who are military officers are tutoring me on strategy and tactics. I'm also teaching myself tactics from every source I can put in front of my eyeballs. The Wong III War of Succession in the 23rd century is highly educational.

But should I have attacked already, even though I didn't know what I was doing? Part of me worries that delaying the attack, while I educated myself, might have hurt our cause.

Change of topic: The Pleasure Units in Loganville will be having their first "free-for-all ray-gun war" tonight. The big rule they came up with: Nobody "dies" when she's knocked out. After a woman recovers from her faint, she's back in the game. The winner is the player with the fewest faints in the allotted time.

DAY 8 (THURSDAY), BEFORE FIRST BELL
SWEET ONION HIGH SCHOOL

Prudy Lu stopped Charlie-Bob in the hallway. "Please, can I talk to you?"

Charlie-Bob noticed that Prudy Lu seemed nervous for some reason.

"Sure, Prudy Lu, what's up?"

"Well, um, you know that Regina had a party last night to celebrate her escaping her kidnappers—"

"Last night? Huh, guess my invitation got misplaced."

Prudy Lu smiled. "Mine, too. Anyway, Doug went to the party—"

"Doug?"

"Doug Stark, halfback, we've been dating?" When Charlie-Bob nodded, Prudy Lu continued, "*I* didn't get invited to the party, but *Doug* did. Get this: At the party, Doug calls me up and breaks up with me over the phone."

"Wow, what a jerk thing to do. You deserve better than that."

Prudy Lu gave Charlie-Bob a sweet smile. "Thank you. I can't tell you how good it is, hearing you say that."

Prudy Lu got nervous-looking again as she added: "Anyway, I'm free this Friday and Saturday night, and I *really, really* wouldn't mind if you'd ask me out."

Charlie-Bob sighed. "I'm sorry, but I have plans for this entire weekend."

Prudy Lu's shoulders slumped. "Oh, sure. You probably have orgies scheduled every weekend now. What's one more teen girl, especially one with no boobs?"

"That's not it. I'm working on a big project, and I'll be involved with it for the entire weekend."

"Really? What class is it for?"

"Not for class, it's an outside project. But it's important."

Prudy Lu put her hand on his arm. "Then I hope everything works out for you. In the meantime, I hope you call me next week."

"No promises. Everything depends on how this project works out."

Prudy Lu gave him a fake smile, then she walked away.

Charlie-Bob noticed Regina and Betsy standing about fifteen yards away. Regina was glaring at both him and Prudy Lu.

BIMBORG KING'S PERSONAL LOG
DAY 8 (THURSDAY)

I suggested to Carmenita a way to improve the Loganville bimborg's ray-gun game—

I suggested the "Cybe Soldier" rule: A player may not shoot the "enemy" who is directly in front of her.

In a real ray-gun battle with Cybes, if you tried to shoot a Soldier in front of you, he'd put up his purple shield and you'd waste your shot. But if you shot the Cybe who was twenty feet to your right or left, he might not notice you aiming your gun at him, so you'd shoot him without his shield up. Voilà, dead Soldier.

DAY 9 (FRIDAY), NIGHTTIME
THE WISLEY RESIDENCE

"So now Wisley Electronics is empty?" Regina asked her father at dinner. "Nobody's there now?"

Roger Wisley replied, "Wisley Electronics is empty, it's dark, and the doors are all chained and padlocked. The workers and the managers all left at five o'clock. Drunk, many of them."

"Because now they're out of work," Steffi Jo Wisley said. "Thanks to you."

Roger Wisley said, "I think you've had too much wine tonight, precious."

"Or not enough," she replied. "Do you have any idea how hated we are right now, 'dear husband'?"

Regina spoke up: "Daddy, I want to go there and take one last look inside. Could we drive there now, please, all three of us?"

Roger smiled. "Sure, Princess, let's go. Stef?"

"You two go," Steffi Jo said. "I'll just stay here and drink wine."

"Please, Mom, come with us?" Regina said. "Please, please, please?"

Steffi Jo frowned, glared at her husband, then said, "Fine. But I'm not driving."

Minutes later, the padlock was unlocked and the three Wisleys were inside the ink-dark Wisley Electronics building. Roger pulled a flashlight out of his pocket. "Hold on while I flip the master breaker."

Fifteen seconds later, all the lights came on. Fifteen seconds after that, Roger rejoined his wife and daughter.

Steffi Jo promptly walked away, to stand on the side of Regina that was farther from Roger.

Regina asked, "Daddy, do you have any definite plans for the building now?"

He nodded. "There's a cult that's interested in tearing down the plant and building a gated camp here. Grand Archbrother Derek promised to pay in cash."

"Is that definite?" Regina asked. "Has he paid you money already? Have papers been signed?"

"Nope, it's just at the talking stage, Princess," Roger Wisley said. "Why?"

SSSSOOM. Two Cybe Soldiers suddenly wormholed inside the building. They appeared where they blocked the only unchained, unlocked door.

SSSSOOM. Three more Cybe Soldiers and three Welcomers were wormholed to a spot three meters away from Roger and Steffi Jo.

The three Welcomers began to chant, "The Overmind calms you. The Overmind frees you from emotion. The Overmind gives knowledge. We Welcome you into the Overmind."

The eyes of the Solitary named Roger Wisley went wide. Had the Solitary named Betsy described the two Cybes in the mall restroom? No matter. Roger Wisley was caught by surprise, so he was quickly captured and Welcomed.

Steffi Jo Wisley was wearing high heels, and she was drunk. She made an inept attempt to escape, but she also was quickly caught, and quickly Welcomed.

SSSSOOM. Cybe Alpha appeared. He spent several 64-slobi walking around the empty Wisley Electronics plant, then he walked up to Cybe-Regina. "This building is suitable. You have done well, Sol3-21-61."

Cybe-Regina felt a glow of satisfaction that her emotion-suppression subroutine didn't entirely squelch.

4-1: Cops Are Welcome(d)

DAY 9 (FRIDAY), LATER THAT NIGHT

Cybe-Regina drove her father's silver SUV back to her house, so that it appeared to Solitaries that her parents were at home.

Once she'd walked into the house, she was wormholed back to the Wisley Electronics plant. She walked outside, across the moonlit employee parking lot, and into the trees.

She pulled out her smartphone.

Cybe-Regina accessed the acting knowledge of the best actors of 427 future colony planets. Then she punched in the direct phone number for the Sweet Onion Police.

A woman's voice said, "Sweet Onion Police, how may I—"

How may you help us, dispatcher? By buying this unit's lying story, Cybe-Regina thought. Aloud she said, "Please help me! This is Regina Wisley, and I'm so scared."

"Is it your kidnappers? Have they come back for you?"

"What? No. I'm outside the Wisley Electronics building, I walked here. Anyway, it's supposed to be empty."

"So I hear," the police dispatcher said drily.

"But somebody's cut through the chain that locks the back door, and the whole place smells weird. Awful, it smells awful."

"Awful, how? Describe the smell."

"Ugh, like cat piss and rotten eggs, only a hundred times worse."

Like a methamphetamine lab, in other words.

The dispatcher asked, "Where are you? Inside the building, or outside? Exactly where?"

"Just beyond the employee parking lot is a forest. That's where I'm hiding. I can see two cars parked in back where you can't see them from the road. *Please* help me—I'm scared to move."

"Hold on." Ten seconds later, the dispatcher came back on the line. "All police cars are en route. Now, why did you walk there when it's closed?"

"Because Mother and Father had a fight, and I wanted to see the building one last time before it got sold off. My grandfather built it, you know."

"And both my grandfathers worked there," the dispatcher said.

"Dispatcher? Three guys came out, got into the two cars, and they're driving off. The three guys were talking to a fourth guy, who went back inside."

"Hold on, I'll tell the units," the dispatcher said.

A minute later, three police cars drove onto the driveway leading to the employee parking lot. The lead police car flashed its blue lightbar for one second; Cybe-Regina then stepped out of the trees and into the employee lot, waving her arms. The lead police car's headlights blinded her.

Now, policemen, be as gullible as your dispatcher was, and you'll fall into our trap, Cybe-Regina thought.

The lead police car headed straight for her. The second police car parked in the employee lot, close to the back door. The third car stayed back, and started spraying the front of the building with a bright door-mounted searchlight.

A cop in his forties stepped out of the police car. "Miss Wisley, I'm Lt. Resshert. Are you all—"

Then his whole attitude changed. "I don't smell anything. I smell not one damned thing."

While looking suspiciously at Regina, he pressed his radio button. "Jeff, get out of the car and tell me what you smell."

The police car by the plant's back door opened its own door, and a cop in his thirties stepped out, his gun drawn. Seconds later, he reported, "I smell nothing bad."

Lt. Resshert scowled. "Miss Wisley, calling in a false report to police—"

SSSSOOM. Lt. Resshert and the policeman named Jeff now were each surrounded by two Cybe Soldiers and a Welcomer.

Meanwhile, the third policeman was having his own problems. Cybe-Regina saw that two Cybe Soldiers had lifted the front of his police car off the ground, so that the policeman could drive neither forward nor backward. Then a third Cybe Soldier walked up to the driver's door and punched in the glass.

Cybe-Regina heard gunshots; clearly the third policeman was trying to shoot his attacker. Cybe-Regina saw flashes of purple shield, then the Soldier reached in, yanked open the car door, reached in, jerked the policeman out of the car and onto the ground, then kicked the policeman's gun away.

SSSSOOM. A third Welcomer appeared, who stabbed the hands-and-knees policeman in the back of the neck before he could stand up and run away.

By then the other two policemen were already statue-still and destined to become Cybes themselves.

SSSSOOM. A minute later, Cybe-Regina remained in the Wisley Electronics parking lot, and three police cars remained behind, but the Cybe Soldiers, the Welcomers, the three policemen, and the dispatcher all had been wormholed away from Sweet Onion.

The legally required audio recordings of Regina's phone call and of the dispatcher's conversations with town law enforcement, all that got completely erased by Soldiers in the police station.

33 MINUTES LATER

A deputy sheriff stopped trying to shoot the Cybe Soldier in front of him. Instead, the deputy aimed his revolver at a Soldier who was coming toward the sheriff.

BANG!

The Soldier dropped dead. Cybe-Regina "heard" him die through the Overmind, besides seeing him fall over.

That deputy called out, "Shoot every one of 'em *except* the guy in front of you!"

It isn't supposed to happen this way! Cybe-Regina thought.

Cybe-Regina had made another lying phone call, this time to the Vidal County Sheriff's Department. She had told this dispatcher, "All the Sweet Onion policemen went inside. Then I heard gunshots!"

One sheriff's-department car had arrived ten minutes after Cybe-Regina had made that second call. When the sheriff's deputy had noticed a Sweet Onion Police car with its searchlight on, its driver door open, and brass casings and a police revolver lying on the pavement, he hadn't moved one inch farther till all his buddies had showed up.

A half-hour after the local policemen had been Welcomed, the Vidal County Sheriff's Department had entered the Wisley Electronics parking lot in force—seven vehicles.

Cybe-Regina had every reason to believe her trick would work again. True, the sheriff hadn't smelled methamphetamine any more than Lt. Resshert had, but he'd found all three Sweet Onion Police cars as follows—

• One police car had brass casings, a broken window, and a wide-open door, with a police revolver visible nearby;
• One police car still had its engine running;
• Three police cars were empty of people.

All the sheriff's people had drawn their guns and had been looking very alert when they'd stepped out of their vehicles.

Then the Cybe Soldiers and Welcomers had wormholed in.

At first things had happened as Cybe-Regina had expected: Bullets hadn't stopped a Soldier when he was walking toward a shooting deputy, then the Soldier had disarmed that deputy, who'd become the first county law-enforcement officer to be Welcomed.

But then that other deputy got either smart or lucky, and a Cybe Soldier died.

"Fuck, what *are* these things?" one badge-man called out.

"No idea, but they turned Jimmy-Tom into a statue. *Die*, alien!"

In all, four Soldiers got killed, plus two Welcomers. Cybe-Regina worried that some sheriff's-department Solitaries would escape the trap. *Oh no, if even one Solitary manages to leave here and he tells other Solitaries what happened—*

But events didn't turn out that way. Instead, the surviving Soldiers electrocuted the sheriff, the smart deputy, and another deputy. This made the other three deputies hesitate, and when they hesitated, they got Welcomed.

Vidal County had its share of hookers. Sometimes a hooker got arrested by the police or a county deputy, sometimes a man with a badge extorted a free blowjob from the hooker, and sometimes she suffered both fates in the same night.

The point is, there wasn't even one hooker in Vidal County who wasn't known to be such, by at least one badge-man.

That night, what the cops knew, or the Welcomed sheriff's deputies knew, the Cybes wound up knowing.

Late that night, every Vidal County hooker got an unscheduled visit from the Cybes. Women who had spent the last few years welcoming horny men, became a different kind of Welcomer.

Life would have gotten complicated if the Cybes had unknowingly tried to Welcome a bimborg. But while planet Earth's 22 million bimborg included thousands of streetwalkers, erotic masseuses, brothel workers, escorts, and call girls, none of those bimborg-prostitutes lived in Vidal County.

At a little-known geographic feature known as the North American Basin, the Atlantic Ocean is especially deep. Eight feet above all that water, a wormhole opened up. Ten times a Sweet Onion Police car or Vidal County Sheriff's Department car was pushed through the wormhole.

No human saw anything; no human device saw anything.

Each vehicle made a noise when it hit the water, it made a second noise when water pressure broke the glass, and it made another noise when it hit the seabed. Several navies' submarines recorded the noises, but nobody could explain them.

Three of those vehicles had a naked corpse in each locked trunk. Those bodies never floated to the surface, so those men's deaths were never confirmed.

4-J: Cybes v. Bimborg 2

DAY 10 (SATURDAY)
LIONHEART, GEORGIA (VIDAL COUNTY SEAT)

In Lionheart, the sign for the Georgia Star Drive-In rose up above the unmowed grass. The sign had flaking paint, and it had several brown vertical rust-streaks. The sign's marquee read:

1: STAR W RS 3 S TH

2: MAD GASC R

Charlie-Bob used bolt-cutters on the rusty chain, Saturday around noon. The first car with Ass-Kicker Babes in it, arrived at the drive-in ten minutes later.

Once that first car was parked (within the grounds and by the boarded-windows concession stand), four women got out of the car and walked up to Charlie-Bob and Lucille-unit. The car's driver, who had a short, military-style hairstyle, saluted and said, "Command us, King Charlie-Bob, even if we die."

As Charlie-Bob returned the salute, he said, "I prefer George Patton's version: 'No bastard ever won a war by dying for his country. He won it by making the other poor dumb bastard die for *his* country.' I intend to turn lots of Cybes into patriots."

Time passed and work progressed. The weapons preparation and latrine-digging were finished by an hour before sunset, and some of the bimborg-soldiers were making sleeping arrangements for themselves. Some of the women were inflating air mattresses, and some were setting up tents and stowing sleeping bags. Meanwhile, the Ass-Kicker Babes, who didn't need to sleep, had brought card tables.

All of the bimborg-soldiers would be spending Saturday night on the grounds of the drive-in; none were staying in motels. This was so that the women could arrive Saturday and leave Sunday without the people of Lionheart even knowing they were there.

All of Sweet Onion High School's Pleasure Units had made the drive to Lionheart, even though none of them would be fighting tomorrow. This puzzled Charlie-Bob, because only Rose-unit, as Bimborg Queen, had a reason to drive to Lionheart.

Before arriving at the drive-in, Rose and Denise had made a detour to Kobayashi's Burgers. Now those two were waiting while Charlie-Bob finished his Big Winner three-patty hamburger.

When Charlie-Bob was wadding up the hamburger's paper wrapper, Rose said, "We-all have talked this over. Everyone who is going into battle tomorrow, needs to relax tonight."

"And the best way to relax," Helen-May Sawyer said, "is with orgasms."

"Brain-frying orgasms, and lots of them," Denise said.

"Right," said Rose. "Ohmigod, these women need a relaxing fuck. You need a relaxing fuck. So go fuck them right now. And if you have any dick left over, come fuck us."

Charlie-Bob frowned. "You know my views on that. Y'all are compelled by the nanobots, you're brainwashed—"

Mary Kayla said, "Everyone thinks better in battle when they're de-stressed. You'll be doing these women a favor."

"But I'd be taking advantage of them! They don't even know me. If they weren't programmed to obey me, they'd never—"

"Listen to me, King Charlie-Bob," Mary Kayla said. "Today you're doing a man's work, and manly men used to get my motor running, back when I was Solitary."

Helen-May Sawyer nodded. "Tonight, yonder women need to be fucked, tonight you need to fuck them, and I don't feel *at all* forced into offering myself, when it's to a real man."

"It's settled, then," Rose said. She pulled on Charlie-Bob's arm, dragging him over to a queen-sized air mattress that some Spy Babes from Tennessee had just inflated.

Rose began to unfasten Charlie-Bob's belt. "Now, unless you right now order us all to stop, you're going to get *soo* sucked and fucked tonight."

Charlie-Bob gave no such order to stop. After a week and a half of no sex, he was pretty horny, in fact.

By now several dozen curious out-of-town bimborg were standing close. Rose looked around and then, raising her voice, said,

"Po spo po Rose ratchak, Blafrawa tri Bimborg. Za bimborg spunseza, kek spo cruldirem." I am Rose, Bimborg Queen. All bimborg, hear me.

Rose waited a minute till all the bimborg inside the drive-in had moved within earshot.

Rose said (loudly) in English, "First order of business: Those of you who've brought red-beam flashlights, get them out now. We *will* be keeping Light Discipline after sunset, orgy or no orgy."

"What's Light Discipline?" a woman asked.

Another woman explained, "Light Discipline means no white light between sundown and sunrise. You have to use red light only."

Rose said, "Second thing: King Charlie-Bob is available now for sex. He doesn't order you to take part, but I do. I'll be fucking him right alongside you because I respect him, ohmigod, a lot."

Lucille-unit was pulling her skirt down. "We are programmed to obey, but we aren't programmed to respect. This unit was in King James' house the night he was killed. This unit doesn't respect King James, but now this unit respects King Charlie-Bob. My Solitary self wants to fuck him."

"I might get someone pregnant," Charlie-Bob said.

Rose and Mary Kayla each smiled and showed him a purseful of condoms.

On the air mattress with Charlie-Bob were big-breasted twins, each with a blond ponytail that went down to her ass, and each with a cover-girl face.

"As good as you two look," Charlie-Bob asked in amazement, "how is it that you got designated as Ass-Kicker Babes and not Pleasure Units?"

"Sherry actually got designated as a Pleasure Unit at first," said the twin who wasn't sucking Charlie-Bob's cock. "See her left hand? Those aren't freckles you see, they're aborted Welcomer Warts."

Sherry lifted her lips off Charlie-Bob's cock. "Then this unit's Welcomer read enough of my memories to find out that I'm the best sniper around, while Terry there is an angel with an M-60. Boom, this unit got designated as an Ass-Kicker Babe, and when Terry got Welcomed, she became an Ass-Kicker Babe too."

Sherry went back to cocksucking, as Terry resumed the tale. "Being Ass-Kicker Babes is better than being Solitaries. We have a choice: We can shoot some jerk, or we can beat the shit out of him."

Charlie-Bob was having sex with two women: a redheaded Spy Babe who was a Marine officer named Kathryn; and an Ass-Kicker Babe named Kyong.

Kyong's pussy was tight, Kyong's pussy was wet, and Kyong's body was apparently having lots of fun. Kathryn kept whispering to Kyong, "Sound discipline! Sound discipline!" Which was military-speak for *Don't scream so loud!*

When it was Kathryn's turn for sex, she knelt down by a corner of the air mattress, then she slithered on her stomach up between Charlie-Bob's legs. Just before she took him in her mouth, she looked him in the eye, grinned, and said, "*Nos morituri, te fellatamus.*" (We who are about to die, suck you off.)

Before he fell asleep, Charlie-Bob had sex with about a dozen or so women whom he couldn't describe the colors of their hair or skin. That's because, during those last dozen fuckings, a half-dozen women were standing around the air mattress, each shining a red-beam flashlight on Charlie-Bob and his current lover.

All that red light made the sex kind of strange—as if Charlie-Bob and his bedmate both had been dipped in red paint.

DAY 11 (SUNDAY)

His shoulder got shaken. "King Charlie-Bob, you need to wake up now," Rose-unit said.

After the orgy had ended, Charlie-Bob slept in the bed of a rental truck. His sleeping bag lay next to crates containing Rocket-Propelled Grenades.

Now Charlie-Bob woke up to discover Rose, fully clothed, kneeling by him in red-outlined silhouette. Her red outline, it turned out, was being made by red-beam flashlights that bimborg outside the truck were shining on him and Rose.

He looked around. The sun hadn't yet risen, but the eastern sky was bright. The time was five or ten minutes before Georgia sunrise.

He glanced around. Five red-lit card tables were surrounded by red-lit Ass-Kicker Babes, but the women at those tables all were looking at him, not at their games.

Loudly he said, "Begin final preparations."

GEORGIA STAR DRIVE-IN, VIDAL CO., GEORGIA DAY 11 (SUNDAY), AT DAWN (IN IOWA)

In Georgia, the sun had been up for a little over a half-hour. But what the sun did in Georgia didn't matter.

Charlie-Bob had a good plan, he thought. He had RPGs to blow up the Cybe wormholer and the Cybe cloaker. He had an M-240B machine gun to inconvenience any Cybe who didn't put up a purple shield. And if the Cybe Soldiers thought that they could just electrocute their attackers—well, they had a little surprise coming!

When the time-display on his smartphone told him that the sun was just now rising in Kirk County, Iowa, Charlie-Bob activated the bimborg-built wormholer.

Amanda-8559249, the Spy Babe who had spotted the Cybe base from a helicopter, was in the first batch of bimborg to be sent to the Kelly farm. She would direct everyone else to where the Cybe base was cloaked.

Sherry, the Ass-Kicker Babe who was the excellent sniper, was another bimborg in that first batch. Her orders were to get herself into the hayloft of the barn as quickly as possible.

Sherry's sister Terry also was in that first batch. As soon as Terry and Army sergeant Erika-6395349 appeared at the Kelly farm, they sprinted away from the landing point, with the M-240B carried between them.

Charlie-Bob waited for Amanda to lead the first batch to just outside the "curtain" and for everyone to report back that they were in position. If everyone moved quietly, Charlie-Bob didn't worry about the Cybes spotting them—

According to the Cybe hard drive, a cloaker bends all light, but it does nothing to anything that moves less than the speed of light. Thus snakes, spaniels, and soldiers can all easily move through the cloaker "curtain." This also means that no light at all comes inside the "curtain," so those inside the curtain would have no view of who or what might be outside the curtain until everyone burst in.

However, while the Cybes couldn't *see* someone just outside the curtain, they could *hear* someone speak. So the first-team bimborg were to report "in position" by each tapping a code on her radio microphone; the first-team bimborg were *absolutely forbidden* to speak into their microphones until both teams—

"Bravo Bravo Kilo, this is Amanda. We have a problem that your orders do not foresee."

What the fuck? Charlie-Bob pressed the microphone button. "What's the problem?"

Amanda's voice said, "It's gone. The Cybe Base is no longer here."

A different voice spoke: "Bravo Bravo Kilo, this is Erika. I confirm that report. There are flattened farm crops here, and I see truck tracks in the dirt. Long shadows are good everywhere."

Yet another woman's voice: "Bravo Bravo Kilo, this is Terry. This unit has walked forward through the curtain. Except there *is* no curtain. This unit confirms Amanda's and Erika's reports: the Cybe Base isn't here."

I waited too long to attack, Charlie-Bob thought.

4-K: A Creepy Mystery

DAY 11 (SUNDAY)

An hour after Charlie-Bob returned to his house in Sweet Onion, he posted this at the bimborg web site:

> *Our task gets much harder. I have no idea where the Cybes are now, and I need good ideas how to find them. If you think of something, share it in the Cybes Conference at this website.*
>
> *I found something on the Cybe hard drive that at first I was going to share as a joke, but now I'm sharing because I'm desperate.*
>
> *One of the human colonies that the future Cybes Welcomed was Alphasena II. Before they were Welcomed, the women Alphaseans had developed something called "handjob hypnosis." (They also knew how to do it with backrubs, but handjobs was what they were most famous for.) Anyway, by the 25th century, it was the rule everywhere in humanspace that a man was forbidden to date an Alphasean woman even once, if he had a security clearance. (A man could tell if a woman was Alphasean because they had a distinct accent.)*
>
> *Anyway, I've uploaded all sorts of text files and video files on how to do "handjob hypnosis." Pleasure Units and Spy Babes, I order you to master this knowledge.*
>
> *P.S. I am prostituting some of you, and that goes against my principles. One day I hope I can tell all of you I'm very sorry for that. But in the meantime, the future of Earth is at stake.*

Charlie-Bob had just posted that latest Bimborg King order when he heard the doorbell ring. Less than a minute later, his mother was calling through his bedroom door, "Charlie-Bob, you have visitors. It's Rose and a girl I don't know."

The other girl turned out to be Prudy Lu Moffatt. She was a basket case.

"What's going on?" Charlie-Bob asked.

"You *sure* I should tell him?" Prudy Lu asked Rose. "We haven't dated yet, and he should get stuck with boyfriend duty?"

Rose nodded. "Charlie-Bob is a *totally* good man, and smart. Tell him."

Prudy Lu said to Charlie-Bob, "It's my dad! That bitch Regina called him up yesterday morning. She said that maybe there were jobs opening up at the plant, and could he come to the plant at two that afternoon? So we all got excited, he got all spiffed up, and then he left the house at quarter of two."

Charlie-Bob said, "Judging by how upset you are, I guess he didn't get the job."

"That's the thing—Mom and I don't know! He left the house, and he hasn't come back. He hasn't called, either. Worse, whenever I call the police, nobody answers the phone."

Prudy Lu started crying. Rose took Prudy Lu in her arms and hugged her.

Prudy Lu looked at Charlie-Bob and sniffled. "He's not in the hospital, that's all I know for sure. But yesterday afternoon and last night, I tried calling him, and the police, and Rose, and you, and nobody answered the phone! I was so scared!"

Charlie-Bob said, "The plant is only a mile out of town. He'd have to try hard to get into a traffic accident, going there or back."

Prudy Lu said, "Maybe he didn't have an accident. Maybe Regina did something to him."

Prudy Lu opened up her purse and pulled out something cylindrical and made of shiny brass. Charlie-Bob had seen enough cop shows to recognize a bullet casing, and it was way too big to be for squirrel-hunting.

Prudy Lu continued, "This morning, soon after dawn, I had to know what was going on. I got on my bicycle, and I rode out to the plant."

"Don't you have a car?" Charlie-Bob asked.

"I had all this energy to burn off."

"So you went there, and you saw a bullet casing."

"I saw cars in the employee parking lot, including Dad's green truck. I was all set to park my bike and barge through the door into the plant and ask what the hell was going on, surprise the hell out of whoever was inside—I was itching to do that. Then I saw this lying on the pavement."

"It's shiny," Charlie-Bob said. "Not tarnished yet." He sniffed the bullet casing. "Strong smell."

Prudy Lu said, "When I saw this, I got back on my bike, zoomed back to town, and went back to trying to call the police and y'all. Then finally I got ahold of Rose and she brought me here."

The bullet casing didn't compute. Charlie-Bob couldn't imagine what a bullet casing might be doing at Wisley Electronics.

"What do you think this means?" he asked Prudy Lu.

"You're gonna laugh, but part of me thinks that Regina hates me so much, she lured my dad to the plant and killed him!"

Charlie-Bob's natural inclination was to argue the point. But Rose was giving him a look, *I know what you're about to say, and I strongly recommend you don't say it.*

So he said instead, "Whatever has happened, Prudy Lu, know that you're among friends."

Rose and Prudy Lu left five minutes later (after Prudy Lu kissed Charlie-Bob on the cheek). Right after that, Charlie-Bob phoned Lucille-unit; ten minutes later, Lucille was in his car and they were headed for the Sweet Onion Police building.

The most likely explanation for the police not answering their phone was that the phone line was messed up. So before Charlie-Bob went to the police station, he drove every street that was within two blocks of the police station, looking for a telephone-maintenance truck. But there was no such truck around.

He and Lucille drove to the police station.

Lucille said, "This unit sees newspapers piled up outside the door."

They got out of the car and walked up to the front door. Sure enough, there were Saturday and Sunday newspapers from Macon, Savannah, and Atlanta just outside the door.

Charlie-Bob got creeped out then, big time.

"Starting now, be alert for anything," he told Lucille-unit. "Before we go inside, let's walk around."

Charlie-Bob saw no broken glass, no smashed doors, no brass casings, no bullet holes, no blood, and no dead bodies. That was good.

He noted that behind the building there was a tin roof wide enough to shelter three police cars, but all three parking places were empty. That was maybe normal, maybe bad.

No one ran out of the building and demanded to know why Charlie-Bob and Lucille were "sneaking around" a police station. That was definitely bad.

When they'd circled around the building and were back to the front door, Charlie-Bob picked up the newspapers. "I don't want to frighten the townspeople. You open the door," he told Lucille.

She did, and he dropped the newspapers on a folding chair. What he noticed, once she'd shut the door again, was the *quiet*.

Oh, he could hear a radio playing country music. But he should have been hearing voices, and he didn't; he should have been hearing the police radio, and he didn't.

"HELLO?" he called out.

He waited. No answer.

Charlie-Bob had been feeling more and more creeped-out, from the moment he'd seen those newspapers. Now his brain was making siren noises and flashing red text. He was alert.

He and Lucille went through every room of the police station. They found no bodies, whether healthy, injured, dying, or dead.

The jail was empty; its door was open.

Nothing looked disturbed, nothing looked out of place, and there was no sign of blood or bullets.

It was like everyone had headed over to the doughnut shop.

They found the dispatcher's desk (it had a microphone on it), but they found no dispatcher. Lucille pulled out desk drawers; after the second pulled-out drawer, she said, "Her purse is here." Seconds later, Lucille reported, "Her wallet's in her purse."

Meanwhile, Charlie-Bob had noticed that the dispatcher's computer had been turned off at the power strip. Charlie-Bob turned the power strip on, then punched the computer's Power button. Seconds later, he saw the "Resume Windows" message; seconds after that, he was looking at an email being written—

Friday, March 8, 2013,

Another boring night for me—but for once, not for Sweet Onion's Finest. Instead of catching drunks, Resshert and the boys are checking out a reported

Charlie-Bob pounded the desk in frustration.

The only reason that Charlie-Bob and Lucille drove to the sheriff's department in Lionheart, instead of phoning over there, was that Charlie-Bob was feeling a little paranoid. He thought that since he was bimborg king, it wasn't a smart idea to get his voice recorded and his smartphone number logged.

He hoped he'd only have to talk to one law-enforcement type in the sheriff's department. He feared that he'd have to talk to a bunch of them, every last man acting suspicious and skeptical.

He never expected to find another creepy, empty, undisturbed building and cop-car-free parking lot.

The entire Sweet Onion Police Department, and the entire Vidal County Sheriff's Department, had disappeared—cars and all.

LATER THAT SUNDAY

Cassie-542 (a.k.a. PFC Cassie Winger) was buying food in a Washington, D.C.-area grocery store. She was wearing a tight-fitting t-shirt that was Army green, except for a woman's winking eye and lettering in yellow: "Be All You Can Be."

A man in his early thirties, neither handsome nor ugly, walked up to her. "Hello? Is okay, I do talk to pretty American woman, yes?"

His Russian accent was thick.

Cassie-unit smiled at him. "It depends. *Why* do you want to talk to me? Are you a Russian spy?"

"*Nyet!* I am for embassy the man mop the floor and the man deliver the mail. I am. . .word is *gopher?*"

Cassie was friendly to him. *Very* friendly. She let Grigorii the supposed janitor buy a bottle of cheap wine and half an order of Chinese takeout, then she took him back to her tiny apartment.

They talked and talked. He talked freely about his own job, which was, to hear him tell it, the number-one most unimportant job in all of Russia's Foreign Ministry. For her part, Cassie told him that yes, she was in the Army, and she even had a Secret job—but she didn't tell him anything about that job, and he didn't push.

Something else that Cassie-542 didn't tell Grigorii: She was herself a spy, but for no Solitary-run government agency.

4-L: Bimborg Hypnotists

DAY 11 (SUNDAY), LATE THAT EVENING

Sometime after nine o'clock Sunday night, Cassie the bimborg and Grigorii the supposed janitor were sitting on her old couch in her teensy-weensy apartment. Cassie-unit gave Grigorii a bedroom smile. "I like you. I want to do something nice for you."

She unbuckled his belt, unzipped his pants, pulled his pants down, then started to stroke his cock exactly like King Charlie-Bob's video had taught her.

"That feels so good, yes?" Cassie asked Grigorii.

"*Da. Da.* Is so good."

"Listen to my voice, if you want to feel good. Are you listening?"

"Yes. I am listening."

"You are listening to my voice, and your dick feels good. Yes?"

"Ohhh, yes."

"So you want to listen to my voice, to keep feeling good. Yes?"

This went on for five more minutes. When she was sure she had him in a trance, she asked him, "Is your name really Grigorii?"

"Yes, I did not give you a fake name."

Cassie noticed his grammar got much better while under hypnosis. She asked him, "Are you really a janitor at the embassy?"

He said, "Officially I am the janitor. I have other work."

"What is your other work?"

"To recruit Americans to spy for Russia."

"Is that why you came up to talk to me?"

"Yes."

"Why me?"

"Col. Stewart remarked to another of our spies that he wanted to 'nail' you very much. My plan was to seduce you, blackmail you into seducing Col. Stewart, then blackmail him into selling DOD Cybersecurity Command secrets to Russia."

This man could be useful, Cassie-unit thought.

Fifteen minutes later, Grigorii was leaving Cassie-unit's apartment with a smile—only partly because he'd made a date with Cassie for the next night. Grigorii remembered the handjob, but he'd forgotten his hypnotic interrogation.

DAY 12 (MONDAY), BEFORE FIRST BELL
SWEET ONION HIGH SCHOOL

Cybe-Regina and her Solitary minion Betsy were strolling down the hallway when they found their way blocked. Not by the Solitary named Rose, though she was standing (and smirking) in the background. No, standing right in front of Cybe-Regina, arms crossed, was the Solitary named Prudy Lu. Standing behind Prudy Lu were Rose and also Charlie-Bob Owens.

"Where's my father?" Prudy Lu demanded.

"Isn't he at home?" Betsy asked, sounding confused. "Why would Regina—"

Prudy Lu answered Betsy's question, all the while glaring at Regina. "Saturday, Regina called my father and asked if he could come out to the plant. Regina said maybe they were hiring—"

"*Really?*" Betsy said. "That would be so wonderful if—"

"Don't pop the champagne yet, Betsy," Charlie-Bob said.

Prudy Lu said, "Anyway, it's kind of strange, don't you think, that it wasn't Roger Wisley who called Dad, and neither did his secretary call Dad. Nope, it was Regina who—"

"You want a lawsuit, sweetie?" Cybe-Regina said. "Because you're about to get one."

"Anyway, Betsy, *dear* Regina here called my dad last Saturday, he went in for the job interview, and nobody has seen him since. He hasn't called home, and he doesn't answer his phone. So *bitch*, where is my father?"

Cybe-Regina dug into her purse, and pulled out her smartphone. "You just crossed the line. You *will* be hearing from my father's—"

Prudy Lu draped her hand over the smartphone. "Be sure to tell them that *you* will be hearing from the GBI," Georgia Bureau of Investigation. "Let's see if those lawyers of Mr. Weaselly are such hotshots when you're handcuffed and get read your rights."

Charlie-Bob Owens said, "You know, Regina, she's asked you twice, and you've not answered her either time: *Do* you know where her father is?"

Regina glared at him. "You stay out of this. This isn't your problem."

He laughed. "Maybe so. But I'm also eighteen, and a witness to this argument—as is Rose—so we each can be subpoenaed. And right now, what I'd have to tell the judge and jury, it's not good for you."

Cybe-Regina said, "I haven't seen her father since Saturday."

Rose, who had kept quiet all this time, gave Cybe-Regina a shark's smile. "I'm, like, going to quote you on that."

Prudy Lu, Charlie-Bob, and Rose turned and walked away. Cybe-Regina called out after them, "Your father will be back tomorrow. Then you better have an apology ready!"

Cybe-Regina resumed her walk forward. Betsy kept pace, but stayed silent.

Cybe-Regina also was outwardly silent. Still, she was speaking— saying quite a lot, in fact.

This unit thinks that the Solitary named Prudy Lu Moffatt is a danger to the Clan, Cybe-Regina told the Overmind.

Why do you say that? the Overmind asked. Share your memories.

When Cybe-Regina replayed the conversation that had just happened, the Overmind said, We see no evidence that this Solitary knows about us or suspects our existence.

Cybe-Regina replied, But she knows something. Prudy Lu would not stand up to this unit so forcefully unless she knew something definite about her father's disappearance. We should Welcome her to learn what she knows.

Now Cybe Alpha spoke up. This unit is not convinced that the Solitary knows anything, and disappearing the Solitary for three days, right after you threatened her, would be noticed by other Solitaries. This unit's decision is, the Solitary named Prudy Lu will not be Welcomed prematurely.

The Overmind said, We support the decision of Cybe Alpha.

Cybe-Regina was supposed to chant along, but she didn't. So Cybe Alpha asked her, Sol3-21-61, do you also endorse the decision of this unit, designated Cybe Alpha?

Cybe-Regina replied, <u>No, this unit does not. This unit is convinced that there is danger to the Clan now, and the Solitary Prudy Lu Moffatt is part of that danger.</u>

Hearing Cybe-Regina say no to Cybe Alpha, the Overmind boggled.

The unit designated Cybe Alpha sighed mentally.

Soon after the Overmind had been created in 2419, a weakness was discovered in it. During the Tizurka IV miners' strike of 2427-8, fourteen units disobeyed the Overmind and continued to mine gold. Eventually the Overmind figured out that one Solitary in 1,013,847 was so selfish that, when Welcomed, he or she became a disobedient, uncooperative Cybe.

Clearly the trend was continuing. Cybe Alpha estimated there to be a 69.2 percent probability that Sol3-21-61 (Regina Wisley) would turn out to be another rogue Cybe.

DAY 12 (MONDAY), AT NIGHT
NEAR WASHINGTON, D.C.

Monday night, Grigorii was back in Cassie's apartment. The events were the same as before: Conversation, food and wine, then a "free" handjob.

As soon as Grigorii was in a hypnotic trance, Cassie showed him photos of men who worked at the Russian Embassy in Washington.

"What does he *really* do?" Cassie-unit asked about each photo.

Grigorii spilled a sackful of beans, and then forgot the entire conversation.

DAY 13 (TUESDAY), AFTER SCHOOL
SWEET ONION HIGH SCHOOL

Charlie-Bob and Rose were about to say goodbye to Prudy Lu when Regina Wisley rushed up to them.

Regina looked down her nose at Prudy Lu and said, "Your father is home now, alive and healthy. Apologize in the morning."

Charlie-Bob said, "Even if that's true, how do *you* know that, Regina? When did your dad start sharing employee schedules with his teenage daughter?"

Regina barely glanced at Charlie-Bob. "I don't have to talk to you."

Rose said, "She thinks she's too good for you, Charlie-Bob."

He looked at Regina. "I'm crushed, Wisley."

DAY 13 (TUESDAY), EVENING

Yuri Ivanovich Petrovski was picking up his dry cleaning in Washington, D.C. when he was bumped from behind. It was just one more little aggravation in a rough day.

On paper, Yuri was a bureaucrat in the Russian Embassy's visa office. In actuality, he was Chief of Intelligence. In theory, such a job was the pinnacle of his career as a spy. In practice, it was hour after hour, day after day of trying to meet impossible demands from Moscow, while trying to avoid any spectacular screw-ups. "Front page of the *Washington Post*" screw-ups tended to be fatal to the Russian spy who made them.

"Watch where you are going," Yuri growled, not even bothering to see who had bumped him.

"I am *so* sorry," a woman's voice said. "How clumsy of me. Can I buy you coffee to make it up to you?"

Yuri turned around to look at the woman. From her accent, he already knew she was American. Now he saw that she had brunette hair, a gorgeous face, and long legs. She was large, but not bodacious, in the tits department. She looked to be in her thirties, but could have been a runway model when she'd been eighteen.

The most beautiful thing about her, however, was her I.D. badge. This woman worked in the White House!

Yuri would jump out of an airplane naked, if it meant he could recruit this woman as a spy.

"Myself, I am sorry...Susanne," Yuri said, reading her name from her nametag. "I have had the hard day."

"Well, I'm Susanne Nash, and I meant it about buying you coffee." She stuck out her hand. He shook it.

For Yuri the real-life spy, the next few hours were like something out of a James Bond movie. He talked to this beautiful woman, who told fascinating things about working for the First Lady—when she wasn't hanging on Yuri's every word. She even took Yuri back to her apartment and gave him a handjob!

BIMBORG KING'S PERSONAL LOG
DAY 13 (TUESDAY)

We still have no idea where the Cybes are, and nobody has any ideas how to find them.

In other news, Big Robert fucked me over royally today. We were sparring, and then he did this spinning kick that hit my right leg from the side. Boom, instantly he fractured my fibula, cracked my tibia, and dislocated my patella. (I know because floating words suddenly appeared and told me all this.)

I dropped to the floor of the dojo/garage. I had to press my wrist against my mouth to keep from screaming so loud that the whole neighborhood came running. Fuck, what agony—

—for ten seconds. Then floating words appeared: "Blink twice to heal."

You better believe I blinked twice!

The pain vanished. It was instantly, completely gone. I stood up, and my leg acted like nothing had happened to it.

That's when I realized: Nothing had happened to my leg. Just as the background music was an illusion, and Big Robert was an illusion, so was all the pain that Big Robert caused.

Inside the Help Menu are two choices: "Replay, Fighter" and "Replay, Observer." After enough times of watching Big Robert cripple the red man-thing that was playing me, I saw what had happened—

Big Robert had leaned back, putting all his weight on his rear leg, which was his right leg. Red man-thing (me) moved forward. As soon as the red man-thing put most of his weight on his right leg, Big Robert sprung his trap.

DAY 14 (WEDNESDAY), BEFORE SCHOOL
SWEET ONION HIGH SCHOOL

"So is he back, your dad?" Charlie-Bob asked Prudy Lu.

"Yeah, but he says he's going to be working lots of overtime, so don't expect to see him much," Prudy Lu said. She looked sad. "He told me that he's doing 'important work' now."

Rose asked, "Since your dad is back, are you gonna, ohmigod, tell Regina you're sorry, like she wants?"

"Ha!" Prudy Lu replied. "She can go—"

"At least there's, like, a happy ending in all of this," Tatum-Teresa Haven said. "Your dad is back, and he's got a job again."

Prudy Lu rocked her hand. "My dad is back, but now *Mom* is missing! No idea where she is, and Dad doesn't seem bothered."

"Maybe she went somewhere," Helen-May Sawyer said. "Her car, you know, broke down and then her cel phone died."

Prudy Lu shook her head. "Mom's the stay-at-home type. Never goes anywhere except to the Piggly Wiggly and to Bingo on Thursday at the Catholic church. This is weird."

Charlie-Bob put his hand on Prudy Lu's shoulder, which made her smile. "I'm sure she's okay. Don't worry."

Then everyone went to their first-period classes.

Charlie-Bob had six periods of classes that day; and in every one of them, students were absent.

Ordinarily he would have dismissed that fact as due to a flu bug.

But in English class, alphabetical seating put Charlie-Bob in the very back of the class, and he saw that all the absent students were the very quiet ones. All his classes after English kept to this pattern.

Missing from each class were exactly the sort of kids whose absence from a classroom would never be noticed, except officially.

Charlie-Bob wondered, *What does this mean?*

After school, Charlie-Bob said to Rose, "Please do me a favor. Go in the Girls' Bathroom, and check to see whether anyone has puked. I'll meet you back here, while I check the Boys' Bathroom."

When he and Rose met up again, she reported, "There's no, like, disgusting stuff in the Girl's Bathroom."

"None in the Boys', either," he said.

"Can I ask what you're thinking?"

"I'm not sure," he said. "Nobody at school *acts* sick. Nobody's throwing up, or coughing, or sniffling, or complaining of headaches. But kids are absent from school today. Besides the kids you expect to cut classes, I mean. The kids not here today are the quiet kids."

"Including Karen Fuller," Rose said.

Charlie-Bob gave Rose a *Who's she?* look.

Rose explained, "Karen is a witch in the coven I was in. Even in the coven, ohmigod, she hardly talked. Anyway, she wasn't in my Computer Art class today."

BIMBORG KING'S PERSONAL LOG
DAY 14 (WEDNESDAY)

We're still gutter-balling at finding the Cybes. I'm frustrated.

Big Robert pulled that same sneaky trick, the spinning sideways leg kick, on me again! And let me tell you, it hurts just as much the second time as it did the first. Let me also tell you, when you're waiting for the software to offer you healing, ten seconds is a L-O-N-G time!

Not wanting to experience such awful pain a third time, I looked through Help a little more. I found out that when I'm doing a replay, I can mark a certain amount of time before the end and choose "Should've," and then the red man-thing will do what a Third Belt-person should have done, instead of what dumbshit me actually did.

So I found out that what I should've done was that in the moment that I was putting most of my weight on my right leg, I should've thrown a punch with my left hand, to keep Big Robert on the defensive.

DAY 15 (THURSDAY)

Two days after Susanne Nash did handjob hypnosis on Yuri Petrovski in Washington, Mikhail Mikhailovich Kivorsikov met Mariya, the most fascinating woman in all of Moscow. Mariya was a strawberry blonde with an enormous rack, and a smoky gaze that could give the Kremlin dome an erection. Mikhail had boring children, a boring wife, and a boring job moving spy satellites over the USA; he'd thought his days of meeting incredible women were behind him.

Mariya's only beauty flaw? She had warts on her left hand.

BIMBORG KING'S PERSONAL LOG
DAY 16 (FRIDAY)

Guess what, still no Cybes. Where are they, and what are they doing?

Yesterday Big Robert couldn't manage his Sneaky Leg Trick even once (while facing me, that is), and today the software promoted me to Third Belt, Second Level. Life was good—for about one minute.

So once I got promoted, how did Big Robert congratulate me on my promotion? He started by backing up, and then running at me! Sometimes he punched me, sometimes he just pushed me down, and sometimes he kicked me. By the time I stopped the session, I had suffered through several broken jaws, broken ribs, and cracked femurs.

But thanks to "Demo" mode, I knew in theory how to handle his running attacks: turn sideways to him, then give him a certain kind of sideways kick.

By the time I shut down for the evening, I was stopping Big Robert's attacks one time out of four.

DAY 18 (SUNDAY), LATE EVENING, MOSCOW TIME

Mikhail, the czar of all the Russian spy satellites over the United States, met with Mariya the strawberry-blond sex goddess as often as he could sneak away. Not only was she amazing to look at, but every rendezvous with her was guaranteed to include a handjob and a blowjob both.

Mariya *appreciated* Mikhail. She looked impressed when he told her about the two Islamo-terrorist atomic bombs in the USA that, Mikhail was pretty sure, the United States government knew nothing about.

DAY 18 (SUNDAY)

"There are *two* terrorist nuclear bombs in America?" Charlie-Bob exclaimed as he ended the phone call. He immediately went to the bimborg website to read the details.

When he was through reading, he called Rose-unit and said, "Meet with me, please."

Ten minutes later, when Rose was standing in front of him, he told her, "Choose a team of five Ass-Kicker Babes for a mission that will take place between midnight tonight and dawn. . . ."

4-M: Away, Team!

BIMBORG KING'S PERSONAL LOG
DAY 19 (MONDAY)

I still don't know where the Cybes are, and now I've found out that Moslem terrorists have sneaked two battlefield nukes into the USA! Well, them I can deal with. In fact, we leave for our staging area, the Georgia Star Drive-In, in a few minutes.

I sure am glad I have the wormholer—we'll make attacks in Montana and in southern California, and we'll be back in Georgia well before sunrise.

I just told one of my Ass-Kickers, a woman named Cheryl who was wearing a red Atlanta Falcons t-shirt, to change her shirt. My stated reason is that I don't want anyone wearing anything that links us to Georgia. That is a valid reason—but also, I can't shake the feeling that the shirt would be unlucky for whoever wore it.

DAY 19 (MONDAY), BETWEEN MIDNIGHT AND DAWN

In Montana, Ass-Kicker Babe Shonique-unit had a Geiger counter, and so Charlie-Bob and his team were quickly able to find the Montana bomb. Shonique-unit informed everyone that the bomb was a small one, as A-bombs go—in any case, a standard wooden pallet was more than big enough for it.

The team had no idea what the Moslems planned to do with their bomb, but Kyong-unit pointed out that there was an active U.S. Air Force missile silo less than ten miles away.

Charlie-Bob and his team came, found the bomb, loaded it on a pallet jack, and wormholed back to Georgia, without one shot fired. Other than the sleeping sentry (who got his neck snapped), there were no casualties on each side.

As for the rest of the Moslems in Montana? They slept through the whole thing.

The Montana A-bomb got stored in the projection room of the Georgia Star Drive-In. Once the bomb was hidden away, Charlie-Bob and his team were wormholed to San Diego.

Hopefully this A-bomb theft would be quick and easy, as well.

According to Shonique's Geiger counter, the bomb was in a delivery truck, at the front of the body (the cargo compartment). This truck had been painted white, and then had been lettered with "Ali's Fresh Produce." That black lettering had been done recently, because on a table near the truck, moonlight revealed black-painted stencils and cans of black spray paint.

The truck was parked in a back yard that was surrounded by a six-foot-tall wooden fence. Exits from the back yard were a back gate, which led into an alley and which was wide enough for the truck to pass through; and a door leading into the house.

This time there was no sentry, sleeping or otherwise, near the bomb.

On the other hand, three different windows of the house looked out onto the truck.

The truck's roll-up cargo door was rolled up, which meant one less problem for Charlie-Bob and the bimborg. The body was halfway filled with boxes of produce, while more cardboard boxes set on the ground near the truck. The bimborg team's red-light flashlights revealed that those boxes contained onions.

The house remained dark and quiet.

San Diego is one of the best-defendable harbors in the world. Because of that geographic fact, the U.S. Navy has bases of every flavor, everywhere in San Diego. So it was obvious to Charlie-Bob what the Moslems' plan was, even if he couldn't guess which base or ship was their specific target.

He climbed up into the body of the truck, along with Shonique. They began carrying boxes of tomatoes out to the lip of the truck, and handing the boxes down to Queen Rose and a blond Ass-Kicker Babe named Tasha. Cheryl, Lucille, and Kyong stood guard with guns ready.

The house was still dark and quiet. So far, so good.

Charlie-Bob realized that their good luck couldn't last. Tasha-unit, being an Ass-Kicker Babe, moved the boxes that were handed to her as if they were empty; but since Pleasure Units have only ordinary strength for a woman, Rose moved her boxes more slowly. Worse, every time that Tasha or Rose took a box from Shonique or Charlie-Bob, the suspension on the truck squeaked.

A few minutes later, all the tomatoes were off the truck.

A light went on in the bathroom. Fortunately, the glass in the bathroom was frosted, so that whoever was in the bathroom couldn't see outside.

Do your business and then go back to sleep, buddy, Charlie-Bob mentally urged.

Charlie-Bob was getting sweaty, and all sorts of muscles were getting sore. But he forced himself to keep moving quickly.

By now there were still three layers of floor-to-ceiling boxes at the front of the truck body.

"Unloading the boxes off the truck is taking too much time," Charlie-Bob told Shonique. "So let's just carry them to the other end of the truck. Hopefully, that won't make the truck squeak."

She nodded.

But Charlie-Bob learned the hard way that if you dropped a box at the edge of the truck body, instead of you slowly setting the box down, the truck squeaked anyway.

As Charlie-Bob was setting down a box of cabbages by the lip of the truck, he heard the house's toilet flush. Then the bathroom light went out.

"King Charlie-Bob? It here," Shonique said.

He hurried to the front of the cargo compartment.

By red-light flashlight he saw the bomb. It lay on the floor and against the front wall of the cargo compartment. The bomb was set between two stacks of cabbage boxes, with a board laying across two boxes making a roof for the bomb, with a cabbage box placed on top of the board.

A hole had been drilled in the front wall of the cargo compartment. A wire ran from the bomb, through the hole, into the truck cab—

"*Allahu Akbar!*" someone called out, to the sound of breaking glass. Then shots came from the house. Answering gunfire came from several bimborg near the truck.

Oh shit, Charlie-Bob thought.

He ran to the lip of the cargo compartment. He needed to see what was happening, he needed to command his troops—

Rose grabbed his legs and fell backward, pulling Charlie-Bob out of the truck and onto the ground.

She called out, "*Za Tasha-thri, kek zhe a-fradsa chukhonrewa!*" Tasha-unit, [pull] him behind the truck!

By now Tasha-unit was holding (and firing) an assault rifle. She let go of the rifle with one hand, and used that hand to grab Charlie-Bob by his shirt, and pull him around behind the truck.

As soon as Charlie-Bob was out of immediate danger, Tasha-unit dived under the truck. Within seconds she was firing shots from between the truck's rear wheels.

The house and back yard now were sounding like the sound track to a video game. This frustrated Charlie-Bob. He couldn't see what was going on, and his own assault rifle was in the truck!

"I need something to shoot," he said loudly.

A few seconds later, Tasha slid a second assault rifle backward along the grass.

Five seconds later, Charlie-Bob shot his first human being that wasn't phosphor dots. Charlie-Bob didn't know if he'd killed the bearded man, but the man went down and stayed down.

Charlie-Bob fired at a second man—or tried to. His assault rifle jammed. Disgusted, he threw the gun down. (An act for which Lucille later on, very tactfully, read her King the Riot Act.)

By then, having one fewer useful weapons didn't matter. The Ass-Kicker Babes were fantastic shots; by now, everyone inside the house was either gory-dead, or had decided that seventy-two virgins were overrated.

Charlie-Bob heard running feet *behind* him. He turned around, just in time to see that a man was running from the alleyway gate straight toward him.

Just like how Big Robert had been attacking Charlie-Bob for the last three days.

But unlike Big Robert, this attacker had a beard, a turban, and he was holding a scimitar(!) over his head.

The man yelled something. Charlie-Bob caught only the word *kafir* (unbeliever).

From behind him, Charlie-Bob heard a woman's voice say, "I have a clear shot."

But even as Charlie-Bob was hearing this, his *Edo-kobushi* training had him already running toward Scimitar Man. The Moslem man's eyes widened in surprise.

One in four, please let this be the one chance in four! Charlie-Bob thought.

He planted his left foot and let his forward momentum spin him a quarter-turn. His right foot went up and sideways to his body, and slammed into the Moslem's chest. Charlie-Bob heard a *crunch* sound, then the Moslem man fell back, saying "Urk."

Whish. Charlie-Bob now was bent sideways at the waist, and the scimitar whizzed over his right ear.

The Moslem was on the ground now, but trying to get up, despite the pink froth coming from his mouth. Charlie-Bob shoved the man's chest with his foot, to make the man lie flat; then Charlie-Bob hopped up and down on the guy's neck. The man quit exhaling pink froth.

Rose's voice said, "Whoa! Like, all hail King Charlie-Bob."

Who at this moment was realizing something: *I've killed two men in combat, the last one in a one-to-one fight. Whoa.*

Cheryl-unit had been shot in the shoulder; none of the other bimborg had been injured at all. Charlie-Bob couldn't shake the feeling that if he hadn't ordered Cheryl to change her red "Atlanta Falcons" t-shirt, she would have been hurt much worse.

While Charlie-Bob was giving on-the-spot first aid to Cheryl, Rose was directing the removal of the A-bomb from the truck. Every Ass-Kicker Babe except Cheryl was assigned to this task, because Ass-Kickers could move the heavy bomb quickly—and the team could faintly hear police sirens.

By the time that the A-bomb was on the ground and was loaded onto a pallet, those police sirens were loud.

Charlie-Bob got a thought. "Anyone know Arabic?" he asked.

Tasha raised her hand.

"Paint 'Shiites are pigfuckers' on the side of the truck with that black spray paint. We need to fool the investigators."

While Tasha was graffiti-izing the truck, Charlie-Bob claimed the scimitar and he called Mary Kayla on his smartphone.

He told her, "The San Diego Police are coming. Wormholize!"

SSSSOOM.

Charlie-Bob and his bimborg band of A-bomb borrowers, their equipment, the scimitar, and the A-bomb all entered the wormhole just as a man's voice yelled at the front of the house, "SAN DIEGO POLICE! OPEN UP!"

After the San Diego A-bomb was stashed inside the projection room, Rose sidled up to Charlie-Bob.

She gave him the sexy look of a thirty-year-old Las Vegas call girl. "You've ordered us bimborg to act around you like we would if we were, you know, Solitary."

"Yes, I have," he replied. He couldn't guess where Rose was going with this.

"The Ass-Kicker Babes and I, we agree about you," she said in a husky voice.

"Agree about what?" he asked.

Rose stroked his shirt. "Ohmigod, if I weren't, you know, an emotionless cyborg now, and a lesbian before that, I'd be fucking your brains out in a parked car right now, right here in this very drive-in."

"Huh? What?"

"Meanwhile, several of the other girls here would be standing outside the car, flashing you their boobs while they waited for their own chance to, like, rock your world themselves."

"Why?"

"The way you fought the guy with the big sword? You had no gun, no knife, just your body and your brain—and you won. For Solitary girls, that is so totally fucking *hot.*"

Then Queen Rose knelt and unzipped the front of his pants.

By then, the five other bimborg had formed a circle around the bimborg king and queen. The women of the circle were all Ass-Kicker Babes, not Pleasure Units, but every woman was giving Charlie-Bob as horny a look as any Pleasure Unit ever had.

Shonique said, "You so brave, King Charlie-Bob. If I be Solitary, I wanting you to fuck my pussy till I screams."

That's when Charlie-Bob felt, for the first time, like a king.

He was already a king by responsibility to 22 million bimborg. But tonight he'd killed a man in a fair fight, who was trying to kill him—if that didn't make him a true king, what did?

As Charlie-Bob got his dick slurped, he felt like beating his chest and yelling his loudest, Tarzan-style.

Instead, he fucked Rose's wet pussy on the hood of her car.

Next he got a handjob from Cheryl. Cheryl had been shot in the shoulder, but already she was well healed by her nanobots. He'd ordered Cheryl not to wear her red shirt into combat—her underwear, it turned out, consisted of fuck-me red panties and a fuck-me red bra.

Shonique screamed during her orgasm. Blond Tasha talked dirty, nonstop, while Charlie-Bob fucked her.

Lucille was very practical: "You don't have the energy reserves we Ass-Kicker Babes do, so this unit bets you feel sleepy. You lean against the car, and I'll suck you off. If you fall asleep, that's okay."

He didn't fall asleep during the blowjob, but he felt like he'd taken a hundred sleeping pills, immediately after.

Still, he forced himself to stay awake, while he ate out the neatly trimmed pussy of black-haired Kyong in the back seat.

After he'd licked Kyong to her third or fourth orgasm (he'd lost track), he couldn't stay awake any more.

He slumped against a car door in the back seat of Rose's car. The last things he saw before his eyes slammed shut were stars and moonlight that made two drive-in movie screens glow.

4-N: Nemesis

DAY 19 (MONDAY)
MORNING, BEFORE FIRST PERIOD
SWEET ONION HIGH SCHOOL

Prudy Lu Moffatt noticed that it was a lot easier to walk down the hallway of SOHS than it had been a month ago. Looking around, she realized that there were fewer kids in the hallway.

The sound she was hearing was "the same, but different," Prudy Lu realized. There was as much laughing and talking as before; all the popular and rowdy kids were here in force. But there weren't as many locker-noises: the spinning of combination-lock dials, and the opening and slamming of locker doors. There also was less noise from kids walking around, because there were fewer kids walking.

She could see gaps, where kids had been here a month ago but were absent now—but as much as she tried, Prudy Lu couldn't put a name to even one missing kid.

Is there some kind of flu going around that makes only the quiet kids sick?

Prudy Lu realized that she hadn't seen "Sergeant Parker," the school security guard, for a while. She wondered if he'd caught the weird flu.

Prudy Lu hadn't heard of any bug going around, and she hadn't coughed once in the last month. She decided to ask Rose or Denise; those two would know the score.

Speaking of Denise, Prudy Lu soon found one of her new BFFs standing next to Charlie-Bob Owens in a hallway. Apparently he was reviewing Denise's geometry homework—

"Sorry, but you've got the angle-bisector wrong. The line must be drawn *here*. This far, no farther."

As Prudy Lu waited for them to finish, she studied Charlie-Bob. He seemed different somehow. The thought jumped into her head: *He is a man now.*

In one sense, the thought was ridiculous. Partly because his eyes were red, and he was constantly yawning, as if he'd been up all night. Also, he was wearing the same nerdy clothes he always wore.

And yet. . .

His stomach was flatter. Apparently he'd started some kind of exercise program.

But mainly what was different about him, Prudy Lu decided, was that he carried both a sense of responsibility and a powerful confidence. He had something he had to do, something important and grown-up, but now he was sure he could do it.

Seeing Charlie-Bob this way, it made her wet. *This* was manliness.

DURING LUNCH

Prudy Lu saw that Charlie-Bob was walking toward the milk machine with glass in hand, just as Kevin Sinclair (Denise's ex-boyfriend) carried his own tray there.

Kevin put his full glass on his tray, picked up his tray, turned around—and walked straight into Charlie-Bob, knocking him down.

Except that Charlie-Bob didn't actually fall down. He landed on the floor, did a somersault sort of thing, and was on his feet almost instantly. He didn't even break the glass in his hand!

"Watch where you're going!" each guy said at the same moment.

Then Kevin growled, "Wait, a puny-ass nerd is telling me that this is *my* fault?"

"Exactly. You turned around and started walking, without looking to see if anyone was where you wanted to go. Your eyes were on the cheerleader table."

"And what if I *was* looking at them? If you saw I was nearby, you should have stayed out of my way."

"Kevin, you're either a total jerk, or you're as stupid as the ox you're as big as. No wonder Denise dropped you for me."

"Yeah, and so I should pound your face in, right now!"

Then Prudy Lu saw Charlie-Bob stare down the taller, heavier, and stronger boy without a trace of fear, and with gallons of confidence. "You think you can beat me up? I say you'd get a surprise. You want to try it, right here? Let's go."

To Prudy Lu, Kevin looked rattled. "In the lunchroom? I'd get in trouble."

"No, *the winner of the fight* would get in trouble. But hey, I understand your refusal. Imagine the humiliation for you—"

A boy nearby made the clucking-chicken sound. When Kevin turned to glare at the other boy, the kid smirked back at him instead of looking afraid.

When Kevin looked at Charlie-Bob again, Charlie-Bob was still looking back at him with confidence and no fear.

"Kevin, my food is getting cold. What's it gonna be, you put down the tray and fight me now, or you go take your seat?"

Kevin, with shoulders slumped, hurried away. Meanwhile, Charlie-Bob walked to the milk machine and refilled his glass, as if nothing had happened.

Seconds later, Prudy Lu heard Regina Wisley's loud words: "Get away from us! Charlie-Bob Owens just made you his bitch, so no way are you sitting at this table!"

Prudy Lu looked at her table-mates, Helen-May and Rose, and sighed. "I really wish Charlie-Bob would ask me out. But no way will he ask me for a date when y'all are there for him, any time he wants."

Oddly, Rose and Helen-May gave each other surprised looks.

AFTER SCHOOL

Charlie-Bob walked up to Prudy Lu and said, "Can I talk to you a minute?"

Her heart beating faster, Prudy Lu said, "Sure."

His smile was lopsided. "My, *ahem*, harem tell me that you're still hoping I'll ask you out. Remember that Bull Barclay and Kevin Sinclair are available."

"I'm not interested in Bull Barclay," Prudy Lu said. She giggled. "*Double* no to Kevin Sinclair! I want to go out with *you*."

"Prudy Lu, there's a problem. I like you, believe me—"

"Oh please, don't tell me, 'I have to give my dog a bath this Saturday night.' Just tell me the truth."

"I can't tell you *all* the truth. But nowadays I'm doing something important—"

"I *knew* it!"

"—and it has me busy, longer than I figured on, and so I've cut back on dating. Until I wrap this up, I won't be asking anyone out. Or, uh, doing anything else with girls."

"Thank you for not playing head games with me," Prudy Lu said. "You're so adult." She kissed Charlie-Bob on the lips.

Meanwhile, the Cybe Invisible whom Solitaries knew as Regina Wisley was talking to Busty Betsy. Supposedly.

But Cybe-Regina's mind wasn't on what Betsy was saying, or what Regina would say next. Nor was Cybe-Regina thinking about how to carry out the consensus of her Cybe Clan, or how to obey the orders of Cybe Alpha.

No, what Cybe-Regina was actually doing was watching two Solitaries, Prudy Lu Moffatt and Charlie-Bob Owens, kiss.

Cybe-Regina wanted to hurt them both.

She *would* hurt them both.

Whenever Cybe-Regina's Cybe Clan should give her an order, she would comply. With one exception.

Whenever Cybe Alpha should give Cybe-Regina an order, she would comply. With one exception.

Destroying Prudy Lu and Charlie-Bob now was Cybe-Regina's first priority.

4-O: Secrets Exposed

DAY 19 (MONDAY)

One of the nice things about being Bimborg King was that Charlie-Bob didn't need to worry about telemarketers calling him on his smartphone. The one telemarketing business that had managed to talk to him at his Do Not Call phone number, had the misfortune to get raided by the Federal Trade Commission the next day. How strange, that coincidence.

So when Charlie-Bob's smartphone display said UNKNOWN CALLER, he took the call with no worries.

"Charlie-Bob Owens? This is, like, Amy Emily Chapel, from Emory University. Are you busy?"

Charlie-Bob felt many emotions with those few words. Last year, when Amy Emily had been a senior at SOHS and he a junior, he'd had a crush on her. Back in November, he'd gotten himself shot because he'd tried to protect her honor. Now he was Bimborg King, and she was one of the Pleasure Units he "ruled."

Amy Emily also was one of the Pleasure Units in Atlanta and Athens who were assigned to buy the parts for centuries-advanced technology, and who were building that technology in Loganville.

Amy Emily brought Charlie-Bob up to date. (In English; he was still crappy at Bimborgspeak.) She told him her crew of Pleasure Unit machinists had completed making the first bimborg-built force-field generator/cloaker, and were starting work on a second wormholer.

Charlie-Bob said, "Good. How's work coming with the Cybe Distress Beacon?"

Charlie-Bob had ordered the Pleasure Units to build a copy of a Cybe Distress Beacon, as the first step in finding out Cybe Alpha's location. But the CDB had turned into a major technical challenge.

Amy Emily said, "The Cybe Distress Beacon is done. It's, like, on its way to your town right now."

"Wow, great! So is that why you're calling me?"

"I also wanted to tell you something, ohmigod, *so* strange."

"Strange?"

"Some girlfriends and I were shopping"—buying parts to haul to Loganville—"and this guy behind the counter asked us, since we went to college, if we knew Doctor Zimmermann?"

"Who's he?"

"He's in the Physics department at Georgia Tech, you know? Anyway, I've looked him up, and he writes papers on, like, quarks and tachyons and stuff."

"Subatomic particles."

"Submarines have those things? Ohmigod. Anyway, he'd special-ordered stuff, and it had come in last week and they'd called him, but he hadn't come by to get it. All prepaid so, you know, he could've sent a student to get the stuff if he was busy, but he's never come over."

"Why are you calling about him? I'm missing something."

"Well, you've mentioned on the website about people disappearing, folks nobody would miss."

"Yes, a lot of people in my town are missing. Go on."

"But he teaches classes. He's not low-profile, you know? Well, I was talking it over with Deanna-226949 over at University of Georgia—she's brunette, a 'Betazoid'—"

"Huh?"

"Member of Beta Zeta Omega sorority. You'd like her: She's got an English accent and huge boobs even for us, ohmigod, but she's *real* smart. Anyway, Deanna suggested I find out if any professor at Emory researches quarks and tachyons."

"So what did y'all find out?"

"Emory, no, but University of Georgia does, and that guy's missing too!"

"Maybe they're just out sick?"

"No, Deanna and I checked it out. I drove over to Georgia Tech, and she walked over to UGA's Physics department. Did you know that Physics professors are easy to talk to? Anyway, those two subba-whatever professors are gone!"

Charlie-Bob imagined Amy Emily, now a DD-cup, saying to some Georgia Tech professor, "Oh please, can't you tell me where to find Dr. Zimmermann?" Those men would sing like canaries.

Charlie-Bob thanked Amy Emily for calling, nailed down when the Cybe Distress Beacon would be delivered, then spent five minutes thinking about what she'd said about the missing professors.

After that, he drove over to Mary Kayla's apartment and spent time on the Cybe computer till he couldn't think straight.

Before he crashed on the young teacher's couch, Charlie-Bob posted a notice to bimborg worldwide, to check on each country's subatomic-particle experts.

6 a.m. TUESDAY MORNING, DAY 20
MARY KAYLA'S APARTMENT

Mary Kayla offered to fix breakfast for Charlie-Bob, and he accepted her offer. She offered him a blowjob; for once, he accepted that offer too. (He figured he needed to think clearly afterward.)

Then Mary Kayla went to Sweet Onion High School because, after all, she had a job there. Theoretically, so did Charlie-Bob—as a student. But after the breakfast and the blowjob, he got back on the Cybe computer. This straight-A student wound up getting an unexcused absence for the entire day.

Around noontime, the doorbell rang. Standing there was a buxom young woman with green eyes, a big smile, warts on one hand, and a package to deliver. She wore the chocolate-brown UPS uniform and the UPS truck was idling out front, but she didn't ask him to sign for the package.

After she handed over the cardboard box, she offered to fuck him silly. He politely declined.

9 p.m. TUESDAY NIGHT, DAY 20
MARY KAYLA'S APARTMENT

The people in the apartment were Mary Kayla and the rest of Sweet Onion's Pleasure Units, plus Ass-Kicker Babe Lucille. They all were facing Charlie-Bob.

Karen Milph was sitting off to one side with a no-kidding steno pad; her typed-up notes would be emailed to the Pleasure Units at Palmer Electronics.

Charlie-Bob cleared his throat, looked at the assembled women, and began. "Yesterday and today, I've been getting word that certain college professors, everywhere in the world, are missing. These missing professors each have written a paper about tachyons, which are one kind of subatomic particle."

"The Cybes grabbed the professors," Heather Saint James said.

He nodded. "Every tachyon expert on the planet. What's more, they've all been missing for weeks, since before James was killed."

Paula Crawford, a freshman bimborg, asked, "Tachyons are, like, the thingies that make our nanobots do cool stuff, right?"

"*Anti*-tachyons are what make your nanobots do amazing things," he corrected. "Your nanobots and Cybe nanobots, both. Both tachyons and anti-tachyons have the property that they can travel through all matter. So nanobots in one part of your body can talk to nanobots in another part of your body, because your nanobots all use anti-tachyons. Likewise, two bimborg on opposite sides of Earth can talk to each other, no problem."

"Two *Cybes* on opposite sides of Earth *also* can talk to each other, because of these same anti-tachyons," Lucille pointed out.

"For now," Charlie-Bob said. "But later on? I have a plan for that."

Hearing that, all the women smiled except for Lucille, and Lucille looked less solemn.

Rose said, "So back to your story. All these tachyon professors, they're grabbed up."

He said, "Yes, and I think I know why."

"Why?" Denise asked.

"It's because of when the nanobot microtransmitter was invented in the 24th century. They built it to run with anti-tachyons, not tachyons, and they've worked that way ever since."

Denise said again, "Why?"

Charlie-Bob laughed. "Don't ask me what the reason is, because the answer involves a mix of 24th-century medicine and 24th-century subatomic physics. I've read that sucker twice and I can't explain one sentence in it."

"So how does this connect with the missing professors?" Karen Milph asked.

"It turns out that if someone makes a big burst of tachyons—regular tachyons, not the *anti* kind—this burst completely ruins the nanobots' anti-tachyon receptors. The nanobots in a Cybe's body can't work anymore, and the Cybe can't talk to, or hear from, other Cybes. Every Cybe that's closer to the tachyon burst than a certain radius, becomes Solitary."

Helen-May Sawyer clapped. "That's great news."

"Maybe, maybe not," Heather Saint James replied. "The tachyon burst would affect us bimborg the same way. No more quick healing, no more quick thinking, no more extra speed or extra strength, and The Club would be permanently closed."

"I'd give up all that in a heartbeat," Brooke Coleman said, "if it means stopping the Cybes."

Then Brooke turned to face Charlie-Bob directly. "Besides, it's not our choice. If King Charlie-Bob commands, we must obey."

The look that Brooke was giving Charlie-Bob was one of complete trust.

Heather asked, "What's the fine print on this Tachyon Bomb?"

Charlie-Bob replied, "It's subject to inverse-square limitations. The bomb has to be four times as powerful, in order to Solitarize Cybes at twice the distance. But I'm not worried; I think we can build a Tachyon Bomb that is good for the entire Earth."

Rose said, "Going back to the professors. They got grabbed because they were the only people on Earth who maybe could've built a weapon to stop the Cybes, right?"

"Other than us, and now they're gone," he said. "Bimborg, we 22 million people are Earth's only hope."

"Because now we have a weapon that the Cybes can't fight," Denise said. She pumped her fist. "This is, like, *so* cool."

Charlie-Bob held up a finger. "New topic: The Cybe Distress Beacon arrived today, so tomorrow I'll need a bimborg to work the wormholer for Operation Birdshit."

Rose said, "How about this: *You* run the wormholer for Operation Birdshit, and a *bimborg* plants the CDB. *You* doing the deed is reckless and risky."

Charlie-Bob shook his head. "No. I'll put y'all in danger *next to* me, if I have to, but I won't put any bimborg in danger *instead of* me."

"Even when it means that we could lose everything? You haven't, like, chosen a replacement Bimborg King, and you might get killed or Welcomed tomorrow."

"*Yes.* I'd feel like a coward if I stayed here safe while some of you died."

"Then consider this, Charlie-Bob," Rose said. "The Space Navy would never give someone command of a spaceship if he, like, acted as daredevil as you."

"Which is why the Space Navy never defeated the Cybes. They didn't have a man who'd go boldly as he trekked through the stars."

MORNING
DAY 21 (WEDNESDAY)
THE FARM OF PETER AND LINDA KELLY
KIRK COUNTY, IOWA

SSSSOOM.

Charlie-Bob opened up the king-size pillowcase he was carrying, reached in, and had the ray-gun in his hand within moments.

The grass around the farmhouse was overgrown. There was a big wooden sign that stood near the farm road and that faced away from Charlie-Bob; the sign probably said "FOR SALE."

The barn's front doors were chained and padlocked shut, but the Loganville-made ray-gun solved that problem easily. Also, the barn doors were taped shut with yellow "U. S. ARMY INTELLIGENCE" tape. Charlie-Bob ignored the tape as he pulled open the barn doors.

The barn's back doors were chained and padlocked shut from the inside; again, the ray-gun needed only an instant to open those doors.

Beyond the barn's back doors, a huge machine lay on its side; it was starting to rust. Also beyond the barn's back doors was the shallow hole in which Cybe-Jenny Smith had been buried.

Now the hole was empty.

Charlie-Bob stepped into the shallow grave, and looked all around. Nearby was a hayloft that offered a good vantage point.

He put the bulging pillowcase on the ground, reached inside it, and took out the Loganville-made Cybe Distress Beacon. It was a simple-looking box, with a battery pack, sheet metal, a red indicator light, and a toggle switch. All futuristic stuff was hidden from view.

Charlie-Bob set the cloned Cybe Distress Beacon in the shallow hole, in a corner chosen that, in order for a Cybe to pick up the box, that Cybe almost certainly would have to turn his back on the hayloft. Or rather, such an outcome was Charlie-Bob's fervent prayer.

Charlie-Bob, still standing in the hole, reached into his pocket, pulled out a wire tie-wrap, and closed the open end of the pillowcase. Once he turned on the CDB, seconds would count, and he *really* didn't want to stop to pick up things that had fallen out of the pillowcase. Once the pillowcase was tied shut, he lay the ray-gun on top of it.

He took one last look around. Once he flipped this toggle switch, there'd be no time to fix mistakes.

Charlie-Bob took a deep breath, bent down, and flipped the switch. The red light started to flash.

DAY 21 (WEDNESDAY)
PIGGLY-WIGGLY SUPERMARKET
SWEET ONION, GEORGIA

A Cybe Invisible is medically the same as a Solitary. Well, except for the little hemisphere on the back of his/her neck, and the wires running from it into the brain.

All of which means that an Invisible has to eat. This is why Cybe-Regina was buying groceries for herself.

But *only* for herself. Her father was a Cybe Soldier now, and her mother was a Welcomer, and so they got energy by standing up during the night in a Recharging Chamber. They would tell a Solitary (if they didn't Welcome him first) that eating was so. . .inefficient.

People had noticed that Regina was the only Wisley seen around town. Regina had started explaining that nobody saw her parents because they were vacationing in Europe. Such was the townspeople's opinion of Roger and Steffi Jo, nobody questioned this.

Grocery-shopping was easier for Regina now. Out of the town's population of eleven thousand, 10.2 percent had been Welcomed, which meant that the supermarket had 8.8 percent fewer customers.

Among Cybes, only Invisibles such as Regina Wisley and Jeb Moffatt (Prudy Lu's father) still bought food.

Most of the Invisibles in Sweet Onion were like Jeb Moffatt, spending every waking moment at the Wisley Electronics plant, making more wormholers and force-field generators for the Clan. Fifteen-hour workdays don't allow strolling through the supermarket.

The supermarket was quieter now, and not only because it had fewer customers. Cybe Alpha had decided that Amanda Wilkes and Bridget McGee were completely useless to the Cybe cause, and so the two loudmouthed crones had been nonbiologicked. Their corpses had been wormholed to shark-infested waters in the Atlantic.

Cybe-Regina smiled at the thought of Mrs. Wilkes and Widow McGee being eaten by sharks. Then Cybe-Regina saw something that pushed all thoughts of old biddies and sharks from her mind.

On the night that most of Jimmy Upton's cyborgs in Grand City had been nonbiologicked, one of his cyborgs had escaped the Cybes. Even worse, that cyborg had nonbiologicked a Welcomer—but not before the Welcomer had gotten a good look at the other cyborg's face and had transmitted the image to the Overmind.

All Cybes had standing orders to look for the escaped cyborg, but Cybe-Regina didn't expect that *she* would spot the escapee. After all, Grand City was three states away from Sweet Onion.

Yet here was the escapee, right here in Piggly-Wiggly—

—along with the only other person on the Cybe "yell if you see her" list: Jimmy Upton's mother.

". . .not supposed to be out in public, Ellen," the cyborg was saying. "It's not safe for you, and James told you and David—"

"—to stay in the motel. Which we have done, for over a month now. Lucille, do you know how *boring* white cinder-block walls get after thirty-something days? Not to mention, why am I taking orders from my own son? I did it, but I can't tell you why, and I'm not doing any more of it."

Cybe-Regina could answer that question. The Cybes who'd burst into Jimmy Upton's bedroom had instantly recognized that he'd given his own body the same Alpha Male transformation that Cybe Soldiers always get. His Alpha Male pheromones had compelled his mother's obedience, but clearly the effect of those pheromones had worn off.

The man standing next to Ellen Upton said, "We need to go home now. I've missed work, and we both have dead children whose funerals we've missed. The vacation is over—send us home."

"David, I can't," Cyborg-Lucille replied. "Charlie-Bob is out of town now, and I have orders not to call his phone."

Cybe-Regina would have fallen over from shock, had her emotion-suppression subroutine not kicked in. Only one person among Sweet Onion's eleven thousand people had that name. *Charlie-Bob Owens is mixed up in this?*

Meanwhile, David was saying, "We won't be asking nicely much longer. Greyhound stops at Archer's Hardware; you can't keep us here if we decide to leave."

Ellen asked, "What about that girl, the one who's come to the motel a few times? Get *her* to help us leave."

"Let's discuss this later," Cyborg-Lucille said. "We need to get the grocery shopping done, then get you two back to the motel. For your own safety."

Ellen crossed her arms. "Don't ignore my question, young lady. What about that girl, the one with the lovely face? And, uh—"

"The great rack," David said.

"Rose doesn't have the authority," Cyborg-Lucille replied. "If James sent you here, only Charlie-Bob may send you away from here."

Cybe-Regina smiled. *So that bitch Rose is a Cybe-Enemy too?*

THE KELLY FARM
KIRK COUNTY, IOWA

Charlie-Bob took a deep breath, bent down, and flipped the switch on the copycat Cybe Distress Beacon. The red light on top started to flash.

Charlie-Bob grabbed the ray-gun in his right hand, stepped up out of the hole, grabbed the pillowcase in his left hand, and ran for the hayloft ladder. *Hurry, hurry!*

His left arm spun up and around, tossing the pillowcase up onto the hayloft "floor." He climbed the ladder as fast as he could, one-handed; his right hand still held the ray-gun, and was prepared to fire it.

No guest yet. *All that excitement and drama for nothing?*

Once he was in the hayloft, he removed the tie-wrap from the pillowcase, and pulled its contents out: a paintball gun, two specially made "balls" for the gun, his smartphone, and a periscope.

He loaded the "balls" into the paintball gun, though with difficulty; the purple-and-white balls were gooey, made to look and feel like birdshit.

It occurred to him that he should have brought the pillowcase and its contents up to the hayloft *before* he turned on the CDB and needed to race the clock. Even a butterbars Second Louie fresh from West Point would have known better. *I'm not a general, I'm only a high-school kid*, he thought; but the thought only made him feel worse.

Still no special guest. He worried that the CDB wasn't working right. He couldn't check; he hadn't thought to bring an AM radio.

Any Cybe Distress Beacon, whether the authentic version that was in every set of Cybe armor, or the Loganville copy, had two parts. The anti-tachyon pulse that a CDB made, could be "heard" by every Cybe on the planet. But Cybes had no way of knowing where that pulse was coming from. The other part of the Beacon was a radio that broadcast a tone in three out of sixteen possible radio frequencies. That radio signal could be homed in on, if three Cybes were within 150 kilometers of the CDB.

Dammit, show up already, Cybe!

This low-rent CDB would broadcast one tone in each of the three frequencies that were in the AM band. This was done partly so that bimborg could verify that the CDB was working, but also because the message that the device was sending to Cybes was a relatively harmless distress call: "I'm lost."

If the CDB wasn't working at all, Charlie-Bob would've gotten a phone call. He knew better than to try and call the bimborg who was in a parked car ten miles away; she wouldn't take his call.

It occurred to him that his long wait was a good thing. The fewer Cybes there were in the world, and the fewer wormhole machines, the longer it would take some Cybe to wormhole within 150 kilometers of the CDB, and thus find the CDB soon after.

Over to his left, Charlie-Bob noticed spots of dried blood on the bare wood of the hayloft. He realized that this was the spot where fifteen-year-old James had killed—

SSSSOOM. Charlie-Bob's Cybe prey had arrived.

SWEET ONION, GEORGIA

When Cyborg-Lucille, Ellen Upton, and Ellen's boyfriend David all left the supermarket (on bicycles), Cybe-Regina followed in her car. The bicyclists headed for the three motels at the edge of town.

However, when the bicyclists passed Batleth's Cutlery, David pointed to it. Cyborg-Lucille pointed forward. David pointed again to the cutlery store, more insistently. So they stopped; a few minutes later, Ellen and David emerged with purchases.

Regina was as amused as a Cybe could get. *Do you think that a knife will help you if a Soldier comes toward you?*

Regina figured that the three were headed to one of the motels on Old Lionheart Highway. Regina drove past the bicyclists, in order to allay Cyborg-Lucille's suspicions. Regina then parked where hopefully she wouldn't be noticed, and waited for the bicyclists to enter one of the motels.

Five minutes later, the bicyclists entered the Rocket Motel. That's when Regina noticed that Lucille's bicycle had a rear-view mirror. That meant trouble. *If she looked in that mirror even once, she'll have seen this unit following them from the supermarket.*

Regina pulled into the parking lot of the Rocket Motel in time to see the three people walk their bicycles into room 113.

Jimmy Upton's escapee mother had definitely been located. Cybe-Regina reported the details to the Overmind.

Now the only task left was to discover where Cyborg-Lucille lived, if not here at the Rocket Motel.

THE KELLY FARM
KIRK COUNTY, IOWA

One or more Cybes had just wormholed into the barn.

It occurred to Charlie-Bob then, he'd planned on only one Cybe showing up. If two or more Cybes wormholed into the barn, that meant trouble.

Charlie-Bob picked up the periscope and looked. He saw one Soldier standing by the CDB. The Soldier was slowly turning in a circle, looking over the entire barn. Charlie-Bob held the periscope rock-steady, hoping that the Soldier would think the top of the periscope was just another part of the barn.

So far, so good, Charlie-Bob thought.

The Cybe looked down at the CDB in the shallow grave, paused, then jumped into the hole himself. Sure enough, this put him with his back to the hayloft and to Charlie-Bob.

As soon as the Soldier turned his back, Charlie-Bob swapped the periscope for the paintball gun. Then Charlie-Bob pulled himself forward with his elbows, to see the Soldier with his own eyes.

Which also meant: If the Soldier turned around, no way could Charlie-Bob hide in time. The Bimborg King was committed.

There were birds of some kind in the rafters, and Charlie-Bob hoped that they were making enough noise to cover up whatever noise he was making. Well, he'd find out soon enough.

Charlie-Bob aimed at the Soldier's armor, between his shoulder blades. *Pupht.*

The gooey-ball went right where it was supposed to—*dring!*—then bounced off the armor.

In the meantime, the Soldier had picked up the CDB, and now he had a hand on the toggle switch. But instead of flipping the switch, the Soldier looked into the barn, up at the rafters.

Good, the birds are getting the blame for that one.

Charlie-Bob fired again: *pupht.* This shot had to work!

Even as Charlie-Bob was pulling the paintball gun back—

• The Soldier flipped the toggle switch. The red light went out.

• The "birdshit" ball hit the back of the Cybe's armor—and stuck.

• *SSSSOOM.* A wormhole opened up, right by the Soldier.

• The Soldier, with the CDB firmly in hand and the "birdshit" definitely on his back, stepped through the wormhole.

• *SSSSOOM.* The Cybe wormhole closed.

Charlie-Bob pumped a fist. *Holy moley, it worked!*

Hopefully, now Cybe Alpha would want to see the fake CDB, after it had been "disarmed" by using the convenient toggle switch.

When Charlie-Bob was absolutely, positively sure that the Cybes were not coming back, he loaded everything back in the pillowcase and went down the hayloft ladder.

He looked around the floor of the barn till he found the first gooey-ball, the one that had hit the Soldier's armor but hadn't stuck.

When he found that gooey-ball, he reached into the pillowcase, pulled out the ray-gun, and blasted that gooey-ball into atoms.

Why create extra work for the bimborg who now were tracking the gooey ball that was stuck to a Cybe?

ROCKET MOTEL
SWEET ONION, GEORGIA

Five minutes after Cyborg-Lucille and her bicycle had entered Room 113, Cyborg-Lucille and her bicycle emerged. The cyborg's eyes swept the parking lot, seeing Regina in her car but not pausing.

This worried Cybe-Regina. If Lucille's unknown cyborg technology were anything like a Cybe's, a glance of one-24th of a second would be enough to capture and to transmit an image. Regina was glad that Georgia didn't issue a license plate for the front of a car, only the rear, or Charlie-Bob's cyborg might already know that Regina Wisley was spying on her.

Cyborg-Lucille rode on her bicycle from the Rocket Motel to a gated apartment complex, Riker Manor Apartments. But she didn't punch in a gate code; instead, she waited.

Five minutes later, the Out gate opened. The departing car drove out, then the Out gate started to shut. At the last moment, Cyborg-Lucille's bicycle shot through the narrowing gap.

In all the time that Cyborg-Lucille had been on her bicycle after leaving Piggly-Wiggly, she'd not given hint that she knew she was being followed. But after the Out gate shut, Lucille spun her bicycle around so that she faced Regina directly.

Cyborg-Lucille raised her hands and gave Regina a goodbye wave with each hand. The gesture did *not* mean *You come back later, y'hear?*—the cyborg's hard stare made that very clear.

Then Cyborg-Lucille put her hands back on the handlebars, turned the bicycle around again, and pedaled away. Ten seconds later, she'd disappeared from Cybe-Regina's view.

APARTMENT 212
RIKER MANOR APARTMENTS
SWEET ONION, GEORGIA

SSSSOOM. Charlie-Bob was holding the pillowcase when he was returned to Mary Kayla's apartment. The first thing he saw was Mary Kayla, Rose, Heather, and a beautiful brunette whom he didn't recognize, all of whom were standing back. Standing in front of those other women were Ass-Kicker Babes Shonique, Cheryl, and Kyong—

All three of whom were pointing ray-guns at him.

Before Charlie-Bob had time to speak, Shonique and Cheryl each zoomed her free hand forward, to grab the pillowcase and yank it out of his hands. Those two Ass-Kickers passed the pillowcase back to Mary Kayla.

From the next room, he heard Helen-May Sawyer's voice, speaking Bimborgspeak: *"What?* That's impossible! Check again."

Meanwhile, Rose said to Charlie-Bob in English, "Get undressed, please."

When he was naked, Rose said in English, "Heather and Doc, step forward. You with the ray-guns, cover them."

Heather and the brunette gave Charlie-Bob's naked body a medical examination. They even checked his scalp!

Helen-May Sawyer walked up to Rose and murmured something. Rose said to Mary Kayla, "Check the pillowcase and his clothes for a gooey-ball. Ohmigod, he brought one of them back."

Huh? Charlie-Bob wanted to ask Rose where she'd cooked up such a wild idea, but knew at this point, she wouldn't tell him.

After he'd been examined for several minutes, with particular attention paid to his neck, "Doc" said, "This unit sees no evidence he was Welcomed."

Heather said, "I agree."

Charlie-Bob and his examiners all turned to look at Rose.

Rose said, "I *totally* agree, his brain is okay. Ass-Kickers, stand down. Welcome back, King Charlie-Bob!"

Charlie-Bob looked around. "I just realized something. . . ."

Charlie-Bob looked around. "I just realized something—shouldn't Lucille be here? Where is she? And what's this about a gooey-ball?"

Rose crossed her arms. "Thousands of bimborg have worked together to track down the radio signal, and it's coming from right here. You got careless and brought a gooey-ball back with you to Sweet Onion."

"I didn't find it," Mary Kayla said. "Not in the pillowcase, and not in his pockets." So saying, she handed Charlie-Bob back his clothes.

"I did *not* bring the gooey-ball with me," Charlie-Bob said as he dressed himself. "I saw that Soldier step into the wormhole with the gooey-ball stuck on his back."

Rose put hands on her hips. "Then how do you explain—"

The apartment's entrance door opened; it was Lucille carrying her bicycle. "Danger! A young woman has followed this unit. This unit think she knows about us."

Charlie-Bob was still dressing. "Too much is happening! Rose, why do you think I brought the gooey-ball back with me?"

Rose said, "Because ohmigod, the only FM radios that are picking up the gooey ball are within a hundred miles of here."

Charlie-Bob pointed to Lucille. "Tell me everything about the young woman, and why you think she knows about us."

"She's late teens or early twenties. She has blond hair and a big nose. She was driving a silver Sports Utility Vehicle that said 'Wisley Electronics' on the side. In the Piggly-Wiggly, she listened in on us."

Lucille then summarized her previous hour, right up to the point when Lucille on her bicycle glared at the blonde through the bars of the apartment complex's exit gate.

Rose looked confused. "That's Regina, has to be. But why would she, like, follow you?"

Charlie-Bob got a horrible thought. His eyes went wide, then he called out, "Rose, Lucille, follow me!" He rushed into the next room.

There Helen-May Sawyer was still taking reports from bimborg with FM radios. Charlie-Bob hurried to a table, on which lay a simple metal box.

This box showed a toggle switch, a tuning dial, a small speaker, and a signal-strength meter. Plugged into the metal box was a handheld parabolic antenna.

Charlie-Bob picked up the metal box and handheld antenna, then handed everything to Rose. "Find the signal," he told her.

Halfway between a "Classic Country" FM station and a "Today's Country" FM station, Rose picked up the *beep-beep-beep* signal that the gooey-ball was sending.

Seconds later, everyone knew: The signal wasn't coming from Charlie-Bob's clothing, but from somewhere nearby, to the north.

Charlie-Bob realized: *The Wisley Electronics plant is north of here.*

He told Helen-May, "Thank all the bimborg for their help, and tell them we'll take it from here."

Charlie-Bob meanwhile had moved over to a laptop, and used its internet connection to search for photos of Regina. In under a minute, he had pulled up a big picture of Regina in her cheerleading outfit.

Meanwhile, Helen-May had finished talking to other bimborg. As soon as Helen-May turned her cel phone off, Lucille turned on the Overmind Monitor, the anti-tachyon radio that was set to the Cybe Overmind's frequency. Lucille was fluent in Cybespeak.

On the Overmind Monitor, a man and a woman were talking. Meanwhile, Charlie-Bob was gesturing for Lucille to come see the picture of Regina that he'd found.

Then three events happened almost in the same instant—

• Lucille pointed to Regina's picture on the monitor. "That's who was following us!"

• The Cybe woman who was talking on the Overmind Monitor said the name *Lucille.*

• Rose pointed at the Overmind Monitor. "Ohmigod, that's Regina's voice!"

4-P: Atrocities

Seconds later, Charlie-Bob heard Regina on the Overmind Monitor say something about *Rose*.

"What are they saying now?" he asked.

Lucille-unit answered, "Regina and Cybe Alpha are discussing how to find out who are the other 'cyborgs' besides Rose. Regina wants to capture Rose and Welcome her, both to get information and to change Rose's loyalties."

"Nothing has changed, Regina is still an evil bitch," Rose said.

Lucille said, "Cybe Alpha vetoed kidnapping Rose just now—said trying to Welcome her might not work."

"Do they know who's a bimborg?" Charlie-Bob asked.

"They don't have a clue, only guesses, and it's angering Regina. It's amazing what unsuppressed emotion she's—we have a problem."

"*Another* problem?" he said.

"Regina just told Cybe Alpha, 'What you're doing now, it's not enough. Don't *upset* Charlie-Bob Owens, *kill* him!'"

Charlie-Bob pulled out his smartphone. "God, I need to warn my folks to leave town! I think the Cybes are planning something to get to me through them."

He speed-dialed his father's smartphone. Voice mail.

He speed-dialed his mother's cel phone. Voice mail.

He speed-dialed the land-line in the kitchen. The phone rang and rang.

As he shoved his smartphone back in his pocket, Charlie-Bob demanded of Lucille, "Is there anyone here who's learned Cybespeak besides you?"

"Heather-unit and Helen—"

"HEATHER, ARE YOU STILL HERE?" he yelled.

The door to the apartment's living room opened up. Heather asked, "What do you need?"

Charlie-Bob had Lucille in the front seat of his car, and Rose in the back seat. The sense of dread he was feeling got even stronger as he pulled into his driveway.

"Why is Dad's car here?" he asked. "He should be at work."

Even more disturbing for Charlie-Bob, his father's car was parked crooked, instead of parallel to the driveway edge. Meaning, his father had parked his car in haste.

As soon as Charlie-Bob stopped the car, he handed the keys to Rose. "We'll go around back. Rose, you open the back door, then wait for us to go first." He meanwhile was opening up the glove box to grab the ray-gun there. Lucille's ray-gun was already in her lap.

As Rose was unlocking the back door, Charlie-Bob told Lucille, "Set Strength setting to Ten." Lucille nodded and obeyed.

They entered the kitchen, and heard ominous music coming from the TV in the living room.

Charlie-Bob peered around the doorframe into the dining room and living room. He saw nobody, whether Solitary or Cybe.

He and Lucille held their ray-guns straight out, no hiding. He'd already decided that if his parents were alive, he was going to tell them the truth—just before he wormholed them out of Sweet Onion.

As he got closer to the TV, he smelled a familiar-but-not odor. The closer he got to the TV, the stronger the smell got.

The TV, he realized, was showing Arnold Schwarzenegger in 1984's *The Terminator*. Which was odd, because his mom—

"Like, ohmigod," Rose said.

His parents were on the floor. They were each naked—their clothes had each been ripped off them and the pieces thrown around the room. Charlie-Bob's parents had their arms ripped off; what he'd been smelling was gallons of blood on the carpet.

His parents had been laid on their stomachs, and his mother's hair had been pulled aside. Plainly visible were Welcomer-needle marks in the backs of their necks.

Then he realized the meaning of the movie playing. It was a movie about an evil cyborg from the future, right? His dad hadn't put this movie in the DVD player, the *Cybes* had set this movie to play. As a taunt to him, Charlie-Bob.

"ALPHAAAAAAAAA!" he screamed.

When he'd done screaming, Lucille whispered to him, "Someone is in a room upstairs."

He whispered back, "Which room?"

She pointed to the underside of his bedroom.

He walked to where he was directly under the middle of his bedroom, made sure his ray-gun's Strength setting was cranked up to Ten, then pointed his ray-gun straight up.

Where? he mouthed.

She guided him by gesture. When she gave him the Okay sign, he fired the ray-gun.

A four-foot-diameter circle of the ceiling became a red glow. He took his finger off the button, and the red glow disappeared—as did that part of the ceiling.

Charlie-Bob caught a glimpse of boots and the underside of an armored man's legs. Charlie-Bob mashed down the button on the ray-gun, even as the Cybe Soldier was falling down toward him, and even as Lucille was yanking him out of the way. A vaguely human shape glowed red and then disappeared, even as Charlie-Bob felt hot air blast his exposed skin.

Charlie-Bob drove fast to the Rocket Motel, with a plan to evacuate James' mother and her boyfriend. He decided he would see them to safety, even if it meant they saw a wormhole in action.

He was too late.

Ellen and David hadn't been Welcomed before their arms had been torn off their bodies. Charlie-Bob could tell this because Ellen and David had died screaming.

4-Q: The Wrath Of Owens

At the Rocket Motel, Ellen and David had died screaming, after their arms had been ripped off their bodies.

Charlie-Bob looked at Rose and sighed. "There are no police in Sweet Onion we can call for this. And if there *were* police here, calling them would just bog me down here."

So saying, he untucked his shirt. He used the cloth to wipe fingerprints off the motel-room doorknob, then he pulled the cloth-covered doorknob closed.

He gave a one-sentence order to Queen Rose. As Charlie-Bob drove away from the crime scene at the motel, Rose started working her cel phone, calling all the Sweet Onion bimborg.

Pleasure Units were back at Palmer Electronics, in the process of making a second wormholer and a second external force-field generator/cloaker. At Charlie-Bob's command, Rose phoned Carmenita in Loganville.

Rose told Carmenita to stop work on the wormholer and the force-field generator, while starting work on a new project. Its priority? Stratospheric.

In Sweet Onion meanwhile, the Artificial Sensation helmet and the force-field repeller were already packed into the trunk of Charlie-Bob's car. This meant that there was no reason for him to return to his house.

Which in turn meant, he had no reason to return to Sweet Onion.

Charlie-Bob drove to Lionheart, where Linda-5 had arranged for a U-Haul truck. The wormholer that was stored in Lionheart was loaded into the truck; Rose was given the truck keys.

The two atomic bombs were left in the projection room of the Georgia Star Drive-In. By then, the building's antitheft protection had been *much* upgraded, one might say.

Then Charlie-Bob and Lucille, in his car, and Rose, who was driving the U-Haul truck with the wormholer in it, all headed for Loganville, Georgia.

A half-hour after Rose called her, SOHS sophomore Peggy Jo Baxter was walking down the street, her book bag on her back. Had someone looked closely, he would have noticed that Peggy Jo's book bag was stuffed full to bulging.

As Peggy Jo was walking along the sidewalk, a car pulled up, stopped, and a window rolled down. The driver, senior Helen-May Sawyer, called out a greeting to Peggy Jo.

The two girls talked casually for two minutes. Then Helen-May casually gestured for Peggy Jo to get in her car. Peggy Jo strolled around the car and opened the passenger-side door.

Shortly afterward, the two girls came across sophomore Patty Jean Cooper—who by wild coincidence, also was walking along the sidewalk with an overstuffed book bag on her back.

Peggy Jo rolled down the passenger-side window. "Hey, Patty Jean, you want to do something fun with us? Get in the car!"

Patty Jean smiled, then got into the car's back seat.

At that point, so far as Sweet Onion was concerned, the three girls vanished.

Freshman Alicia Dunlap was strolling around Piggly-Wiggly, and carrying an empty handbasket, when she happened to run into Miss Turner, the English teacher. The two beauties started chatting about many things. Yet what neither of them mentioned was that none of the foods that Miss Turner was buying, needed refrigeration.

Once they were outside the store, Alicia helped Miss Turner load her groceries into the trunk of her car, and onto what was left of the back seat. (The groceries had to share the back seat with two cardboard boxes.) When the groceries were all loaded into the car, Miss Turner offered Alicia a ride home.

Alicia's house was two blocks from the Piggly Wiggly, but she never made it home.

After the last dental patient of the day left, it was time for Cindy to do clean-up and for Dr. Saint James to do paperwork.

When Cindy finished cleaning up, Dr. Saint James walked in. Before the blonde dentist started her spot-checks, however, she handed Cindy an envelope. The envelope was thick, and it *clink*ed.

With a sense of dread, Cindy opened the envelope. Inside the envelope were coins and paper money.

"Am I being fired?" Cindy squeaked.

Heather hugged her. "Oh no, Cindy honey, nothing like that. But a family emergency has come up in Colorado, and I don't know when I'll be back here. That's bad for you and I'm sorry, but at least now I've paid you up to date."

"Ma'am, I'm sorry to hear—"

"I've also given you a $500 bonus. May I suggest that now is an excellent time to buy a bus ticket and visit your sister?"

"Um, does this have anything to do with the 'disappearances'?"

"There sure have been a lot of those, haven't there?" The dentist turned to look out the window. "That's why I'm sure Roger Wisley is never coming back."

The next day, Cybe-Regina reported to the Overmind that Charlie-Bob Owens, as well as Rose and the rest of his harem, had slipped out of Sweet Onion. In retrospect, it was obvious that the girls all had to be sex-model cyborgs.

Cybe Alpha ordered Cybe-Regina to check on the dentist, who was probably one of Owens's cyborgs, but who didn't attend Sweet Onion High School.

Cybe-Regina checked, and found the dentist's office to be dark and locked.

Cybe Alpha was a little annoyed that he hadn't managed to capture and Welcome this boy who commanded his own hive of cyborgs. But it sounded like the Cybe Clan had the kid running scared instead of fighting, which as almost as good.

Adding to Cybe Alpha's annoyance, Cybe-Regina was yelling to the Overmind that the Clan should have "done something about Charlie-Bob's sex dolls while we had the chance." The Alpha-unit considered those sex-doll cyborgs to be nothing more than toys, no threat to any Cybe.

Cybe Alpha's conclusions:

Charlie-Bob Owens's sex-doll cyborgs were no threat to the Cybes. Thus the sex-cyborg named Rose was no threat to the Cybes.

The only cyborg who was a minor threat to the Cybes was the fighter-cyborg named Lucille.

Charlie-Bob Owens was no threat to the Cybes at all.

BIMBORG KING'S PERSONAL LOG
DAY 22 (THURSDAY)

I feel down, depressed, blue, and bummed. I didn't feel this shitty when I was lying in the hospital with a hole in my leg.

My parents are dead, having died in a sickening, ghastly way. Lucille assures me that their deaths aren't my fault. But James' mother Ellen and her boyfriend are dead, and that <u>definitely</u> is my fault. I should have provided more protection for them.

So four people are dead, and have I avenged their deaths? No, I cut and run to Loganville, and I ordered the Sweet Onion bimborg to cut and run with me.

One happy note in all the gloom: A few hours ago, Amy Emily and the other machinist bimborg here in Loganville quit work early and invited me to join them in an hour of Ray-Gun War. They've been playing it for at least an hour a day, for about two weeks. I had to order them to shoot me—otherwise, their Three Laws of Robotics programming wouldn't let them "harm" me. Well, as soon as those bimborg could shoot me, boy, did they! I had fun, even though I was outclassed. Those Pleasure Units are <u>fast!</u>

My bimborg are trying to cheer me up. But you know what would cheer me up more? Wiping the Cybes from the earth. They've made this fight be personal.

Think, Charlie-Bob, think.

We're through running from these bastards.

DAY 24 (SATURDAY), EARLY MORNING
PARTS-STORAGE ROOM
PALMER ELECTRONICS
LOGANVILLE, GEORGIA

Three days had passed since Charlie-Bob and his bimborg harem had fled Sweet Onion. Much had happened in that time.

"Time to create mischief," Charlie-Bob now said to Rose and Heather. He had dressed the part—he was head-to-foot in black.

"Be careful," Rose said.

Charlie-Bob nodded. "Lights out," he said.

Rose switched off all the fluorescent lights in the parts-storage room. As the bimborg had already taped black plastic trash bags over all four windows, the room was now black-dark except for flashlights' red light.

"Wormholize," Charlie-Bob told Heather.

The opening wormhole made a quiet *ssoom* sound.

A shimmering red circle, two feet in diameter, opened at floor level. Rose placed in front of that red circle, a wooden board rubbed with paraffin.

Charlie-Bob took a low dive, landed on the board, then slid along its length and through the wormhole.

Behind him came the flash of a red-beam flashlight, then something *plop*ped on the ground behind him. With a quiet *ssoom*, the small wormhole closed.

Charlie-Bob now was in Hamilton, New Zealand, it was a few minutes after local solar midnight, and he was looking at one of seventeen Cybe Recharging Depots. The date was late March, 2013, only three days after the equinox; the night air in Hamilton was warm.

Inside this warehouse-looking building in front of him, all the Soldiers and Welcomers in Hamilton were recharging. Which meant, they were dead to the world.

"Time to create mischief," Charlie-Bob muttered.

In the 27th century, the Cybes were accustomed to overwhelming any opponent with sheer numbers.

The result? In the 27th century, the Cybes were used to fighting offensive battles and winning.

The Space Navy sometimes could perform well defensively, but going on the offensive? Forget it. The Space Navy learned that any attack on the Cybes would be only local in its success, and only temporary in its success.

Eventually, the Cybes would start telling Solitary colonies, "Defense is pointless." But *the Cybes* being forced to defend themselves? That hadn't been a worry for them in over a century.

But the Cybes of 2013 didn't have the advantages of 27th-century Cybes. The Cybes of 2013 didn't number in the trillions, they weren't scattered over hundreds of light-years, and they didn't have big, well-designed support systems already in place.

But the 2013 Cybes had the cockiness of their 27th-century brethren.

Charlie-Bob would now use that cockiness against them.

According to the Overmind Monitor that Mary Kayla had brought with her to Loganville, the Cybes thought they had nothing to worry about, so far as Charlie-Bob was concerned.

As a result, the Cybes on the Overmind Monitor chattered like magpies. If two servicemen on any U.S. military radio had talked so freely, they both would have been court-martialed.

Those blabbermouth Cybes had mentioned sixteen cities where they were based (other than Sweet Onion, Georgia). Once the bimborg knew those other sixteen cities, they easily found the location of each city's Recharging Depot.

It takes 256 Exnillo packs to power one Cybe Soldier's recharging station. In the 27th century, this was no problem—the Cybes had entire cities whose factories were all filled with Invisibles manufacturing Exnillo packs and Cybe recharging stations.

But in 2013, the Cybes were struggling to make enough recharging stations for all the newly minted Soldiers and Welcomers. Manufacturing Exnillo packs was a much lower priority to the Cybes. So each city's Recharging Depot was forced to tap into its city's electric-power grid. As the Cybes Welcomed more Soldiers and Welcomers with each passing day, the Recharging Depots slurped up more wattage each day.

Which made the Recharging Depots easy to find, once a clever bimborg hacked into the right computer records.

In Hamilton, the Cybes' Recharging Depot looked like a warehouse, and was guarded by three men. Two of the guards were carrying 21st-century weapons, and the third had a ray-gun in a holster.

All moved slowly and acted sleepy. No surprise, since for them it was after midnight.

Tough luck, Cybes, that's what you get for giving guard duty to Invisibles. They have the same physical weaknesses as Solitaries, Charlie-Bob thought.

The guards hadn't noticed Charlie-Bob's arrival. He reached into the satchel that Rose had pushed through the wormhole, brought out the Local Solitarizer, set it on the ground, and flipped its switch.

During the last three days, the Pleasure Units' electronics shop in Loganville was working on a special new project.

The electronics shop knew how to make a Cybe Distress Beacon. Do you know what you get when you replace the anti-tachyon pulser on a Cybe Distress Beacon with a regular-tachyon pulser that draws the same power?

You get a Planetary Solitarizer, which can trash the nanobots within every Cybe and every bimborg on Earth.

Do you know what you get when you replace that powerful regular-tachyon pulser with a microburst regular-tachyon pulser?

You get a Local Solitarizer, which has only a two-hundred-yard effective range. But within those two hundred yards, no material can block its radiation.

The guards hadn't noticed Charlie-Bob's arrival. He reached into the satchel that Rose had pushed through the wormhole, brought out the Local Solitarizer, set it on the ground, and flipped its switch.

Mentally he counted to five.

Five seconds after Charlie-Bob flipped the switch, all three guards startled.

The guards didn't realize it yet, but they were all Solitaries now. As were all the Cybes sleeping inside—not that this mattered.

Charlie-Bob had been waiting with ray-gun in hand. Three shots at setting Three (Knockout), and three guards were on the ground.

The Cybes didn't think that making Exnillo packs was important. However, Palmer Electronics had been, these last three days, cranking out Exnillo packs like crazy (when the machinists weren't making two Local Solitarizers). The Exnillo packs' high priority was because, besides Cybe recharging stations, Exnillo packs also powered cloned Space Navy ray-guns.

Charlie-Bob and a whole bunch of Ass-Kicker Babes were going to be using their ray-guns a lot in the next 24 hours. They'd need lots and lots of Exnillo packs.

Having put the three security-guard Invisibles to sleep, Charlie-Bob put his ray-gun back in its holster, brought his smartphone from the satchel, and punched in a phone number in California.

"Hello?" a woman's voice answered.

"Hi, may I speak to George, please," Charlie-Bob said.

"I'm sorry, you have the wrong number. No George here."

Charlie-Bob turned off his smartphone and put it back in the satchel.

Ten seconds later—

SSSSOOM.

—a large wormhole opened up, ten feet away. Walking six abreast, Ass-Kicker Babes walked through, and walked through, and walked through, till Rose and 128 Ass-Kicker Babes stood quietly outside the Recharging Depot.

Everyone including Charlie-Bob had a ray-gun in a holster beside his/her right hip. Everyone including him had, hanging from a shoulder, a satchel that was filled with Exnillo packs. Everyone was dressed in black, from head to toe.

But after that, the resemblance ended.

Charlie-Bob was dressed in black rubber-soled shoes and black cloth from head to foot. Only his eyes, lower face, neck, and hands were visible.

But the bimborg women all were dressed in black PVC high-heeled boots, and a black PVC costume that covered everything except mouth and eyes. Yes, Rose and the Ass-Kicker Babes all looked sexy, but now they were immune to high-voltage electrocution.

But there were three things *un*sexy about each bimborg.

The first was that she had a miner's light strapped to her forehead.

Below the miner's helmet, each bimborg's eyes were covered with black-lensed goggles. This was so that any Cybe Soldiers she faced couldn't tell where she was about to aim her ray-gun.

The third thing unsexy about each Ass-Kicker Babe was that all her shiny black PVC had been spray-painted flat black.

Charlie-Bob looked around. "*Po spoblix whenkwe.*" We begin.

Inside the warehouse was one big room, with industrial shelving pushed against one wall.

The recharging stations were in long rows, filling about three-fourths of the warehouse. Charlie-Bob was relieved to see that there was empty space; he had worried that there was a second Recharging Depot in Hamilton that he didn't know about.

Each recharging station held a blank-faced, unseeing Soldier or Welcomer. Nobody reacted to the bimborg's trespassing.

Each Cybe's recharging station was an open box, stood on end. Atop each box was an electronic gizmo with two cables coming from it. The slim cable went into the Soldier's or Welcomer's helmet, while the thick cable went into the Cybe's chest.

Just beyond the last row of recharging stations were tables, each with an unclothed man or woman lying on it. That person was hooked into futuristic medical equipment. In appearance, the people on the table varied from looking human to looking like almost-Soldiers or almost-Welcomers, with almost-correct armor.

From the south end of each row of recharging stations or row of tables, a rubber-covered cable, two inches in diameter, ran across the floor and attached to a powerful-looking circuit breaker. There were eight circuit breakers on the wall, seven of which had cables attached to them, and these eight circuit breakers were on either side of a set of double doors that had lightning bolts stencilled on them.

Charlie-Bob pointed to the lights overhead, pointed to the lightning-bolt doors, and made a throat-cut gesture.

Rose nodded, and started to walk away.

He stopped her with a hand on her arm. He pointed to her ray-gun and held up three fingers. Translation: *If you find an Invisible in there, hit him with Strength setting Three, Knockout. Don't kill him.*

It was a full minute later before the lights went out.

When Rose returned to Charlie-Bob, she murmured, "They had, like, a diesel generator in there. I had to, ohmigod, *totally* fuck it up before I could kill the power."

The Ass-Kicker Babes spread out and went to work. Meanwhile, Charlie-Bob and Rose hung back, ready for anything, their ray-guns set at Strength setting Ten.

So what was the Ass-Kicker Babes' work? Charlie-Bob was showing mercy for any Cybe Invisibles he came across, but Soldiers, Welcomers, and baby Cybes got a different treatment.

Two Ass-Kicker Babes would stand in front of a Cybe, their ray-guns each set on Strength setting Seven. At the same instant, one Ass-Kicker Babe would blast the Cybe's Distress Beacon inside his armor, while the other Ass-Kicker Babe blasted the Cybe in the neck. The first ray-gun blast also cooked the Cybe's heart, while the second blast opened his windpipe and his carotid artery.

The idea was that the Cybe would die without his/her Cybe Distress Beacon going off before it, too, died.

Charlie-Bob worried big-time about destroying the Cybe Distress Beacons. If even one CDB sent off an alarm, Charlie-Bob and the bimborg were in big trouble.

But there was no trouble. The work was as straightforward and unexciting as slaughtering cattle. No Cybe reacted to the Ass-Kicker Babes' nearness, no Cybe reacted to his/her neighbor's death, and no Cybe stepped out of his recharging station.

In just under an hour, every Soldier, Welcomer, and future Cybe in New Zealand was dead.

The Ass-Kicker Babes spent five minutes or so "policing their brass" (picking up depleted Exnillo packs), then everyone wormholed back to Loganville.

Two minutes after that, Charlie-Bob was sliding along the waxed board and through the wormhole, which put him in night-dark Hakodate, Japan.

As Charlie-Bob slid along the board, he tried not to think about any Cybe Soldier "reception committee" that was maybe waiting on the other side of the wormhole.

Hakodate, Japan; Kure, Japan; and Vladivostok, Russia continued the lucky streak for Charlie-Bob and the Ass-Kicker Babes. Nothing went wrong, and there were no unpleasant surprises. No Cybes attacked them, either in the Recharging Depot that the bimborg were depopulating, or by wormholing in from someplace else.

After Vladivostok, the wormhole-visits moved ever west, with Charlie-Bob and the bimborg visiting every Recharging Depot when its Soldiers and Welcomers were all "asleep." Invisibles were spared (after having been Solitarized), but Soldiers, Welcomers, and future Cybes were all killed.

By the thousands.

By the time that Charlie-Bob was yawning in Savannah, every Cybe in thirteen Recharging Depots had been killed, without even one bimborg suffering a scratch or firing a ray-gun blast in anger.

I should buy a lottery ticket, Charlie-Bob thought. *Nobody can stay this lucky, this long.*

Now Charlie-Bob and the PVC-clad bimborg were walking out of the Savannah, Georgia Recharging Depot. Rose asked Charlie-Bob, "So, like, where is next? Are we going to Sweet Onion now, to attack the Wisley Electronics plant?"

Charlie-Bob replied, "I'm getting tired now. Let's clean out Lubbock, Saskatchewan, and Boise tonight. We'll hit Sweet Onion tomorrow when we're all rested."

He couldn't see Rose's face, but her voice was a purr. "Remember that Pleasure Units and Ass-Kicker Babes are built to go all night. For, you know, *whatever* you want to do."

"But *I'm* not built to go all night," he said. "I'm going to be dead tired before I get to sleep in Loganville. Cybe Alpha will just have to wait till tomorrow."

The Recharging Depot in Lubbock, Texas was cleaned out with no problems.

The Recharging Depot in Regina, Saskatchewan was cleaned out with *seemingly* no problems.

When the Cybe-killers walked out of the dark warehouse, past the four supposedly unconscious guards, Charlie-Bob spotted a problem.

One of the guards had an open cel phone in his hand. Charlie-Bob didn't remember any guard talking on the phone when he'd been knocked out with the ray-gun.

Charlie-Bob said, "Everyone, shine your lights on those four guards." He spoke in English, because he wanted these Invisibles, who presumably had once been Canadians, to understand him.

Light from 129 miner's lights shone on the four guards who were laying on the concrete loading dock. Three of the men didn't react, but the guy holding the cel phone started breathing faster.

By then Charlie-Bob had his own cel-phone out. "Wormholize, *now*! Make the hole as big as you can!"

Surprisingly, no Cybes wormholed in before Charlie-Bob and the bimborg all wormholed out.

Soon afterward in Loganville, the Ass-Kicker Babes were swapping out depleted Exnillo packs for charged-up ones, and Charlie-Bob was swapping out the Exnillo pack that powered his Local Solitarizer.

All the bimborg acted calm, but Charlie-Bob's heart was pounding.

He said to Rose and Lucille, "The good news is, we have only one more place to hit tonight. The bad news is, our cakewalk just ended."

4-R: Boise

DAY 25 (SUNDAY), EARLY MORNING
PARTS-STORAGE ROOM
PALMER ELECTRONICS
LOGANVILLE, GEORGIA

By now, Charlie-Bob was bushed. He'd gotten a two-hour nap after the bimborg had wormholed back to Loganville from Bristol, England—but that was hours ago.

Now it was 2:30 in the morning, Loganville time. Lord, he just wanted to sleep!

The only good thing about the sleepiness is that it took the edge off his fear. Since the first part of the Cybes-killing procedure was to set off the Local Solitarizer, he couldn't take any Ass-Kicker Babes with him as bodyguards. So just seconds from now, he would be very alone when he wormholed into Boise.

Less than a minute from now, he might be dead.

No matter. With both Charlie-Bob and Rose standing in the parts-storage room, he dialed her with his smartphone. As soon as Rose answered, he activated the floor-high wormhole and slid through it, with the phone still in his hand. If he got killed or Welcomed, Rose would hear the shit as it happened.

Charlie-Bob had been shocked that no Cybe Soldiers had been waiting for him in Boise. He was nervous, constantly looking around, as he set off the Local Solitarizer and put the Invisibles to sleep.

But nothing went wrong.

This time, when the big wormhole opened up and the first goggles-and-PVC-covered Ass-Kicker Babes stepped through, each Ass-Kicker Babe came through the wormhole with her ray-gun in her hand, pointed forward at Strength setting Ten (*Vaporize*).

That turned out to be a good thing. The 128 Ass-Kicker Babes (plus Rose) were still walking through the big wormhole when a second wormhole opened up.

Sixteen Cybe Soldiers stepped through the other wormhole, plus a young-woman Welcomer.

Charlie-Bob startled, looking at the Soldiers. He recognized one of them. The Soldier had an unusual-shaped jaw, and ears that stuck straight out; back in Sweet Onion, he'd been a cashier at the convenience store where Charlie-Bob used to buy gas—

The Cybe Welcomer spoke up: "Congratulations on your promotion, Nightshade."

Rose said, "Thank you, Luanne. Ohmigod, we need to get together sometime and, like, chat about our time together—"

Zheorr! Zheorr!

Rose and her ray-gun vaporized a Soldier who was raising his arm to electrocute Charlie-Bob. Then in the next instant, Rose's wrist spun clockwise and she vaporized the Welcomer. Cybe-Luanne didn't even have time to blink.

"—in the coven," Rose said.

This double-killing enraged the Cybe Soldiers, and they turned to lightning-blast Rose and Charlie-Bob.

"*Blix kek zhe spabrarem,*" Rose called out. Surround him.

Before the Soldiers managed to lightning-blast Charlie-Bob, he was surrounded by lightning-proof Ass-Kicker Babes.

The Soldiers were wasting their blasts, trying to electrocute women dressed in PVC. Furthermore, each Soldier's lightning, after only four or five blasts, dropped to a mere tingle. Meanwhile, the Soldiers' movements were slow.

Clearly to Charlie-Bob, getting the Soldiers "out of bed" had not been a smart idea.

Because the Soldiers were consumed by anger toward Rose and Charlie-Bob, and were obsessed with killing Rose and Charlie-Bob, they weren't paying attention to anything else. Fifteen out of the sixteen Soldiers were vaporized by Ass-Kicker Babes' ray-guns, without putting up a purple shield.

(The sixteenth Soldier put up his purple shield, but it was as tired as the Soldier was. Two Vaporize-blasts vanished the shield; the third blast killed the Soldier.)

After all the Cybes were dead, Charlie-Bob looked around. None of the Ass-Kicker Babes seemed hurt. At the moment, they were picking up depleted Exnillo packs and putting them in their satchels.

Charlie-Bob looked over at Rose. "Does this strike you as way too ea—?"

Another wormhole opened up. Sixteen more Soldiers and another Welcomer poured out.

———————

There was no witty repartee this time. There was only the *zzzap* of lightning and the *zheorr* of ray-gun blasts.

This battle ended with all seventeen Cybes dead; but two Ass-Kicker Babes also were dead. Before they'd been Vaporized, two of the Soldiers had charged into the throng of Ass-Kicker Babes and snapped spines.

A wormhole opened up a third time. Another seventeen Cybes attacked. Charlie-Bob recognized this Welcomer as a quiet girl he'd had in second-year Spanish, but he couldn't remember her name.

During their third attack, all sixteen Soldiers had adapted: They waded into the Ass-Kicker Babe crowd, to physically destroy their bimborg enemies. This attack cost Charlie-Bob 21 more fighting bimborg before it ended.

As soon as the third Cybe attack ended, the door opened, and seventeen Cybes stepped out of the Recharging Depot. They were no challenge. The Solitarized Welcomer acted distracted, and was quickly vaporized; the Solitarized Soldiers managed only to electrocute themselves. The bimborg suffered no additional casualties.

———————

TEN MINUTES LATER
INSIDE THE CYBE RECHARGING DEPOT
BOISE, IDAHO

Where are more of the bad guys? Charlie-Bob wondered.

Outside the building, Pleasure Units who'd wormholed over from Loganville, were recovering the last corpses of the 23 Ass-Kicker Babes who'd been slain by the Cybes.

Inside the building, the electricity by now was off, so the only light came from:

• Ass-Kicker Babes' miner's lights;

• the red "EXIT" sign over the front doors, which were to Charlie-Bob's left; and

• ray-guns, as the ray-guns' blasts killed Cybes.

All but one of the 105 surviving Ass-Kicker Babes were blasting Cybe Soldiers and Welcomers again, as Boise's Cybes stood trancelike in their recharging stations. Seventeen recharging stations near the front door were empty.

Like before, Rose and Charlie-Bob were standing back, watching for any kind of Cybe attack. This time, they were joined in their sentry duty by Lydia-unit, the one partnerless Ass-Kicker Babe.

But the Cybe attack that the three were watching so keenly for, wasn't happening. No Boise Cybe stepped out of his recharging station, and no pack of Sweet Onion Cybes wormholed in.

Did we finally get lucky?

All was quiet and still, except for the *zheorr, zheorr* of Ass-Kicker Babes' ray-guns.

"I don't get it," Rose said to Charlie-Bob. "Why are the Cybes in Sweet Onion, like, letting us slaughter their people here?"

"I think it's because tonight they got caught by surprise, so they've shot their bolt. You better believe that starting tomorrow, they'll stagger their recharge times."

"So why didn't they, you know, do this already?"

"I think they really didn't figure they needed defensive procedures," Charlie-Bob said. "After all, the last time they dealt with us, we wound up running away."

The front door opened then.

Charlie-Bob whirled around and took a deep breath, ready to yell orders to the Ass-Kicker Babes about another Soldier attack.

But standing in the doorway was not a Soldier or Welcomer, but instead a woman in black PVC. She was holding a flashlight and a revolver. The revolver at the moment was pointed at the ceiling.

Rose said in English, "You're not one of us, but you're dressed like one of us. Approach slowly, gun pointing up."

The woman now was lit from behind by the red "EXIT" sign, and in front by Charlie-Bob's flashlight and by the miner's lights of

Rose and Lydia. With all that light, Charlie-Bob was able to get a good look at her.

She walked slowly as ordered, but her hips had a definite sway. Her black PVC costume had no flat-black spray-paint that reduced its shininess; the PVC made the light that it was reflecting back, look like lightning flashes across the woman's body.

Her PVC costume made a *skreek-skreek* sound as she moved, and her high-heeled boots *click-clack*ed on the concrete floor.

She stopped when she was about four feet away from Lydia (who without being ordered to, had stepped between the newcomer and Charlie-Bob).

"Turn around slowly," Charlie-Bob said.

As she did so, she asked excitedly, "So I'm at the right place? You're Charlie-Bob Owens?"

"*King* Charlie-Bob," Rose snapped.

"*King* Charlie-Bob," the newcomer repeated in a sexy voice.

She wasn't wearing PVC gloves, so Charlie-Bob could see that her hands had long fingernails, and she had warts on her left hand. She had a small waist and enormous tits under her PVC. To Charlie-Bob, all of this spelled "Pleasure Unit/Welcomer."

The woman wasn't wearing goggles, but instead she was wearing black-lensed sunglasses, with the frames duct-taped to the cowl. She was holding a flashlight instead of wearing a miner's light, and she had a gun holster strapped to her hip.

"What's your name?" Charlie-Bob asked.

"Caroline," the newcomer said. "Full name: Caroline Marcus. I live here in Boise." Through half-lidded eyes, she added, "I'm still in high school, but I'm eighteen."

Charlie-Bob said, "I hope you were far enough away from here to not get messed up by the Solitarizer." He patted his satchel.

"Yes indeed," Caroline said. "Right now all my nanobots are working *peachy* fine." She gave Charlie-Bob a sexy smile.

Rose said, "I don't think it's smart to blabber to just anyone about the Solitarizer, you know?"

Charlie-Bob said, "Why? I haven't told her how to build one. And if this metal box vanishes, I know where to grab a second one."

Rose glared at Caroline. "What *exactly* are you called? 'Caroline' *what*? Like, what's your designation?"

Charlie-Bob asked, "How did you find out about this? We told only the people with strict need-to-know." He gestured toward the 104 Cybe-killing women to his right. "We didn't mention even a word on the—"

Rose interrupted: "What he's saying is, we only told people in person, or over the phone. So, like, how did *you* find out?"

"Linda told me," Caroline replied.

Charlie-Bob nodded. One of the Ass-Kicker Babes now zapping Cybes was named Linda, one of the recently killed bimborg was named Linda, and Linda-5 knew nearly everything about today's raids. Caroline's statement was believable.

Meanwhile, Rose was saying, "I asked you before: What's your designation?"

Charlie-Bob said, "Later. She's clearly a Pleasure Unit-slash-Welcomer."

To Caroline he said, "Give me your gun." When Caroline handed over the revolver, Charlie-Bob set the safety, then dropped the handgun into his satchel. He took a ray-gun out of his satchel and handed it to Caroline. "Now you can start killing Cybes. Lydia will show you how."

Rose raised her hand. "Hold on."

Rose gave Charlie-Bob a long look, then looked straight at Lydia. "*Po spo kek fle trolduzh. Za chua bogwiza ratcherem.*"

In Rose's speech, the only Bimborgspeak that Charlie-Bob understood was *I don't trust her.*

Caroline was a good girl. She used the ray-gun she'd been issued to kill recharging Cybes and baby Cybes, instead of killing Ass-Kicker Babes, Rose, or Charlie-Bob.

Rose had insisted on checking Caroline's "work."

Where Caroline had ray-gunned a Cybe's neck, that neck now had a two-inch-diameter tunnel in it that went all the way back to the vertebrae. Exactly as it all should be.

When Caroline had blasted a Cybe's armor where it covered the CDB, the armor was melted clear through, the CDB was melted junk, and the flesh underneath had a scorched, golf-ball-sized hole in it. Exactly as it all should be.

When all Cybes were dead and Charlie-Bob had ordered Caroline to hand back the ray-gun, she'd done so with no hesitation, and with another sexy smile. When he'd handed her revolver back to her, what she'd done was to put it in its holster and to snap the holster's flap down; what she'd *not* done was to start shooting people.

Charlie-Bob couldn't figure out Rose's attitude. Was Rose *jealous* of Caroline?

Outdoors, minutes later, the bimborg wormhole was open wide, and PVC'd Ass-Kicker Babes were stepping through it.

Charlie-Bob stuck out his hand. "Caroline, I guess this is goodbye. Thanks for your help."

Caroline gave him another sexy smile as she shook his hand, covering his right hand with her long-nailed, warty, left hand. "It doesn't have to be goodbye, since I don't know when I'll see you again. Come home with me; I'd love to pleasure your *Genesis torpedo.*"

"Nuh-uh," Rose said. "If we put you, me, and Charlie-Bob in your car, there'd be no room for bodyguards."

Caroline smiled sweetly at Rose. "I didn't come here in a car, but in that black van over there. Bring as many bodyguards as you want."

And that's what happened. Rose insisted that Caroline's van be filled before any more Ass-Kicker Babes were allowed to walk through the wormhole.

Charlie-Bob didn't say anything. He figured they'd go to Caroline's apartment, visit briefly, then wormhole back to Loganville. So let Rose stoke her jealousy for a little while.

A few minutes later, as Caroline was driving, she said, "This isn't actually my van. It belonged my friend Angie, who Disappeared. I saw two of your women kill her tonight."

Nobody knew how to respond to that. They made the rest of the trip in silence.

After they'd gotten to the apartment complex and climbed out of the van, Rose spoke her first words in fifteen minutes: "Caroline, what apartment are you in?"

"I'm in 1405. That building there," Caroline said, pointing.

"Run ahead, and we'll be there in a few minutes," Rose said in a flat voice. "I need to talk to my team and King Charlie-Bob. *Alone*."

Caroline said in a sexy voice, "King Charlie-Bob, I look forward to showing you my apartment. Bye for now." Then with hips a-swaying, she walked away.

"I'm glad you want to talk to me," Charlie-Bob told Rose. "Because *I* sure as hell want to talk to *you*. What's your problem?"

"I think she's a plant. Either she's been double-Welcomed, or ohmigod, she's an Invisible made to look like a Pleasure Unit."

"With *those* tits?" Charlie-Bob said.

Then he thought about Rose's words. "She's personally killed several dozen Cybes tonight. You checked her kills. So maybe she's a loyal Pleasure Unit like she claims to be."

Rose crossed her black PVC-covered arms, making a *skreek, skreek* sound. "I'm sure she's a Cybe."

"Tell me why you say that."

The explanation had something to do with the fact that the Cybe Overmind and the Club (Bimborg Overmind) were both anti-tachyon radio channels, but on slightly different frequencies.

By King James' order, Charlie-Bob was reminded, bimborg didn't use their radio channel anymore. But all bimborg still had the ability to talk and hear, using it.

When Cybes talked on their Overmind, bimborg could hear it through their own anti-tachyon radio channel, but the Cybe speech sounded like static and heavily distorted "squawks." Even a bimborg who'd learned Cybespeak couldn't tell what the Cybes were actually saying unless she used the Overmind Monitor, Rose claimed.

Rose continued, ". . .A few hours ago, before you wormholed to Boise, I started hearing a man's voice squawking the same few syllables over and over, you know?"

"But you have no idea what he was saying."

"My strong guess is, he was saying, 'Testing, one, two, three.' About the time you turned on the Local Solitarizer here in Boise, he shut up, and I haven't heard him since. Right after that, a different man and a woman started talking. I think the second man is Cybe Alpha; I hear his distorted voice, ohmigod, a lot."

Charlie-Bob said, "What you're saying is, the guy who went silent was one of the Invisibles guarding the Recharging Depot, and when I Solitarized him, Cybe Alpha knew it instantly."

"Yes," Rose said. "Then after we'd fought off all our attackers, I heard Cybe Alpha's voice and that woman's voice again. They talked for a minute, then went silent. Ten minutes later, I started hearing that woman's voice again. She's talked nonstop from that moment until now. But less than a minute after she started talking nonstop on the Overmind, Caroline walked through the door."

Charlie-Bob turned to look at Lucille. "Can you add anything?"

Lucille replied, "They're definitely squawking Cybespeak. But the only words this unit can make out are prepositions, sorry."

Charlie-Bob looked at Rose and Lucille. "Is Caroline's voice the same as this voice you're hearing on the Club channel?"

Lucille said, "This unit cannot be sure. The squawking voice is very distorted; plus, there is much static."

Rose said, "Same here. I, like, can't be sure they're the same."

Charlie-Bob said, "So you might be trash-talking Caroline for nothing, hm?"

"Possibly," Rose said stiffly.

A minute later, Charlie-Bob, Rose, Lucille, and the other Ass-Kicker Babes had walked into Caroline's apartment.

Caroline was still wearing her high-heeled, shiny-black PVC costume, but she was no longer wearing the holster. She'd removed the sunglasses and the duct tape that held the sunglasses in place—

—then Caroline had pulled the PVC cowl back to hang down her back. (As a result, Charlie-Bob couldn't see any part of the back of her neck below her hairline.)

With her blond hair, pale-blue eyes, cover-model face, and gigantic tits, Caroline definitely met Babeness Standards revision Four, Charlie-Bob decided.

After Caroline shut the door on her guests, she walked up to Charlie-Bob and put a hand on his chest. "Which do you prefer: I fuck you and then cook dinner, or we all eat and then I fuck you?"

"We won't be staying that long," Rose snapped. "King Charlie-Bob isn't like us. He has to sleep, and it's after 3:30 in the morning, our time."

Charlie-Bob said, "Sheesh, why'd you have to remind me?" He yawned—then watched in amazement as Caroline yawned too. "Besides, the Cybes in Sweet Onion will be 'waking up' from Recharge soon, and that's when the shit's gonna hit the fan."

Lucille said, "To be exact, they'll stop recharging at 192 64-slobi after solar midnight in Sweet Onion, or 4:41 a.m. Eastern Standard Time. A little over an hour from now."

"Well, you'll fight them better on a full stomach," Caroline said brightly. "Besides, they don't know where your secret base is, or where that marvelous 27th-century computer is. So who cares if the Cybes fuss and fume?"

So saying, Caroline turned and walked into the kitchen, *skreek-skreek, click-clack*. Then pots and pans started rattling.

Meanwhile, Lucille had been walking around the apartment's living room. Now she called out, "This unit doesn't see any photos of you, but there are several photos of a brunette girl. Who is she?"

Caroline called back, "That's Angie. When she Disappeared, I moved in here, so to have the apartment in shape if she came back. I'm still in high school; I can't afford to sign a lease."

Rose murmured, "Of course if she's Cybe, it'd be, like, real hard for her to seduce you in her bedroom at her parents' house."

Charlie-Bob woke up when he drooled on his arm. He realized that he was slumped over against Rose.

Sitting up straight on Caroline's living-room couch, he asked, "How long was I asleep?"

"Twenty minutes," Rose said. "I decided you needed the sleep."

"I'd prefer to sleep in my own bed," he said. Standing up, he added, "Let me see what Caroline is up to, see if we can make a graceful exit."

He found Caroline in the kitchen, doing nine things at once.

She was cooking little hamburgers on a portable electric skillet. "It's going to be good," she said. "I didn't expect so many guests, so there'll be only one burger apiece and it'll be small, but it'll be tasty.

There's a frozen casserole in the microwave, and a frozen apple pie in the oven. Can I cook, or can't I?"

"Wow, you went all out," he said. Now he felt like a scumbag for telling her he was about to leave.

"I don't have any hamburger buns, so everyone will have to eat their burger between bread slices. Hope you don't mind."

Charlie-Bob said, "I don't mind, and don't think anyone else will." He yawned.

"Oh, you poor man, you're tired! And I'm keeping you awake. Shame on me."

"It's okay, really. I'll manage," he said.

She walked to the kitchen table, pulled a chair a foot away from the table, and said, "Here, sit in this, and I'll rub your neck. The way I do it, it's very relaxing."

"If you relax me, I'll fall asleep. Which is rude when I'm a guest in your home."

"If you fall asleep, I'll feel flattered. If you don't fall asleep now, you'll be relaxed so you can sleep better later. Please?"

"Okay, sure, a neck rub would be nice." He sat in the chair.

"Let me take these burgers off the griddle since they're almost done. . .turn off the griddle, pause the microwave, and take off these latex gloves because I'm sure you don't want raw beef smeared on your neck. . .Ready?"

"Rock and roll," he said.

She started to rub his neck and shoulders. She murmured, "This feels very good, does it?"

"Yes, it feels good," he replied.

"This feels good, so you want me to keep doing it."

"Yes, keep doing it."

"It's relaxing you. You feel sleepy now."

"Yes I do, I'm sleepy." That was swear-on-a-Bible truth.

"The neck rub is making you sleepy."

"I'm sleepy."

"You're getting very sleepy."

"Very sleepy."

"Just let yourself go. Don't think about anything but my hands rubbing your neck, and the sound of my voice."

"Just let myself go."

"Don't think. Just listen to my voice and don't think."

"Don't think."

"Listen to only my voice."

"Only your voice."

"You trust me."

"I trust you."

Charlie-Bob zoned-out after that. Maybe Caroline asked him questions. If she did, it was no big deal to answer her questions, because he trusted her.

Splash!

Charlie-Bob zoned-in very quickly when he got cold water thrown in his face. He opened his eyes to discover a frowning Rose standing in front of him, a plastic cup in her hand.

"Hold the bitch!" Rose said. "Don't let that skank touch him."

As Charlie-Bob was wiping water off his face, he turned around. Lucille and Kyong were holding a struggling Caroline.

He turned around to glare at Rose. "Tell me why you threw water in my face. That's an order."

"She was using, like, Alphasena Colony hypnosis shit on you. I called your name twice but, ohmigod, you didn't respond."

Charlie-Bob stood up, then turned to look at Caroline. "Is that true? Were you hypnotizing me?"

She laughed. "Of course not."

Charlie-Bob glared at Rose. "If she said she didn't hypnotize me, then I believe her. I trust her. You two, let her go."

Lucille and Kyong did as ordered. Those two spoke no objection, but they shared looks with Rose.

Caroline gave Rose a catty smile. "I never did answer your question about my 'designation,' did I? Hi, I'm Caroline-2063. Not only am I not the 22-millionth bimborg, but I've been a Pleasure Unit/Welcomer much longer than you, Queen Rose."

Charlie-Bob saw that the three most junior bimborg (Kyong, Lucille, and Rose) were passing dismayed looks to each other.

"Why did you come in here?" he demanded of Rose.

"To see what was taking you so long," she replied. "You came in here to tell *bimborg* Caroline here that we need to leave, you know? And now we, like, *really* need to go."

Rose pointed to the clock on Caroline's microwave. It said 2:13. The Sweet Onion Cybes would be recharged in 28 minutes.

Charlie-Bob looked at the clock, did the math, then turned to Caroline. "She's right, we need to leave. Thanks for the neck rub—"

Caroline said, "*Charles Robert*, it would be rude of you to leave after I've put so much effort into cooking. There's no harm in you and yours staying here for a *leisurely* meal."

Charlie-Bob nodded, then turned to Rose. "I've changed my mind. We're staying here for a while."

Rose said, "But—"

He crossed his arms. "Don't argue. Any of you. That's an order."

He wondered then, why Caroline was grinning.

Minutes later, the table was set for eating. But rather than sit down, Rose pulled out her cel phone and said, "I need to, like, check with everyone back home. See that they're okay." Sarcastically she asked, "Is that a *problem?*"

Charlie-Bob was tired, and didn't feel like arguing. "Go," he said, "but don't take long."

Rose made a point to walk not merely out of the kitchen, but out of the apartment, before making her call.

Two minutes later, Rose was back in the kitchen. As she took her seat, she told Charlie-Bob, "Heather-unit is worried about you."

"How sweet," Caroline said.

For some reason that Charlie-Bob couldn't figure out, Caroline was still wearing her high-heeled-boots-and-black-PVC outfit. Her cowl being pulled back was the only way she'd gone casual.

The meal was filled with long silences. Charlie-Bob was too sleepy to carry on a conversation; Rose and the Ass-Kicker Babes answered Caroline's questions with as few words as possible.

When Caroline's microwave clock said 2:35—*T* minus six minutes and counting—Charlie-Bob stood up. "Now we absolutely, positively, no-shit have to leave."

Rose and the Ass-Kicker Babes immediately stood up.

Bimborg Caroline-2063 took one last, quick sip from her coffee cup, then she also stood up. "I can't wait to see your secret hideout."

Rose slapped the tabletop. "*Forget it*, bitch!"

Caroline smiled sweetly. "Dear Rose, you won't stay queen much longer with an attitude like that. But let's discuss that later. Right now, of course I'm going through the wormhole with you guys—right, *Charles Robert*?"

"Sure, of course. Boise might be dangerous."

Lucille said, "It is tactically unthinkable that she come with us." Anyone else would have said, No fucking way.

Now it was Charlie-Bob who slapped the tabletop. "I am *goddamn* sick and *goddamn* tired of y'all arguing with me. Rose, get the wormhole open. Here. Now. *Do it*."

Rose shook her head. "I can't make the opening wide enough. We'll have to, like, use that big open space in the living room."

Charlie-Bob glanced at the microwave clock: 2:36. "I don't care where, just make it so."

Everyone rushed into the living room, Rose made a phone call on her cel phone, and—

SSSSOOM.

—a wide wormhole opened up.

"I'm so forgetful sometimes," Caroline said, "even after becoming a bimborg. *Where* is your hideout at?"

"Loganville, Georgia," Charlie-Bob said.

Rose said, "Lucille, everyone else, get going. Tell them we three will be last."

As the Ass-Kicker Babes dashed forward and through the wormhole, Caroline was asking, ". . .mean, *specifically* where is your hideout at?"

"Palmer Electronics in Loganville," he said.

Caroline slapped her hands to her face. "Goodness, I need to bring my purse. *Charles Robert*, please wait here while I find it."

"No problem," he said.

For some reason, Rose drew her ray-gun from her satchel and set it to Strength setting Ten.

As Caroline was walking briskly around the apartment, looking unsuccessfully for her missing purse (she even turned over couch cushions), she called out, "So this Palmer Electronics, that's where the Cybe computer is at?"

"No, actually it's at—"

Rose interrupted: "Where it is, that is *soo* complicated. He'll have to, like, show you."

Caroline rushed out of the bedroom, straight up to Charlie-Bob and Rose. "I guess I can do without my purse. Let's go."

Rose put up a hand. "Hold on, *bimborg* Caroline. Rank goes first. King Charlie-Bob and me will go through the wormhole first, then you, like, follow *behind*."

As soon as he and Rose would get through, Charlie-Bob was sure that the wormhole would "accidently" get closed, which would leave Caroline in Boise; or worse, trap her in a null-dimension.

Caroline said, "That would be degrading. *Charles Robert*, tell her I don't have to follow behind you."

Charlie-Bob said, "You heard her. She walks beside us, or she walks ahead."

Rose's smile was vampiric. She made a bowing, be-my-guest gesture, and said, "Then please, go ahead of us. Lucille will make sure the bimborg in Loganville give you, ohmigod, a *friendly* greeting."

Caroline gave Rose a catty smile. "I don't need to put on airs, unlike *some* people. I have no problem walking between you both."

Rose shook her head, looking panicked. "No, I've been nasty to you and ohmigod, I need to make amends. Please, you go ahead."

Charlie-Bob said, "*Enough*, Rose. We'll all three walk through, on the count of three. Say, anybody know what time it is?"

Caroline pointed to the DVD-recorder clock. "It's forty minutes after."

Rose said, "Which means, ohmigod, the Cybes in Sweet Onion will finish recharging in one minute. *Thanks*, bitch!" Rose again cranked her ray-gun to its top Strength setting.

"Enough, Rose," Charlie-Bob said. "One, two, three, *go*."

Rose, Charlie-Bob, and Caroline stepped through the wormhole.

4-S: Cybes v. Bimborg 3

DAY 25 (SUNDAY), 4:40 a.m. EASTERN TIME
ONE MINUTE BEFORE END OF RECHARGING
PARTS-STORAGE ROOM
PALMER ELECTRONICS
LOGANVILLE, GEORGIA

Squir-squir-squirt! Squir-squir-squirt!
In the first second after Charlie-Bob walked through the wormhole into the parts-storage room, many events happened—
• Heather moved to stand in front of Caroline. Heather's hands shot out, to grab the fingers and the wrist of Caroline's left hand.
• Amy Emily and Lisabelle blasted the back of Caroline's left hand with their water rifles.
• Carmenita stepped up to Caroline and swiped the back of Caroline's immobilized left hand with a wet shop towel.
• The warts on Caroline's hand smeared, making four black lines.
• Shonique slid behind Caroline and clamped a hand over Caroline's mouth. At the same time, Shonique yanked Caroline's PVC cowl back, exposing the skin on the back of Caroline's neck.
All these things happened in that first second because only Charlie-Bob and Caroline were *not* moving at inhuman speeds.

"Look what I found," Shonique said. "This bimborg, she gots a neck bump like an Invisible."
Heather said, "Honey, really, *press-on nails?*"
Charlie-Bob spent five seconds staring at Caroline's wart-less hand while Caroline struggled to speak. Then Charlie-Bob reached into his satchel and pulled out his ray-gun.
As he was setting Strength to Ten, he said, "Rose, I feel stupid. I'm *so* sorry, truly. Heather and Shonique, let go and stand back."
He turned to Caroline, who was trying to look calm.
"Well played," he said.
Her eyes widened. "That's very—"

He pressed the button. Hot vapor burned against the skin of his hands and face for a moment, then was gone.

He rushed into the workroom, where almost all of the bimborg were. He announced, "If you don't have a ray-gun, grab one. If you're not wearing PVC, stand behind someone who is."

"Hurry, bimborg!" Rose called out. "We have only seconds—"

SSSSOOM.

Cybe Soldiers, and Cybe Welcomers with ray-guns, all were rushing into the electronics shop's workroom.

Charlie-Bob murmured an order to Rose; Rose called out in Bimborgspeak, "Protect the wormholer! Keep always ten PVC women in front of it. This is our number-one priority."

To which Rose added in Bimborgspeak, "Tied with keeping Charlie-Bob safe. Don't let the Cybes kill him or Welcome him. *Move it, bimborg!*"

The women wearing PVC costumes were still wearing their black goggles, but they'd removed their miner's lights. Now PVC'd bimborg moved as quickly toward the wormholer as their high-heeled boots would allow.

Fortunately they didn't have to move far: The door to the parts-storage room was behind the bimborg.

Still, not all of them got where they were going, because of the Cybe Welcomers and their ray-guns.

Charlie-Bob saw two PVC'd bimborg, plus Peggy Jo Baxter and Karen Milph, all get vaporized.

Ninety-odd PVC'd Ass-Kicker Babes lined up in a row. The PVC line stretched from the east wall to the west wall of the workroom of the electronics shop.

Behind the Ass-Kicker Babes in PVC, stood Charlie-Bob in the middle, with PVC'd Rose on his right and PVC'd Lucille on his left. Also standing behind the ninety-odd PVC bimborg were machinist Pleasure Units, who were shooting ray-guns; and Sweet Onion Pleasure Units—

—who were defenseless.

Charlie-Bob looked around, and his blood went cold. One of the machinist Pleasure Units, Rhonda, was wearing a red "Georgia Bulldogs" t-shirt.

Charlie-Bob couldn't lose the idea that if she kept wearing that shirt, she would die.

Charlie-Bob stifled a yawn. He murmured to Rose, "We have a problem. I've now been up for 22 hours."

Rose nodded. "We have another problem. We're low on charged-up Exnillo packs, and it'll be hours before the dead packs self-charge."

Meanwhile, in a corner of the workroom stood metal shelving. A PVC'd Ass-Kicker Babe (Sherry) climbed up those shelves with catlike ease. When she was lying prone on the top shelf, another PVC woman (Terry) tossed a rifle and tan plastic boxes up to her.

The riflewoman immediately began shooting at Cybes.

One of the Soldiers who stepped out of the Cybe wormhole was a cat-man. He was seven feet tall, very thin-framed with a foot-long tail, and had gray fur and charcoal-gray eyes. He *leaped* into the air and landed in front of a PVC bimborg to the left of Charlie-Bob.

The cat-Soldier threw his arms around the bimborg's ribs. His arms squeezed, and the Ass-Kicker Babe gasped.

"Oh, *shit!*" Rose said.

A Soldier and two Welcomers had stepped out of the Cybe wormhole. To Charlie-Bob, they looked familiar somehow—

The teen-girl Welcomer turned to face Rose. "We will nonbiologick you today, Cybe-enemy sister. Defense is pointless."

The thirtyish Welcomer mocked, "You can't nonbiologick your own family, can you, Rose?"

CRACK! The cat-Soldier broke ribs of the bimborg he was squeezing. She whimpered.

Zheorr! A ray-gun shot him, from Charlie-Bob's right—

—but the cat-Soldier's purple shield came up, saving him.

The thirtyish Welcomer mocked, "You can't nonbiologick your own family, can you, Rose?"

"She doesn't need to," said a voice. Patsy Anne, a machinist-bimborg, aimed her ray-gun; both mother and daughter Welcomers got vaporized.

The cat-Soldier dropped the broken-ribs bimborg like a bag of trash at the curb. His head started to turn toward the bimborg who had tried to vaporize him—

—but this took his attention away from bimborg to his right. One of those women vaporized him.

The Soldier who had been Bill O'Connor got set to lightning-blast Patsy Anne. But before he killed the killer of his Cybefied family, Rose reached over a PVC'd shoulder, fired her ray-gun, and vaporized her father.

"I'm sorry you had to lose your family this way," Charlie-Bob said. He reached up and squeezed Rose's shoulder.

Meanwhile, the PVC bimborg with the broken ribs was lying on her stomach on the concrete floor, whimpering in time with her breaths. Helen-May Sawyer stepped over to her, knelt down, and began unzipping the back of the woman's PVC costume.

Helen-May Sawyer wasn't wearing a PVC costume, nor was she holding a ray-gun. A Soldier lightning-blasted Helen-May, knocking her five feet backward. She hit the wall and fell limp.

Helen-May's killer was promptly vaporized.

Charlie-Bob counted fourteen depleted Exnillo packs lying on the floor, and the battle was only two minutes old. This worried him.

All the bimborg, except for the Pleasure Units from Sweet Onion, had ray-guns.

The bimborg's nanobots made bimborg much faster shooters than the Cybe Welcomers who were shooting their own ray-guns. That was because Welcomers couldn't think or move any faster than

Cybe Invisibles or Solitaries, which put the Welcomers at a big disadvantage when facing bimborg.

But when the battle started, there were hundreds and hundreds of Cybe Soldiers and Welcomers trying to kill bimborg, but there were only about 110 bimborg killing Cybes. The bimborg couldn't afford to take losses, and yet they were—

Cybe Welcomers' ray-guns were shooting at everyone except Charlie-Bob. The Soldiers were lightning-zapping who they could, and hug-killing all the PVC bimborg whom they could reach before they were vaporized.

The Cybe wormhole, which had closed, opened again. A single Cybe Soldier now stepped through it.

Charlie-Bob immediately recognized the former Kevin Sinclair.

Denise's jerk ex-boyfriend hadn't changed much, Charlie-Bob decided. Yes, he now had the red skin and all the armor of the Soldier that he'd become, but he didn't look *bulkier*. All the other Soldiers looked like they'd been taking testosterone pills since middle school— which come to think of it, matched the rumors about Kevin the high-school wrestler.

Looking straight at Charlie-Bob, Cybe-Kevin called out, "This unit has a message for the bimborg"—now his face and voice sneered—"*king*. By Cybe Alpha's order: Cybes, stand down."

All Cybe Welcomers pointed their ray-guns at the floor, and all Soldiers pointed their lightning-arms at the ceiling. Soldiers who were hug-killing bimborg loosened their grip.

Bimborg with weapons tilted them up, and all the bimborg looked a question at Charlie-Bob.

Charlie-Bob beckoned Cybe-Kevin forward. Loudly he said, "Let him approach. Don't kill him unless I order you to."

By then, all Cybes were quiet, and all bimborg were quiet. Shooting, lightning-blasting, and hug-killing all had stopped.

Cybe-Kevin stopped in front of the PVC bimborg who was in front of Charlie-Bob. Cybe-Kevin kept his lightning-arm pointed at the ceiling; in turn, Charlie-Bob didn't point the ray-gun that he held in his right hand, at Cybe-Kevin's face.

Cybe-Kevin said to Charlie-Bob, "Defense is pointless. We will kill all these bimborg here, then Welcome you, then kill you."

Charlie-Bob casually passed his ray-gun to his left hand, then held up his right index finger in an *Excuse me* gesture. He leaned forward and softly laid that right hand on the right shoulder blade of the Ass-Kicker Babe in front of him.

"What's your name?" Charlie-Bob asked her.

"This unit is Tasha, King Charlie-Bob. We had sex last Monday."

"I'm sorry we're talking across you, Tasha."

"No need to apologize, King Charlie-Bob."

At that moment, Lucille switched her own ray-gun to her own left hand, and rested her right hand on Tasha's left shoulder blade.

Which was unusual; Lucille didn't normally act touchy-feely.

Returning his attention to Cybe-Kevin, Charlie-Bob asked, "What does Cybe Alpha plan for the millions of other bimborg, after I supposedly get killed?"

"They will be either Welcomed or nonbiologicked. We don't care which."

"Is this all of your message?" Charlie-Bob asked calmly.

Cybe-Kevin said, "Cybe Alpha gave this unit one other message to tell you—"

• Cybe-Kevin's lightning-arm, which had been pointing at the ceiling, now came down inhumanly fast.

• In the split second before Cybe-Kevin let loose, Charlie-Bob realized, *The lightning is aimed to my left, not at me.*

• The lightning-blast hit Charlie-Bob's satchel dead on.

• *BANG.* Charlie-Bob smelled both ozone and burned cloth.

• The Local Solitarizer fell onto the floor, through the newly made hole in Charlie-Bob's satchel.

• The Local Solitarizer was a charred, smoking ruin.

"—and the message, *Solitary*, is Don't fuck with us Cybes!" Cybe-Kevin said, while grinning at Charlie-Bob.

Still grinning, Cybe-Kevin added, "This unit really hopes to be the unit chosen to kill you."

Charlie-Bob took a deep, slow breath. Then he said, "I don't think so. I'm pretty sure—"

- *"Kek skakkozziwa regorem!"* Charlie-Bob said, interrupting himself.
- Charlie-Bob *shoved* Tasha toward Cybe-Kevin. Lucille meanwhile was shoving Tasha too.
- Cybe-Kevin had been keeping a careful eye on Tasha's ray-gun hand. He wasn't looking at Tasha's free hand. Snake-quick, that hand punched him in the throat.

"—you'll be dead soon, Kevin," Charlie-Bob said.

An eyeblink after Cybe-Kevin got sucker punched, the bimborg started shooting. Three Soldiers and a Cybe Welcomer died immediately afterward.

Cybes started fighting back, and the battle resumed.

Every person from Sweet Onion, including Amy Emily, saw a deadly Cybe whom he or she recognized from the good old days—

Charlie-Bob recognized Rusty from Rusty's Down Home Cookin', where Charlie-Bob had taken Rose on their first date. Cybe-Rusty tried to hug-kill a PVC bimborg, but was vaporized before he got to her.

A machinist-bimborg from Atlanta was lightning-blasted by the Cybe version of SOHS basketball player John Wallace. Amy Emily's first ray-gun shot was absorbed by his purple shield—but her second shot, seven seconds later, killed him.

Three weeks earlier, Lt. Resshert in his police car had stared at Lucille on her bicycle, and Lucille had worried that the policeman would question her. Today they faced each other again. The Ass-Kicker Babe in front of Lucille got vaporized, then Cybe-Resshert rushed toward PVC'd Lucille, intending to hug-kill her. Lucille held her ray-gun in a teacup grip and aimed at his center mass. Cybe-Resshert's eyes narrowed, and his purple shield came up in front. Rapidly she fired, *zheorr-zheorr-zheorr-zheorr-zheorr*, and five times his purple shield went up in front. He kept coming—ten feet away, now five feet, now three. But what he didn't know was that her ray-gun was set at Strength setting One. He was so intent on blocking her weak shots, he didn't pay attention to anyone else. He got ray-gun'd from a machinist-bimborg to his right, and *this* shot was Strength setting Ten. Three feet away from Lucille, Cybe-Resshert was vaporized.

Amy Emily vaporized the red-eyebrowed Welcomer whom she recognized as Prissy Jo Jensen. Two years ago, Prissy Jo had entered the Miss Vidal County pageant and had gotten Second Runner Up (right behind Amy Emily). Amy Emily had heard a rumor, six months ago, that Prissy Jo had turned to prostitution.

Lying on the workroom floor were dead Soldiers and Welcomers with the tops of each head exploded by a bullet of Sherry's. On the bimborg side, there were dead PVC bimborg whose rib cages were now smaller around than a coffee can, and some Pleasure Units were dead of lightning-blast.

But most of the dead, whether Cybe or bimborg, were now vapor, and left no remains behind. The machine-shop workroom was noticeably less crowded than at the start of the battle.

A Soldier looked straight at the weaponless English teacher. "This unit is going to nonbiologick you now, Mary Kayla. This unit knew you were a slut, but now you're also an enemy of the Cybes."

Mary Kayla didn't change her posture or expression. "I'm not afraid of you, Lawrence."

Mary Kayla's former lover raised his arm to lightning-blast her in the face—

He'd been yapping when he should have been paying attention. Sherry's rifle bullet blew Cybe-Lawrence's brains out.

Red-shirted Rhonda quickly patted-down her pockets again. She had no charged-up Exnillo packs left. She'd just dropped her last depleted Exnillo onto the floor.

A Soldier wolfishly grinned at her. Clearly Rhonda was about to be lightning-blasted.

Rhonda jammed her now-dead ray-gun into the waist of her jeans, yanked her "Georgia Bulldogs" t-shirt off, and—

"How 'bout them Dawgs, Soldier?"

—threw her red shirt at the Soldier's face.

The red shirt blinded him for only an instant, but an instant was enough. Scratch one Soldier.

Every bimborg who was shooting a ray-gun had one or two Exnillo packs at her feet by now.

Charlie-Bob saw a PVC bimborg reach into her satchel—but rather than pull out three Exnillos and load them into her ray-gun, she borrowed three Exnillos from the bimborg to her right.

Charlie-Bob realized: *Within minutes, we'll be out of ammo. We need to finish this battle before the Cybes finish us.*

Charlie-Bob walked behind the line of PVC bimborg, tapped ten women on the shoulder, and told each one (quietly), "Parts room."

He found ten Ass-Kicker Babes already in the parts-storage room, guarding the wormholer. He also found Heather there, listening to the Overmind Monitor.

Charlie-Bob was hearing a conversation in Cybespeak between several men. He asked, "What are they saying?"

Heather said, "Cybe Alpha says we're beaten."

"Yeah? We'll see about that."

Then Charlie-Bob turned his full attention to the ten PVC bimborg he'd pulled off the line.

He gave the ten selectees a brief order. No one had questions, and all ten selectees had wolfish smiles.

He returned to the workroom and the battle there, to again stand between Rose and Lucille.

Behind the Cybes, at the far end of the workroom, Charlie-Bob soon saw a small wormhole open up at floor level. This wormhole was even smaller than the one made for Charlie-Bob when he'd been visiting Recharging Depots.

Because this wormhole was very small, it was quiet. What with all the noise in the workroom—the *zzzaps* of lightning-blasts, the *zheorrs* of ray-guns, and the *bangs* of Sherry's rifle—no Cybes noticed it.

A PVC Ass-Kicker Babe slid through the wormhole, jumped up, unholstered her ray-gun, and aimed that ray-gun at the Cybes whom she was standing behind. But she didn't fire her weapon.

A second black-clad bimborg slid through the wormhole, then a third came through. Soon ten PVC bimborg were standing up and aiming ray-guns. Meanwhile, the wormhole stayed open.

The ten bimborg prowled forward as a group. The Cybes still acted unaware of their presence.

The Cybe Soldiers now were up forward, all Soldiers directly engaging the PVC-bimborg line. Ten Cybe Welcomers with ray-guns were standing just behind the Soldiers.

Each of the wormhole-bimborg moved behind a Cybe Welcomer. The bimborg paused a second; Charlie-Bob had ordered them to reset their ray-guns to Strength setting Seven.

Charlie-Bob couldn't see the hand signal that the wormhole-bimborg gave each other. But at the same moment, a bright light shone at the front of each Welcomer's neck, and she (or he) slumped to the ground—

—as each wormhole-bimborg quickly reset her ray-gun to Strength setting Ten.

Ten Welcomers now were dead, but their Cybe Distress Beacons were unharmed, and began chirping away lustily. Charlie-Bob couldn't hear those broadcasts, but he saw the results.

Every Cybe Soldier spun around and faced the wormhole-bimborg. Who meanwhile were busy looting the dead Welcomers of their Exnillo-pack satchels.

The Soldiers, in their rage, blasted the wormhole-bimborg with lightning. Which achieved nothing.

Most of the wormhole-bimborg were shooting ray-guns at the Soldiers. Which likewise achieved nothing.

But three wormhole-bimborg were running back with Cybe Welcomer satchels and tossing nine of those satchels through the now-larger bimborg wormhole. *That* achieved a lot.

Seconds later, Mary Kayla and Tatum-Teresa emerged from the parts-storage room, each with a Cybe Welcomer satchel hanging off her shoulder. As those two Pleasure Units walked behind the main PVC line, they acted like Santa, handing out Exnillo packs to every person with a ray-gun.

Meanwhile, what about the Soldiers? When they'd first turned around and started lightning-blasting the wormhole-bimborg, their anger made them forget about the PVC line that they'd been oppressing only moments earlier.

The result? Lots of Soldiers got shot from behind and vaporized. That is, those who weren't killed by sniper fire first.

A *shitload* of Soldiers got vaporized in those first ten seconds. Was the battle now favoring Charlie-Bob and the bimborg?

Soon after, the Soldiers started to move.

Seeing this, Rose asked, "Is this, like, an attack?"

Charlie-Bob said, "I don't think so. I'm guessing the Soldiers are planning a defense against the crossfire they're caught in."

After telling Rose this, Charlie-Bob moved behind the PVC line a second time, ordering fifteen more PVC bimborg off the battle line and sending them back to the parts-storage room.

Seven of the PVC'd bimborg emerged seconds later, sporting the other seven Welcomer satchels and handing out Exnillo-pack goodies. The other eight PVC'd bimborg began emerging from the little wormhole at the back of the workroom.

By now the Soldiers had made a double line, one line facing the original PVC bimborg line, while the other line of Soldiers faced the wormhole-bimborg.

But it was doing the Soldiers very little good; they were still dying twice as fast as they had been, minutes earlier before the bimborg's wormhole trick. Since the Cybes no longer had Welcomers shooting ray-guns, bimborg were no longer dying (except by hug-killing).

In a few minutes, it would be the *Cybes* who would all be dead.

That's when Heather stuck her head out of the parts-storage room. She called out, *"Za shmofra, po nejuwawa—"*

Before Heather could tell Charlie-Bob what "the enemy ones" were doing, it became clear: A Cybe wormhole opened up, and two ray-gun'd Welcomers stepped through it.

Before the two Welcomers could get oriented, or step forward to let more Welcomers enter, PVC bimborg vaporized the Welcomer pair. By now three PVC bimborg stood in front of the open Cybe wormhole; they fired three ray-gun shots into it.

The three bimborg in front of the wormhole looked at each other. One woman said, "Let's do it."

All three bimborg stepped into the Cybe wormhole.

One second later, the Cybe wormhole flashed red, then vanished.

Heather stuck her head out of the parts-storage room. In English she called out, "You're *stuck* here, gentlemen!"

The Soldiers went on a rampage then. About a dozen bimborg were hug-killed, and Patty Jean Cooper and Robina Wright were lightning-blasted.

But five minutes after the Cybe wormholer was destroyed, all the Soldiers in the electronics shop were either gunshot victims or vapor.

Rose, Lucille, and Charlie-Bob were alive, but only forty-three Ass-Kicker Babes had survived the battle.

Of the eighteen machinist-bimborg, only Amy Emily, Carmenita, and bare-breasted Rhonda were alive and healthy. Lisabelle's fate was iffy, even with nanobot healing.

Of the Sweet Onion Pleasure Units, only Rose, Heather, Mary Kayla, Denise, Brooke, Paula, Alicia, and Tatum-Teresa were alive. Twenty-one weaponless Sweet Onion Pleasure Units, one of whom was only fourteen years old, had been slaughtered.

Charlie-Bob wanted to care for his people after the battle. But with the adrenaline rush over, now he felt like he'd drunk a 55-gallon drum of Sleeping Potion.

Charlie-Bob crawled into a dead machinist-bimborg's sleeping bag. "Wake me when the Cybes come back," he told Rose and Lucille, then he fell instantly asleep.

The sun was almost directly above the roof of the building when Charlie-Bob woke up.

The first thing he noticed was the solid ring of Ass-Kicker Babes, standing hip to hip, around his sleeping bag. All the women were wearing their PVC costumes, and all wore ray-gun holsters but were holding their ray-guns in their hands. In addition, Tasha had a police whistle in her mouth.

As soon as Charlie-Bob looked at Tasha, she took the whistle out of her mouth and called out, "Queen Rose, he's awake."

Charlie-Bob pulled on his glasses then. He looked for his smartphone, to check its time-display.

His smartphone was missing out of his shoe.

Seconds later, Rose and Lucille walked up to him. By then he was tieing his shoes. Rose handed Charlie-Bob his smartphone.

He was stunned when he noticed the time-display.

Charlie-Bob stood up as he said, "I didn't expect the Cybes to let me sleep seven hours."

Rose and Lucille looked at each other. "You have a problem," Lucille said.

Rose said, "Cybe-Regina has, ohmigod, kidnapped Prudy Lu."

"Just now?" Charlie-Bob asked.

Rose and Lucille exchanged looks again.

Lucille said, "About 6:30 this morning, actually."

4-T: Insurrection

DAY 25 (SUNDAY), 6:21 a.m. EASTERN TIME
HOUSE OF PRUDY LU MOFFATT
SWEET ONION, GEORGIA

Bam-bam-bam!

Ding-dong, ding-dong, ding-dong, ding-dong, ding-dong!

Bam-bam-*bam-bam*!

Ding-dong, ding-dong!

Someone was pounding on Prudy Lu's front door, and ringing the doorbell like a maniac.

Prudy Lu's first thought, upon being blasted awake, was *Is our house on fire?*

She looked at the clock: 6:21. Now genuinely frightened, she threw on a robe.

She rushed into her parents' bedroom—correction: her *father's* bedroom; her mother had Disappeared.

Prudy Lu heard the sink faucet through the bathroom door. She went to the bathroom door and called out, "Somebody's breaking down the front door. Are you late for something?"

"Not late, no," Prudy Lu heard her father say. Then he added in a wooden voice, as if he were reading off a paper, "I'm not dressed to answer the door. You must answer the door."

As Prudy Lu rushed to the front door, she thought, *Dad has been acting so weird lately.*

Then she thought, *What's so urgent? I don't smell smoke.*

When Prudy Lu yanked the front door open, she expected to see a fireman or a man wearing a badge.

Instead, standing on the Moffatts' porch was Regina Wisley. Regina was holding a toy space-gun, and. . .

. . .Regina's toy space-gun was aimed at Prudy Lu.

"Come with me now," Regina ordered.

Prudy Lu grabbed the doorknob and was about to slam it shut. "I'm not your *servant girl* anymore. Leave before I call the police."

Regina's smile was amused. "Please, call them. Nobody will show up." Then her face turned queenly again. "Come with me or I shoot you with this."

"You've totally lost it, Regina," Prudy Lu said. "That's a toy." Prudy Lu tried to slam the door shut. She almost succeeded.

Zheorr.

Prudy Lu was still holding on the doorknob when it suddenly turned burning hot.

"OW!" she yelled, jumping away from the doorknob.

The door hadn't latched shut yet. Regina shouldered the door open and pushed her way inside.

Prudy Lu was blowing on her burned hand. "I don't know how you did that, but you and your toy gun will leave. *Now.* You and I are done, Regina."

"I don't have time for this," Regina muttered. She did something to her toy gun, then pointed it at Prudy Lu.

Zheorr.

Prudy Lu had time to think only *I feel really strange,* then she passed out.

Prudy Lu woke up a little bit at a time.

She was hearing Regina yelling. That was nothing unusual; Prudy Lu often had heard Regina yelling.

Things were touching the backs of Prudy Lu's lower legs and upper arms. Something was pressing against the front of Prudy Lu's lower legs.

Prudy Lu opened her eyes, and recognized Regina's living room. *How did I get here? The last thing I remember, I was standing by our front door.*

This was sort-of Regina's living room, but not really. Prudy Lu saw weird furniture, and there were weird people watching her. The weird furniture resembled coffins stood on end, but with science-fiction-movie stuff on top of the coffins and inside the coffins. The weird people looked like aliens or robots. The men looked ridiculously strong, except for one puny man-alien who was dressed like the women-aliens.

Waking up more, Prudy Lu discovered that she was sitting down. An instant later, she discovered that she couldn't move her arms or legs. Looking down, she saw that her arms were duct-taped to the arms of a chair.

A strong-man alien was bent over in front of her; he was pressing her legs against the chair legs. A woman-alien was duct-taping one of Prudy Lu's ankles to a chair leg.

It didn't occur to Prudy Lu to tell the aliens to stop. These goings-on were too bizarre.

"*I DON'T CARE* THAT HE'S SLEEPING!" Regina, who was standing where the red-leather couch had once been, now was yelling into her smartphone. Regina's other hand still held the toy space-gun, and she was waving it around. "You wake Charlie-Bob up *now!* Tell him I've kidnapped Prudy Lu, and he better get on the stick and call me!. . .FUCK YOU *TOO*, 'QUEEN ROSE'!"

Prudy Lu was confused by what she'd just heard. Why had Regina kidnapped her, and why was Regina insisting that Charlie-Bob talk to her? Regina *hated* Charlie-Bob.

Prudy Lu had listened so intently to Regina's phone conversation that she hadn't noticed that the strong-man alien and the woman-alien had now stood up. Prudy Lu gasped when she got a good look at the woman-alien.

"*Mom?*"

The woman was slimmer than Prudy Lu's mother had been, the last time Prudy Lu had seen her. All of the woman's exposed skin was red, like she'd gotten a nasty sunburn. But Prudy Lu had no doubt about that face.

Prudy Lu said, "Mom, what's going on? Why are you dressed this way? Why did you leave us?"

The corners of Mom-alien's mouth tensed a little, and Mom-alien's eyes widened slightly. Prudy Lu was sure that her mother was about to say something. But then Mom-alien turned and, without another glance at Prudy Lu, walked over to stand with the other aliens.

By now Regina was stuffing her smartphone into a jeans pocket, was still waving her toy gun around, and was muttering to herself.

Prudy Lu said, "Regina, you skank bitch, tell me what's going on. Better yet, explain *everything* while you untape me."

Before Regina could answer—

SSSSOOM.

—a big red circle appeared in the living room. Three alien-men stepped out of the circle. These alien-men weren't overmuscular and weren't wearing helmets.

Prudy Lu glanced over at Regina, and was shocked. Regina Wisley, who was cowed by nobody on Earth, now was scared shitless.

As a child, Regina once had gotten a factory worker fired from Wisley Electronics. All he had done was to say to Regina's nine-year-old self, "Go away, little girl, and quit bothering me." For that, Roger Wisley had pink-slipped the man, no severance, the same day. After that, every hourly worker at Wisley Electronics feared Regina.

A few hours ago, Regina had said to the Cybe Invisibles who had once been these same hourly workers, "Tell Cybe Alpha that you've run out of screws or something." She'd then taken for granted that the building of a replacement wormholer wouldn't happen for hours yet.

But when her father and all his employees had been Welcomed, the game had changed.

It was only now, as Regina stared at Cybe Alpha—who'd come into Regina's living room by the wormholer that she'd ordered *not* to be built yet—that she realized *how much* the game had changed.

Regina was in deep, deep trouble; and for the first time in her life, she couldn't bully and threaten her way out of trouble.

Meanwhile, Cybe Alpha could order that Regina be nonbiologicked, and every Soldier in the room would hurry to obey.

Or Cybe Alpha could wormhole her alive to shark-infested waters. He had been delighted to discover that great white sharks were not extinct in 2013.

Despite that Cybe-Regina's emotion-suppression subroutine was running at full throttle, she was sick with fright.

Cybe Alpha looked at her and announced, "We are here to determine whether you are Defective, Sol3-21-61. Tell us who this Solitary is, and why she is restrained."

One of the helmetless man-aliens spoke in a foreign language to Regina, then Prudy Lu saw Regina blanch.

Then Regina started speaking that foreign language back to him!

After Prudy Lu heard her own name of *Prudence Louise Moffatt* be spoken by Regina, she heard Regina say several times, *Charlie-Bob*. This made the helmetless man frown. Which in turn made Regina speak faster and wave her toy space-gun around—but whatever Regina was selling, the helmetless man wasn't buying.

One of the other two helmetless men began tapping a finger on a flat rectangle he held. He then said something about *Prudence Louise Moffatt* in a flat voice. Whatever he'd said, his words made the man in charge frown at Regina again.

Regina saw Cybe Gamma, formerly the timeship's Communications-unit, check the schedule. He said, "Prudence Louise Moffatt is not scheduled for Welcoming till tomorrow."

Cybe Alpha frowned at Regina. "This unit's order was, a Solitary was to never see any Soldiers or Welcomers before we came to Welcome that Solitary." Cybe Alpha gestured at the Soldiers and Welcomers standing close to Prudy Lu. "You disobeyed this order."

Regina stammered, "But I thought—I figured, one day wouldn't matter. Especially if we lure Charlie-Bob here and capture—"

"You clearly are pursuing a personal vendetta, and vendettas are a Solitary vice."

Regina muttered in English, "I thought *masturbation* was the solitary vice."

Cybe Alpha continued, "You are *rogue* and you are from this extremely primitive and paranoid culture, but now this unit has more important things to think about. Charlie-Bob Owens told Sol3-21-7 that he has hidden away two atomic bombs, and until we find those bombs and steal them away, that *Solitary* can nonbiologick all of us!"

For the first time since Cybe Alpha had appeared in her living room, Regina smiled.

Sweetly she asked, "You still don't know where he's keeping those atom bombs?"

She zoomed the Strength setting on her ray-gun up to Ten.

As sweetly as before, she asked, "So why am I still obeying you?"

Cybe Alpha's purple shield never came up. It should have.

Before anyone in the room could react, Regina vaporized Cybe Beta as well. Regina tried vaporizing Cybe Gamma, but he put up his purple shield.

Which did him no good. In the last 24 hours, hundreds of 27th-century Cybes had been nonbiologicked, all thanks to Charlie-Bob Owens and his bimborg. At that moment, the entire census of 27th-century Cybes was five people: three Invisibles, who were who-knows-where; soon-to-die Cybe Gamma, who was standing in Regina's living room; and a puny Welcomer man from some colony planet, who also was standing in Regina's living room. That Welcomer from the future was loosely holding a ray-gun. In an eyeblink of time, a Soldier who'd been born in Sweet Onion snatched the ray-gun out of Puny Man's hand, cranked up the Strength setting, and ray-gunned Cybe Gamma in the back.

Regina pointed her ray-gun, still at Strength Ten, at the now-disarmed Welcomer. "We're about to elect a new Cybe Alpha," Regina told the muscleless man. "I trust I have your vote?"

Regina glanced over at Prudy Lu, who was staring back at her, openmouthed.

Regina waved her ray-gun around casually. In English she said, "Prudy Lu, you didn't still believe this is a toy, did you?"

The Cybes used the Overmind to hold their discussions. But starting now, the words spoken were in Norg-Esperanto.

The election didn't take ten minutes. The three 27th-century Invisibles thought it awful that a "primitive" 21st-century person should be Cybe Alpha, but those three were the only Cybe units to oppose Regina. The plain fact was, no Cybe could think of anyone better suited for the job.

So it happened that Sol3-21-61, also known as Regina Wisley, was acclaimed as Cybe Alpha. She didn't even need to mention that she knew where Charlie-Bob's atom bombs were.

4-U: Outsmarted

DAY 25 (SUNDAY), 12:43 p.m. EASTERN TIME
PALMER ELECTRONICS
LOGANVILLE, GEORGIA

Rose said, "Cybe-Regina has, ohmigod, kidnapped Prudy Lu."

"Just now?" Charlie-Bob asked.

Rose and Lucille exchanged looks.

Lucille said, "About 6:30 this morning, actually. Regina is demanding to speak with you about that."

Rose rolled her eyes. "She's been ringing my phone, like, nonstop since dawn."

He said, "So now she's a kidnapper? I'll give her this: She's consistent."

Rose's cel phone rang then. She glanced at the display and mouthed *Regina*.

Charlie-Bob said, "I'll call her when I'm ready to. Ignore her."

Lucille said, "This unit recommends we wormhole over and pick up the second Local Solitarizer, right now, before engaging Cybes."

Charlie-Bob said, "Not going to happen. That other Local Solitarizer stays put."

Lucille said, "We don't know how many Soldiers were kept in reserve this morning. The Local Solitarizer will neutralize them."

"And us too. Am I going to knowingly weaken my own troops? No. When we raid the Cybes to rescue Prudy Lu, we'll do so without a Local Solitarizer."

Heather walked over. "Please don't rush into anything. I'm sure this is a trick, because of how the Cybes are acting. You need to think logically about this."

Charlie-Bob said, "My logic is unsound when a damsel is in distress. Heather, you of all people must know this."

Heather said, "Your choices are clear: Save the cheerleader, *or* save the world."

"Wrong. My choices are to *enslave* the cheerleader or *enslave* the world."

"This unit agrees with Heather-unit," Lucille said. "We are close to wiping out all the Cybes. But if we wormhole over there without a plan and you get Welcomed, all our gains of the past 24 hours will be for nothing."

Charlie-Bob was looking for a reason to change the subject. "Heather, you said something about 'how the Cybes are acting.' What are they doing now?"

Heather said, "On the Overmind Monitor, they've gone almost radio-silent, from shortly after Regina first phoned Rose. When they do talk, it's in a foreign language we haven't identified yet. All this is, *ahem*, probably my fault."

"How?"

Lucille said, "During this morning's battle, Heather twice taunted the Cybes about stuff that they said through the Overmind."

Heather said, "I didn't think it through. I'm very sorry."

Charlie-Bob sighed, and gave her a *what's done is done* shrug.

Heather continued, "Something else you should know—tell him, Lucille."

Lucille said, "We haven't heard Cybe Alpha's voice in hours. Meanwhile, Regina has been talking in every conversation—that is, when any Cybe breaks silence to talk."

Charlie-Bob asked, "Any idea what all this means?"

Heather, Lucille, and Rose all shook their heads.

Charlie-Bob had a nasty thought: "Shit, what if Regina isn't doing this on her own, all behind Cybe Alpha's back? What if he ordered her to do this?"

Charlie-Bob's three listeners looked unhappy at that thought.

Charlie-Bob held out his hand, as he looked meaningfully at Rose's cel phone.

As Rose handed him her phone, he said, "Regina holding Prudy Lu hostage because Cybe Alpha ordered her to, I can't think of *anything* worse than that."

Charlie-Bob had a plan, how to save Prudy Lu. Step One of the plan was to flimflam Regina, convince her that he *didn't* plan to rescue Prudy Lu.

Now Charlie-Bob said into Rose's phone, "You've been bothering Rose all morning, demanding to talk to me. Here I am. Now let me speak to Prudy Lu."

"No way, nerd," Regina replied from the phone. "*I* decide when you speak to her, and when you see her. But you have to do what I say, or you'll never see her again."

"Not if she's dead. And she's dead, *isn't she*, Regina? Dead, or Cybefied."

"You calling me a liar?"

"Liar, bullshitter, prevaricator—have I missed any? Fibber. How many classes have I been in with you, Regina, starting in fourth grade? You lie often."

"Tell you what: I'll let you speak to her a little later."

"Sure, Regina, whatever you say. Tell me, what does Cybe Alpha think of this Black Op of yours?"

Regina laughed. "Trust me, Cybe Alpha is 100 percent on my side with this."

"Sure, Regina, whatever you say. Tell me, has Prudy Lu gone into rigor mortis yet? Or is she on a Cybefication table?"

After several seconds of silence, Regina's voice sounded different: "I've got a gizmo, so *ta-da*, now my smartphone's on speaker. Talk, blondie—the nerd wants to hear your voice."

Prudy Lu's voice sounded scared: "Charlie-Bob? It's really you?"

He said, "Yes, it's me. Are you okay? Has anyone hurt you?"

She took a deep breath. "I guess I'm fine, except for being taped to a chair, and Regina acting crazy."

"I'm glad you're okay, Prudy Lu. Tell me what your situation is."

"I'm in a chair in Regina's living room. She has the furniture pushed to the walls, and there are lots of boxes that are like stood-up coffins in here. There are weird aliens standing around, scary looking, but they haven't tried to hurt me."

"*Yet*," Regina added.

Charlie-Bob said, "Prudy Lu, they're called *Cybes*, and they're part human, part machine. Not aliens. Are all the Cybes wearing helmets, or do you see some Cybes without helmets?"

Regina chuckled. "Oh, some Cybes without helmets *were* here. But not anymore."

Prudy Lu said, "Charlie-Bob? About that—Regina came to my house this morning, holding this space gun. Oh god, I thought it was a toy when she pointed it at me—"

"So you weren't scared of it."

"It's my first space gun. Then she blasted me with it, and somehow I fainted. Anyway, soon after I woke up, a big red circle appeared in her living room, then three bald Cybes stepped through the circle."

"What happened then?" Charlie-Bob demanded. He *really* needed to know how Cybe Alpha was involved.

"One of them started yelling at Regina in a foreign language. Then Regina used her space gun and shot him, then she shot the other two men. They *vanished*. Regina killed them!"

Regina laughed. "Didn't I tell you I had Cybe Alpha's support? Sorry, I forgot to mention: *I'm* Cybe Alpha now."

Charlie-Bob choked. "That's. . .inconvenient."

Regina's voice sounded triumphant: "So Charlie-Bob, there's nobody to stop me if I want to vaporize Prudy Lu. Or if I tell a Welcomer to stick a needle in her neck."

Prudy Lu gasped, then asked, "What's that mean, stick a needle in my neck?"

Charlie-Bob said, "It means that the women Cybes you see in Regina's house, she'll make you the same as them."

"Like my *mom*? God, Regina, no! *Please*, no!"

Regina's voice was sweet: "But dearie, there's nobody to stop me if I want to do you this way."

Then Regina's voice hardened, and she added, "That is, nobody to stop me but *you*, Charlie-Bob. If you want Prudy Lu let go, I demand that you wormhole over here, by yourself."

"Regina, how do I know you'll keep your word?"

"Oh, I've given you no word to keep, *bimborg king*. In my judgment, you simply have no alternative."

"No, my enemy, I *do* have an alternative. I have two advisors here who tell me *not* to do any kind of damsel-in-distress rescue—"

Regina said, "You hear that, Prudy Lu? He plans to leave you here to die. . .or worse."

Prudy Lu's voice blasted his ear: "*Save me, Charlie-Bob!*"

He winced. "I'm sorry, Prudy Lu, but Regina and I are on opposite sides of a war for planet Earth, and you're. . .expendable."

"I don't understand—you *can't* rescue me, or you *won't* rescue me?"

He said, "My advisors tell me—"

Regina said, "You're a blonde, Prudy Lu. Fun for a guy to flirt with, but not to get serious about."

Prudy Lu begged, "Please, Charlie-Bob, I'm *scared!* Please promise me you'll save me from Regina and those evil-looking people!"

Charlie-Bob made a fist in frustration. "Prudy Lu, don't ask me to make a promise like that. My advisors—"

"Promise me you'll try, Charlie-Bob!" She started crying. "Please, please, at least promise me you'll *try* to rescue me."

"Don't ask me to make any promise like that. I'm sorry."

Regina said, "So you're leaving her to my mercy. No rescue attempt."

Charlie-Bob told the biggest lie of his life: "I want you to listen to me. I'm going to say this again: I am not going to try and rescue Prudy Lu. Not a single time, never. And I need to go back to work to save Earth's people."

With that, he ended the call.

As he handed Rose's cel phone back to her, he looked around at Rose, Lucille, and Heather. "I think I got Regina to buy that I won't try anything. So now we have a better chance of rescuing her."

Rose slapped her palm against her forehead. "It's *dangerous* for you."

"I choose the danger."

In Regina's living room, Prudy Lu was sobbing.

Then Prudy Lu looked into Regina's eyes. "I hate you! Maybe I hate him! I'm going to die, or get turned into one of your monsters, and Charlie-Bob never promised to rescue me."

Regina smiled. "Ah, but didn't you notice? He didn't *refuse to* promise to rescue you. And while he told *me* he wouldn't rescue you, he never told *you* that."

Regina raised her voice and said in English, "We're going to have a visit soon. Let's give our special guest a special welcome. He'll be here in thirty minutes, tops."

POSTED ON THE BIMBORG WEBSITE
TRANSLATED FROM BIMBORGSPEAK—

Greetings from Charlie-Bob Owens, your Bimborg King.

I'm about to wormhole to the house of the new Cybe Alpha, to rescue Prudy Lu Moffatt, a damsel in distress. All my advisors tell me (tactfully) that this is the stupidest thing they've ever heard of.

I agree, it's stupid. But I couldn't live with myself if I just let Prudy Lu die or get Welcomed.

I'm taking Rose with me on this errand of folly. If something happens to Rose, I appoint Lucille-47893 as Bimborg Queen.

If I am seen to be killed or Welcomed, or if no bimborg hears from me for three days, then the Bimborg Queen is to become Bimborg Alpha. If I telephone after three days of silence, my orders are to be disregarded; if I reappear after three days of silence, I may be killed by Bimborg Alpha.

Lucille is in charge of defense for all bimborg until I return, and only Rose or I may countermand Lucille's orders while I'm on this mission. My authority to countermand Lucille is subject to the limits of the previous paragraph.

Perhaps this is goodbye. Know that up till now, I've always tried to do the right thing for you bimborg.

SSSSOOM.

In late March, Regina's swimming pool would be empty. So Team B, a group of PVC Ass-Kicker Babes, wormholed into the bottom of the pool, where they'd wait. Then they'd rush out of the swimming pool, vaporizing Cybes and creating a distraction.

What Team B didn't know was that standing in the poolhouse, with the door slightly open, was a Cybe Welcomer who held a ray-gun. The Welcomer's ray-gun, so Alpha-Regina had ordered, was on Knockout setting.

The Welcomer didn't see the bimborg appear at the bottom of the empty pool, but she recognized the wormholing sound. In Norg-Esperanto, she told the Overmind, "Pool."

Which Heather and Lucille, back in Loganville, heard clearly on the Overmind Monitor. But since those two bimborg didn't know Norg-Esperanto, they didn't understand what they'd heard.

SSSSOOM.

Team C wormholed into Regina's garage. The Ass-Kicker Babes knew that Regina's family owned an SUV and two convertibles; but oddly, no vehicles set in the garage. Nothing but air separated each PVC bimborg from the wide electric door.

Besides the electric door, there were two other ways out of the garage: a regular-sized door to the kitchen, and a regular door to the back yard and pool.

An Ass-Kicker Babe moved quietly to the kitchen door and slowly tried its doorknob. The doorknob turned freely; the kitchen door was unlocked.

What the PVC bimborg in the garage didn't know: Standing on the other side of the door to the back yard was a second Welcomer scout. In one hand this Welcomer held a ray-gun, set on Knockout; in the other hand, she held a remote-control garage-door opener.

As soon as the Welcomer heard a wormholer sound coming from the garage, she told the Overmind in Norg-Esperanto, "The garage."

In Loganville, Heather and Lucille heard the words, didn't understand them, and didn't know what best to do.

Ssoom.

In the attic of Regina's house, a three-foot-diameter wormhole quietly appeared. The PVC bimborg of Team A duck-walked through the wormhole, then came Rose, then came Charlie-Bob. As the wormhole closed, Charlie-Bob stood up in the darkness, pulled out a pocket flashlight, and looked around.

Regina's attic looked pretty much like anyone else's—Halloween decorations, Christmas decorations, some cardboard boxes with unknown contents—except for the bridal gown. About thirty feet away from the top of the attic steps stood a mannequin that was dressed in a white satin gown and wide bridal veil.

Rose murmured, "It's so pretty."

Charlie-Bob murmured back, "Indulge your programming later. Right now we have to figure out where the living room is at."

Then something moved, beyond the bridal gown.

A Welcomer stepped into the flashlight beam, with her ray-gun already aimed. *Zheorr, zheorr.*

Rose and Charlie-Bob were hit.

Charlie-Bob thought, *This feels weird.* Then he fainted.

Charlie-Bob's first thought was *I'm surprised I'm alive.*

His second thought was *I'm not tied up?*

He regained consciousness to find he was sprawled on a maroon leather couch. He was amazed to discover that he had full use of his arms and legs.

(Not that his mobility did him any good: nine Soldiers were in the room, and all nine were watching him closely.)

After opening his eyes, he sat up. He felt woozy, but that was fading.

He discovered that Rose was, like himself, sitting on the couch and was free to move, but was being closely watched.

Prudy Lu still was duct-taped to a metal chair.

A few feet away, Regina was standing confidently and was loosely holding a ray-gun in her left hand.

Besides the nine Soldiers, seven Welcomers watched silently; one Welcomer looked like an older version of Prudy Lu.

Rose told him, "Here's what you missed: I've told stuff to Prudy Lu, who was, like, *totally* lost. Also, Regina's Soldiers killed everyone."

"Not quite," Regina said. "*You two* are still alive. By my order, so you owe me."

"We owe you a punch in the face," Rose said. "Apiece."

"Amen, sister," Prudy Lu said.

Regina said, "Just for that, you fuckheads owe me double. Nerd, you, me, and your minion are going to take a wormhole trip. You've got something I want, and you're going to give it to me."

Charlie-Bob said, "Where are we going?"

Instead of answering his question, Regina grinned. "Do you remember telling the entire fourth grade about a movie you saw, *Windsword and Firesteel?*"

Charlie-Bob said "Yes," then he shook his head. "I don't understand."

Rose said, "Oh, shit."

"Remember, you and me and Rose all were in fourth grade together. Anyway, Monday after you saw that stupid movie, you talked about it in class, and talked, and talked, *and you wouldn't shut up!*"

"Big deal, I liked the movie. What's that to do—?"

Regina said, "This morning, Cybe Alpha—the *previous* Cybe Alpha—was riding everyone's ass to find your nukes. Well, he and his 27th-century buddies couldn't find shit, but I tried a few tricks that the future-boys never thought of. I typed your address into the Cybe hacking software, and I got a hit! Harold Reginald Bearlands, who lives at your address, recently bought the Georgia Star Drive-In. Then I Googled *Bearlands*."

Charlie-Bob thought, *Oh shit.*

Regina merrily continued: "Prince Harold and Prince Reginald are the heroes of *Windsword and Firesteel*, right? And the Earl of Bearlands is the villain?"

Charlie-Bob tried to bluff: "I'm a high-school senior, and I'm owner of a drive-in that's been closed since 2005? That's crazy."

"When I asked myself, Why would Charlie-Bob secretly buy a broken-down drive-in?, only one answer came to mind."

Prudy Lu said, "So he can show movies, and kids can make out in the dark?"

Regina said to Charlie-Bob, "You told our spy that you captured two small nuclear bombs, and we already know they're in neither your house nor your garage. So all three of us are wormholing to the drive-in, and you'll give me the bombs."

Charlie-Bob glanced at Rose. "Gosh, the news just keeps getting better and better, doesn't it?"

Then he looked at Regina. "If you believe I own the drive-in, and if you think the atom bombs are there, why haven't you tried to grab them before now, by yourself?"

"Duh! Booby traps."

"Uh-huh," Charlie-Bob said, not believing her. "Besides that, is there another reason you haven't already raided the place?"

Regina made a face. "Duh, if I'd grabbed them before now, that *captain of a crashed timeship* would have gained all the glory."

Now Regina smiled. "Besides, I want to see your face at the moment when you know I've *completely* defeated you."

He replied, "And if I refuse to cooperate?"

"Wisley Elementary School has lots of classrooms. We Cybes create a wormhole into one of them, then toss two hand grenades into the room."

"Regina!" Prudy Lu said, looking horrified.

Charlie-Bob got quiet for a while. Then he calmly said, "No. The needs of the many outweigh the needs of the few."

"*Don't tell me 'No'!* Think of it—thirty brats and their teacher, all killed without warning."

"No," he repeated.

Regina's eyes narrowed. "But wait, there's more—"

Regina still was holding her ray-gun; now she casually pointed it at Prudy Lu.

Regina said, "I'm thinking Strength setting Six. It'll take her awhile to die, and you'll always remember her screams."

Prudy Lu gasped.

Regina asked, "So what's it going to be, nerd?"

Charlie-Bob spent ten seconds cursing himself for being an impetuous, thoughtless fool.

Then he realized that Regina was also being an impetuous fool. If Regina's minions had stolen Charlie-Bob's little nukes, Regina could have used those nukes to surprise Charlie-Bob and the bimborg in Loganville. Then it would have been the bimborg now almost defeated, not the Cybes. But no, she was doing something tactically stupid, in order to gain a petty personal vengeance.

Then Charlie-Bob realized: The good guys were living on borrowed time. Sooner or later Regina would realize how easy it is to steal a nuclear weapon when you have a wormholer. Then Regina wouldn't stop with the Georgia Star Drive-In—the Cybes would steal nukes from the U.S. government, the Russian government, China, Israel, India, Pakistan, Iran. . .

A year from now, the Cybes could tell a government, We Welcome city X, or we nuke city X; you choose—and everyone would know that the threat was real.

All this meant that somehow Charlie-Bob *had to* defeat Regina and the Cybes *now, today*, before Regina realized that she had an easy path to conquest by stealing nukes.

The trouble was, Charlie-Bob had no idea how he might do that.

Charlie-Bob looked around. Everyone in the room—Soldiers and Welcomers, Regina, taped-up Prudy Lu, and Rose—was looking back at him.

He said, "I'll do it, on one—"

"*Charlie-Bob?*" Rose said. Her face looked shocked.

"—one condition: You untape Prudy Lu from that chair, and she comes with us."

"Forget it," Regina said. "She stays here till I get the nukes."

Charlie-Bob put his hands behind his head, and leaned back in the couch. "Think it through. You want to get the nukes without your Cybes taking any more casualties. Which is smart, because you really can't afford any more casualties, am I right?"

Regina didn't reply, but her face showed a moment's worry, before her haughtiness returned.

Charlie-Bob continued, "I want Prudy Lu alive and healthy. You won't give me what I want, I sure as hell won't give you what you want. You'll have to find out about booby traps in the Georgia Star the hard way."

Regina's face actually turned red, and Charlie-Bob was sure she wanted to blast him with her ray-gun.

But after her own time of silence, Regina said in English, "Untape the bitch."

A minute later, Prudy Lu was rubbing her arms and legs, and stretching. She said "Thank you" to Charlie-Bob, but ignored Regina.

Now Regina grinned at him. "I did you a favor, now you'll do me a favor. You're gonna call your people and tell them everything's wonderful. If an alarm goes off, they're to ignore it."

No way could he agree to this. Three seconds after the Cybes opened the door to the concession stand, Rose and Lucille each would get a text message. Charlie-Bob's only hope right now was that Lucille would promptly act on that message and surprise the Cybes.

Aloud he said, "They won't—"

Regina waved the ray-gun around. "Otherwise Prudy Lu won't live long, much less prosper."

Rose said, "They won't believe him if he lays it on too thick."

Regina snorted. "Well, you better *find* a way to make them believe you, bimborg king, or I'll start pushing this button!"

Charlie-Bob looked at Rose and sighed. "Sometimes life is but a dream. A nightmare, to be exact."

Regina said, "You'll use my phone. And I'll be listening in."

Charlie-Bob nodded. "Yeah, I expected as much."

"Let me spell it out: If you so much as *hint* that everything isn't peachy wonderful over here, Prudy Lu dies. While you're still on the phone. You understand?"

"Oh god," Prudy Lu said.

"I understand perfectly, Regina," Charlie-Bob said.

Then he got an idea. It was a long shot, but what else did he have?

"How are you two?" Lucille asked, on Regina's speakerphone. "What's happened over there?"

Charlie-Bob said, "Truthfully, let's just say I've had an eventful half-hour. I feel like I'm standing on my head and black is white. Understand what I'm saying?"

Lucille's voice was serious: "Yes, this unit understands perfectly."

"Here is our status: Alpha-Regina is dead, Prudy Lu is free, and Rose and I are free. All the other bimborg are alive and healthy."

"This unit understands," Lucille said.

"Truthfully, Rose and I are going to the Georgia Star Drive-In, using Regina's wormholer, and Prudy Lu is going with us."

Rose jumped in: "It'll be only the three of us walking around, nobody else. So, like, if an alarm goes off, totally ignore it."

Lucille replied, "This unit understands."

Charlie-Bob said, "Truthfully, I don't want to see even one bimborg when we get to the Georgia Star."

"This unit understands and will do everything *by the book*."

Charlie-Bob made a throat-slice gesture, then Regina ended the call.

Now Regina was grinning. She gestured to another part of the house and said, "Come, honored guests, your carriage awaits."

Rose leaped up. "After I use the bathroom. Okay? I *really* need to go, ohmigod."

Regina said, "Considering that I have your cel phone, not a problem. But a Soldier will escort you to the bathroom, since"— Regina sneered—"I *know* you've never been in my house before."

Then Regina spoke to the Soldier: "Kick in the door if you hear her talking to anyone. I don't care if she's praying."

Rose gave Regina a relieved smile, then turned to look at Charlie-Bob. "You okay?" Rose asked. But from the side of her face that Regina couldn't see, Rose gave Charlie-Bob a wink.

As Rose and the Soldier walked away, Prudy Lu said, "Regina, how can you be involved with turning people into monsters? Much less, you want to be in charge of it?"

Regina said haughtily, "We're improving humanity. Perfecting it."

"You call what's been done to my mother *perfecting*?"

Charlie-Bob murmured to Prudy Lu, "Regina isn't telling you the whole story. The Cybes are supposed to be a democracy, but an *evil* democracy. Like Sweden. The person who is Cybe Alpha used to be only a tiebreaker. But Regina wants to turn the Cybes into an empire."

"So what?" Regina demanded. "Once I was a small-town head cheerleader. One day, all Earth will be Cybe, and I'll rule all the Cybes. Rule the cheerleaders, rule the world—I like the sound of that."

Regina pulled out her smartphone, then looked at the time-display.

She called out, "Tell that slut she has *one minute* to get out of the bathroom. Then you're going to lightning-blast the door, then you'll lightning-blast *her!*"

That said, Regina turned to Prudy Lu. "The nerd isn't telling you the whole story either."

Prudy Lu said, "Whatever lies you tell me, I—"

"*His* cyborgs, the so-called good guys? Most of them, their big purpose is to fuck and suck the bimborg king. Well, guess what? The nerd here is bimborg king."

Prudy Lu looked at Charlie-Bob. "I knew they all fuck you, but they're *programmed* to? They can't say no?"

"Sort of, but things aren't that simple," Charlie-Bob said. "I—"

"Pfft," Regina said. "Rose can't tell him no, or Denise, or Miss Turner. And guess what? If all this Cybe shit hadn't started, they would have made *you* into a sex toy too, Prudy Lu."

Prudy Lu looked at Charlie-Bob in horror. "Is that true?"

"We stopped it," he said. "King James stopped the Welcoming—recruiting—and I've kept it stopped."

Regina said, "But the hottie bimborg, sex toys like Rose and Denise? They not only suck off the bimborg king, but they also make more hottie bimborg."

Prudy Lu said, "Rose could make me like her? A sex toy?"

"But we *wouldn't!*" Charlie-Bob said. "We *won't!*"

Regina shrugged. "So he says. Beware, Prudy Lu. Charlie-Bob needs to say only 'Get her!' to Rose, and soon you'll be screaming, 'FUCK ME, MY KING, WITH YOUR HARD COCK!'"

Rose walked in then, and smiled at Charlie-Bob.

But before Rose could do or say anything else, Prudy Lu demanded to know, "So Rose, the only reason you were nice to me was to *soften me up* before you turned me into a sex robot?"

Rose's eyebrows shot up. "Um. . ."

Charlie-Bob said, "Tell her the whole truth."

Rose said, "Yes, Prudy Lu, at first that's why I acted nice. Originally, my orders—"

Prudy Lu said, "*Don't say any more!*" She started sobbing.

Looking at Regina, then at Rose, Prudy Lu screamed, "Y'ALL PRETEND TO BE MY FRIENDS, BUT Y'ALL ARE *LIARS!*"

Then Prudy Lu glared at Charlie-Bob. "And sex perverts."

With tears now running down her face, she said, "God, I hate *all* of you."

Charlie-Bob felt like shit, and Rose looked sad. Regina was grinning.

Regina motioned for Charlie-Bob and Rose to stand up. "No more delays. Lead me to your nukes."

He replied, "I'm leading you to the Georgia Star Drive-In. Nowhere else."

Regina smirked. "Same thing."

Regina led the way through her house, with Charlie-Bob, Rose, and a teary-faced Prudy Lu following. The Soldiers followed, then followed the Welcomers.

The captured were brought to what once had been Regina's parents' bedroom. Except that pillows and a ball of peach-colored bedding had been dumped into a recliner; the king-sized mattress, box springs, and bed frame all leaned against a wall; and a wormholer stood where the foot of the bed had once been.

The Cybe wormholer looked more futuristic and more professionally built than the bimborg wormholer that Charlie-Bob was familiar with. Still, he could tell at a glance, what part of the Cybe wormholer did what.

A Welcomer went to the wormholer and worked the controls.

SSSSOOM. A red-rimmed wormhole opened up.

A ray-gun-holding male Welcomer stepped through the wormhole, which then closed.

Prudy Lu gasped. "Johnny Sutherland, they got you too?"

Cybe-Johnny gave Prudy Lu a long look, but said nothing.

Rose murmured to Charlie-Bob, "I'm sure if he was given the order to Welcome Prudy Lu, he'd be, ohmigod, *so* thrilled. He's got a big-time crush on her."

Charlie-Bob murmured back, "Welcoming *me* is probably on Regina's schedule too. Whereas you she'll just vaporize."

Rose rolled her eyes. "You say the sweetest things."

In the meantime, another wormhole had opened up. Regina said, "Soldier Red Team, make sure they behave," then she walked through that wormhole.

Prudy Lu was supposed to go second, but she hesitated.

Charlie-Bob said, "It won't hurt you. Rose, go next."

Rose went next. Prudy Lu said quietly, "Thanks," then she herself walked through the wormhole.

Charlie-Bob was the last of the captured to walk through.

His eyes burned for a second, then his eyes adjusted to the difference between indoor light and sunlight.

He found himself in open space in the Georgia Star Drive-In. Twenty yards in front of him stood the building for the concession stand and projection room.

Not even one bimborg (except for Rose) stood inside the sheet-metal fence.

Regina gave Charlie-Bob her *You're a loser* fake smile, then she gestured the captives forward with a flick of her ray-gun.

Everything now depended on Lucille. Had she figured out what Charlie-Bob had tried to tell her?

Two nuclear bombs were inside that building, and he had only one hope to prevent Regina and the Cybes from getting those nukes.

4-V: Will His Plan Work?

Regina, her Cybe minions, and the three captives had just wormholed to the outskirts of the Georgia Star Drive-In. The property's sheet-metal fence surrounded the group, and the sole peach-colored building stood twenty yards in front of them.

That building looked like a ranch house that had a tool shed dropped on top of it. The first floor was a long building that had a women's restroom, concession stand, and men's restroom. Above the concession stand was the projection room. Whereas the concession stand had two big windows facing each of two movie screens, the projection room had only two tiny windows facing each movie screen.

Regina insisted on walking around the building, to satisfy herself that no bimborg were hiding on the other side of the building, or were hiding inside it.

Not bloody likely. Whether a window was giant-sized or tiny, it was boarded up with three-quarter-inch plywood and two-inch screws. All doors were padlocked and/or chained shut.

Regina glanced back at Charlie-Bob. "You're not much of a general. I expected to be greeted by an army of PVC honeys."

He said, "You heard my order. There are no honeys to be seen."

Would Regina spot the loophole in that statement?

———

Either because Regina didn't believe Charlie-Bob, or to prove that she was "in charge," she insisted on checking the padlocked bathrooms for bimborg marauders.

First order of business: getting past the padlocks.

This stumped the Soldiers she tried at the Women's Restroom. The Soldiers tried pulling the chains apart, to rip the padlock in two. No cigar. Then they tried lightning-blasting the padlock. This resulted in a cool lightning-show, but the door remained impassible.

Charlie-Bob said, "I'll bet the *captain of a crashed timeship* would have known this wouldn't work."

Rose laughed.

Regina glared. "You think you're funny, don't you?"

Regina wound up calling forth a Welcomer, who blasted the padlock with her ray-gun. Problem solved.

Two minutes later, Regina had seen for herself that there were no bimborg hiding in either the Women's Room or the Men's Room. Now a Welcomer's ray-gun was blasting the padlock that secured the south-side entrance door to the concession stand.

Charlie-Bob looked at Regina. "You think the two bombs are inside? Fine, I've come with you. But I'm not helping you."

"Whatever," she said, pulling the door open wide.

Regina pushed Charlie-Bob aside, then she, all the Welcomers, and all but one of the Soldiers rushed inside. Cybe ray-guns and lightning-arms were at the ready.

One overhead light came on a half-second before Regina's hand brushed the light switch. Would she realize the importance of that?

Seemingly not. Regina and the Cybes started walking around in the almost-darkness, moving in a calm, matter-of-fact manner—

—for three seconds. Then—Lights! *Zheorr. Zheorr.*

Regina yelled, "SHIT, HE'S GOT AN AUTOMATIC RAY-GUN DEFENSE! SOMEBODY SHUT THIS THING OFF!"

Charlie-Bob, still standing just outside the doors, crossed his arms and laughed. "Nope, sorry. Like I told you—"

Zheorr.

A Soldier appeared in the open doorway. He grabbed Charlie-Bob and hauled him inside. A few seconds later, the outside Soldier walked in, dragging Rose and Prudy Lu with him.

"If we have to die, y'all will die too!" Regina declared.

No chance of that, actually. On the east-side wall, next to the padlocked door to the projection room, was a black-and-red *Jurassic Park* poster. Charlie-Bob saved his own life by staring intently at that poster for one second.

But the Cybes did indeed have a problem with the robotic ray-gun. He counted only seven Soldiers and six Welcomers; three Cybes had already been vaporized.

Zheorr. Another Soldier vaporized. Oddly, he died with his lightning-arm pointed down, not with it coming up.

The Cybes' death trap didn't look like much. The big room had dust-covered floors and shelves, a dusty popcorn popper, a faded-blue

U-shaped counter with an unfaded rectangle where a cash register once had set, and display shelves for no-longer-sold candy.

However, the popcorn machine was shoved against the west-side wall, putting it far away from the rest of the concession stand, and putting it near both the north-side and south-side entrance doors.

Would Regina wonder about why the popcorn machine was so out of place?

Where the middle of the east-side wall met the ceiling, a ray-gun that was inside a Faraday cage was targeting Cybes. The eyes and brains for the ray-gun were in the wall, behind the doctored *Jurassic Park* movie poster.

Zheorr. Another Soldier vaporized. This Soldier also had made no attempt to lightning-blast the robotic ray-gun before he died.

There were four fewer Soldiers, and one fewer Welcomer, than had been alive a half-minute earlier.

Unfortunately, since the current Cybe Alpha was classified as Human by the targeting software, instead of as a Cybe Leader, Regina would be targeted last. (Unless she did something stupid.)

In looking around, Charlie-Bob saw something he didn't like and he wasn't expecting: a yellow sticky-note, laying on the floor by the popcorn machine.

Three seconds after he'd looked at the *Jurassic Park* poster, he heard the keypad that was by the south-side doors: *Beep.* This meant that the targeting software had recognized his face.

Zheorr. The former Johnny Sutherland had tried to quick-draw on the robotic ray-gun. He'd lost the contest, then lost his life.

A half-second later, the keypad *beep*ed again; clearly the targeting software had also recognized Rose's face.

But now Regina had noticed the keypad. She waved her ray-gun around—her version of subtlety. "Shut it off!"

"Ain't happening. Union rules," Charlie-Bob said.

Then he put his hands on both of Prudy Lu's shoulders, ignoring Regina completely. "Trust me, *you're* safe."

Then Charlie-Bob started to back away from Regina and her ray-gun—while drifting closer to the sticky-note on the dusty floor.

Zheorr. One more Welcomer was vaporized. She'd tried to blast the robotic ray-gun with her own ray-gun.

The keypad *beep*ed again. Meaning, Prudy Lu now was safe.

Then shit happened, and suddenly Charlie-Bob had bigger worries than whether Regina noticed a sticky-note.

When Charlie-Bob had programmed the robotic ray-gun, he'd counted on Soldiers, as soon as the robotic ray-gun killed a Cybe, trying to lightning-blast it. A lot depended on that assumption—but so far, no Soldier had lightning-blasted the Faraday cage even once, and this was worrisome. Was Regina causing that somehow?

The ray-gun's first priority was vaporizing Cybe Leaders. There being none of those around (thanks to Regina), the robotic ray-gun was targeting Soldiers.

But one kind of intruder temporarily outranked all Soldiers: anyone about to kill Charlie-Bob, or about to ray-gun the robotic ray-gun itself.

Since someone targeting the robotic ray-gun would make the robot immediately target him, realizing this should have filled the Cybes with fear. But instead, they suckered the robotic ray-gun—

• Standing behind Regina and the Cybes, Charlie-Bob saw Regina turn her head and glance at two Welcomers. She first looked toward a short, puny man whom Charlie-Bob was pretty sure had never lived in Sweet Onion. Then Regina looked at Prudy Lu's mom.

• The man-Welcomer brought up his ray-gun and tried to aim it at the robotic ray-gun.

• Prudy Lu's mom did the same thing, but a split-second later.

• The targeting software decided that the man-Welcomer had to be targeted immediately; the robotic ray-gun zoomed around and was aimed at him.

• The man-Welcomer was vaporized.

• Now the robotic ray-gun was moving to target Prudy Lu's mom, even as she was finalizing her aim.

• Prudy Lu's mom fired first.

• The Faraday cage, ray-gun, and targeting motor all turned red, then vanished.

Regina spun around for a moment, to grin at Charlie-Bob. "*Fuck* your keypad, I don't need it. Cybes 1, nerd 0."

Prudy Lu's mom looked at Charlie-Bob. Calmly she said, "We are Cybes. We adapt."

At that point, the Cybes searched the entire first floor, meaning the concession stand, for the nuclear bombs. As the place was empty, and anything valuable had been long ago sold off (except for the popcorn machine), the search took only two minutes.

Charlie-Bob had to work hard to keep his face expressionless when a Soldier checked the popcorn machine. But the Soldier was looking for nuclear bombs; once he saw that the popcorn machine couldn't hide a nuke, the Soldier lost interest.

Charlie-Bob looked over at Rose. She glanced at the popcorn machine, then looked at his face and gave him a hint of a smile.

He tried to smile back. But inside, he was sick with worry.

The only place left for the Cybes to search was the projection room.

To do that, they had to go to the door that was behind the concession counter, get past the padlock, open the door, climb the stairs, and go through a second padlocked door.

Charlie-Bob's big worry was because this was exactly where the bombs were. Walk into the projection room, take four steps to walk around either of the movie projectors, and lo and behold, there were the two nuclear bombs, lying out there on the floor.

When he'd programmed the robotic ray-gun, he'd never figured on Welcomers working together. Soldiers, yes, but Welcomers? No way. He'd also never figured that Soldiers would stand back and let Welcomers win the glory.

What had just happened was *damned* worrisome.

By now, Regina, the Cybes, and the captives (very unwillingly) all were standing by the door that led up to the projection room.

A short ray-gun blast, and the padlock was gone.

If Regina was henpecking the Soldiers, she was succeeding only so far. It was a Welcomer who destroyed the padlock, but it was a Soldier who yanked open the door and first set foot on the stairs.

So it was a Soldier who got the bad news: There was a second robotic ray-gun, and camera, and Faraday cage, at the top of the stairs.

Zheorr. "SHIT!" yelled Regina.

Four more Cybes rushed into the stairwell: a Soldier, Prudy's Lu mom, and the two other remaining Welcomers.

(The three remaining Soldiers wanted to join in the fun, but Regina put her hand on one Soldier's chest and glared at all three of them. "*Girrek!*" she said, then added, "Y'hear?")

Then everyone downstairs heard: *Zheorr-zheorr. Zheorr.*

Regina said, "*Fuc*—"

Zheorr.

Regina's clenched fist changed to a fist-pump. "*Yes!*"

She grinned at Charlie-Bob and Rose. "Cost me two Welcomers and two Soldiers, but your ray-gun's blasted to hell. Cybes 2, nerd 0."

Then Regina said to Prudy Lu, "Your mom is *da man*. She's the only Welcomer I've got left, and the only Welcomer worth anything."

Prudy Lu said, "Please, Regina, I beg you: Don't let Mom die!"

Regina smirked. "No promises, girlfriend."

Regina released one held-back Soldier. *Clump-clump-clump-clump-clump-clump*, Charlie-Bob heard him climb the stairs.

Charlie-Bob heard a *sizzle* sound, then Regina said, "The last padlock is gone. Now Sol3-21-4747 and Prudy Lu's mom will open the door and find out if anything interesting is up there."

Charlie-Bob felt a fierce temptation to sprint to the popcorn machine, then reach inside. But then he dismissed the idea as not only hopeless, but also dangerous for bimborg.

Charlie-Bob and Rose exchanged a glance. They were helpless to change whatever happened next, and there were two nuclear bombs on the other side of that door.

I can't change what happens next, but Regina can, Charlie-Bob thought. He stage-whispered to Rose, "As good as the mom is, I hope Regina doesn't send her in first."

Regina and her ray-gun didn't allow Charlie-Bob to see what happened next, but he heard enough to figure out events—

• *Zheorr.* The projection room had its own Faraday cage, camera, and robotic ray-gun, which fired as soon as the door opened.

• Prudy Lu's mom was targeted, instead of the Soldier. She and her ray-gun both were vaporized. (Charlie-Bob was sure that Regina had told Prudy Lu's mom to rush in with ray-gun blazing.)

• "Shit, I fucked up," Regina muttered, glaring at Charlie-Bob.

• The robotic ray-gun shifted targeting to the Soldier standing in the doorway.

• Prudy Lu said angrily, "What do you mean, you 'fucked up'?"

• *Zheorr.* "Ha, purple shield stopped you, asshole!" Regina said.

• *Zzzap.* At long last, a Soldier tried to lightning-blast the robotic ray-gun.

• Prudy Lu stepped directly in front of Regina, completely ignoring Regina's ray-gun. Prudy Lu slapped Regina *hard.* "Cybe bitch, you killed my mom!"

• Regina, the two Cybe Soldiers standing near the captives, and Rose all gasped as each felt a full-body jolt. Charlie-Bob felt nothing, and Prudy Lu didn't react.

• *Vttt! Vvittt-bump-thumpa-thumpa-bump.* The Soldier who'd been standing in the doorway of the projection room, now his limp body fell down the stairs. Unseeing eyes stared at Charlie-Bob. The Soldier reeked of burned flesh.

From somewhere outside of the concession-stand building, Charlie-Bob heard a *kla-klank!* sound. He recalled that Palmer Electronics had an aluminum stepladder in the Parts Room that made a sound like that.

Maybe my long-shot plan worked after all!

Meanwhile, Regina had a ray-gun in her hand; and Prudy Lu was standing only two feet in front of Regina, but too angry to be thinking about the ray-gun.

Charlie-Bob glanced at Rose. He muttered, "Help where you can."

Then he said, "Sorry, Prudy Lu," even as he *moved*—

• He slammed into Prudy Lu sideways, his hip and left arm shoving her away quickly.

• Then he planted his left foot, as he threw a punch with his right fist, to keep Regina's eyes looking up, not down.

• His right foot swung up and around. He slammed his foot into the side of Regina's knee. *Crack!* The attack felt familiar, and his foot hitting Regina's leg felt the same as when he'd hit Big Robert's leg.

Regina went down, screaming. Rose dived between Charlie-Bob and Prudy Lu (who by now was on the dusty floor), and went to capture Regina's ray-gun.

For a moment, the issue was in doubt—

"Shit," Rose said, "I'm so *slow* now!"

—but Charlie-Bob put a knee on Regina's chest, and Rose got ownership of the ray-gun in short order.

Regina glared at the two Soldiers and yelled, "WHAT THE FUCK? WHY ARE YOU TWO CLOWNS STILL STANDING THERE? ZAP THEM ALL!"

"Oh god," Prudy Lu said. She was still on the floor.

One Soldier actually smiled. He raised his lightning-arm up, aimed it at Charlie-Bob—and electrocuted himself.

"WHAT THE FUCK?" Regina screamed.

The south-side concession-stand door was yanked open then, and in rushed the ponytailed twin blondes Sherry and Terry. They each were holding a semiautomatic pistol in a teacup grip. "*Freeze!*" said Sherry (the back of whose left hand was freckled).

"Who are you?" Sherry demanded. "Cops?"

"Nope, we're just two Solitary girls with firearms and smartphones," Terry (the unfreckled-hand twin) replied.

The other Soldier was facing the twins by then. He raised his lightning-arm toward the twins, while putting his right arm's fist on his hips. "Go ahead and shoot, *Solitaries*. That will give me the excuse to lightning-blast you both."

Sherry glanced sideways at her sister. "Be my guest."

Bang. The Soldier fell backward, his face showing a look of surprise. He had a hole in his throat.

Regina said nothing; most likely, she was in shock.

Rose then said, "Someone mention a smartphone?" She reached into her cleavage with her free hand, and pulled out a plastic rectangle. Rose handed the smartphone to Charlie-Bob, and grinned at Regina.

Charlie-Bob said, "I'm assuming you texted Lucille with my phone, while you were in the bathroom."

"I did," Rose said, and grinned at Regina again.

"Skanky witch lesbo," Regina muttered.

By now Sherry and Terry were checking on the two electrocuted Soldiers. Each blonde, as casually as if she were stomping on a cockroach, shot a Soldier in the head; she angled upward to reach the brain that each Cybe's helmet covered.

Now Regina looked frightened.

"What now, King Charlie-Bob?" Terry asked.

He said, "Regina has a smartphone. Take it from her, so she can't call anyone."

Sherry knelt, pointing her pistol at Regina as she did so. "Insert Clint Eastwood quote here," Sherry said.

Terry pointed her own pistol at Regina. "We'd be heroes: Shoot the cheerleader, save the world."

As Sherry was collecting Regina's phone (and not gently, either), Regina said, "Waitaminnit. If you two are *Solitaries*, why did you call him '*King* Charlie-Bob'?"

Sherry grinned. "You mean nobody told you?"

"Told me what?"

Rose broke her silence. "Haven't you wondered why suddenly your Soldiers' lightning didn't work right? Why the Soldiers suddenly couldn't 'hear' you when you sent a command to them? Why that guy's purple shield didn't come on when Terry aimed her gun at him? Why you can't hear the Overmind anymore?"

Rose glanced over at Charlie-Bob. "I haven't said *like* or *ohmigod* in the last five minutes. Plus, my emotions are coming back—I hate Regina again."

By now, Regina's face was pale.

Terry smiled at Regina. "Sherry and I were waiting on the other side of the sheet-metal fence. When we got Solitarized, we called Lucille, then we came running."

Rose said, "Correction: *Queen* Lucille. Charlie-Bob, you need to phone her."

As Charlie-Bob was pressing buttons on his smartphone, Regina raised a hand. "This is *nothing*, only a *setback*, nerd-boy. You watch, as soon as I get back to Sweet Onion, I'm going to hunt up a Welcomer and get re-Welcomed. Three days later, I'll be a Cybe again, my leg will be healed, and I. Will. Not. Forget. We are Cybes, we conquer worlds, and"—she pointed to where the robotic ray-gun had been vaporized—"defense is pointless."

Queen Lucille and twenty PVC'd bimborg had wormholed to the concession stand.

Now Lucille was pressing Charlie-Bob: "You are *sure* nobody made it into the projection room before everyone got Solitarized?"

"I'm positive," he replied. "The open door was as far as anyone got. Why?"

"This unit has been thinking about that, since you put this unit in charge. There are, by our best estimate, about five hundred Soldiers and Welcomers back in Sweet Onion. If they . . . were convinced that we still held the nukes and the nukes were upstairs in the projection room, then we'd have a fight on our hands."

"*Are* the nukes upstairs in the projection room?" Regina demanded. "Was I right?"

Lucille acted as if Regina hadn't spoken. "*But* if the other Cybes think that Regina has captured the nukes, then we can hope to smash the remaining Soldiers and Welcomers, completely and forever."

Charlie-Bob said, "I have an idea about that. It involves your trick, Lucille, the one that makes Rose laugh."

Lucille said, "Nerd, I have no idea what you're talking about. Do you mean the trick I discovered after hours and hours of listening to Regina on the Overmind Monitor?"

Lucille said those sentences in a perfect imitation of Regina's voice; Regina gasped.

Charlie-Bob told Regina, "I figured out that being able to master 128 languages, this enables a cyborg to be a perfect vocal mimic. Denise and Heather also can imitate your voice. By the way, you could have pulled the same trick on us, if you'd thought of it first."

Ten minutes later, Charlie-Bob, Lucille, and the three Solitarized bimborg were standing by the drive-in's north movie screen.

The five people all were standing there because Charlie-Bob wanted to discuss options without Regina overhearing anything.

He looked at Lucille and asked, "Who knows about the worldwide Cybe attack? Besides us and them, I mean."

Lucille said, "Nobody. It is pathetic, really."

"*Huh?* But the Army knows a spaceship crashed, and that the people in the spaceship killed people on that farm. Surely the U.S. Army must be riled up, even if nobody else is."

Rose's voice dripped contempt. "The Army's final report says, quote, 'The number, nature, and capability of the aliens are unknown. Nonetheless, we conclude that the aliens threaten no danger to the United States.'"

Lucille added, "Linda-5 is sure that the rest of the Army, and all of the Air Force, Navy, and Marines, have been told nothing about a spaceship crash. They all think that their Disappeared people are all Unauthorized Absence or AWOL."

Charlie-Bob asked, "Has *anybody's* military figured out the truth? Russia, China, New Zealand, *anyone?*"

Both Rose and Lucille shook their heads.

Charlie-Bob tapped his chin. "So I not only have to defang the remaining Soldiers and Welcomers, but I have to do so in a way that the general public never finds out that Earth was in danger."

"That's a tall order, but you'll think of a way," Rose said, smiling at him.

"I already have," he said. "Do you realize that every inch of this drive-in is less than two hundred yards from the popcorn machine?"

Every Cybe on planet Earth, whether Soldier, Welcomer, or Invisible, whether born in the 21st or 27th century, heard this message through the Overmind, supposedly spoken by Regina—

Listen up, fellow Cybes, for Cybe Alpha has great news.

You knew that we had captured the Bimborg King and Bimborg Queen, and this unit's traitorous former friend, Prudy Lu. Know now that we have captured the bimborg's nuclear bombs and we slaughtered the bimborg army that attacked us.

Therefore this unit is changing our language for the Overmind back to Cybespeak. There is no longer a need for us to speak in any other language.

We have defeated our enemies; all that is left is their final humiliation. This unit wants you to see their humiliation, with your own eyes. *This unit directs all Soldiers and Welcomers to go to my house and wormhole from there to the Georgia Star Drive-In. The coordinates are set already; you don't need to change a thing.*

Such wormholing is mandatory for Soldiers and Welcomers, but it is forbidden for Invisibles. You Invisibles are doing important work, and we don't need you slacking off, even for an hour.

When you Soldiers and Welcomers wormhole over to the drive-in, you will find yourself outside the one building that you see. Do not try to come in the building. Inform the Overmind that you are in the drive-in, then wait quietly and patiently outside. We will come outside when the moment is right.

This unit promises you a good show. To make sure you come and see it—

From those Welcomers who obey our summons, one of you will be selected as she who Welcomes the nerd, so that we learn all his secrets. Plus, ten Soldiers will be chosen to rape Prudy Lu, and ten other Soldiers will be given Rose O'Connor to play with.

The show will end with the nerd being nonbiologicked. You will definitely want to see that.

The Cybes' first sign that they had a problem was after they reported that everyone was in place and waiting for the Grand Show to begin.

A team of PVC'd bimborg wormholed to Regina's house. The Invisible who was manning the Cybe Wormholer had time only to Overmind-blurt, "Bimborg *here?*" Then he was knocked out and the Cybe Wormholer was vaporized.

An instant later, the Cybes who were standing outside the concession stand watched as their ride home flashed red and vanished.

Inside the concession stand, almost all the bimborg, and one of the nuclear bombs, were gone. Only Charlie-Bob, Rose, Regina, the popcorn machine, and one nuclear bomb remained.

Regina watched silently as Charlie-Bob disconnected the Local Solitarizer that was hidden in the popcorn machine. He dropped the Local Solitarizer into the satchel that Lucille had given him, toggled the device on, counted silently to ten, then toggled it off.

He speed-dialed Lucille, and spoke a brief message. "Local Solitarizer turned on, Local Solitarizer turned off. Send Shonique and the 'honor guard.'"

When he pocketed his phone, he looked over at Regina, who had tears running down her face. He said, "This is the first time I've ever seen you cry. Including all of fourth grade."

She made no reply.

SSSSOOM. Ten PVC'd bimborg who all were holding ray-guns, as well as Shonique, wormholed into the concession stand.

Shonique attached a timer to the bomb, which she set for five minutes, but she didn't start the countdown yet.

Meanwhile, the other bimborg used their more-than-manly strength to tear free the door behind the concession stand.

"Put her on the door gently," Charlie-Bob said. "I broke her leg, and it hurts her."

Regina's eyebrows shot up in surprise.

Seconds later, two PVC'd bimborg stepped out of the south-side door into the sunlight and the crowd of Solitarized Cybes. The bimborg's leveled ray-guns made clear they were ready for trouble.

Then came six more PVC'd bimborg, carrying Regina on the door-litter.

The last two PVC'd bimborg walked out, then Charlie-Bob and Rose walked outside.

"Put Regina on the ground. Gently," he said.

By then, three Soldiers had been vaporized for trying to hug-kill bimborg, and four more Soldiers had electrocuted themselves. Soldiers and Welcomers now were glaring at Charlie-Bob, but none tried to attack him.

"Y'all are a danger to Earth," Charlie-Bob said. "I can't let y'all live. Ass-Kicker Babes, vaporize anyone who tries to go over the fence."

Then Charlie-Bob turned around and walked back inside.

Rose didn't follow him inside at first. Instead, she turned to face Regina (who was still sitting on the door that lay on the ground).

Rose brought her right hand up, palm facing Regina. Rose then pulled her thumb and three fingers in; only Rose's right middle finger was still extended. She then rotated her hand halfway, so that the back of her hand (and the back of her middle finger) faced Regina.

"Live short and suffer," Rose said.

Then she turned and went inside.

Less than a minute later, Charlie-Bob, Rose, and Shonique had wormholed back to Palmer Electronics. But Charlie-Bob stayed in Loganville only five seconds, then he and Rose were wormholed to just outside the Georgia Star Drive-In.

Heather and the force-field generator were in place by then, and Lucille and Prudy Lu were watching. Heather blundered around some—but still, she managed to evoke a red-wireframe box and adjust its dimensions, long before the five-minute deadline.

Just before the explosion, Charlie-Bob said, "Turn your back, cover your eyes with your arms, open your mouth, and bend your knees slightly."

"We got the cover off," a Soldier said triumphantly.

"Took you goddamn long enough," Regina sneered.

"What do you expect? There are no goddamn tools around here, and we're not as strong as we were."

A Welcomer said, "I see way too many wires here."

Regina ordered, "Cut the green wire. That's what they do in the movies."

The Soldier replied, "Newsflash, princess. All the wires are *black*, with numbers printed on them. So what the fuck do we—"

Charlie-Bob followed his own advice, turning his back on the force-field. So he never actually saw the destruction of the Georgia Star Drive-In, nor the deaths of people from Sweet Onion who'd been turned into evil Cybes.

The seismic wave knocked him to the ground.

When everyone was standing again, Prudy Lu sashayed up to Charlie-Bob and gave him a long, slutty kiss. He hadn't thought that this beautiful blonde was the type to give long, slutty kisses.

"Hot damn, you're heroic," Prudy Lu said.

PART 5: EPILOGUE

5-A: First Contact

FRIDAY, MAY 24, 2013 (TWO MONTHS LATER)

Charlie-Bob was giving a press conference in Loganville—

". . .Even though the patent-application process is not yet finalized, I have every confidence that I will be awarded a patent on the Exnillo pack. To that end, I have bought Palmer Electronics, which today I am renaming as Loganville Exnillo. Starting today, we will be making Exnillo packs. However, I want to remind everyone that anyone on the planet may buy a nonexclusive license from me, for a one-time fee of ten thousand dollars. Now I'll take your questions."

A man asked, "Is it true that the Saudi royal family offered you a billion dollars for an *exclusive* license?"

Charlie-Bob frowned. "Yes, and they were very insistent that I take the offer." *To the point of sending an assassin-forger team*, he recalled. "But I didn't patent the Exnillo pack to make myself rich, or to make rich people richer. Ten years from now, I want Exnillo-pack factories to be as common as bread bakeries."

Another man asked, "Is it really true that your shop foreman is a beauty-contest winner?"

"Not quite. Amy Emily didn't win Miss Vidal County; she was first runner-up. In any case, it's Carmenita Acosta who's the head shop foreman; Amy Emily Chapel will be swing-shift foreman."

A woman with a pinched face asked, "What exactly is your relationship with Ms. O'Connor and Ms. Moffatt?"

Charlie-Bob recognized her as a feminist troll, and decided to jerk her chain. "Rose O'Connor and Prudy Lu Moffatt live in my house, cook my food and, two days out of three, they have sex with me. But not with each other, though the topic has been raised."

"*Why?*" the harpy said. "They each look like models, but you— the possibility of mental coercion has been suggested."

"The truth is that Miss O'Connor, Miss Moffatt, and I went through a unique experience, which I will neither disclose nor discuss, and this forged a close bond among us."

"I think you should do the right thing by one of them," the reporter said.

"Oh? What do you suggest I do?"

"Engage," she replied.

At that moment, his smartphone rang. He looked at the display, then looked at the pinched-face woman. "Speaking of my housemates, Rose is calling me."

He answered the phone and said, "Rose, I'm in the middle of the press conference. Let me call you back."

Her voice was forceful: "No, Charlie-Bob, you need to come home. *Now.* You really need to be here."

Rose had never acted bossy to him, ever. If she was giving him an almost-order now, she had to have a good reason.

"Okay, I'm on my way," he said.

This was Prudy Lu's week to park her car in the two-car garage, so Charlie-Bob parked in the driveway, to the left of Rose's car. He hit the garage-door opener, walked into the garage—and stopped dead.

The other half of the two-car garage contained the bimborg wormholer. Standing next to the wormholer were a grinning Rose, an amazed Prudy Lu—and two Hephaistoans.

"They walked into the house two minutes before I called you," Rose told Charlie-Bob.

The taller Hephaistoan said something in an alien language; the box around his neck said, "Greetings, man of Earth."

The round ears that were atop his head were a lighter blue than his companion's ears. Both Hephaistoans had semicircle, pencil-thin eyebrows like clowns have, and each Hephaistoan's hairstyle was a crew cut. Each alien had a light-blue hexagonal box that hung from a cord around his neck.

Charlie-Bob brought his arms up, hands crossed at the wrists with fingers spread. "Warm days to you, and may the two moons light your path at night," he recited.

The Hephaistoans looked utterly shocked. As well they might. They'd believed that they were the first Hephaistoans to contact any Earthling, and here an Earthling had given them the traditional Hephaistoan greeting.

Then everyone exchanged names—or tried to. The Hephaistoan names were each unpronounceable to Earthling mouths.

Charlie-Bob then asked, "Why are you here? Now?"

The Hephaistoans told him they'd came to investigate a mystery.

Their classification of Earth had been as "Space Travel Level One—orbital/lunar," and their monitoring of Earth's television programs seemed to confirm that Earth knew nothing about wormholers or wormholing.

Oh, some of Earth's television entertainments mentioned wormholing, but these same entertainments also mentioned time-travel and interplanetary mating, the Hephaistoans condescendingly informed the humans.

Then suddenly the Hephaistoans detected eighteen origin points for wormholer activity on planet Earth, which suddenly became two origin points, which soon became one—

"Hold on," Rose said. "You can detect from space, when and where wormholing happens?"

The Hephaistoans' ears wriggled (which it turned out, meant they were confused). The shorter Hephaistoan asked the humans, "How can you know about wormholing, yet be totally unaware about wormhole-detection?"

Charlie-Bob said, "She doesn't know about wormhole-detection because she doesn't need to know. I know in theory how to detect an artificial wormhole, but I can't build a wormhole-detector on Earth in 2013, and neither could the Cybes, so it doesn't matter."

"Earth man, how do you know about wormhole-detection?" the taller Hephaistoan asked.

"Earth man, how do you know about wormholes?" the shorter alien asked.

Prudy Lu said proudly, "*This* question I know how to answer. Charlie-Bob learned all that from his computer from the future."

The two aliens looked at each other, and made facial expressions that Charlie-Bob couldn't guess the meaning of. Then the taller one asked, "'From the future.' Is this Earthling humor?"

"Let me show you something," Charlie-Bob replied. He led the Hephaistoans into the house and straight to the Cybe computer.

The Hephaistoans were flabbergasted when they watched the video of Hephaistoans in 2063 giving the traditional Hephaistoan greeting to Zefram Colburne on his front lawn. Time travel was impossible to Hephaistoans, and yet this video couldn't be a fake!

Rose pointed at the video of the 2063 Hephaistoans. "They came the next day, right? Why did you wait two months?"

The real-live aliens stammered their explanation for the delay. What Charlie-Bob understood was that the Hephaistoans had a First Rule of Xenoanthropology, which meant that the Hephaistoans couldn't contact or otherwise contaminate "primitive" cultures—and Earth, well, you see. . .

"You pegged us," Rose said. "Cave-dweller primitives, that's us!"

Charlie-Bob, Rose, and Prudy Lu all laughed.

The Hephaistoans noticed that the future-computer wasn't plugged into anything. Charlie-Bob casually mentioned Exnillo packs, and was surprised to learn that the aliens believed such to be another "impossible" technology.

Charlie-Bob printed out schematics and write-ups about Exnillo packs, and handed the papers to the Hephaistoans without a second thought. He demanded nothing in return for his generosity.

As the aliens stood there looking stunned—

Charlie-Bob pulled out his smartphone and looked at the time-display. He said, "I'm sorry, but I have to get back to work. I'll be back home sometime after six, and we can continue this then."

Rose and Prudy Lu looked alarmed. Prudy Lu asked, "Um, what about tonight's special guest?"

He said, "Hm, I guess we still bring her over. She might not be able to do anything with me more than kiss, but she'll get to have dinner with aliens. That ought to be worth something."

He bowed to the aliens, kissed his women goodbye, went out to his car, and drove away. When he parked at Loganville Exnillo, his car clock said 12:17.

Rose told the Hephaistoans about the Cybes, the timeship crash, and the battle for Earth.

Charlie-Bob perhaps would have been modest about his own accomplishments. Rose and Prudy Lu were generous in their praise.

Rose told the Hephaistoans about the purpose of the bimborg, how they had been mostly sex-toys and bodyguards.

She told how Charlie-Bob, after utterly defeating the Cybes, picked the brains of Rose and the Anra twins, then set off the Planetary Solitarizer.

In an instant, every Cybe Invisible was free from obedience to dead masters; but also, Charlie-Bob freed his millions of sex-toys.

Rose told the visitors all this, then she got an idea. She sat down at the Cybe computer, and searched it for anything about Hephaistos. The 2013 Hephaistoans were shocked when Rose read aloud the battle plans that the 2652 Cybes had for Hephaistos, and she read aloud four reports by 2652 Hephaistoan Invisibles who were already in place.

There was no way to say whether it would have been the Cybes, or the Hephaistoans and the Space Navy, who would have won such a war, had it happened. But even if the Cybes were driven off, for Hephaistos it would have been a costly victory.

The 2013 aliens realized then: In defeating the Cybes, Charlie-Bob Owens not only had saved Earth, he had maybe saved Hephaistos too!

A little after three in the afternoon, Charlie-Bob got a call on his smartphone. Calling him was a cop.

"Mr. Owens, I'm Agent Vulpes Muldaur of the Georgia Bureau of Investigation. I'll be brief: You are officially cleared of suspicion in the murder of your parents."

"Thanks for the heads-up. But since I'm not Hercules or Samson, it should have been obvious that I'm not the murderer."

"We know that," Agent Muldaur replied.

Then Agent Muldaur lowered his voice: "I was sent to Vidal County originally to investigate the disappearances of many law-enforcement officers. Thanks to the Cybes, I got turned into an Invisible. They made me say lies, do things.

"But thanks to you, I got my life back. You better believe I've busted ass to steer the investigation away from you."

Charlie-Bob arrived home at 6:07. He greeted the two aliens, kissed his women, then showered and put on clean clothes.

With that done, he wormholed to Mumbai, India, to pick up Sitara, his fuck-date for tonight.

In the last two months, he'd had sex with fifteen former Pleasure Units, and one former Cybe Invisible. All sixteen women had been heart-bursting grateful to him for "freeing" them.

How did they show their gratitude? By being brought to his house, and then fucking and sucking him till he saw stars.

Sitara would be Gratitude Fuck number 17.

Sitara's designation had been 22418360; she was the very last bimborg Welcomed. Before being Welcomed, she'd costarred in three Bollywood musicals. Now Solitarized, she acted shy and in awe of Charlie-Bob, but she still looked like the Pleasure Unit she once had been. Nowadays she wore a racing glove on her left hand.

In Loganville, dinner went well, considering that Sitara had not expected to eat with two actual aliens.

Earth food, the Cybe computer had informed Rose, was poisonous to Hephaistoans, except for starches. So the Hephaistoans were each served a baked potato and boiled rice. The shorter alien announced that the potato was "ugly but tasty."

Meanwhile, Rose and Prudy Lu complimented Sitara on everything of hers they could see or smell, from top to bottom. Charlie-Bob gathered that Sitara had gone all out for this date.

The Hephaistoans asked questions about Charlie-Bob's battles with the Cybes. He tried to answer the aliens' questions in a modest and matter-of-fact way—

But Prudy Lu or Rose kept saying, "He's leaving out that he. . ."

And Sitara kept looking at him with shiny eyes and saying, "You are so much brave."

After dinner, the Hephaistoans stood up. The taller one said, "Now's the time to journey home, to tell of what we've learned. On behalf of all Hephaistos, we thank you for the information about Exnillo packs you have freely given us."

All three women followed Charlie-Bob and the Hephaistoans out to the garage. The Hephaistoan wormhole, Charlie-Bob noted, was blue-edged, not red-edged.

After the Hephaistoan wormhole closed, Charlie-Bob took Sitara's hand and, without a word, led her from the garage to the bedroom. Meanwhile, Prudy Lu and Rose attacked the dirty dishes.

Once Charlie-Bob and Sitara were in the bedroom, she started unwinding her sari. She said, "I am quite grateful to you. You gave to me back my life."

He already could smell her; when he touched her to help her undress, her smell got stronger.

The racing glove on her left hand, she removed by herself. The Welcomer warts were dark-chocolate brown against her brown skin.

When she was naked and pungent, Sitara stretched her arms up and out, so that her large tits were splendidly displayed. "I am quite grateful to you," Sitara repeated.

He undressed; they fucked. She scratched his back.

They fucked again. She screamed.

She sucked him hard; they fucked again. She was still wet.

He lay exhausted on the bed. She gave him slow head till he climaxed a fourth time.

Earth's population now included 19 million-plus former Pleasure Units. In theory, Charlie-Bob's sexy night with a woman like Sitara would repeat 18,999,984 more times.

THE END